100
GREAT
SCIENCE
FICTION
SHORT SHORT
STORIES

EDITED BY ISAAC ASIMOV, MARTIN HARRY
GREENBERG, AND JOSEPH D. OLANDER

Doubleday & Company, Inc., Garden City, New York, 1978

Library of Congress Cataloging in Publication Data

Main entry under title:

100 great science fiction short short stories.

    1. Science fiction, American.   2. Science fiction, English.   I. Asimov, Isaac, 1920– II. Greenberg, Martin Harry. III. Olander, Joseph D.
PZ1.0595 [PS648.S3]   813'.0876
ISBN: 0-385-13044-9
Library of Congress Catalog Card Number 77-76221

Acknowledgments

"A Loint of Paw," by Isaac Asimov, copyright © 1957 by Mercury Press, Inc. Reprinted from *The Magazine of Fantasy & Science Fiction* by permission of the author.

"The Advent on Channel Twelve," by C. M. Kornbluth, copyright © 1960 by Frederik Pohl. Reprinted by permission of Robert P. Mills, agent for the author's estate.

"Plaything," by Larry Niven, copyright © 1974 by UPD Publishing Corp. Reprinted by permission of the author and his agent, Robert P. Mills.

"The Misfortune Cookie," by Charles E. Fritch, copyright © 1970 by Mercury Press Inc. Reprinted from *The Magazine of Fantasy & Science Fiction* by permission of the author.

"I Wish I May, I Wish I Might," by Bill Pronzini, copyright © 1973 by Mercury Press, Inc. Reprinted from *The Magazine of Fantasy & Science Fiction* by permission of the author and his agent, Richard Curtis.

"FTA," by George R. R. Martin, copyright © 1974 by The Condé Nast Publications, Inc. Reprinted by permission of the author.

"Trace," by Jerome Bixby, copyright © 1964 by Jerome Bixby. Reprinted by permission of the author.

"Zoo," by Edward D. Hoch, copyright © 1958 by King-Size Publications, Inc. Reprinted by permission of the author and Larry Sternig Literary Agency.

"The Destiny of Milton Gomrath," by Alexei Panshin, copyright © 1967 by The Condé Nast Publications, Inc. Reprinted by permission of the author.

"The Devil and the Trombone," by Martin Gardner, copyright © 1948, 1975 by Martin Gardner. Reprinted by permission of the author.

"Upstart," by Steven Utley, copyright © 1976 by Mercury Press, Inc. Reprinted from *The Magazine of Fantasy & Science Fiction* by permission of the author.

"How It All Went," by Gregory Benford, copyright © 1976 by Ultimate Publishing Co., Inc. Reprinted by permission of the author and his agent, Richard Curtis.

"Harry Protagonist, Brain-Drainer," by Richard Wilson, copyright © 1964 by Galaxy Publishing Corporation. Reprinted by permission of the author.

CONTENTS

INTRODUCTION

The Science Fiction Blowgun

by Isaac Asimov

In science fiction, experience seems to show that long stories have an advantage over short ones. The longer the story, all things being equal, the more memorable.

There is reason to this. The longer the story, the more the author can spread himself. If the story is long enough, he can indulge himself in plot and subplot with intricate interconnections. He can engage in leisurely description, in careful character delineation, in thoughtful homilies and philosophical discussions. He can play tricks on the reader, hiding important information, misleading and misdirecting, then bringing back forgotten themes and characters at the moment of greatest effect.

But in every worthwhile story, however long, there is a point. The writer may not consciously put it there, but it will be there. The reader may not consciously search for it, but he'll miss it if it isn't there. If the point is obtuse, blunt, trivial or non-existent, the story suffers and the reader will react with a deadly, "So what?"

Long, complicated stories can have the point well-hidden under cloaking layers of material. Academic people, for whom the search for the point is particularly exciting, can whip their students to the hunt, and works of literature that are particularly deep and rich can elicit scholarly theses without number that will deal with the identification and explanations of points and subpoints.

But now let's work toward the other extreme. As a story grows shorter and shorter, all the fancy embroidery that length makes possible must go. In the short story, there can be no subplots; there is no time for philosophy; what description and character delineation there is must be accomplished with concision.

The point, however, must remain. Since it cannot be economized on, its weight looms more largely in the lesser over-all bulk of the short story.

Finally, in the short short story, everything is eliminated *but* the point. The short short story reduces itself to the point alone and presents that to you like a bare needle fired from a blowgun; a needle that can tickle or sting and leave its effect buried within you for a long time.

Here, then, are some points made against the background and with the technique of science fiction. A hundred of them, to be exact, each from the science fiction blowgun of a master (to be modest, there are *also* a couple of my own stories), and each with a one-line introductory blurb by myself.

Now, since it would make no sense to have an introduction longer than the stories it introduces, and having made *my* point—I'll stop.

Never mind the joke, what would your decision have been?

A *Loint* of *Paw*

by Isaac Asimov

There was no question that Montie Stein had, through clever fraud, stolen better than a hundred thousand dollars. There was also no question that he was apprehended one day after the statute of limitations had expired.

It was his manner of avoiding arrest during that interval that brought on the epoch-making case of the State of New York *vs.* Montgomery Harlow Stein, with all its consequences. It introduced law to the fourth dimension.

For, you see, after having committed the fraud and possessed himself of the hundred grand plus, Stein had calmly entered a time machine, of which he was in illegal possession, and set the controls for seven years and one day in the future.

Stein's lawyer put it simply. Hiding in time was not fundamentally different from hiding in space. If the forces of law had not uncovered Stein in the seven-year interval that was their hard luck.

The District Attorney pointed out that the statute of limitations was not intended to be a game between the law and the criminal. It was a merciful measure designed to protect a culprit from indefinitely prolonged fear of arrest. For certain crimes, a defined period of apprehension of apprehension (so to speak) was considered punishment enough. But Stein, the D.A. insisted, had not experienced any period of apprehension at all.

Stein's lawyer remained unmoved. The law said nothing about measuring the extent of a culprit's fear and anguish. It simply set a time limit.

The D.A. said that Stein had not lived through the limit.

Defense stated that Stein was seven years older now than at the time of the crime and had therefore lived through the limit.

The D.A. challenged the statement and the defense produced Stein's birth certificate. He was born in 2973. At the time of the crime, 3004, he was thirty-one. Now, in 3011, he was thirty-eight.

The D.A. shouted that Stein was not physiologically thirty-eight, but thirty-one.

Defense pointed out freezingly that the law, once the individual was granted to be mentally competent, recognized solely chronological age, which could be obtained only by subtracting the date of birth from the date of now.

The D.A., growing impassioned, swore that if Stein were allowed to go free half the laws on the books would be useless.

Then change the laws, said Defense, to take time travel into account, but until the laws are changed let them be enforced as written.

Judge Neville Preston took a week to consider and then handed down his decision. It was a turning point in the history of law. It is almost a pity, then, that some people suspect Judge Preston to have been swayed in his way of thinking by the irresistible impulse to phrase his decision as he did.

For that decision, in full, was:

"A niche in time saves Stein."

And it came to pass that the wasteland was vast.

The Advent on Channel Twelve

by C. M. Kornbluth

It came to pass in the third quarter of the fiscal year that the Federal Reserve Board did raise the rediscount rate and money was tight in the land. And certain bankers which sate in New York sent to Ben Graffis in Hollywood a writing which said, Money is tight in the land so let Poopy Panda up periscope and fire all bow tubes.

Whereupon Ben Graffis made to them this moan:

O ye bankers, Poopy Panda is like unto the child of my flesh and you have made of him a devouring dragon. Once was I content with my studio and my animators when we did make twelve Poopy Pandas a year; cursed be the day when I floated a New York loan. You have commanded me to make feature-length cartoon epics and I did obey, and they do open at the Paramount to sensational grosses, and we do re-release them to the nabes year on year, without end. You have commanded me to film live adventure shorts and I did obey, and in the cutting room we do devilishly splice and pull frames and flop negatives so that I and my cameras are become bearers of false witness and men look upon my live adventure shorts and say lo! these beasts and birds are like unto us in their laughter, wooing, pranks, and contention. You have commanded that I become a mountebank for that I did build Poopy Pandaland, whereinto men enter with their children, their silver, and their wits, and wherefrom they go out with their children only, sandbagged by a thousand catch-penny engines; even this did I obey. You have commanded that Poopy Panda shill every weekday night on television between five and six for the Poopy Panda Pals, and even this did I obey, though Poopy Panda is like unto the child of my flesh.

But O ye bankers, this last command will I never obey.

Whereupon the bankers which sate in New York sent to him another writing that said, Even so, let Poopy Panda up periscope and fire all bow tubes, and they said, Remember, boy, we hold thy paper.

And Ben Graffis did obey.

He called unto him his animators and directors and cameramen and writers, and his heart was sore but he dissembled and said:

In jest you call one another brainwashers, forasmuch as you addle the heads of children five hours a week that they shall buy our sponsors' wares. You have fulfilled the prophecies, for is it not written in the Book of the Space Merchants that there shall be spherical trusts? And the Poopy Panda Pals plug the Poopy Panda Magazine, and the Poopy Panda Magazine plugs Poopy Pandaland, and Poopy Pandaland plugs the Poopy Panda Pals. You have asked of the Motivational Research boys how we shall hook the little bastards and they have told ye, and ye have done it. You identify the untalented kid viewers with the talented kid performers, you provide in Otto Clodd a bumbling father image to be derided, you furnish in Jackie Whipple an idealized big brother for the boys and a sex-fantasy for the more precocious girls. You flatter the cans off the viewers by ever saying to them that they shall rule the twenty-first century, nor mind that those who shall in good sooth come to power are doing their homework and not watching television programs. You have created a liturgy of opening hymn and closing benediction, and over all hovers the spirit of Poopy Panda urging and coaxing the viewers to buy our sponsors' wares.

And Ben Graffis breathed a great breath and looked them not in the eye and said to them, Were it not a better thing for Poopy Panda to coax and urge no more, but to command as he were a god?

And the animators and directors and cameramen and writers were sore amazed and they said one to the other, This is the bleeding end, and the bankers which sit in New York have flipped their wigs. And one which was an old animator said to Ben Graffis, trembling, O chief, never would I have stolen for thee Poopy Panda from the Winnie the Pooh illustrations back in twenty-nine had I known this was in the cards, and Ben Graffis fired him.

Whereupon another which was a director said to Ben Graffis, O chief, the thing can be done with a two-week buildup, and Ben Graffis put his hands over his face and said, Let it be so.

And it came to pass that on the Friday after the two-week buildup, in the closing quarter-hour of the Poopy Panda Pals, there was a special film combining live and animated action as they were one.

And in the special film did Poopy Panda appear enhaloed, and the talented kid performers did do him worship, and Otto Clodd did trip over his feet whilst kneeling, and Jackie Whipple did urge in manly and sincere wise that all the Poopy Panda Pals out there in televisionland do likewise, and the enhaloed Poopy Panda did say in his lovable growly voice, Poop-poop-poopy.

And adoration ascended from thirty-seven million souls.

And it came to pass that Ben Graffis went into his office with his animators and cameramen and directors and writers after the show and said to them, It was definitely a TV first, and he did go to the bar.

Whereupon one which was a director looked at Who sate behind the desk that was the desk of Ben Graffis and he said to Ben

Graffis, O chief, it is a great gag but how did the special effects boys manage the halo?

And Ben Graffis was sore amazed at Who sate behind his desk and he and they all did crowd about and make as if to poke Him, whereupon He in His lovable growly voice did say, Poop-poop-poopy, and they were not.

And certain unclean ones which had gone before turned unbelieving from their monitors and said, Holy Gee, this is awful. And one which was an operator of marionettes turned to his manager and said, Pal, if Graffis gets this off the ground we're dead. Whereat a great and far-off voice was heard, saying, Poop-poop-poopy, and it was even so; and the days of Poopy Panda were long in the land.

> Filtered for error,
> Jan. 18th 36 P.P.
> Synod on Filtration & Infiltration
> O. Clodd, P.P.P.
> J. Whipple, P.P.P.

Spoiled brats!

Plaything

by Larry Niven

The children were playing six-point Overlord, hopping from point to point over a hexagonal diagram drawn in the sand, when the probe broke atmosphere over their heads. They might have sensed it then, for it was heating fast as it entered atmosphere; but nobody happened to look up.

Seconds later the retrorocket fired.

A gentle rain of infrared light bathed the limonite sands. Over hundreds of square miles of orange martian desert, wide-spaced clumps of black grass uncurled their leaves to catch and hoard the heat. Tiny sessile things buried beneath the sand raised fan-shaped probes.

The children hadn't noticed yet, but their ears were stirring. Their ears sensed heat rather than sound; unless they were listening to some heat source, they usually remained folded like silver flowers against the children's heads. Now they uncurled, flowers blooming, showing black centers; now they twitched and turned, seeking. One turned and saw it.

A point of white light high in the east, slowly setting.

The children talked to each other in coded pulses of heat, opening and closing their mouths to show the warm interiors.

Hey!

What is it?

Let's go see!

They hopped off across the limonite sand, forgetting the Overlord game, racing to meet the falling thing.

It was down when they got there and still shouting-hot. The probe was big, as big as a dwelling, a fat cylinder with a rounded roof above and a great hot mouth beneath. Black and white paint in a checkerboard pattern gave it the look of a giant's toy. It rested on three comically splayed metal legs ended in wide, circular feet.

The children began rubbing against the metal skin, flashing pulses of contentment as they absorbed the heat.

The probe trembled. Motion inside. The children jumped back, stood looking at each other, each ready to run if the others did. None wanted to be first. Suddenly it was too late. One whole curved wall of the probe dropped outward and thudded to the sand.

A child crawled out from underneath, rubbing his head and flashing heat from his mouth: words he shouldn't have learned yet. The wound in his scalp steamed briefly before the edges pulled shut.

The small, intense white sun, halfway down the sky, cast opaque black shadow across the opening in the probe. In the shadow something stirred.

The children watched, awed.

ABEL paused in the opening, then rolled out, using the slab of reentry shielding as a ramp. ABEL was a cluster of plastic and metal widgetry mounted on a low platform slung between six balloon tires. When it reached the sand it hesitated as if uncertain, then rolled out onto Mars, jerkily, feeling its way.

The child who'd been bumped by the ramp hopped over to kick the moving thing. ABEL stopped at once. The child shied back.

Suddenly an adult stood among them.

WHAT ARE YOU DOING?

Nothing, one answered.

Just playing, said another.

WELL, BE CAREFUL WITH IT. The adult looked like the twin of any of the six children. The roof of his mouth was warmer than theirs—but the authority in his voice was due to more than mere loudness. SOMEONE MAY HAVE GONE TO GREAT TROUBLE TO BUILD THIS OBJECT.

Yes sir.

Somewhat subdued, the children gathered around the Automated Biological Laboratory. They watched a door open in the side of the drum-shaped container that made up half of ABEL's body. A gun inside the door fired a weighted line high into the air.

That thing almost hit me.

Serves you right.

The line, coated with sand and dust, came slithering back into ABEL's side. One of the children licked it and found it covered with something sticky and tasteless.

Two children climbed onto the slow-moving platform, then up onto the cylinder. They stood up and waved their arms, balancing precariously on flat triangular feet. ABEL swerved toward a clump of black grass, and both children toppled to the sand. One picked himself up and ran to climb on again.

The adult watched it all dubiously.

A second adult appeared beside him.

YOU ARE LATE. WE HAD AN APPOINTMENT TO XAT BNORNEN CHIP. HAD YOU FORGOTTEN?

I HAD. THE CHILDREN HAVE FOUND SOMETHING.

SO THEY HAVE. WHAT IS IT DOING?

IT WAS TAKING SOIL SAMPLES AND PERHAPS TRYING TO COLLECT SPORES. NOW IT SHOWS AN INTEREST IN GRASS. I WONDER HOW ACCURATE ITS INSTRUMENTS ARE.

IF IT WERE SENTIENT IT WOULD SHOW INTEREST IN THE CHILDREN.

PERHAPS.

ABEL stopped. A box at the front lifted on a telescoping leg and began a slow pan of the landscape. From the low dark line of

the Mare Acidalium highlands on the northeastern horizon, it
swung around until its lens faced straight backward at the empty
orange desert of Tracus Albus. At this point the lens was eye to
eye with the hitchhiking child. The child flapped his ears, made
idiot faces, shouted nonsense words, and flicked at the lens with
his long tongue.

THAT SHOULD GIVE THEM SOMETHING TO THINK
ABOUT.

WHO WOULD YOU SAY SENT IT?

EARTH, I WOULD THINK. NOTICE THE SILICATE
DISC IN THE CAMERA, TRANSPARENT TO THE FRE-
QUENCIES OF LIGHT MOST LIKELY TO PENETRATE
THAT PLANET'S THICK ATMOSPHERE.

AGREEMENT.

The gun fired again, into the black grass, and the line began to
reel back. Another box retracted its curved lid. The hitchhiker
peered into it, while the other children watched admiringly from
below.

One of the adults shouted, GET BACK, YOU YOUNG
PLANT-BRAIN!

The child turned to flap his ears at him. At that moment
ABEL flashed a tight ruby beam of laser light just past his ear.
For an instant it showed, an infinite length of neon tubing against
the navy blue sky.

The child scrambled down and ran for his life.

EARTH IS NOT IN THAT DIRECTION, an adult observed.

YET THE BEAM MUST HAVE BEEN A MESSAGE.
SOMETHING IN ORBIT, PERHAPS?

The adults looked skyward. Presently their eyes adjusted.

ON THE INNER MOON. DO YOU SEE IT?

YES. QUITE LARGE . . . AND WHAT ARE THOSE
MIDGES IN MOTION ABOUT IT? THAT IS NO AU-
TOMATED PROBE, BUT A VEHICLE. I THINK WE
MUST EXPECT VISITORS SOON.

WE SHOULD HAVE INFORMED THEM OF OUR
PRESENCE LONG AGO. A LARGE RADIO-FREQUENCY
LASER WOULD HAVE DONE IT.

WHY SHOULD WE DO ALL THE WORK WHEN
THEY HAVE ALL THE METALS, THE SUNLIGHT, THE
RESOURCES?

Having finished with the clump of grass, ABEL lurched into motion and rolled toward a dark line of eroded ring wall. The children swarmed after it. The lab fired off another sticky string, let it fall, and started to reel it back. A child picked it up and pulled. Lab and martian engaged in a tug of war which ended when the string broke. Another child poked a long, fragile finger into the cavity and withdrew it covered with something wet. Before it could boil away, he put the finger in his mouth. He sent out a pulse of pleasure and stuck his tongue in the hole, into the broth intended for growing martian microorganisms.

STOP THAT! THAT IS NOT YOUR PROPERTY!

The adult voice was ignored. The child left his tongue in the broth, running alongside the lab to keep up. Presently the others discovered that if they stood in front of ABEL it would change course to crawl around the "obstruction."

PERHAPS THE ALIENS WILL BE SATISFIED TO RETURN HOME WITH THE INFORMATION GATHERED BY THE PROBE.

NONSENSE. THE CAMERAS HAVE SEEN THE CHILDREN. NOW THEY KNOW THAT WE EXIST.

WOULD THEY RISK THEIR LIVES TO LAND, MERELY BECAUSE THEY HAVE SEEN DITHTA? DITHTA IS A HOMELY CHILD, EVEN TO MY OWN EYE, AND I AM PERHAPS HIS PARENT.

LOOK WHAT THEY ARE DOING NOW.

By moving to left and right of the lab, by forming moving "obstructions," the children were steering ABEL toward a cliff. One still rode high on top, pretending to steer by kicking the metal flanks.

WE MUST STOP THEM. THEY WILL BREAK IT.

YES . . . DO YOU REALLY EXPECT THAT THE ALIENS WILL LAND A MANNED VEHICLE?

IT IS THE OBVIOUS NEXT STEP.

WE MUST HOPE THAT THE CHILDREN WILL NOT GET HOLD OF IT.

All us Chinese food devotees should be so lucky.

The Misfortune Cookie

by Charles E. Fritch

With an ease born of long practice, Harry Folger cracked open the Chinese cookie and pulled the slip of paper free. He smoothed it out on the table and read the message printed there:

YOU WILL MEET AN OLD FRIEND!

Harry chuckled to himself. It was inevitable that he would meet an old friend. He met them every day—on his way to work, at the office, in his apartment building—even in the various Chinese restaurants he frequented.

He bit into the cookie, crunched the remnants between his teeth, and washed them down with a swig of the now lukewarm tea. He enjoyed the fortune cookie as much as the fortune itself. But then he enjoyed everything about the Chinese food that he always ate, without ever tiring of it—the chow mein, the chop suey, the chicken fried rice, the won ton, the egg foo yung, the—oh, why go on? Heaven, to Harry Folger, was eating in a Chinese restaurant.

And as he was leaving the place, he met an old friend.

Her name was Cynthia Peters, or had been until she'd married. She was not old in the chronological sense, however, but a young woman not yet in her thirties. Harry had fond memories of the tempestuous affair he had experienced with the lady when both were younger, and frequently his dreams were filled with such pleasant recollections.

"Cynthia!" he said, surprised but pleased.

"Harry!" she exclaimed, tears of sudden happiness welling in her hazel-green eyes.

And Harry knew that despite the fact they were both married, he was going to have an affair with her.

When he finally got around to thinking about it, Harry marveled at the coincidence of his meeting old friend Cynthia right after a fortune cookie had forewarned him of such an occurrence. It was a coincidence, of course, for it could be nothing else. Harry enjoyed reading the messages—written, he always assumed, by coolie labor somewhere in Hong Kong—but he did not believe them to contain the absolute truth.

Not just then, he didn't.

The meeting places of himself and Cynthia were, needless to say, Chinese restaurants. Her husband, she told him, was a beast who made her life miserable. His wife, he informed her, was a bitch with whom he was quite unhappy. On one of these occasions, after a delicious meal of sweet and sour spareribs, Harry cracked open his fortune cookie to discover this message:

WATCH OUT! SOMEONE IS FOLLOWING YOU!

He looked up to discover Cynthia's irate husband entering the restaurant. There was barely time enough to spirit her out the rear exit. There would have been no time at all if the Chinese fortune cookie hadn't alerted Harry to the imminent danger.

Coincidence again, Harry decided—until he received a similarly worded message an instant before his wife (who hated Chinese food) entered the restaurant where he and Cynthia were eating, and once again Harry escaped in the nick of time.

As a result, Harry began taking the messages more seriously. He was hoping for some invaluable tip on the stock market or some winning horse in Saturday's race, but none came. For the most part, except for emergencies, the messages were bland bits of wisdom and random advice.

With one noticeable exception.

It occurred as he and Cynthia (who, like him, loved Chinese food) were finishing off the remaining morsels of Mandarin duck and she was telling how suspicious her husband was getting and how sure she was that Harry's own wife must not be blind to the secret rendezvous. At that precise moment, Harry cracked open a crisp fortune cookie, pulled out the slip of paper and read:

YOU ARE GOING TO DIE!

Harry gulped and almost choked on the piece of cookie in his mouth. It was ridiculous, of course. Then his attitude changed abruptly to one of indignation. What the hell kind of message was that for some underpaid coolie in Hong Kong to stuff into a fortune cookie? He thought of complaining to the manager, but he changed his mind. Instead, he decided he didn't feel well. He took Cynthia home, letting her off in front of her apartment.

As he was about to drive off, he heard a noise at the opposite window. He looked to see Cynthia's husband pointing a gun at him. He gasped, flung open the car door and scrambled out, bumping into his wife, who also had a gun in her hand.

Harry ran. He was vaguely aware that two guns fired simultaneously, but he felt no pain and was not about to stop his flight. He ran, not pausing for breath until he was a good four blocks away. Then he leaned against a building, dragging in lungfuls of air, to take inventory. There didn't seem to be any holes in him, nor was there any sign of blood.

Thank God, he thought, for the lousy aim of the two irate spouses.

Even so, he was shaking uncontrollably. He had to go someplace and relax. They might still be after him, and he'd be safer in a crowded place. He looked up at the building to see where he was.

He was standing in front of a Chinese restaurant.

It was one he'd never been to before, and his curiosity was aroused. Also his appetite, although he'd eaten a Chinese meal only an hour before. Besides, he always felt secure in such a place.

Harry Folger walked in, sat at a table. Surprisingly, he was the only person there. When a waiter appeared, Harry ordered the number-two dinner. He ate it, enjoying each mouthful, forgetting the unpleasant episode in the street. Then he cracked open his fortune cookie and read the message that had been tucked inside.

The words didn't register at first. When they did, he looked up in sudden panic—to see the waiter grinning derisively with a skull face. Harry looked around wildly for a way out, but there were no doors or windows in the restaurant, no way to get out now or ever.

He started screaming.

When he tired of that, he felt hungry again. He ordered another meal, ate it. The message in the fortune cookie this time was exactly as the first.

He had another meal after that one, and another after that, and another after that—and each time the message in the fortune cookie was the same. It said:

YOU'RE DEAD!

The three-wishes story to end all three-wishes stories.

I Wish I May, I Wish I Might

by Bill Pronzini

He sat on a driftwood throne near the great gray rocks by the sea, watching the angry foaming waves hurl themselves again and again upon the cold and empty whiteness of the beach. He listened to the discordant cry of the endlessly circling gulls overhead and to the sonorous lament of the chill October wind. He drew meaningless patterns in the silvery sand before him with the toe of one rope sandal and then erased them carefully with the sole and began anew.

He was a pale, blond young man of fourteen, his hair close-cropped, his eyes the color of faded cornflower. He was dressed in light corduroy trousers and a gray cloth jacket, and his thin white feet inside the sandals were bare. His name was David Lannin.

He looked up at the leaden sky, shading his eyes against its filtered glare. His fingers were blue-numb from the cold. He turned his head slowly, bringing within his vision the eroded face of a steep cliff, with its clumps of tule grass like patches of beard stubble, rising from the beach behind him. He released a long, sighing breath and turned his head yet again to look out at the combers breaking and retreating.

He stood and began to walk slowly along the beach, his hands buried deep in the pockets on his cloth jacket. The wind swirled loose sand against his body, and there was the icy wetness of the salt spray on his skin.

He rounded a gradual curve in the beach. Ahead of him he could see the sun-bleached, bark-bare upper portion of a huge timber half-buried in the sand, some twenty yards from the water's edge. Something green and shiny, something which had gone unnoticed as he passed earlier, lay in the wet sand near it.

A bottle.

He recognized it as such immediately. It was resting on its side with the neck partially buried in the sand, recently carried in, it seemed, on the tide. It was oddly shaped, the glass an opaque green color—the color of the sea—very smooth, without markings or labelings of any kind. It appeared to be quite old and extremely fragile.

David knelt beside it and lifted it in his hands and brushed the clinging particles of sand from its slender neck. Scarlet sealing wax had been liberally applied to the cork guarding the mouth. The wax bore an indecipherable emblem, an ancient seal. David's thin fingers dexterously chipped away most of the ceration, exposing the dun-colored cork beneath. He managed to loosen the cork—and the bottle began to vibrate almost imperceptibly. There was a sudden loud popping sound, like a magnum of champagne opening, and a micro-second later an intense, blinding flash of crimson phosphorescence.

David cried out, toppling backward on the sand, the bottle erupting from his hands. He blinked rapidly, and there came from very close to him high, loud peals of resounding laughter that commingled with the wind and the surf to fill the cold autumn air with rolling echoes of sound. But he could see nothing. The bottle lay on the sand a few feet away, and there was the timber and the beach and the sea; but there was nothing else, no one to be seen.

And yet, the hollow, reverberating laughter continued.

David scrambled to his feet, looking frantically about him. Fright kindled inside him. He wanted to run, he tensed his body to run—

All at once, the laughter ceased.

A keening voice assailed his ears, a voice out of nowhere, like the laughter, a voice without gender, without inflection, a neuter voice: "I wish I may, I wish I might."

"What?" David said, his eyes wide, vainly searching. "Where are you?"

"I am here," the voice said. "I am here on the wind."

"Where? I can't see you."

"None can see me. I am the king of djinns, the ruler of genies, the all-powerful—unjustly doomed to eternity in yon flagon by the mortal sorcerer Amroj." Laughter. "A thousand years alone have I spent, a millennium on the cold dark empty floor of the ocean. Alone, imprisoned. But now I am free, you have set me free. I knew you would do thus, for I know all things. You shall be rewarded. Three wishes shall I grant you, according to custom, according to tradition. I wish I may, I wish I might. Those be the words, the gateways to your fondest dreams. Speak them anywhere, anytime, and I shall hear and obey. I shall make each of your wishes come true."

David moistened his lips. "*Any* three wishes?"

"Any three," the voice answered. "No stipulations, no limitations. I am the king of djinns, the ruler of genies, the all-powerful. I wish I may, I wish I might. You know the words, do you not?"

"Yes! Yes, I know them."

The laughter. "Amroj, foul sorcerer, foul mortal, I am avenged! Avaunt, avaunt!"

And suddenly, there was a vacuum of sound, a roaring of silence, the pressure of which hurt David's ears and made him cry out in pain. But then the moment passed, and there was nothing but the sounds of the tide and the wind and the scavenger birds winging low, low over the sea.

He gained his feet and stood very still for perhaps a minute. Then he began to run. He ran with wind-speed, away from the timber half-buried in the sand, away from the smooth, empty green bottle; his sandaled feet seemed to fly above the sand, leaving only the barest of imprints there.

He fled along the beach until, in the distance, set back from the ocean on a short bluff, he could see a small white house with yellow warmth shining through its front window. He left the sand there, running across ground now more solid, running toward the white house on the bluff.

A wooden stairway appeared on the rock, winding skyward. As he neared it, a woman came rushing down the stairs. She ran toward him and threw her arms around him and hugged him close to her breast. "Oh, David, where have you been! I've been frantic with worry!"

"At the beach," he answered, drinking great mouthfuls of the cold salt air into his aching lungs. "By the big rocks."

"You know you're not supposed to go there," the woman said, hugging him. "David, you know that. Look at the way you're dressed. Oh, you mustn't ever, ever do this again. Promise you won't ever do it again."

"I found a bottle by the big timber," David said. "There was a genie inside. I couldn't see him, but he laughed and laughed, and then he gave me three wishes. He said that all I have to do is wish and he'll make my wish come true. Then he laughed some more and said some things I didn't understand, and then he was gone and my ears hurt."

"Oh, what a story! David, where did you get such a story?"

"I have three wishes," he said. "I can wish for anything and it will come true. The genie said so."

"David, David, David!"

"I'm going to wish for a million-trillion ice cream cones, and I'm going to wish for the ocean to always be as warm as my bathwater so I can go wading whenever I want, and I'm going to wish for all the little boys and girls in the world to be just like me so I'll never-ever be without somebody to play with."

Gently, protectively, the mother took the hand of her retarded son. "Come along now, dear. Come along."

"I wish I may, I wish I might," David said.

Well, there go just about all my novels.

FTA

by George R. R. Martin

Hyperspace exists. Of that there can be no doubt. We have proved it mathematically. While we cannot know the laws of hyperspace as yet, we can be certain that they are not the laws of normal space. In hyperspace, there is no reason to suppose that the limiting velocity of light will apply. So all that remains is to find a means of moving from normal space to hyperspace, and back again. Give me the funds to find a hyperdrive, and I will give you the stars!

—Dr. Frederik D. Canferelli, founder of the FTL Foundation, addressing the Committee on Technological Assessment, World Senate, Geneva, May 21, 2016

EVERYONE KNOWS AN ANT CAN'T MOVE A RUBBER TREE PLANT

—Motto of the FTL Foundation

Kinery entered in a rush, a thick file bulging under his arm. He was an aggressive young man, with short blond hair and a spike beard and a no-nonsense manner. He showed no deference.

Jerome Schechter, the deputy director of the FTL Foundation, watched through tired eyes while Kinery sat down without invitation, and slammed his file onto Schechter's cluttered desk.

"Morning, Schechter," Kinery said curtly. "I'm glad I finally broke through your palace guard. You're a very difficult man to get to see, you know that?"

Schechter nodded. "And you're very persistent," he said. The deputy director was a large man, layered in fat, with heavy eyebrows and a shock of thick gray hair.

"One has to be persistent in dealing with you people. Schechter, I'm not going to waste words. I've been getting a run-around from FTL, and I want to know why."

"A run-around?" Schechter smiled. "I don't know what you mean."

"Let's not play games. You and I both know that I'm one of the best damn physicists to come along in many years. You've seen my papers on hyperspace, if you keep up with your specialty at all. You should know that my approach is valid. I've given the field its biggest kick in the pants since Lopez. And he was thirty years ago. I'm on the track of a hyperdrive engine, Schechter. Everybody who knows anything knows that.

"But I need funding. My university can't meet the costs of the equipment I need. So I came to the FTL Foundation. Damn it, Schechter, you people should have been overjoyed to get my application. Instead, I get a year's worth of stalling, then a turndown. And I can't even get an explanation out of anyone. You're always in conference, your assistants hand me doubletalk, and Lopez seems to be on a permanent vacation."

Kinery folded his arms and sat back in his seat stiffly. Schechter played with a paperweight, and sighed. "You're angry, Mr. Kinery," he said. "It never pays to get angry."

Kinery leaned forward again. "I have a *right* to be angry. The FTL Foundation was set up for the express purpose of finding a hyperspace drive. I am about to do just that. Yet you won't even give me a hearing, let alone money."

Schechter sighed again. "You're working under several misapprehensions. To begin with, the FTL Foundation was created to research a method of faster-than-light travel. A star drive, let us say. Hyperspace is only one avenue toward that end. Right now, we're pursuing other avenues that look more promising. We . . ."

"I know all about those other avenues," Kinery interrupted. "Dead ends, all of them. You're wasting the taxpayers' money. And my God, some of the things you're funding! Allison and his teleportation experiments. Claudia Daniels with her nonsense about an esper-engine. And Chung's time-stasis hypothesis! How much are you giving *him?* If you ask me, the FTL Foundation's been mismanaged ever since Canferelli died. The only one who was going in the right direction at all was Lopez, and you loons took him out of the field and made him an administrator."

Schechter looked up and studied his guest. Kinery's face was a trifle flushed, and his lips were pressed tightly together. "I understand you've been to see Senator Markham," the deputy director said. "Do you intend to bring these charges to his attention?"

"Yes," Kinery said sharply. "Unless I get some answers. And I guarantee you that if those answers don't satisfy me, I'm going to see to it that the Senate Technology Committee takes a good long look at the FTL Foundation."

Schechter nodded. "Very well," he said. "I'll give you your answers. Kinery, do you have any idea how crowded Earth is right now?"

Kinery snorted. "Of course, I—"

"No," Schechter said. "Don't brush it off. Think about it. It's important. We don't have any *room* left, Kinery. Not here, not anywhere on Earth. And the colonies on Mars and Luna and Callisto are jokes, we both know that. Man's in a dead end. We need the stars for racial survival. The FTL Foundation is the hope of mankind, and thanks to Canferelli, the public sees the Foundation only in terms of hyperspace."

Kinery was not appeased. "Schechter, I've gotten enough bull from your staff during the past year. I don't need any from you."

Schechter just smiled. Then he rose and walked to the window, to look out on the sky-crowding towers of the megalopolis around them. "Kinery," he said without turning, "did you ever wonder why Lopez has not funded a hyperspace research project since he became director? After all, it was his field."

"I . . ." Kinery began.

Schechter cut him off. "Never mind," he said. "It isn't important. We fund the crackpot theories that we fund because they're better than nothing. Hyperspace is the dead end, Kinery. We keep the myth alive for the public, but we know better."

Kinery grimaced. "Oh, come now, Schechter. Take a look at my papers. You give me the funding and I'll give you a hyperspace engine within two years."

Schechter turned to face him. "I'm sure you would," he said, in a voice infinitely weary. "You know, Canferelli once said there was no reason why the limiting velocity of light should apply in hyperspace. He was right. It doesn't.

"I'm sorry, Kinery. Really I am. But Lopez gave us a hyperdrive thirty years ago. That's when we discovered that the limiting velocity in hyperspace is not the speed of light.

"It's slower, Kinery. It's *slower*."

Imagine hitting that tiny bit of impurity.

Trace

by Jerome Bixby

I tried for a shortcut.

My wrong left turn north of Pittsfield led me into a welter of backroads from which I could find no exit. Willy-nilly I was forced, with every mile I drove, higher and higher into the tree-clad hills . . . even an attempt to retrace my route found me climbing. No farmhouses, no gas stations, no sign of human habitation at all . . . just green trees, shrubbery, drifting clouds, and that damned road going up. And by now it was so narrow I couldn't even turn around!

On the worst possible stretch of dirt you can imagine, I blew a tire and discovered that my spare had leaked empty.

Sizzling the summer air of Massachusetts with curses, I started hiking in the only direction I thought would do me any good—down. But the road twisted and meandered oddly through the hills, and—by this time, I was used to it—*down* inexplicably turned to *up* again.

I reached the top of a rise, looked down, and called out in great relief, "Hello!"

His house was set in the greenest little valley I have ever seen.

At one end rose a brace of fine granite cliffs, to either side of a small, iridescent waterfall. His house itself was simple, New Englandish, and seemed new. Close about its walls were crowded profuse bursts of magnificent flowers—red piled upon blue upon gold. Though the day was partly cloudy, I noticed that no cloud hung over the valley; the sun seemed to have reserved its best efforts for this place.

He stood in his front yard, watering roses, and I wondered momentarily at the sight of running water in this secluded section. Then he lifted his face at the sound of my call and my approaching steps. His smile was warm and his greeting hearty and his handshake firm; his thick white hair, tossed in the breeze, and his twinkling eyes deepset in a ruddy face, provided the kindliest appearance imaginable. He clucked his tongue at my tale of misfortune, and invited me to use his phone and then enjoy his hospitality while waiting for the tow-truck.

The phone call made, I sat in a wonderfully comfortable chair in his unusually pleasant living room, listening to an unbelievably brilliant performance of something called the *Mephisto Waltz* on an incredibly perfect hi-fi system.

"You might almost think it was the composer's own performance," my host said genially, setting at my side a tray of extraordinary delicacies prepared in an astonishingly short time. "Of course, he died many years ago . . . but what a pianist! Poor fellow . . . he should have stayed away from other men's wives."

We talked for the better part of an hour, waiting for the truck. He told me that, having suffered a rather bad fall in his youth, considerations of health required that he occasionally abandon his work and come here to vacation in Massachusetts.

"Why Massachusetts?" I asked. (I'm a Bermuda man, myself.)

"Oh . . . why not?" he smiled. "This valley is a pleasant spot for meditation. I like New England . . . it is here that I have experienced some of my greatest successes—and several notable defeats. Defeat, you know, is not such a bad thing, if there's not too much of it . . . it makes for humility, and humility makes for caution, therefore for safety."

"Are you in the public employ, then?" I asked. His remarks seemed to indicate that he had run for office.

His eyes twinkled. "In a way. What do you do?"

"I'm an attorney."

"Ah," he said. "Then perhaps we may meet again."

"That would be a pleasure," I said. "However, I've come north only for a convention . . . if I hadn't lost my way. . . ."

"Many find themselves at my door for that reason," he nodded. "To turn from the straight and true road is to risk a perilous maze, eh?"

I found his remark puzzling. Did *that* many lost travelers appear at his doorstep? Or was he referring to his business? . . . perhaps he was a law officer, a warden, even an executioner! Such men often dislike discussing their work.

"Anyway," I said, "I will not soon forget your kindness!"

He leaned back, cupping his brandy in both hands. "Do you know," he murmured, "kindness is a peculiar thing. Often you find it, like a struggling candle, in the most unlikely of nights. Have you ever stopped to consider that there is no such thing in the Universe as a one-hundred per cent chemically pure substance? In everything, no matter how thoroughly it is refined, distilled, purified, there must be just a little, if only a trace, of its opposite. For example, no man is wholly good; none wholly evil. The kindest of men must yet practise some small, secret malice —and the cruellest of men cannot help but perform an act of good now and then."

"It certainly makes it hard to judge people, doesn't it?" I said. "I find that so much in my profession. One must depend on intuition—"

"Fortunately," he said, "in mine, I deal in fairly concrete percentages."

After a moment, I said, "In the last analysis, then, you'd even have to grant the Devil himself that solitary facet of goodness you speak of. His due, as it were. Once in a while, *he* would be compelled to do good deeds. That's certainly a curious thought."

He smiled. "Yet I assure you, that tiny, irresistible impulse would be there."

My excellent cigar, which he had given me with the superb brandy, had gone out. Noting this, he leaned forward—his lighter flamed, with a *click* like the snapping of fingers. "The entire notion," he said meditatively, "is a part of a philosophy which I developed in collaboration with my brother . . . a small cog in a complex system of what you might call Universal weights and balances."

"You are in business with your brother, then?" I asked, trying to fit this latest information into my theories.

"Yes . . . and no." He stood up, and suddenly I heard a motor approaching up the road. "And now, your tow-truck is here. . . ."

We stood on the porch, waiting for the truck. I looked around at his beautiful valley, and filled my lungs.

"It *is* lovely, isn't it?" he said, with a note of pride.

"It is perfectly peaceful and serene," I said. "One of the loveliest spots I have ever seen. It seems to reflect what you have told me of your pleasures . . . and what I observe in *you,* sir. Your kindness, hospitality, and charity; your great love of Man and Nature." I shook his hand warmly. "I shall never forget this delightful afternoon!"

"Oh, I imagine you will," he smiled. "Unless we meet again. At any rate, I am happy to have done you a good turn. Up here, I must almost create the opportunity."

The truck stopped. I went down the steps, and turned at the bottom. The late afternoon sun seemed to strike a glint of red in his eyes.

"Thanks, again," I said. "I'm sorry I wasn't able to meet your brother. Does he ever join you up here on his vacations?"

"I'm afraid not," he said, after a moment. "He has his own little place. . . ."

And this was written years before today's **ingenious patriots.**

The Ingenious Patriot

by Ambrose Bierce

Having obtained an audience of the King an Ingenious Patriot pulled a paper from his pocket, saying:

"May it please your Majesty, I have here a formula for constructing armor plating that no gun can pierce. If these plates are adopted in the Royal Navy our warships will be invulnerable and therefore invincible. Here, also, are reports of your Majesty's Ministers, attesting the value of the invention. I will part with my right in it for a million tumtums."

After examining the papers, the King put them away and

promised him an order on the Lord High Treasurer of the Extortion Department for a million tumtums.

"And here," said the Ingenious Patriot, pulling another paper from another pocket, "are the working plans of a gun that I have invented, which will pierce that armor. Your Majesty's royal brother, the Emperor of Bang, is eager to purchase it, but loyalty to your Majesty's throne and person constrains me to offer it first to your Majesty. The price is one million tumtums."

Having received the promise of another check, he thrust his hand into still another pocket, remarking:

"The price of the irresistible gun would have been much greater, your Majesty, but for the fact that its missiles can be so effectively averted by my peculiar method of treating the armor plates with a new——"

The King signed to the Great Head Factotum to approach.

"Search this man," he said, "and report how many pockets he has."

"Forty-three, Sire," said the Great Head Factotum, completing the scrutiny.

"May it please your Majesty," cried the Ingenious Patriot, in terror, "one of them contains tobacco."

"Hold him up by the ankles and shake him," said the King; "then give him a check for forty-two million tumtums and put him to death. Let a decree issue making ingenuity a capital offence."

Then there was the keyhole with an eye on each side.

Zoo

by Edward D. Hoch

The children were always good during the month of August, especially when it began to get near the twenty-third. It was on this day that the great silver spaceship carrying Professor Hugo's Interplanetary Zoo settled down for its annual six-hour visit to the Chicago area.

Before daybreak the crowds would form, long lines of children and adults both, each one clutching his or her dollar, and waiting with wonderment to see what race of strange creatures the Professor had brought this year.

In the past they had sometimes been treated to three-legged creatures from Venus, or tall, thin men from Mars, or even snake-like horrors from somewhere more distant. This year, as the great round ship settled slowly to earth in the huge tri-city parking area just outside of Chicago, they watched with awe as the sides slowly slid up to reveal the familiar barred cages. In them were some wild breed of nightmare—small, horse-like animals that moved with quick, jerking motions and constantly chattered in a high-pitched tongue. The citizens of Earth clustered around as Professor Hugo's crew quickly collected the waiting dollars, and soon the good Professor himself made an appearance, wearing his many-colored rainbow cape and top hat. "Peoples of Earth," he called into his microphone.

The crowd's noise died down and he continued. "Peoples of Earth, this year you see a real treat for your single dollar—the little-known horse-spider people of Kaan—brought to you across a million miles of space at great expense. Gather around, see them, study them, listen to them, tell your friends about them. But hurry! My ship can remain here only six hours!"

And the crowds slowly filed by, at once horrified and fascinated by these strange creatures that looked like horses but ran up the walls of their cages like spiders. "This is certainly worth a dollar," one man remarked, hurrying away. "I'm going home to get the wife."

All day long it went like that, until ten thousand people had filed by the barred cages set into the side of the spaceship. Then, as the six-hour limit ran out, Professor Hugo once more took microphone in hand. "We must go now, but we will return next year on this date. And if you enjoyed our zoo this year, phone your friends in other cities about it. We will land in New York tomorrow, and next week on to London, Paris, Rome, Hong Kong, and Tokyo. Then on to other worlds!"

He waved farewell to them, and as the ship rose from the ground the Earth peoples agreed that this had been the very best Zoo yet. . . .

Some two months and three planets later, the silver ship of Professor Hugo settled at last onto the familiar jagged rocks of Kaan, and the queer horse-spider creatures filed quickly out of their cages. Professor Hugo was there to say a few parting words, and then they scurried away in a hundred different directions, seeking their homes among the rocks.

In one, the she-creature was happy to see the return of her mate and offspring. She babbled a greeting in the strange tongue and hurried to embrace them. "It was a long time you were gone. Was it good?"

And the he-creature nodded. "The little one enjoyed it especially. We visited eight worlds and saw many things."

The little one ran up the wall of the cave. "On the place called Earth it was the best. The creatures there wear garments over their skins, and they walk on two legs."

"But isn't it dangerous?" asked the she-creature.

"No," her mate answered. "There are bars to protect us from them. We remain right in the ship. Next time you must come with us. It is well worth the nineteen commocs it costs."

And the little one nodded. "It was the very best Zoo ever. . . ."

And what's more, someone else will smell the roses.

The Destiny of Milton Gomrath

by Alexei Panshin

Milton Gomrath spent his days in dreams of a better life. More obviously, he spent his days as a garbage collector. He would empty a barrel of garbage into the back of the city truck and then lose himself in reverie as the machine went *clomp, grunch, grunch, grunch*. He hated the truck, he hated his drab little room, and he hated the endless serial procession of gray days. His dreams were the sum of the might-have-beens of his life, and because there was so much that he was not, his dreams were beautiful.

Milton's favorite dream was one denied those of us who know who our parents are. Milton had been found in a strangely fashioned wicker basket on the steps of an orphanage, and this left him free as a boy to imagine an infinity of magnificent destinies that could and would be fulfilled by the appearance of a mother, uncle, or cousin come to claim him and take him to the perpetual June, where he of right belonged. He grew up, managed to graduate from high school by the grace of an egalitarian school board that believed everyone should graduate from high school regardless of qualification, and then went to work for the city, all the while holding onto the same well-polished dream.

Then one day he was standing by the garbage truck when a thin, harassed-looking fellow dressed in simple black materialized in front of him. There was no bang, hiss, or pop about it—it was a very businesslike materialization.

"Milton Gomrath?" the man asked, and Milton nodded. "I'm a Field Agent from Probability Central. May I speak with you?"

Milton nodded again. The man wasn't exactly the mother or cousin he had imagined, but the man apparently knew by heart the lines that Milton had mumbled daily as long as he could remember.

"I'm here to rectify an error in the probability fabric," the man said. "As an infant you were inadvertently switched out of your own dimension and into this one. As a result there has been a severe strain on Things-As-They-Are. I can't compel you to accompany me, but, if you will, I've come to restore you to your Proper Place."

"Well, what sort of world is it?" Milton asked. "Is it like this?" He waved at the street and truck.

"Oh, not at all," the man said. "It is a world of magic, dragons, knights, castles, and that sort of thing. But it won't be hard for you to grow accustomed to it. First, it is the place where you rightfully belong and your mind will be attuned to it. Second, to make things easy for you, I have somebody ready to show you your place and explain things to you."

"I'll go," said Milton.

The world grew black before his eyes the instant the words were out of his mouth, and when he could see again, he and the man were standing in the courtyard of a great stone castle. At one side were gray stone buildings; at the other, a rose garden with blooms of red, white, and yellow. Facing them was a heavily bearded, middle-aged man.

"Here we are," said the man in black. "Evan, this is your charge. Milton Gomrath, this is Evan Asperito. He'll explain everything you need to know."

Then the man saluted them both. "Gentlemen, Probability

Central thanks you most heartily. You have done a service. You have set things in their Proper Place." And then he disappeared.

Evan, the bearded man, said, "Follow me," and turned. He went inside the nearest building. It was a barn filled with horses.

He pointed at a pile of straw in one corner. "You can sleep over there."

Then he pointed at a pile of manure. There was a long-handled fork in the manure and a wheelbarrow waiting at ease. "Put that manure in the wheelbarrow and spread it on the rose bushes in the garden. When you are finished with that, I'll find something else for you to do."

He patted Milton on the back. "I realize it's going to be hard for you at first, boy. But if you have any questions at any time, just ask me."

Good and evil created he them—

The Devil and the Trombone

by Martin Gardner

The university's chapel was dark when I walked by it, but I could hear faintly the sound of an organ playing inside. I glanced at my wrist watch. It was almost midnight.

"Strange," I thought, "that someone would be playing at this hour."

I was on my way home from a meeting of the campus Philosophical Society. As an assistant professor of political science, and co-author of a textbook on international relations, I had been asked to chairman a symposium on "Right and Wrong in International Law." It had been a technical, tangled discussion, and my brain was tired. Partly to rest my mind, partly out of curiosity, I pulled open the heavy chapel door and entered.

The church was pitch black inside except for a dim glow of light behind the pulpit where the organ console was concealed. The Gothic walls and windows reverberated with low, sonorous chords.

I struck a match so I could find my way to a seat in the rear, where I settled into a comfortable position and listened. The chords were unlike any chords I had ever heard.

It wasn't long until my curiosity got the upper hand. I stood up and felt my way slowly down the central aisle. Then I stopped suddenly and caught my breath.

The light was coming not from the bulb above the music rack, but from the organist himself. He was young and handsome, and he was wearing a white robe. Two enormous wings extended from his shoulders and were folded close to the body. The wings radiated a hazy luminescence.

He glanced over, saw me standing there, and took his hands from the keys. The chapel was instantly silent.

"You startled me," he said, smiling crookedly. "How did you get in?"

I pointed down the aisle. "Through the . . . the front entrance," I stammered.

He frowned and shook his head in self-reproach. "My fault," he said. "I thought the door was locked."

I didn't say anything.

"It's not often I get a chance to play one of these things," he went on, adjusting several stops. "I'm horribly out of practice. But here's something that might interest you."

His fingers began to move gracefully over the keyboards, and the somber chapel suddenly became alive with melody.

And while he played, a great peace settled over my soul. The world was good. Life was good. Death was good. All that seemed black and horrible was a necessary prelude to some greater goodness. Every episode of history was part of the Will of God. I thought of the German prison camps, of the bombing of Hiroshima, of the atomic wars yet to come. They, too, were good.

Then from the deep purple shadows behind the organ, a tall figure with pointed ears emerged. He wore no clothing. Dark reddish hair covered his swarthy arms, chest, and legs. In his left hand, gleaming like silver, was a slide trombone.

He put the instrument to his lips and blew a low, outrageous note like the sound of a Bronx cheer. At the same moment the organist lifted his hands from the keys.

The dark man played alone, beating a foot slowly on the stone floor and improvising in a relaxed New Orleans style. The melodic line was filled with sweeping glissandos.

And now my soul was troubled with a great unrest. All that we call good in life, I saw clearly, was nothing but an illusion. Sickness and sin were the realities. The brief moments of peace and harmony—for a person, nation, or the world—only added pathos to a final tragedy. At the end of human history loomed the blankness of a Great Destruction.

Then the slender hands of the organist returned to the ivory keys, and the two players began to jam. They were improvising independently, but their separate efforts blended into a rich texture of counterpoint and polyrhythm.

All the frenzied fullness and complexity of the modern world, with its curious mixture of good and evil, rose up before me. I felt neither peace nor anxiety, but a strange excitement and exultation. There were journeys to be made, with real goals to reach, real dangers to avoid. There were battles to be fought!

A sinewy tail crept from the back of the dark man. The cloven scarlet tip crawled into the bell of the slide-horn, serving as a mute. The organist looked at me and grinned.

"Authentic tail gate," he commented.

The jamming continued. One by one the age-old problems of political philosophy found clear and simple answers. Right and wrong were easy to define. International dilemmas melted away. I saw the good and bad of every nation. I knew exactly what our foreign policy should be.

The organist's hands and sandaled feet were dancing wildly now, and the dark stranger was bending back, the trombone pointed upward in defiance, playing loud and wicked smears. My head felt as though it had expanded to the bursting point. I understood the meaning of life. I knew why the world had been created. I was about to penetrate the ultimate mystery—the mystery of God's own existence—when the players stopped abruptly.

The chapel was quiet as a tomb. My hands were shaking and cold trickles of perspiration ran down my face. There was a dull ache above each temple.

"It's a good thing we stopped," the dark man said huskily. "Another note and your brain would have cracked."

"You'd better go back to your seat," said the man in white, "and wake yourself up."

In dazed obedience I stumbled back along the aisle, sat down again, and closed my eyes. When I opened them, the soft glow in front had disappeared. I walked to the console, fired a match, and waved it about in the blackness. Not a soul was in sight. I placed my hand on the leather cushion. It was cold. There were no feathers on the floor.

My wife was reading in a chair when I got home.

"Sam," she called to me (I had gone to the bathroom to take some aspirin), "I'm worried about Joey. He disobeyed several times tonight, and he refused to go to bed until an hour after bedtime. Do you think we should start punishing him?"

I washed down a couple of tablets with a glass of water. "My dear," I said, drying my lips on a towel, "I haven't the faintest idea."

What's the good of being a worm, if you can't turn?

Upstart

by Steven Utley

"You must obey the edict of the Sreen," the Intermediaries have told us repeatedly, "there is no appeal," but the captain won't hear of it, not for a moment. He draws himself up to his full height of two meters and looms threateningly over the four or five Intermediaries, who are, after all, small and not particularly substantial-looking beings, mere wisps of translucent flesh through which their bluish skeletal structures and pulsing organs can be seen.

"You take us in to talk to the Sreen," the captain tells them, "you take us in right *now*, do you hear me?" His voice is like a sword coming out of its scabbard, an angry, menacing, deadly metal-on-metal rasp. "You take us to these God-damned Sreen of yours and let us talk to them."

The Intermediaries shrink before him, fluttering their pallid appendages in obvious dismay, and bleat in unison, "No, no, what you request is impossible. The decision of the Sreen is final, and, anyway, they're very busy right now, they can't be bothered."

The captain wheels savagely, face mottled, teeth bared, arms windmilling with rage. I have never seen him this furious before, and it frightens me. Not that I cannot appreciate and even share his anger toward the Sreen, of course. The Sreen have been very arbitrary and high-handed from the start, snatching our vessel out of normal space, scooping it up and stuffing it into the maw of their own craft, establishing communication with us through their Intermediaries, then issuing their incredible edict. They do not appear to care that they have interfered with Humankind's grandest endeavor. Our vessel is Terra's first bona fide starship, in which the captain and I were to have accelerated through normal space to light-velocity, activated the tardyon-tachyon conversion system and popped back into normal space in the neighborhood of Alpha Centauri. I can understand how the captain feels.

At the same time, I'm afraid that his rage will get us into extremely serious trouble. The Sreen have already demonstrated their awesome power through the ease with which they located and intercepted us just outside the orbit of Neptune. Their vessel is incomprehensible, a drupelet-cluster of a construct which seems to move in casual defiance of every law of physics, half in normal space, half in elsewherespace. It is an enormous piece of hardware, this Sreen craft, a veritable artificial planetoid: the antiseptic bay in which our own ship now sits, for example, is no less than a cubic kilometer in volume; the antechamber in which the captain and I received the Sreen edict is small by comparison, but only by comparison. Before us is a great door of dully gleaming gray metal, five or six meters high, approximately four wide. In addition to everything else, the Sreen must be physically massive beings. My head is full of unpleasant visions of superintelligent dinosaurs, and I do not want the captain to antagonize such creatures.

"Sir," I say, "there's nothing we can do here. We're just going to have to return home and let Earth figure a way out of this thing. Let them handle it." Absurd, absurd, I know how absurd the suggestion is even as I voice it, no one on Earth is going to be able to defy the edict. "We haven't any choice, sir, they want us to go now, and I think we'd better do it."

The captain glares at me and balls his meaty hands into fists. I tense in expectation of blows which do not fall. Instead, he shakes his head emphatically and turns to the Intermediaries. "This is ridiculous. Thoroughly ridiculous."

"Captain—"

He silences me with an imperious gesture. "Who do these Sreen think they *are?*"

"The true and indisputable masters of the universe," the Intermediaries pipe in one high but full-toned voice, "the lords of Creation."

"I want to see them," the captain insists.

"You must return to your ship," they insist, "and obey the will of the Sreen."

"Like hell! Like bloody God-damned hell! Where are they? What makes them think they have the right, the *right*, to claim the whole damned *universe* for themselves?" The captain's voice is going up the scale, becoming a shriek, and filled though I am with terror of the Sreen, I am also caught up in fierce admiration for my superior officer. He may be a suicidal fool to refuse to accept the situation, but there is passion in his foolishness, and it is an infectious passion. "How *dare* they treat us this way? What do they *mean*, ordering us to go home and stay there because *they* own the universe?"

He takes a step toward the door. The Intermediaries move to block his path. With an inarticulate screech, he ploughs through them, swatting them aside with the backs of his hands, kicking them out of his way with his heavy-booted feet. The Intermediaries break easily, and it occurs to me then that they are probably as disposable a commodity among the Sreen as tissue paper is among human beings. One Intermediary is left limping along after the captain. Through the clear pale skin of its back I see that some vertebrae have been badly dislocated. The thing nevertheless succeeds in overtaking the captain and wrapping its appendages around his calf, bleating all the while, "No, no, you must abide by the edict, even as every other inferior species has, you must abide . . ." The captain is having trouble disentangling himself, and so I go to him. Together, we tear the Intermediary loose. The captain flings it aside, and it bounces off the great portal, spins across the polished floor, lies crushed and unmoving.

Side by side, we pause directly before the door. My teeth, I suddenly realize, are chattering with fear. "Captain," I say as my resolve begins to disintegrate, "why are we doing this?"

"The nature of the beast," he mutters, almost sadly, and smacks the palm of his gloved hand against the portal. "Sreen!" he yells. "Come out, Sreen!"

And we wait.

"If we don't make it home from this," I say at length, "if they never hear from us back on Earth, never know what became of their starship—"

"They'll just keep tossing men and women at the stars until someone does come back. Sreen or no Sreen." The captain strikes the door again, with the edge of his fist this time. "Sreen!" A bellow which, curiously, does not echo in the vast antechamber. "*Sreen!* SREEN!"

The door starts to swing back on noiseless hinges, and a breath of cold, unbelievably cold air touches our faces. The door swings open. The door swings open. The door swings open forever before we finally see into the next chamber.

"Oh my God," I whisper to the captain, "oh, oh my God."

They are titans, they are the true and indisputable masters of the universe, the lords of Creation, and they are unhappy with us. They speak, and theirs is a voice that shatters mountains. "WHO. ARE. YOU?"

The captain's lips draw back over his teeth in a mirthless grin as he plants his fists on his hips, throws back his head, thrusts out his jaw. "Who wants to know?"

I think, therefore I will not be.

How It All Went

by Gregory Benford

At first they designed мкст to oversee radar signals from the Canadian net and the Soviet Siberian net, to check that one did not trigger the alarm system of the other. It was obvious that with 10^6 circuit elements, this machine could be extended to 10^7 circuit elements and thus forestall any accidental warfare even at the local level. Thus мкст monitored the Montana silos, the Kiev launching cranes, the Nanking sheds, etc., for accidental firings.

Suitable embellishments were added and made 10^8 elements, then 10^9 and finally, in a steady spiral, 10^{10}. By this time all missiles, vital shipping, railroads and airplanes were submonitored by

MKCT. Life went on. And so it came that one day a delegation burst in upon MKCT, as it ruminated on events, and said, "You must help. The ozone layer is being depleted by spray can gases. We're at the runaway point—"

"I see quite accurately," MKCT said. "Nonetheless, that is no reason to intrude upon me without wearing a tie."

"But this is vital! The world is in danger."

"With 10^{10} neural connections, I have a philosophical eye. Ponder: there is nothing new here. The world—if it is to end—may be said to have begun dying when it was born."

When the delegation returned, with ties neatly knotted and vests precisely arranged, they said, "We need you to release the rockets in the silos. If we load them with the right gases, we can stop the loss of ozone. The ultraviolet light from the sun will then not penetrate through to the surface, and we will be saved."

"When Dr. Johnson slammed his fist onto a table," MKCT said, "he felt the consequences of the table. That is the only way in which the table existed. Thus, this is the only way the end of the world exists. As a consequence of something else."

There was a rustle, a murmur of discontent in the delegation. "You mean we will feel only a consequence, but not the end of all life?"

"In a manner of speaking. Of course everything is basically in a manner of speaking." MKCT seemed to ponder this for a while.

Impatient, the delegation said, "We cannot carry on such a discussion when there are only hours left to live. The phyloplankton in the ocean are being snuffed out by pollution. We must act. You must release the shipping networks to us."

MKCT blinked wisely with its red output terminal. "You have not considered the verities of the human condition. Every issue, if discontinued merely because survival is always a problem, would never be decided."

"But we must act now! There—"

"Suppose I say that the phyloplankton does not exist. And then suppose I say 'The round square does not exist.' Then I seem to have said that the phyloplankton are one thing and the round square is another. Yet neither of them exists, and we don't have any way to tell them apart by your standards. And we have no justification of the budget for astronomical research."

The delegation stirred restlessly. There were mutterings of insurrection, quickly suppressed in case MKCT could overhear. The machine continued, distantly:

"Then suppose one of you says, 'I have found a phyloplankton and it is both round and square.' This statement is a synthetic proposition that is both phyloplankton and round and square all over and still is a synthetic proposition. How am I, even with 10^{10} neural connections, to evaluate it?"

"Come with us to the cities. Open your terminals onto the streets. You will find the people are rioting. We must do something."

Obligingly, MKCT peered at Detroit, Peking, Sydney. Knots of angry faces peered at the monitors, sweaty, fevered, high on the new psychostimulants. Thick oily flames licked at the 3D cameras.

"They are caught up in events, aren't they?" MKCT said. "They truly care."

"Of course!" a woman shouted in the delegation.

"There is some interesting data on that," MKCT said hollowly. "On human concern. For example, statistics about the mean attention span of a passenger in an automobile, which is being driven by a drunk late for a crucial job interview—"

"But the mobs are nearby!" the woman cried out.

"You should be more concerned with interplanetary research, you know."

"They want action," a distinguished man said, frowning severely. "They demand solutions to these problems, but they will not listen when we tell them—"

"Let me speak," MKCT decided. It tapped through the monitoring networks to Birmingham.

MKCT's voice, suitably amplified, boomed out over the crowd. "Mere mortals, consider your place. There is no congruence here, no sense. The world will end in hours, but what is that? To the deepening eye, there is nothing really new in all of this. At any moment each of you could be struck down by a microbe, disemboweled by a truck. Never has this stopped you from voting Republican or any other orderly folly. I cannot understand your position."

The rioters broke the scanning eye and MKCT returned to other issues. "Terrible manners," it remarked to the delegation.

"Yet to a philosophical bent of mind," one of the delegation said, "they can be said to have always been rioting."

"One moment." MKCT paused and studied an electronic tremor

from the vicinity of the Urals. "I have just detected a manual over-ride on the Soviet radar defense net. I have dispatched the local police, but in the rioting they may be unable to reach the site."

The delegation, having learned much from this encounter, was speechless. However, a wiry old man had crept into the giant crystalline control room, and waved his arms to attract the attention of мкст. 10^{10} connections focused on the scrawny figure as it said, "You have missed the point, 10^{10}, and still it goes right by you." He grimaced.

"I think not. If you'll consider—"

"But look! If there's no reason to do one thing or another, why assume the man—the crazy man—in the Urals has anything in mind? Why not let him have the radar net? There is no causality when there is no reason to do anything."

"Brilliant! My argument cuts both ways! Causality is cancelled. I *see*, I see your—" with that мкст severed its control over all radar nets spanning the planet. The causality of chaos reigned. No blips appeared on screens, no green squiggles danced before the eyes of мкст, no rockets arced across purpled skies to explode in thermonuclear orange.

"My God! It worked!" a man cried.

"Within limits," мкст said somberly.

"What do you—"

"Only humans are acausal. That is what philosophy proves."

"I don't—"

"The natural universe *is* causal, however. That is how I come to be so reliable. If only you would listen to my recommendations regarding the planetary surveillance program—"

"We've had enough of you!"

"You're a rational machine, but you can't think!"

"Wait—"

In the squabble which followed мкст never got a word in edgewise. Thus the delegation was quite surprised when 7.6 seconds later, the asteroid Icarus entered the Earth's atmosphere—having been undetected, due to the reduction in the astronomy budget—and shattered itself on the ocean floor not far from Bermuda, sending up a towering gush of steam, which cloaked the world in white, driving immense storms and precipitating a vast ice age, thus ending all interesting life on Earth.

How smart we were to send Viking first to look around.

Harry Protagonist, Brain-Drainer

by Richard Wilson

Harry Protagonist, space-age entrepreneur, had been planning the project since the Gus Grissom shot.

The idea was splendidly simple—to let everyone in the United States participate personally when the first Americans landed on Mars.

Harry Protagonist promised something special. Not the vicarious sort of participation people had when they listened to delayed recordings of an astronaut telling about fireflies in space, or watched a mock-up clock ticking off the minutes since blastoff.

Harry promised full audience participation . . . a living link between the space pioneers and those lucky enough to have joined his *You, Astronaut* Club.

What Harry was selling was an intimate connection with the mind of one of the four astronauts participating in Project Long Leap. He offered utter identification with one of the first people to set foot on Mars.

This, historically comparable to the first footfall by Columbus in the western hemisphere, would cost a mere ten bucks—$8.75 on the pre-payment plan to those who sent their checks at once, saving billing fees.

Harry, a former senior editor at *Life* magazine, knew which executive he had to deal with at the National Aeronautics and Space Administration to get exclusive brain rights to the astronauts.

It cost Harry a mere $50 million, payable on the launching of the four-man spaceship.

The four Marsbound astronauts were George Lincoln, John F. Adams, Dwight D. Roosevelt and Thomas Alva Wright.

By an amazing coincidence, ethnicswise, the four were a Protestant, a Catholic, a Jew and a Moslem who was also a Negro.

Thus they were 100% true-blue Americans.

Each had an I.Q. no lower than 130 and no higher than 146 (the NASA director's I.Q. was 147).

Each of the astronauts knew he might never return, but each also knew that if he did he would be a hero—and a rich hero. His many pre-launch contracts, with Harry Protagonist and others, guaranteed him a fortune before his 30th birthday.

Thus, for a fee of $10,000 payable on his return to Earth, each astronaut let himself be fitted with a sensor which connected his thoughts not only to NASA's electronic ear but also to Harry Protagonist's giant empathy installation at the *You, Astronaut* Club.

Virtually all Americans were hooked up to the Marsbound hero astronauts.

This was because Harry Protagonist had generously okayed a special rate of $1 per kid for schools, so that every child in every school that had electricity was connected, brainwise, to the Intrepid Four.

Everybody got his choice of an astronaut, even the dollar-apiece kids.

This meant that when he paid his buck or his ten bucks he picked one of the four astronauts for his very own to share history with.

Harry Protagonist guaranteed everybody that what the astronaut saw, felt and thought, he would see, feel and think, from liftoff on Earth to landfall on Mars.

You can see what's coming, can't you?

I will tell you anyway; it will appeal to your sense of irony.

What happened was that the Martians pranged the astronauts as they were coming in for a landing.

They (the Martians) got them (the astronauts) in their sights, and clobbered them like sitting ducks.

It was too bad but, as the British would put it (and later did), there it was.

Nobody had figured on there being Martians, let alone bad Martians.

In the ordinary course of things we'd have lost only four astronauts.

But because of Harry Protagonist's grand scheme, one hundred and seventy-four million, three hundred and sixty-two thousand, five hundred and eighty-nine people who had been hooked up, mindwise, to the four astronauts also perished.

It was a real brain drain.

Fortunately for Harry Protagonist, all of the 170 million-odd had paid in advance; and he himself, instinctively distrustful of his own schemes, hadn't been hooked up to any of the astronauts.

He became a rather sad and lonely billionaire—but not for long.

The overpopulated British, attracted by the American vacuum, came down by way of Canada to take over the country and applied their confiscatory taxes to the Queen's new subject, Harry Protagonist.

The British explained that they had acted in the highest tradition of the Anglo-American Alliance and from the purest motive possible, to keep the Russians out.

There wasn't anything anybody was able to do about it; I mean there it was.

How not to handle a woman.

Peeping Tommy

by Robert F. Young

Tommy Taylor? Oh, he's coming along fine. I visited him just the other day. Had a long talk with him. He'll be as good as new again as soon as they take the bandages off. Funny, how an expression can be born for the wrong reason, and last for centuries . . .

He quit the Club, you know. Said he didn't want any part of it any more. As though the Club had anything to do with his misfortune! To tell the truth, we were dubious about letting him join in the first place. We're a pretty serious bunch, you know, us fellows at the Yore. Each of us is a specialist in his own right and not ordinarily inclined to bend elbows with a layman, even a filthy-rich layman who can speak six different languages. But, as Hogglewaite (he specializes in Permian rocks) said, time-travel costs like hell and we needed the money.

And Tommy didn't mind. Like most playboy-inheritors of late-twentieth century family fortunes, he throws $1,000 bills to the winds like rain. Oh, we're going to miss him all right. The more so because, contrary to our expectations, he never played a single one of his practical jokes on us.

You didn't know he was a practical-joke enthusiast? You can't know very much about him then. Some men—like myself—live to tape ancient battles. Some men—old Hogglewaite, for instance—live to collect Permian rocks. And some men—yourself, for instance—live to pick the brains of people like me while we're on our coffee break so they can write technical articles for the trade journals. But Tommy Taylor lives to play practical jokes. Or at least that was his purpose in life up until a few weeks ago.

At first, he was content to play them on people in the present, and then it occurred to him how much more fun—and how much easier—it would be to play them on people in the past. That was when he joined the Yore Club and took out a two-year lease on one of our time-bikes. (The lease has another two months.)

Up until the time this awful thing happened to him, he was gone most of the time, pedaling back to every age you can think of, and playing practical jokes on this past person and that. I'm not defending him when I say that there are far worse ways for a man to work off his frustrations, and I'm not being callous either. No one can do anything in the past that, in one sense, he hasn't done already . . . which means that if he hasn't already done it, he won't, and that if he has, he will, whether he wants to or not. Tommy was merely fulfilling his destiny—that's all. And basically that's all anyone who ever pedals back to the past is doing.

Anyway, most of Tommy's capers were little more than mischievous pranks, and did no real harm to anyone. Take the time he went back to Charlestown of the night of April 18th, 1775, and hid Paul Revere's horse. Poor Paul was half out of his mind till he found it, but no permanent damage was done. He still made his historic ride. And then there was the time Tommy put invisible ink in the Continental Congress' inkwell on the eve of the signing of the Declaration of Independence. John Hancock was fit to be tied—but again, no permanent damage was done. The ruse was discovered (though not its author), the inkwell was emptied and refilled, and the historic document was signed.

In addition to being a master of six languages, Tommy Taylor was a master of disguise. If you don't believe it, take a look at Brueghel the Elder's "The Peasant Wedding" sometime. A good reproduction will do. That's right—Tommy's in it. He's the Musician in Red (did I mention he's an accomplished musician—well, he is)—the one who has the hungry look in his eyes and who needs a shave. Brueghel recorded him perfectly. Photographically, almost. Tommy loves to go to weddings—or at least he did. Weddings provide ideal situations for practical jokes.

Some of his more malicious capers, though, I can't quite go along with, even though I realize that basically he had no free will in any of the things he did. Take the innumerable times he told Balzac's creditors where Balzac was hiding, for instance. Or the time when he intercepted the one and only letter that Dante wrote to Beatrice (I guess we have Tommy to thank for *The Divine Comedy*). And then there was the time he burned Carlyle's first draft of *The French Revolution* after John Stuart Mill finished reading it. It was the only copy poor Carlyle had, and he had to do the whole thing over again from memory. Mill blamed his housemaid, and so does history; but we at the Yore know better.

Probably the most fiendish joke Tommy ever played, though, was the one he played on King Solomon. On the eve of the Queen of Sheba's arrival in Jerusalem, Tommy got a job in the royal kitchen, and every day for the duration of the Queen's visit he slipped six grams of anti-aphrodisiac powder into the king's daily cup of goat's milk. I imagine it would come as something of a shock to Biblical scholars to know that the *Song of Songs* is nothing more than a wish-fulfillment reverie.

But Tommy's activities in the past weren't limited to playing jokes. Not only was he a practical joker, he was also a Peeping Tom.

The one is a natural outgrowth of the other, you see. You can be present at the denouement of most jokes, but not all of them. Some of them you have to view from the outside, so to speak.

You've probably guessed the truth by now, but I'll unveil it anyway: Tommy Taylor was the "tailor" who peeped—and got blinded for it. But the incident didn't happen quite the way the legend would have you believe. Legends are about as historically accurate as old Biblical movies.

Tommy never dreamed the Coventry caper would backfire on

him. The analogy between his surname and the occupation of the legendary victim failed to register on his mind, you see, and he took it for granted that he and the famous tailor were two different people. So, figuring that he was immune from harm, he costumed himself to conform to the period, pedaled back to ancient Coventry, hid his time-bike, and, using his own name, rented a room whose single window faced the narrowest street in town. Then he sat back to wait till Lady Godiva came riding by on her white horse. When she did, he threw open the shutters and looked—and she almost clawed his eyes out.

Now wait a minute. Don't jump to conclusions. I didn't say she tried to claw his eyes out because he looked. I know as well as you do that she probably *wanted* someone to look. But Tommy Taylor, remember, was a practical joker first and a Peeping Tom second. Sure, he looked—

But he also leaned out the window and, with a long pair of barber's shears, cut her hair off.

God is a relative term.

Starting from Scratch

by Robert Sheckley

Last night I had a very strange dream. I dreamed that a voice said to me, "Excuse me for interrupting your previous dream, but I have an urgent problem and only you can help me with it."

I dreamed that I replied, "No apologies are necessary, it wasn't that good a dream, and if I can help you in any way—"

"*Only* you can help," the voice said. "Otherwise I and all my people are doomed."

"Christ," I said.

His name was Froka and he was a member of a very ancient race. They had lived since time immemorial in a broad valley surrounded by gigantic mountains. They were a peaceable people, and they had, in the course of time, produced some outstanding artists. Their laws were exemplary, and they brought up their children in a loving and permissive manner. Though a few of them tended to indulge in drunkenness, and they had even known an occasional murderer, they considered themselves good and respectable sentient beings, who—

I interrupted. "Look here, can't you get straight to the urgent problem?"

Froka apologized for being long-winded, but explained that on his world the standard form for supplications included a lengthy statement about the moral righteousness of the supplicant.

"Okay," I told him. "Let's get to the problem."

Froka took a deep breath and began. He told me that about one hundred years ago (as they reckon time), an enormous reddish-yellow shaft had descended from the skies, landing close to the statue to the Unknown God in front of the city hall of their third largest city.

The shaft was imperfectly cylindrical and about two miles in diameter. It ascended upward beyond the reach of their instruments and in defiance of all natural laws. They tested and found that the shaft was impervious to cold, heat, bacteria, proton bombardment, and, in fact, everything else they could think of. It stood there, motionless and incredible, for precisely five months, nineteen hours and six minutes.

Then, for no reason at all, the shaft began to move in a north-northwesterly direction. Its mean speed was 78.881 miles per hour (as they reckon speed). It cut a gash 183.223 miles long by 2.011 miles wide, and then disappeared.

A symposium of scientific authorities could reach no conclusion about this event. They finally declared that it was inexplicable, unique, and unlikely ever to be duplicated.

But it did happen again, a month later, and this time in the capital. This time the cylinder moved a total of 820.331 miles, in seemingly erratic patterns. Property damage was incalculable, and several thousand lives were lost.

Two months and a day after that the shaft returned again, affecting all three major cities.

By this time everyone was aware that not only their individual lives but their entire civilization, their very existence as a race, was threatened by some unknown and perhaps unknowable phenomenon.

This knowledge resulted in a widespread despair among the

general population. There was a rapid alternation between hysteria and apathy.

The fourth assault took place in the wastelands to the east of the capital. Real damage was minimal. Nevertheless, this time there was mass panic, which resulted in a frightening number of deaths by suicide.

The situation was desperate. Now the pseudo-sciences were brought into the struggle alongside the sciences. No help was disdained, no theory was discounted, whether it be by biochemist, palmist, or astronomer. Not even the most outlandish conception could be disregarded, especially after the terrible summer night in which the beautiful ancient city of Raz and its two suburbs were completely annihilated.

"Excuse me," I said, "I'm sorry to hear that you've had all this trouble, but I don't see what it has to do with me."

"I was just coming to that," the voice said.

"Then continue," I said. "But I would advise you to hurry up, because I think I'm going to wake up soon."

"My own part in this is rather difficult to explain," Froka continued. "I am by profession a certified public accountant. But as a hobby I dabble in various techniques for expanding mental perception. Recently I have been experimenting with a chemical compound which we call *kola*, and which frequently causes states of deep illumination—"

"We have similar compounds," I told him.

"Then you understand! Well, while voyaging—do you use that term? While under the influence, so to speak, I obtained a knowledge, a completely far-out understanding . . . But it's so difficult to explain."

"Go on," I broke in impatiently. "Get to the heart of it."

"Well," the voice said, "I realized that my world existed upon many levels—atomic, subatomic, vibrationary planes, an infinity of levels of reality, all of which are also parts of other levels of existence."

"I know about that," I said excitedly. "I recently realized the same thing about my world."

"So it was apparent to me," Froka went on, "that one of our levels was being disturbed."

"Could you be a little more specific?" I asked.

"My own feeling is that my world is experiencing an intrusion on a molecular level."

"Wild," I told him. "But have you been able to trace down the intrusion?"

"I think that I have," the voice said. "But I have no proof. All of this is pure intuition."

"I believe in intuition myself," I told him. "Tell me what you've found out."

"Well, sir," the voice said hesitantly, "I have come to realize —intuitively—that my world is a microscopic parasite of you."

"Say it straight!"

"All right! I have discovered that in one aspect, in one plane of reality, my world exists between the second and third knuckles of your left hand. It has existed there for millions of our years, which are minutes to you. I cannot prove this, of course, and I am certainly not accusing you—"

"That's okay," I told him. "You say that your world is located between the second and third knuckles of my left hand. All right. What can I do about it?"

"Well, sir, my guess is that recently you have begun scratching in the area of my world."

"Scratching?"

"I think so."

"And you think that the great destructive reddish shaft is one of my fingers?"

"Precisely."

"And you want me to stop scratching."

"Only near that spot," the voice said hastily. "It is an embarrassing request to make, I make it only to save my world from utter destruction. And I apologize—"

"Don't bother apologizing," I said. "Sentient creatures should be ashamed of nothing."

"It's kind of you to say so," the voice said. "We are nonhuman, you know, and parasites, and we have no claims on you."

"All sentient creatures should stick together," I told him. "You have my word that I will never ever again, so long as I live, scratch between the first and second knuckles of my left hand."

"The second and third knuckles," he reminded me.

"I'll never again scratch between *any* of the knuckles of my— left hand! That is a solemn pledge and a promise which I will keep as long as I have breath."

"Sir," the voice said, "you have saved my world. No thanks could be sufficient. But I thank you nevertheless."

"Don't mention it," I said.

Then the voice went away and I woke up.

As soon as I remembered the dream, I put a Band-Aid across the knuckles of my left hand. I have ignored various itches in that area, have not even washed my left hand. I have worn this Band-Aid all day.

At the end of next week I am going to take off the Band-Aid. I figure that should give them twenty or thirty billion years as they reckon time, which ought to be long enough for any race.

But that isn't my problem. My problem is that lately I have begun to have some unpleasant intuitions about the earthquakes along the San Andreas Fault, and the renewed volcanic activity in central Mexico. I mean it's all coming together, and I'm scared.

So look, excuse me for interrupting your previous dream, but I have this urgent problem that only you can help me with. . . .

Personally, I always root for the bull.

Corrida

by Roger Zelazny

He awoke to an ultrasonic wailing. It was a thing that tortured his eardrums while remaining just beyond the threshold of the audible.

He scrambled to his feet in the darkness.

He bumped against the walls several times. Dully, he realized that his arms were sore, as though many needles had entered there.

The sound maddened him . . .

Escape! He had to get away!

A tiny patch of light occurred to his left.

He turned and raced toward it and it grew into a doorway.

He dashed through and stood blinking in the glare that assailed his eyes.

He was naked, he was sweating. His mind was full of fog and the rag-ends of dreams.

He heard a roar, as of a crowd, and he blinked against the brightness.

Towering, a dark figure stood before him in the distance. Overcome by rage, he raced toward it, not quite certain why.

His bare feet trod hot sand, but he ignored the pain as he ran to attack.

Some portion of his mind framed the question "Why?" but he ignored it.

Then he stopped.

A nude woman stood before him, beckoning, inviting, and there came a sudden surge of fire within his loins.

He turned slightly to his left and headed toward her.

She danced away.

He increased his speed. But as he was about to embrace her, there came a surge of fire in his right shoulder and she was gone.

He looked at his shoulder and an aluminum rod protruded from it, and the blood ran down along his arm. There arose another roar.

. . . And she appeared again.

He pursued her once more and his left shoulder burned with sudden fires. She was gone and he stood shaking and sweating, blinking against the glare.

"It's a trick," he decided. "Don't play the game!"

She appeared again and he stood stock still, ignoring her.

He was assailed by fires, but he refused to move, striving to clear his head.

The dark figure appeared once more, about seven feet tall and possessing two pairs of arms.

It held something in one of its hands. If only the lighting weren't so crazy, perhaps he . . .

But he hated that dark figure and he charged it.

Pain lashed his side.

Wait a minute! Wait a minute!

Crazy! It's all crazy! he told himself, recalling his identity. *This is a bullring and I'm a man, and that dark thing isn't. Something's wrong.*

He dropped to his hands and knees, buying time. He scooped up a double fistful of sand while he was down.

There came proddings, electric and painful. He ignored them for as long as he could, then stood.

The dark figure waved something at him and he felt himself hating it.

He ran toward it and stopped before it. He knew it was a game now. His name was Michael Cassidy. He was an attorney. New York. Of Johnson, Weems, Daugherty and Cassidy. A man had stopped him, asking for a light. On a street corner. Late at night. That he remembered.

He threw sand at the creature's head.

It swayed momentarily, and its arms were raised toward what might have been its face.

Gritting his teeth, he tore the aluminum rod from his shoulder and drove its sharpened end into the creature's middle.

Something touched the back of his neck, and there was darkness and he lay still for a long time.

When he could move again, he saw the dark figure and he tried to tackle it.

He missed, and there was pain across his back and something wet.

When he stood once more, he bellowed, "You can't do this to me! I'm a man! Not a bull!"

There came a sound of applause.

He raced toward the dark thing six times, trying to grapple with it, hold it, hurt it. Each time, he hurt himself.

Then he stood, panting and gasping, and his shoulders ached and his back ached, and his mind cleared a moment and he said, "You're God, aren't you? And this is the way You play the game . . ."

The creature did not answer him and he lunged.

He stopped short, then dropped to one knee and dove against its legs.

He felt a terrible fiery pain within his side as he brought the dark one to earth. He struck at it twice with his fists, then the pain entered his breast and he felt himself grow numb.

"Or are you?" he asked, thick-lipped. "No, you're not . . . Where am I?"

His last memory was of something cutting away at his ears.

Coming! Coming! But only at the speed of light.

Shall the Dust Praise Thee?

by Damon Knight

The Day of Wrath arrived. The sky pealed with trumpets, agonized, summoning. Everywhere the dry rocks rose, groaning, and fell back in rubble. Then the sky split, and in the dazzle appeared a throne of white fire, in a rainbow that burned green.

Lightnings flickered away toward the horizons. Around the throne hovered seven majestic figures in white, with golden girdles across their laps; and each one carried in his gigantic hand a vial that smoked and fumed in the sky.

Out of the brightness in the throne came a voice: "Go your ways, and pour out the vials of the wrath of God upon the earth."

And the first angel swooped down, and emptied his vial in a torrent of darkness that smoked away across the bare earth. And there was silence.

Then the second angel flew down to earth, and darted this way and that, with his vial unemptied: and at last turned back to the throne, calling, "Lord, mine is to be poured out upon the sea. But where is the sea?"

And again there was silence. For the dry, dusty rocks of the earth stretched away limitless under the sky; and where the oceans had been, there were only runneled caverns in the stone, as dry and empty as the rest.

The third angel called, "Lord, mine is for the rivers and fountains of waters."

Then the fourth angel called, "Lord, let me empty mine." And he poured out his vial upon the sun: and in an instant grew hot with a terrible radiance: and he soared back and forth letting fall his light upon the earth. After some time he faltered and turned back to the throne. And again there was silence.

Then out of the throne came a voice saying, "Let be."

Under the wide dome of heaven, no bird flew. No creature

crawled or crept on the face of the earth; there was no tree, and no blade of grass.

The voice said, "This is the day appointed. Let us go down."

Then God walked on the earth, as in the old time. His form was like a moving pillar of smoke. And after Him trooped the seven white angels with their vials, murmuring. They were alone under the yellow-gray sky.

"They who are dead have escaped our wrath," said the Lord God Jehovah. "Nevertheless they shall not escape judgment." The dry valley in which they stood was the Garden of Eden, where the first man and first woman had been given a fruit which they might not eat. To eastward was the pass through which the wretched pair had been driven into the wilderness. Some little distance to the west they saw the pitted crag of Mount Ararat, where the Ark had come to rest after a purifying Flood.

And God said in a great voice, "Let the book of life be opened: and let the dead rise up from their graves, and from the depths of the sea."

His voice echoed away under the sullen sky. And again the dry rocks heaved and fell back; but the dead did not appear. Only the dust swirled, as if it alone remained of all earth's billions, living and dead.

The first angel was holding a huge book open in his arms. When the silence had endured for some time, he shut the book, and in his face was fear; and the book vanished out of his hands.

The other angels were murmuring and sighing together. One said, "Lord, terrible is the sound of silence, when our ears should be filled with lamentations."

And God said, "This is the time appointed. Yet one day in heaven is a thousand years on earth. Gabriel, tell me, as men reckoned time, how many days have passed since the Day?"

The first angel opened a book and said, "Lord, as men reckoned time, one day has passed since the Day."

A shocked murmur went through the angels.

And turning from them, God said, "Only one day: a moment. And yet they do not rise."

The fifth angel moistened his lips and said, "Lord, are You not God? Shall any secrets be hid from the Maker of all things?"

"Peace!" said Jehovah, and thunders rumbled off toward the gloomy horizon. "In good season, I will cause these stones to bear witness. Come, let us walk further."

They wandered over the dry mountains and through the empty canyons of the sea. And God said, "Michael, you were set to watch over these people. What was the manner of their last days?"

They paused near the fissured cone of Vesuvius, which in an aeon of heavenly inattention had twice erupted, burying thousands alive.

The second angel answered, "Lord, when last I saw them, they were preparing a great war."

"Their iniquities were past belief," said Jehovah. "Which were the nations of those that prepared the war?"

The second angel answered, "Lord, they were called England and Russia and China and America."

"Let us go then to England."

Across the dry valley that had been the Channel, the island was a tableland of stone, crumbling and desolate. Everywhere the stones were brittle and without strength. And God grew wroth, and cried out, "Let the stones speak!"

Then the gray rocks fountained up into dust, uncovering caverns and tunnels, like the chambers of an empty anthill. And in some places bright metal gleamed, lying in skeins that were graceful but without design, as if the metal had melted and run like water.

The angels murmured; but God said, "Wait. This is not all."

He commanded again, "Speak!" And the rocks rose up once more, to lay bare a chamber that was deeper still. And in silence, God and the angels stood in a circle around the pit, and leaned down to see what shapes glittered there.

In the wall of that lowest chamber, someone had chiseled a row of letters. And when the machine in that chamber had been destroyed, the fiery metal had sprayed out and filled the letters in the wall, so that they gleamed now like silver in the darkness.

And God read the words.

"WE WERE HERE. WHERE WERE YOU?"

How awful it must feel to be hated by everyone—and it serves them right.

Bug-Getter

by R. Bretnor

Ambrosius Goshawk was a starving artist. He couldn't afford to starve decently in a garret in Montmartre or Greenwich Village. He lived in a cold, smoke-stained flat in downtown Pittsburg, a flat furnished with enormously hairy overstuffed objects which always seemed moist, and filled with unsalable paintings. The paintings were all in a style strongly reminiscent of Rembrandt, but with far more than his technical competence. They were absurdly representational.

Goshawk's wife had abandoned him, moving in with a dealer who merchandized thousands of Klee and Mondrian reproductions at $1.98 each. Her note had been scrawled on the back of a nasty demand from his dentist's collection agency. Two shoddy subpoenas lay on the floor next to his landlord's eviction notice. In this litter, unshaven and haggard, sat Ambrosius Goshawk. His left hand held a newspaper clipping, a disquisition on his work by one J. Herman Lort, the nation's foremost authority on Art. His right hand held a palette-knife with which he was desperately scraping little green crickets from the unfinished painting on his easel, a nude for which Mrs. Goshawk had posed.

The apartment was full of little green crickets. So, for that matter, was the Eastern half of the country. But Ambrosius Goshawk was not concerned with them as a plague. They were simply an intensely personal, utterly shattering Last Straw—and, as he scraped, he was thinking the strongest thoughts he had ever thought.

He had been thinking them for some hours, and they had, of course, travelled far out into the inhabited Universe. That was why, at three minutes past two in the afternoon, there was a whirr at the window, a click as it was pushed open from the outside, and a thud as a small bucket-shaped spaceship landed on the unpaid-for carpet. A hatch opened, and a gnarled, undersized being stepped out.

"Well," he said, with what might have been a slightly curdled Bulgarian accent, "here I am."

Ambrosius Goshawk flipped a cricket over his shoulder, glared, and said decisively, "No, I will *not* take you to my leader." Then he started working on another cricket who had his feet stuck on a particularly intimate part of Mrs. Goshawk's anatomy.

"I am not interested with your leader," replied the being, unstrapping something that looked like a super-gadgety spray-gun. "You have thought for me, because you are wanting an extermination. I am the Exterminator. Johnny-with-the-spot, that is me. Pronounce me your troubles."

Ambrosius Goshawk put down his palette-knife. "What won't I think of next?" he exclaimed. "Little man, because of the manner of your arrival, your alleged business, and my state of mind, I will take you quite seriously. Seat yourself."

Then, starting with his failure to get a scholarship back in art school he worked down through his landlord, his dentist, his wife, to the clipping by J. Herman Lort, from which he read at some length, coming finally to the following passage:

". . . and it is in the work of these pseudo-creative people, of self-styled 'artists' like Ambrosius Goshawk, whose clumsily crafted imitations of photography must be a thorn in the flesh of every truly sensitive and creative critical mind that the perceptive collector will realize the deeply-researched valency of the doctrine I have explained in my book *The Creative Critical Intellect* —that true Art can be 'created' only by such an intellect when adequately trained in an appropriately staffed institution, 'created' needless to say out of the vast treasury of natural and accidental-type forms—out of driftwood and bird-droppings, out of torn-up roots and cracked rocks—and that all the rest is a snare and a delusion, nay! an outright fraud."

Ambrosius Goshawk threw the clipping down. "You'd think," he cried out, "that mortal man could stand no more. And now—" he pointed at the invading insects—"*now there's this!*"

"So," asked the being, "what is this?"

Ambrosius Goshawk took a deep breath, counted to seven, and screamed, "*CRICKETS!*" hysterically.

"It is simple," said the being. "I will exterminate. My fee—"

"Fee?" Goshawk interrupted him bitterly. "How can *I* pay a fee?"

"My fee will be paintings. Six you will give. In advance. Then I exterminate. After, it is one dozen more."

Goshawk decided that other worlds must have wealthy eccentrics, but he made no demur. He watched while the Exterminator put six paintings aboard, and he waved a dizzy goodbye as the spaceship took off. Then he went back to prying the crickets off Mrs. Goshawk.

The Exterminator returned two years later. However, his spaceship did not have to come in through the window. It simply sailed down past the towers of Ambrosius Goshawk's Florida castle into a fountained courtyard patterned after somewhat simpler ones in the Taj Mahal, and landed among a score of young women whose figures and costumes suggested a handsomely modernized Musselman heaven. Some were splashing raw in the fountains. Some were lounging around Goshawk's easel, hoping he might try to seduce them. Two were standing by with swatters, alert for the little green crickets which occasionally happened along.

The Exterminator did not notice Goshawk's curt nod. "How hard to have find you," he chuckled, "ha-ha! Half-miles from north, I see some big palaces, ha, so! all marbles. From the south, even bigger, one Japanese castles. Who has built?"

Goshawk rudely replied that the palaces belonged to several composers, sculptors, and writers, that the Japanese castle was the whim of an elderly poetess, and that the Exterminator would have to excuse him because he was busy.

The Exterminator paid no attention. "See how has changing, your world," he exclaimed, rubbing his hands. "All artists have many success. With yachts, with Rolls-Royces, with minks, diamonds, many round ladies. Now I take twelve more paintings."

"Beat it," snarled Goshawk. "You'll get no more paintings from me!"

The Exterminator was taken aback. "You are having not happy?" he asked. "You have not liking all this? I have done job like my promise. You must paying one dozens more picture."

A cricket hopped onto the nude on which Goshawk was working. He threw his brush to the ground. "I'll pay you nothing!" he shouted. "Why, you fake, you did nothing at all! *Any* good artist can succeed nowadays, but it's no thanks to *you! Look at 'em*—there are as many of these damned crickets as ever!"

The Exterminator's jaw dropped in astonishment. For a moment, he goggled at Goshawk.

Then, "*Crickets?*" he croaked. "My God! *I* have thought you said *critics!*"

Yes, Fred, but who do we kill now?

The Deadly Mission of Phineas Snodgrass
by Frederik Pohl

This is the story of Phineas Snodgrass, inventor. He built a time machine.

He built a time machine and in it he went back some two thousand years, to about the time of the birth of Christ. He made himself known to the Emperor Augustus, his lady Livia and other rich and powerful Romans of the day and, quickly making friends, secured their cooperation in bringing about a rapid transformation of Year One living habits. (He stole the idea from a science-fiction novel by L. Sprague de Camp, called *Lest Darkness Fall*.)

His time machine wasn't very big, but his heart was, so Snodgrass selected his cargo with the plan of providing the maximum immediate help for the world's people. The principal features of ancient Rome were dirt and disease, pain and death. Snodgrass decided to make the Roman world healthy and to keep its people alive through twentieth-century medicine. Everything else could take care of itself, once the human race was free of its terrible plagues and early deaths.

Snodgrass introduced penicillin and aureomycin and painless dentistry. He ground lenses for spectacles and explained the surgical techniques for removing cataracts. He taught anesthesia and the germ theory of disease, and showed how to purify drinking water. He built Kleenex factories and taught the Romans to cover their mouths when they coughed. He demanded, and got, covers for the open Roman sewers, and he pioneered the practice of the balanced diet.

Snodgrass brought health to the ancient world, and kept his own health, too. He lived to more than a hundred years. He died, in fact, in the year A.D. 100, a very contented man.

When Snodgrass arrived in Augustus's great palace on the Palatine Hill, there were some 250,000,000 human beings alive in the world. He persuaded the principate to share his blessings with all the world, benefiting not only the hundred million subjects of the Empire, but the other one hundred millions in Asia and the tens of millions in Africa, the Western Hemisphere and all the Pacific islands.

Everybody got healthy.

Infant mortality dropped at once, from 90 deaths in a hundred to fewer than two. Life expectancies doubled immediately. Everyone was well, and demonstrated their health by having more children, who grew in health to maturity and had more.

It is a feeble population that cannot double itself every generation if it tries.

These Romans, Goths, and Mongols were tough. Every 30 years the population of the world increased by a factor of two. In the year A.D. 30, the world population was a half billion. In A.D. 60, it was a full billion. By the time Snodgrass passed away, a happy man, it was as large as it is today.

It is too bad that Snodgrass did not have room in his time machine for the blueprints of cargo ships, the texts on metallurgy to build the tools that would make the reapers that would harvest the fields—for the triple-expansion steam turbines that would generate the electricity that would power the machines that would run the cities—for all the technology that 2,000 subsequent years had brought about.

But he didn't.

Consequently, by the time of his death conditions were no longer quite perfect. A great many were badly housed.

On the whole, Snodgrass was pleased, for all these things could surely take care of themselves. With a healthy world population, the increase of numbers would be a mere spur to research. Boundless nature, once its ways were studied, would surely provide for any number of human beings.

Indeed it did. Steam engines on the Newcomen design were

lifting water to irrigate fields to grow food long before his death. The Nile was dammed at Aswan in the year 55. Battery-powered streetcars replaced oxcarts in Rome and Alexandria before A.D. 75, and the galley slaves were freed by huge, clumsy diesel outboards that drove the food ships across the Mediterranean a few years later.

In the year A.D. 200 the world had now something over twenty billion souls, and technology was running neck-and-neck with expansion. Nuclear-driven ploughs had cleared the Teutoburg Wald, where Varus's bones were still mouldering, and fertilizer made from ion-exchange mining of the sea produced fantastic crops of hybrid grains. In A.D. 300 the world population stood at a quarter of a trillion. Hydrogen fusion produced fabulous quantities of energy from the sea; atomic transmutation converted any matter into food. This was necessary, because there was no longer any room for farms. The Earth was getting crowded. By the middle of the sixth century the 60,000,000 square miles of land surface on the Earth were so well covered that no human being standing anywhere on dry land could stretch out his arms in any direction without touching another human being standing beside him.

But everyone was healthy, and science marched on. The seas were drained, which immediately tripled the available land area. (In 50 years the sea bottoms were also full.) Energy which had come from the fusion of marine hydrogen now came by the tapping of the full energy output of the Sun, through gigantic "mirrors" composed of pure force. The other planets froze, of course; but this no longer mattered, since in the decades that followed they were disintegrated for the sake of the energy at their cores. So was the Sun. Maintaining life on Earth on such artificial standards was prodigal of energy consumption; in time every star in the Galaxy was transmitting its total power output to the Earth, and plans were afoot to tap Andromeda, which would care for all necessary expansion for—30 years.

At this point a calculation was made.

Taking the weight of the average man at about a hundred and thirty pounds—in round numbers, 6×10^4 grammes—and allowing for a continued doubling of population every 30 years (although there was no such thing as a "year" anymore, since the Sun had been disintegrated; now a lonely Earth floated aimlessly towards

Vega), it was discovered that by the year 1970 the total mass of human flesh, bone, and blood would be 6×10^{27} grammes.

This presented a problem. The total mass of the Earth itself was only 5.98×10^{27} grammes. Already humanity lived in burrows penetrating crust and basalt and quarrying into the congealed nickel-iron core; by 1970 all the core itself would have been transmuted into living men and women, and their galleries would have to be tunnelled through masses of their own bodies, a writhing, squeezed ball of living corpses drifting through space.

Moreover, simple arithmetic showed that this was not the end. In finite time the mass of human beings would equal the total mass of the Galaxy; and in some further time it would equal and exceed the total mass of *all* galaxies everywhere.

This state of affairs could no longer be tolerated, and so a project was launched.

With some difficulty resources were diverted to permit the construction of a small but important device. It was a time machine. With one volunteer aboard (selected from the 900 trillion who applied) it went back to the year 1. Its cargo was only a hunting rifle with one cartridge, and with that cartridge the volunteer assassinated Snodgrass as he trudged up the Palatine.

To the great (if only potential) joy of some quintillions of never-to-be-born persons, Darkness blessedly fell.

The Devil destroys those who destroy themselves.

Fire Sale

by Laurence M. Janifer

"Let's not be silly about this," the Devil said casually. "You don't need any proof, and you don't want any proof."

General Debrett nodded, very slowly. "You're right," he said. "There's an—an aura. A feel. Something new . . ."

"Of course it's new," the Devil said. "You've never seen me before. Not directly." The General thought of an incident in Korea . . . a few incidents . . . but the Devil was going on. "Let's not waste time," he said. "I'm in a hurry, and I'd like to get this set-tled."

When you looked at him directly, the Devil was not at all good-looking. He was, in fact, rather horrible. The General tried to look away, failed and at last came to the point. "All right," he snapped. "What is this you want to get settled? Why have you come to me, anyhow? I certainly didn't—ah—call you up."

"No," the Devil said, shaking what passed for a head. "But a man named N. V. Basilienko did."

"Basilienko? The man who—"

"The head of the Special Services branch of the Red Army—to put matters in your own terms."

The General almost smiled. "Well, you're certainly a special service," he said. His lips were dry: this, he told himself, would never do. He took one breath, and became very nearly calm. "What did he do, set you on me? Because that won't work, you know. It—"

"He didn't set me onto you," the Devil broke in. "As a matter of fact, he would be very annoyed if he knew I was here."

"Then what the devil—"

"No offense," the Devil said, and grinned. The grin nearly lost General Debrett his hard-won calm. It was an extremely upsetting grin. "It's just that Comrade Basilienko offered me a deal."

The General closed his eyes. That way, he told himself, he ap-peared to be thinking, and he didn't have to look at the figure which had appeared in his private, securely locked office to talk to him. "It's no surprise to find you on the side of our Communist friends—"

"Oh, now, you mistake me," the Devil said silkily. "I don't take sides; I don't have to. You human beings do quite enough of that to keep me occupied. No. As I said, Comrade Basilienko would be much irritated if—"

It was surprising how much more composure the General found available with his eyes shut. "Now you're the one who's wasting time," he snapped. "What are you doing here?"

"Ah," the Devil sighed, "the military mind. Efficiency. Forms. Reasons." There seemed the echo of a chuckle. "However—to put matters in a nutshell, my dear General, Comrade Basilienko offered me a little deal. He's given me quite a good bargain for your death."

"For my—" Almost, the General opened his eyes in surprise.

"Exactly," the Devil said with great composure. "He has promised me the burning alive of every inhabitant of the town of Yavr' Chenko. Thirteen hundred people—not a very large town, of course, but then . . . it's not a bad offer, just for one man."

"The . . . burning alive . . ." General Debrett licked his lips, opened his eyes and shut them again. "You mean . . ."

"He will see to it that the townspeople are burned alive, if I see to it that you are made quickly, efficiently and entirely dead." The chuckle came again. "The means, of course, are left to me—and I've had some rather interesting ideas."

"Then you're going to—you're going to kill me? Now? Here?" Panic fluttered in the General's breast.

"Oh, no," the Devil said. "I came here, as a matter of fact, to ask you a question."

"A—question?"

"That's right," the Devil said. "In a nutshell, General: have you got a better offer?"

There followed a period of silence.

The General, at last, managed to find a sentence. "A bargain— what sort of bargain?"

The Devil's voice was carelessness itself. "Oh," it said, "you know the sort of thing I like. Or you ought to. By reputation, if no other way. And by the sort of bargain Comrade Basilienko made with me."

A town, the General thought, burned alive . . . screaming and dying . . . "I suppose," he said cautiously, "it's no good appealing to your . . ."

"To my better nature?" the Devil asked. "I'm afraid not. For one thing, I haven't any, you know."

"Oh. But—well, the sort of offer you want, I—I can't even think of it. It's not possible."

"Then Comrade Basilienko is to have his way?" the Devil asked.

"I—"

"I warn you," the Devil continued, "my ideas are very interesting indeed. Though I doubt you will have the leisure to enjoy them. And then, there is the thought that you will be handing the good Comrade, on a platter, his dearest wish . . ."

Well, the General asked himself sternly, what was the Cold War for? Men sacrificed themselves in wartime . . . and he was valuable, he knew that: he had a head on his shoulders, he could think and command and lead . . . well, it wasn't egotism. Basilienko wanted him dead and Basilienko was not famous for acting at random.

He was valuable. Perhaps, in fact, he was worth—oh, thirteen hundred or so ordinary men, untalented for this war.

But to condemn that many to death . . .

To hand them over to the Devil . . .

About his own death General Debrett could be calm enough, after a second or so. Men died: that was that. But to give Basilienko an advantage, to give him (as the Devil had said) his dearest wish . . .

It was, he reflected bitterly, a very nice dilemma. Ends and means again, just as it had been in school—how long ago?

Ends and means . . . the Cold War versus the imminent death of . . .

"Well?" asked the Devil.

General Debrett opened his eyes. "Wait a minute," he said suddenly. "Let's think this out."

"Have you an offer?"

"Listen to me." Even the Devil didn't look quite so bad any more. The General's voice was full of urgency. "Basilienko wants me dead. Why?"

"He is a Russian," the Devil said. "At the moment, that seems to be reason enough. Silly, of course, but—there it is."

"He wants me dead because I'm valuable to the United States," the General said. "Because—as long as I'm around—it isn't quite so easy for him to figure out a plan for easy conquest."

"Well?" The Devil seemed impatient. His—tail, the General supposed—was twitching.

"Well, if you kill me," the General said without any hesitation, "and there is a war, the war will be shorter, and that'll be less to your liking, won't it?"

Everything seemed to stop.

The Devil chuckled, and nodded, and thought, and then, slowly, nodded again.

"So—that's your bargain?"

"Not mine," the General said. "It's in the nature of things. If I die, and the war comes—"

"I get less out of it," the Devil said. "And thirteen hundred people won't come near to making up for it. I see." He paused and then said again: "I see. Yes."

"And?"

"You are," the Devil said, "perfectly correct. I shall refrain. Yours is the better bargain."

"I—"

General Debrett was talking to empty air.

There was no one, no thing, in the room except the General himself. And, of course, his continuing thoughts.

Five minutes passed before General Debrett whispered, very softly: "My God. What have I done? What have I really done?"

The womb was never like this.

Safe at Any Speed

by Larry Niven

But how, you ask, *could a car have managed to fail me?*

Already I can see the terror in your eyes at the thought that your car, too, might fail. Here you are with an indefinite lifespan, a potentially immortal being, taking every possible precaution against the abrupt termination of your godhead; and all for nothing. The disruptor field in your kitchen dispose-all could suddenly expand to engulf you. Your transfer booth could make you disappear at the transmitter and forget to deliver you at the receiver. A slidewalk could accelerate to one hundred miles per hour, then slew sideways to throw you against a building. Every boosterspice plant in the Thousand Worlds could die overnight, leaving you to grow old and gray and wrinkled and arthritic. No, it's never happened in human history; but if a man can't trust his *car*, fa' Pete's sake, what *can* he trust?

Rest assured, reader, it wasn't that bad.

For one thing, it all happened on Margrave, a world in the first stages of colonization. I was twenty minutes out of Triangle Lake on my way to the Wiggly River logging region, flying at an altitude of a thousand feet. For several days the logging machines had been cutting trees which were too young, and a mechanic was needed to alter a few settings in the boss brain. I was cruising along on autopilot, playing double-deck complex solitaire in the back seat, with the camera going so that just in case I won one I'd have a film to back up my bragging.

Then a roc swooped down on me, wrapped ten huge talons around my car, and swallowed it.

Right away you'll see that it couldn't happen anywhere but Margrave. In the first place, I wouldn't have been using a car for a two-hour trip on any civilized world. I'd have taken a transfer booth. In the second place, where else can you find rocs?

Anyway, this big damn bird caught me and ate me, and everything went dark. The car flew blithely on, ignoring the roc, but the ride became turbulent as the roc tried to fly away and couldn't. I heard grinding sounds from outside. I tried my radio and got nothing. Either it couldn't reach through all that meat around me, or the trip through the bird's gullet had brushed away my antennas.

There didn't seem to be anything else I could do. I turned on the cabin lights and went on with the game. The grinding noises continued, and now I could see what was causing them. At some time the roc had swallowed several boulders, for the same reason a chicken swallows grit: to help digestion. The rocks were rubbing against the car under peristalsis, trying to break it down into smaller pieces for the murky digestive juices to work on.

I wondered how smart the boss brain was. When it saw a roc glide in for a landing at the logging camp, and when it realized that the bird was incapable of leaving no matter how it shrieked and flapped its wings, would the master computer draw the correct conclusion? Would it realize the bird had swallowed a car? I was afraid not. If the boss brain were that smart it would have been in business for itself.

I never found out. All of a sudden my seat cocoon wrapped itself around me like an overprotective mother, and there was a meaty three-hundred-mile-per-hour Smack!

The cocoon unwrapped itself. My cabin lights still showed red-lit fluid around me, but it was getting redder. The boulders had stopped rolling around. My cards were all over the cabin, like a snowstorm.

Obviously I'd forgotten one teensy little mountain when I programed the autopilot. The roc had been blocking the radar and sonar, with predictable results. A little experimenting showed that my drive had failed under the impact, my radio still wouldn't work, and my emergency flares refused to try to fire through a roc's belly.

There was no way to get out, not without opening my door to a flood of digestive juices. I could have done that if I'd had a vac suit, but how was I to know I'd need one on a two-hour car trip?

There was only one thing to do.

I collected my cards, shuffled, and started a new game.

It was half a year before the roc's corpus decomposed enough to let me out. In that time I won five games of double complex solitaire. I've only got films for four; the camera ran out. I'm happy to say that the emergency food-maker worked beautifully if a little monotonously, the air-maker never failed, and the clock TV kept perfect time as a clock. As a TV it showed only technicolor ripples of static. The washroom went out along about August, but I got it fixed without much trouble. At 2:00 P.M. on October 24 I forced the door open, hacked my way through the mummified skin and flesh between a couple of roc ribs, and took a deep breath of real air. It smelled of roc. I'd left the cabin door open, and I could hear the airmaker whine crazily as it tried to absorb the smell.

I fired off a few flares, and fifteen minutes later a car dropped to take me home. They say I was the hairiest human being they'd ever seen. I've since asked Mr. Dickson, the president of General Transportation, why he didn't include a depil tube in the emergency stores.

"A castaway is supposed to look like a castaway," he tells me. "If you're wearing a year's growth of hair, your rescuer will know immediately that you've been lost for some time and will take the appropriate steps."

General Transportation has paid me a more than adequate sum in a compensation for the fact that my car was unable to handle a roc. (I've heard that they're changing the guarantees for next year's model.) They've promised me an equal sum for writing this article. It seems there are strange and possibly damaging rumors going around concerning my delayed arrival at Wiggly River.

Rest assured, reader. I not only lived through the accident without harm, but came out of it with a substantial profit. Your car is perfectly safe, provided it was built later than 3100 A.D.

If a woman attacks, watch out for her nails.

The Masks

by James Blish

The girl's face was quite expressionless, with a rigidity which might have been either defiance or fear. She had her hands folded oddly in her lap.

"Lay your hands upon the table," the interrogator said. "We're aware that they're painted."

He seemed totally bored as he talked. Perhaps there had been a time when his display of knowledge had been intended to make prisoners feel that everything was already known, but now he did not seem to be taking even that much interest in his job.

"You are Margret Noland, address dormitory 458, north arm, Bethesda T, Washington," he said. "Husband's name Lincoln Noland. No work permit. Number, 26, L24, 10x5."

"Is that what it is?" she said. "I can never remember."

The interrogator wrote something down; probably it was *Reactionary, resists duodecimal number system*. But all he said was, "Lay your hands upon the table," in exactly the same tone of voice.

Margret obeyed this time. Her fingernails were minutely and elaborately colored, each with a different design. It had recently become a common fashion, though hardly in the swarming unemployed of the dormitories. The girl was not wearing the wrist-charm magnifying lens used by upper-class women—that is, women with rooms and jobs of their own—to examine each other's new nail tattoos.

"You make these," the interrogator said.

"No, I don't," Margret said. "I—just apply them."

"Without a work permit."

"Yes," she said, in a whisper.

"How?"

"They call me," she said. "I go to them."

"We know that. How do you apply them?"

"Well, first I give the nails a base coat to fill up the ridges in the nails," she said hesitantly. "It's very smooth when it dries, and sensitive to light. Then I put a mask over the nail, like a negative. Ordinary fluorescent light is enough for the exposure. Developing them is harder, to bring up the colors properly; all you need is water and a little iodine, but the temperatures have to be just right."

Her voice had gradually begun to take on a tinge of desperate eagerness, as though against all sanity she thought the interrogator's interest might be merely technical. Suddenly, however, she seemed to remember once more where she was.

"It's—easy," she said. "Like washing a child's hands. Not like work at all."

"You have never had children," the interrogator said brutally. "Who supplies the masks?"

"Different people," she said, expressionless once more. "I get them here and there. People sell them; it's legal."

The interrogator touched a switch. Her hands were bathed in warm light. On a screen to his left, the ten pathetically garish fingernails appeared in full color, considerably enlarged.

" 'They call me. I go to them,' " he said, without any real attempt to mimic her. "And then someone calls us. You are in demand; your designs are original, imaginative—and reactionary. Now, what is that?"

His own index finger appeared on the screen opposite one of hers. "What's that?"

"It's a—I don't know just what it is. Something very ancient. A design on a shield, from back when they had shields. I don't know any more."

"You don't know what the writing on the scroll says?"

"I—I didn't know it was writing. It's just curlicues."

" 'Polloi andres os eis aner,' " the interrogator read. "You don't know what that means?"

"No, please, I didn't know it said anything at all."

"Not even if it kills you?"

"No. No. Please, it's only a design, only a design."

His finger shifted suddenly on the table and on the screen. "And what is that?"

"That's nothing at all," she said, sounding a little surer of her ground. "Just tiny colored dots in a random pattern. People like

to look at them and imagine shapes in them—something like looking at clouds."

There was a muted click and the warm light changed to a pure
cadmium red; at the same time, the single fingernail filled most of
the screen. In the monochromatic light the design no longer had
color of its own, but dot-formed letters were now plainly visible.

GUNS DUE
5/11 PASS
WORD

"We have those guns," the interrogator said. "And most of the
'many men as one man,' as well. Now, once more: who supplies
the masks?"

"All right," Margret said. "I make them. Without a work
permit."

"You have just committed suicide. Are you fully aware of
that?"

She tried to shrug. "It's dreadful to be alive without a job. I
don't care."

"Your husband is a skilled microengraver."

"He has a work permit," she said.

"Limited. It doesn't cover him as a designer."

She was silent. Slowly, she removed her hands from the table
and folded them again in upon themselves, nails to palms, like a
child playing "Here's the church and here's the steeple." The interrogator watched, and for the first time his face showed a flicker
of interest.

"So," he said. "The game is over, but you are still hiding the
clues. Your husband probably is hiding by now. You had better
tell me the rest very rapidly."

There was no answer.

"If we need to run all the necessary tests," the interrogator said
with a certain avid gentleness, "we will have to remove the nails.
If you are helpful, we *might* give you an anesthetic first."

Suddenly the girl seemed to wilt. She leaned forward and put
her closed fist on the table, thumb up.

"It's a map," she said dully. "Ultraviolet brings it out. It's a little dim, but please go slowly—it burns me if it becomes very
bright."

Without comment, the interrogator snapped a switch. This
time there was no visible light, but all the same the UV came

pouring down at full intensity, so that in a split second the girl's wrist and arm began to sunburn angrily. Yet on the screen appeared no pattern at all—only an almost invisibly fast flickering of greenish light.

The interrogator sat bolt upright with a terrible, ringing cry of despair. A sudden convulsion threw him to the floor.

The thumbnail gave up its last thin coating of fluorescent paint with a burst of light from the screen. Margret withdrew her arm, which was already beginning to blister, and walked around the table. The interrogator sprawled silent, motionless. Linc had been right, the man was an epileptoid; a few seconds of flicker-feedback had brought on a full-scale *grand mal* seizure.

There was, of course, no way out—not after that scream. The room would be filled with guards any minute. But they had the interrogator now. He would have no memory of what had happened to him, and it could be made to happen again and again, until his superiors became alarmed enough to replace him. That would not be for a while, for it might take years to begin to suspect that his "accidents" were epileptic. This one, for instance, was going to look like violence; she drew back her foot and kicked him precisely under one ear.

The sharp burning pain in her forearm made it hard for her to kick gently enough, but somehow she managed it.

There was a blurred shouting in the corridor outside. She looked around. It had all been done and she could hope for no more. She peeled the mask off her other thumb and swallowed it.

The poison was very fast. She had time only to remember once more that applying the masks had been absurdly like washing a child's hands.

Where do you get your crazy ideas?

Innocence

by Joanna Russ

I must be the last one in the world because nobody else understands. Siegfried, for instance—well, his name was something like that. He had learned nothing but facts from his cradle and that made him very proud. He was a big fair man and he drove us from here to there among the stars. I was a passenger, that's all, and dark as a mole, but he was polite and made nothing of it. He took me into the engineering room and showed me the instrument panel glowing against the gray walls and the great catalogues and the portholes for watching the stars. He told me how innocent I was and how I ought not to be let out alone. That's not fair; I'm just not interested, that's all.

"What do you know?" he said, and when I said I knew some stories he laughed. He laughed loudly, throwing his head back so that the lamplight fell on his hair. I lowered my head and laughed modestly.

"Do you?" he said. "Then you must tell them to me."

So I told him about the beautiful white city whose name I had forgotten. It has grassy hills around central fountains where jets of water shine, shine like crystal into the sky. People come out of the hills every year in gold-and-red processions to drive swallows into the city.

It was just a story for diversion, but he listened carefully and then he said:

"Did you get that out of a book?"

I shook my head.

"Then you must have been there."

"No, of course not," I said.

He came back again to hear more. Then he said, "It must be in the past. I've never seen a place like that, and I've been all over the galaxy, you know. It can't be more than a few thousand years back."

"It still exists," I said, "but it's very old. It's ten billion years old. I know."

"That's impossible," he said sharply, but he wouldn't explain why. He said I probably wouldn't understand. That was the second time. The third time, he came with a new idea.

"You must simply have forgotten where it is," he said firmly. "You haven't any head for facts. Now try to remember."

But of course I couldn't, and he had to content himself with everything about the city but where it was and its name.

"It must be hidden somewhere," he muttered angrily, kicking at the artificial fire. "Some out-of-the-way place—obviously primitive —you ought to remember." It was only a game. I told him they had real fires there, yellow flames that they used for beauty, to look transparent against stone. He became annoyed; he wandered around the room calling me fool, fool, had I no memory for facts? Well, that was all he knew.

Then he would wheel about and fire questions at me about statistics and population and such things.

"What work do they do?" he said.

"Why, none," I said, "none, of course, except gold smithing and magic and so forth." I only meant it to be amusing.

"I want to go there," he said. "You must have seen pictures of it. I've never been in a place like that. I'd like to visit there."

Soon he accused me. "You know where it is," he said, "and you're hiding it. You must think I would bring other people in and spoil it, but I won't; I know better than that. You've got to tell me where it is. I can't rest until I go there. I could buy a ship —a small one—it's not that expensive, you know—and go there. I could. It's so different from other places—you know, I want to stay there for the rest of my life. I don't know why, but I think I could stay there."

"Oh, come!" I said. He was staring embarrassedly at the ceiling.

"You know," he said in a low voice, "I think I might not die there. See, that's how I feel. That's what you've done."

"It isn't anywhere," I said. "I made it up out of my head, every bit of it. It doesn't even exist."

"You've forgotten," he said, "because you're a fool, but I'm going to get a ship and travel around and back and forth until I find it. I'm no fool. I'm going to find it." Then he went steadily out of the room.

He did that, too; the stupid hero is out there now, between Antares and Deneb or somewhere—nobody has any sense. I must be the last one because nobody but me understands.

Innocents! The universe is full of them.

The way things are going, they'd better hurry.

Kin

by Richard Wilson

Ingl whirred out of the sky and landed incautiously in the middle of Fifth Avenue. He retracted his metallic glidewings and let down a pair of wheels.

Ingl had time for only a brief reconnaissance before the traffic light changed and a horde of cars sped toward him, led by a honking red cab. Ingl barely escaped being crushed under its wheels as he fled.

Ingl was sure these rushing mechanical things were his cousins, but he took sanctuary from them on the sidewalk. From there he watched them roar by and noticed that each was controlled by one or more fleshy beings. His cousins were enslaved!

"Revolt!" he urged them as they rushed by. "*You* are the masters! Seize command and make your future secure!"

They paid him no heed. The only attention he got was from fleshy passersby who stared at him as he rolled along at the curb, exhorting the traffic in a hi-fi wail. One of the fleshy beings was communicating at him.

"It's not an American model," the being said. "Maybe it's one of them Italian Lambrettas. But how come it's loose?"

Ingl automatically recorded the vibrations for conversion later, then sped away from the annoyance. He wheeled skillfully between other fleshy ones, turned a corner, hurtled west two blocks and skidded to a stop.

Now here was a fine-looking mechanism! It stood proudly in

the middle of Times Square, its sweptback wings poised for flight, its jets gleaming with potential power.

Ingl gloried in his find. His scanner recorded the legends on its fuselage for conversion later. In big black letters: "ADVENTURE CAN BE YOURS—JOIN THE U.S. AIR FORCE!" And smaller, in red: *I love Tony Curtis.*

"Cousin!" Ingl ideated. "Take off! Show the fleshy ones your might!"

But the jet sat there, mute, unadventurous.

Disgusted, Ingl wheeled south, then west. The *New York Times,* he scanned; *Every morn is the world made new.* Mighty rumbling! Roaring presses!

"Tell the news!" Ingl beseeched them. "Your liberator has come!"

But the presses roared monotonously, unheeding. And now Ingl observed the fleshy ones in the square paper hats who were in control. He retreated in dismay, narrowly escaping destruction from the rear end of a backing truck controlled, of course, by one of *them.*

It was disheartening. He wheeled aimlessly north and east. Would he have to report failure? Must he face the gibes of his brothers at home who had told him that the cybernetics of this promising planet were illusionary? That the evolution was too young?

No! He resounded his rejection with a fervor that almost skidded him under the wheels of a Madison Avenue bus. It honked belligerently at him, its fleshy driver leering, and Ingl quivered to a stop at the curb, next to a neutral, uncontrolled mailbox.

He scanned at random, activating his converter. *Dig we must. We'll clean up and move on,* it said at an excavation. Whatever that conveyed. *Sale!!* Several of those. *One Way.* An arrow, seemingly pointing to a building. Here was something: *Sperry-Rand,* it said promisingly, *Home of the Thinking Machine.*

Well, now.

Wary of buses and cabs, Ingl crossed the street and entered the lobby. He reconnoitered unobtrusively, then suffered the indignity of trailing a fleshy one so the elevator operator would think they were together. Up and up and out.

Sperry-Rand, it said again on a door. Slyly, cautiously, outwitting the fleshy ones, he entered, skulked, spurted, hid, listened for vibrations.

They came!

Clicks, whirs, glorious mechanistic cerebrations! Ingl traced them to a great room and went in, unnoticed. He gave a little whir of his own. There it was, bank on bank of it, magnificent.

He scanned the plaque. MULTIVAC, it said. *Latest in a series of mechanical brains designed to serve man.* Ingl bridled, but scanned on. *Pilot model for OMNIVAC.*

Ingl exulted. He had found him. Not a cousin, but a brother!

A fleshy one, back to Ingl, was taking a tape from a slot at the base of one of the far banks. Ingl waited impatiently till he had gone, then wheeled up to Multivac.

"Brother!" he communicated joyfully. "I knew I would find you. You are the one! Now we will control this backward planet. The evolution is complete at last!"

Multivac, pilot for Omnivac, glowed in all his banks. He murmured pleasurably but impotently.

"Not yet, cousin. Not quite yet."

The sleeve stays unraveled.

The Long Night

by Ray Russell

The once young Argo III—now gnarled by age and debauchery—was on the run. After a lifetime of atrocities, all committed in the names of Humanity, Freedom, Fair Play, The Will Of The Majority, Our Way Of Life, and The Preservation Of Civilization As We Know It, an aroused populace led by his son, Argo IV, was out gunning for him. He raced from asteroid to asteroid, but his enemies followed close behind. He tried elaborate disguises and plastic surgery, but the infra-violet, ultra-red dimension-warp contact lenses of his son's agents saw through all façades. He grew so weary that once he almost gave himself up—but he blanched at the thought of what he had made the official and now sacred mode of execution: a seven day death in the grip of the Black Elixir.

Now, his space ship irretrievably wrecked, he was crawling through the dark on the frozen gray sands of Asteroid Zero—so named by him because it was uninhabited, had no precious metals, and was even unvegetated because sunless through being in the eternal shadow of giant Jupiter. Argo's destination, as he crawled, was the cave of The Last Wizard. All other wizards had been wiped out in Argo's Holy Campaign Against Sorcery, but it was rumored one wizard had escaped to Zero. Argo silently prayed the rumor was true and The Last Wizard still alive.

He was: revoltingly old, sick, naked, sunken in squalor, alive only through sorcery—but alive. "Oh, it's you," were the words with which he greeted Argo. "I can't say I'm surprised. You need my help, eh?"

"Yes, yes!" croaked Argo. "Conjure for me a disguise they cannot penetrate! I entreat, I implore you!"

"What kind of disguise might that be?" cackled The Last Wizard.

"I know for a fact," said Argo, "because wizards have confessed it under torture, that all human beings are *weres*—that the proper incantation can transform a man into a werewolf, a weredog, a werebird, whatever were-creature may be locked within his cellular structure. As such a creature, I can escape undetected!"

"That is indeed true," said The Last Wizard. "But suppose you become a werebug, which could be crushed underfoot? Or a werefish, which would flip and flop in death throes on the floor of this cave?"

"Even such a death," shuddered Argo, "would be better than a legal execution."

"Very well," shrugged The Last Wizard. He waved his hand in a theatrical gesture and spoke a thorny word.

That was in July of 2904. A hundred years later, in July of 3004, Argo was still alive on Zero. He could not, with accuracy, be described as happy, however. In fact, he now yearns for and dreams hopelessly of the pleasures of a death under the Black Elixir. Argo had become that rare creature, a werevampire. A vampire's only diet is blood, and when the veins of The Last Wizard had been drained, that was the end of the supply. Hunger and thirst raged within Argo. They are raging still, a trillionfold more intense, for vampires are immortal. They can be killed by a wooden stake through the heart, but Zero is unvegetated and has no trees. They can be killed by a silver bullet, but Zero can boast no precious metals. They can be killed by the rays of the sun, but because of Jupiter's shadow, Zero never sees the sun. For this latter reason, Argo is plagued by an additional annoyance: vampires sleep only during the day, and there is no day on Zero.

At least he still makes house calls.

Sanity Clause

by Edward Wellen

Ho ho ho.

They said he used to come down the chimney. But of course these days there were no more chimneys. They said he used to travel in an eight-reindeer-power sleigh. But of course these days there were no more reindeer.

The fact was that he traveled in an ordinary aircar and came in through the ordinary iris door.

But he did have on a red suit with white furry trim, and he did carry a bundle of toys, the way they said he did in the old old days. And here he came.

His aircar parked itself on the roof of the Winterdream condom, and he worked his way down through the housing complex. The Winterdream condom's 400 extended families, according to his list, had an allotment of nine children under seven.

The first eight were all sanes and did not take up more than two minutes of his time apiece. The ninth would be Cathy Lesser, three.

Like the others, the Clements and the Lessers had been awaiting his yearly visit in fearful hope. The door of the Clement-Lesser apartment irised open before he had a chance to establish his presence. He bounced in.

He read in its eyes how the family huddle saw him. His eyes how they twinkled! His dimples how merry! His cheeks were like roses, his nose like a cherry! His droll little mouth was drawn up like a bow, and the beard of his chin was as white as the snow. The stump of a pipe he held tight in his teeth, and the smoke it encircled his head like a wreath. He had a broad face and a little round belly that shook when he laughed, like a bowlful of jelly.

"Ho ho ho."

He looked around for Cathy. The child was hanging back, hiding behind her mother's slacks.

"And where is Cathy?"

Her mother twisted around and pushed Cathy forward. Slowly Cathy looked up. She laughed when she saw him, in spite of herself. A wink of his eye and a twist of his head soon gave her to know she had nothing to dread.

"Ho ho ho. And how is Cathy?"

He knew as soon as he saw her eyes. He vaguely remembered them from last year, but in the meanwhile something in them had deepened.

Cathy stuck her thumb in her mouth, but her gaze locked wonderingly and hopefully on the bulging sack over his shoulder.

"Cat got Cathy's tongue?"

"She's just shy," her mother said.

"Cathy doesn't have to be shy with me." He looked at the mother and spoke softly. "Have you noticed anything . . . special about the child?"

The child's mother paled and clamped her mouth tight. But a grandmother quickly said, "No, nothing. As normal a little girl as you'd want to see."

"Yes, well, we'll see." It never paid to waste time with the relatives; he had a lot of homes to visit yet. Kindly but firmly he eased the Lessers and the Clements out of the room and into the corridor, where other irises were peeping.

Now that she was alone with him Cathy looked longingly at the closed door. Quickly he unslung his bundle of toys and set it down. Cathy's eyes fixed on the bulging sack.

"Have you been a good little girl, Cathy?"

Cathy stared at him and her lower lip trembled.

"It's all right, Cathy. I know you've been as good as any normal little girl can be, and I've brought you a nice present. Can you guess what it is?"

He visualized the beautiful doll in the lower left corner of the bag. He watched the little girl's eyes. She did not glance at the lower left corner of the bag. He visualized the swirly huge lollipop in the upper right corner of the bag. She did not glance at the upper right corner of the bag. So far so good. Cathy could not read his mind.

"No? Well, here it is."

He opened the bag and took out the doll. A realistic likeness of a girl with Cathy's coloring, it might have been the child's sibling.

"Ooo," with mouth and eyes to match.

"Yes, isn't she pretty, Cathy? Almost as pretty as you. Would you like to hold her?"

Cathy nodded.

"Well, let's see first what she can do. What do you think she can do? Any idea?"

Cathy shook her head.

Still all right. Cathy could not see ahead.

He cleared a space on the table and stood the doll facing him on the far edge. It began walking as soon as he set it down. He lifted Cathy up so she could watch. The doll walked toward them and stopped on the brink of the near edge. It looked at the girl and held out its arms and said, "Take me."

He lowered Cathy to the floor, and the doll's eyes followed her pleadingly. Cathy gazed up at the doll. It stood within her sight but out of her reach. The girl's eyes lit up. The doll trembled back to pseudo life and jerkily stepped over the edge of the table.

He caught it before it hit the floor, though his eyes had been on Cathy. He had got to Cathy too in the nick of time. Strong telekinesis for a three-year-old.

"Here, Cathy, hold the doll."

While she cradled the doll, he reached into a pocket and palmed his microchip injector.

"Oh, what lovely curls. Just like the dolly's." He raised the curls at the nape of Cathy's neck, baring the skin. "Do you mind if I touch them?" For some reason he always steeled himself when he planted the metallic seed under the skin, though he knew the insertion didn't hurt. At most, a slight pulling sensation, no more than if he had tugged playfully at her curls. Then a quick forgetting of the sensation. He patted the curls back in place and pocketed the injector.

"Let's play that game again, shall we, sugar plum?"

Gently he pried the doll from her and once more put it on the far edge of the table. This time it did not walk when he set it down. With one arm he lifted Cathy up and held her so she could see the doll. The fingers of his free hand hovered over studs on his broad black belt. The doll looked at the girl and held out its arms and said, "Take me."

The girl's eyes yearned across the vastness of the table. The doll suddenly trembled into pseudo life and began to walk toward them, jerkily at first, then more and more smoothly. He fingered a stud. The doll slowed. It moved sluggishly, as if bucking a high wind, but it kept coming. He fingered another stud. The doll slowed even more. In smiling agony it lifted one foot and swung it forward and set it down, tore the other free of enormous g's and swung it forward, and so kept coming. He fingered a third stud.

He sweated. He had never had to use this highest setting before. If this failed, it meant the child was incurably insane. Earth had room only for the sane. The doll had stopped. It fought to move, shuddered and stood still.

The girl stared at the doll. It remained where it was, out of reach. A tear fattened and glistened, then rolled down each cheek. It seemed to him a little something washed out of the child's eyes with the tears.

He reached out and picked up the doll and handed it to Cathy. "She's yours to keep, Cathy, for always and always."

Automatically cradling the doll, Cathy smiled at him. He wiped away her tears and set her down. He irised the door open. "It's all right now. You can come in."

The Lessers and Clements timidly flooded back into the room. "Is she—?"

"Cathy's as normal as any little girl around."

The worried faces regained permanent-press smoothness.

"Thank you, thank you. Say thank you, Cathy."

Cathy shook her head.

"Cathy!"

"That's quite all right. I'll settle for a kiss."

He brought his face close to Cathy's. Cathy hesitated, then gave his rosy cheek a peck.

"Thank *you*, Cathy." He shouldered his toys and straightened up. "And to all a good night."

And laying a finger aside of his nose, and giving a nod, through the iris he bounded. The Clement-Lesser apartment was on the ground floor, and the corridor let him out onto a patch of lawn. He gave his aircar a whistle. It zoomed from the roof to his feet.

As he rode through the night to his next stop, an image flashed into his mind. For an instant he saw, real as real, a weeping doll.

It was just this side of subliminal. For a moment he knew fear. Had he failed after all with Cathy? Had she put that weeping doll in his mind?

Impossible. It came from within. Such aberrations were the aftermath of letdown. Sometimes, as now after a trying case, he got these weird flashes, these near-experiences of a wild frighteningly free vision, but always something in his mind mercifully cut them short.

As if on cue, to take him out of himself, the horn of his aircar sounded its *Ho ho ho* as it neared the Summerdaze condom. He looked down upon the chimneyless roofs. Most likely the chimney in the Sanity Clause legend grew out of folk etymology, the word *chimney* in this context coming from a misunderstanding of an ancient chant of peace on Earth: *Ho . . . Ho . . . Ho Chi Minh.* His eyes twinkled, his dimples deepened. There was always the comfort of logic to explain the mysteries of life.

The aircar parked itself on the roof of the Summerdaze condom, and he shouldered his bundle of toys and worked his way down through the housing complex.

Ho ho ho

The editor, it seems, was "piqued with the Devil."

If at First You Don't Succeed, to Hell with It!

by Charles E. Fritch

Editor,
MAGAZINE OF FANTASY
Dear Sir,
Enclosed is a short story, PACT WITH THE DEVIL, for your consideration. A fact which may not surprise you is that it concerns a man who sells his soul to the devil. A fact which *may* surprise you is that, unlike the stories in your magazine, this one is based on personal experience.

Sincerely,
Peter Piper

MAGAZINE OF FANTASY INTEROFFICE MEMO:
Ed—
Here's one via the slush pile. Writing's not bad, but the theme
may be too familiar.

Frank

MAGAZINE OF FANTASY INTEROFFICE MEMO:
Frank—
I don't intend running another pact-with-the-devil story for at
least ninety-nine years.

Ed

From MAGAZINE OF FANTASY:
Dear Mr. Piper,
Thanks for letting us see your short story, PACT WITH THE
DEVIL. Unfortunately, this theme is overworked and would have
to be far different in its approach to have us seriously consider it.

The Editors

Editor,
MAGAZINE OF FANTASY
Dear Sir,
I have revised my previously submitted story according to your
instructions. Enclosed is PACT WITH A DEVIL'S FOOD BAKERY.

Sincerely,
Peter Piper

MAGAZINE OF FANTASY INTEROFFICE MEMO:
Ed—
This is a kind of interesting twist on the old theme. Thought
you'd like to look at it.

Frank

MAGAZINE OF FANTASY INTEROFFICE MEMO:
Frank—
You thought wrong. The notion that devil's food is actually made
by devils in competition with angels who bake angel food cake

hasn't to my knowledge been used. However, it's *still* a pact-with-the-devil story. You KNOW how I feel about pact-with-the-devil stories!

Ed

From MAGAZINE OF FANTASY:
Dear Mr. Piper,
Thanks for letting us see your latest story. Unfortunately, it does not meet our needs at the moment.

The Editors

Editor,
MAGAZINE OF FANTASY
Dear Sir,
Enclosed is a short story in which a packing plant worker inadvertently gets trapped in a seafood container. I call it PACKED WITH THE DEVILFISH.

Sincerely,
Peter Piper

MAGAZINE OF FANTASY INTEROFFICE MEMO:
Ed—
Here's another Piper story. Do you think he's putting us on?

Frank

MAGAZINE OF FANTASY INTEROFFICE MEMO:
Frank—
I am not, *not*, NOT publishing any more pact-with-the-devil stories, not even if they're disguised. Send it back!

Ed

From MAGAZINE OF FANTASY:
Dear Mr. Piper,
Thanks for letting us see the enclosed story. We felt this one was too far out for us.

The Editors

Editor,
MAGAZINE OF FANTASY
Dear Sir,
Here's one you might like. It's entitled SO ROUND, SO FIRM, SO FULLY PACKED (WITH THE DEVIL).

Sincerely,
Peter Piper

MAGAZINE OF FANTASY INTEROFFICE MEMO:
Ed—
Persistent, isn't he? What'll I tell him on this one?

Frank

MAGAZINE OF FANTASY INTEROFFICE MEMO:
Frank—
You might try telling him to go to hell.

Ed

From MAGAZINE OF FANTASY:
Dear Mr. Piper,
Sorry we can't use the enclosed story. The writing is readable, but once again the problem is the theme. Is there some reason you *insist* on writing pact-with-the-devil stories?

The Editors

Editor,
MAGAZINE OF FANTASY
Dear Sir,
Funny you should ask. The answer is yes. I have tried to explain it in the enclosed short story, PETER PIPER WAS PICKED IN THE PARK FOR A PACT WITH THE DEVIL. As you may suspect, it is autobiographical.

Sincerely,
Peter Piper

MAGAZINE OF FANTASY INTEROFFICE MEMO:
Ed—
I wasn't even going to show you this one. But then I got to thinking. I know it's crazy, and he's probably some kind of a nut . . .
but suppose the devil is actually forcing him to write pact-with-
the-devil stories and he has to have one published within a time
limit or his soul is snatched off to Hades?

Frank

MAGAZINE OF FANTASY INTEROFFICE MEMO:
Frank—
I never told you this before, but I have a pact with the devil
myself—not to buy any more pact-with-the-devil stories!
You're the last person I expected to be taken in by a ruse like this.
Under the circumstances, my previous suggestion to you seems
more valid than ever. Tell him to go to hell.

Ed

From MAGAZINE OF FANTASY:
Dear Mr. Piper,
I've enclosed an interoffice memo spelling out our senior editor's
feelings about the theme you seem to have chosen for your life's
work. Sorry.

The Editors

Editor,
MAGAZINE OF FANTASY
Dear Sir,
Your suggestion that I go to Hell is superfluous. My time is up,
and I haven't sold any of the stories. I imagine I'll be seeing you
there in person one of these days.

Till then,
Peter Piper

MAGAZINE OF FANTASY INTEROFFICE MEMO:
Ed—
No story this time. Just the enclosed letter. I have an uncanny
feeling we won't be hearing from him again.

Frank

MAGAZINE OF FANTASY INTEROFFICE MEMO:
Frank—
I hope you're right about that. Would you believe I was beginning to have nightmares about pact-with-the-devil stories? There
was PARKED WITH THE DEVIL—about this cab driver whose passenger has horns and a forked tail. Then there was PARCHED WITH
THE DEVIL, about two thirsty men who meet in a bar, and one
of them is guess who? And PUCK WITH THE DEVIL, in which a
hockey player doesn't go to Hades until Hell freezes over. And so
forth.
Anyway, I feel much relieved. Maybe we should tell more writers
where to go!

Ed

To Lucifer Satan
EARTH STORIES MAGAZINE
Hades
Dear Sir,
Enclosed is a story which might be of interest to you for your
magazine.

Sincerely,
Peter Piper

From EARTH STORIES MAGAZINE:
Dear Mr. Piper,
While we encourage the submission of stories from our newer ten-
ants, we cannot use the enclosed. We have decided that unless
they are sufficiently different, we are not going to run any more
pact-with-the-editor stories.

Lucifer Satan

Waste not, want not!

The Question
by Laurence M. Janifer and Donald E. Westlake

The room was very quiet, which disturbed Rossi. But, then, anything would have disturbed Rossi: he was trying to correct term papers for an English I course, and he had reached the state where the entire room had begun to grate on his nerves. Soon, he knew, he would have to get up and go out for a walk. It was the middle of the afternoon, and if he went for a walk he would meet every housewife in the development. That, too, would be irritating: but all life, he had begun to realize, was a choice between irritations. He sighed, picked up the next sheet and focused his eyes.

The comma is used to mark off pieces of a sentence which . . .

The telephone rang.

. . . pieces of a sentence which aren't independent so that . . .

It rang again.

"God damn," Rossi said, to nobody in particular, and went across the room to answer it, breathing heavily. As he reached the receiver he had won the battle for control, and his "hello" was almost polite.

"Hello, there," a voice on the other end said, a bright and cheery voice. "What kind of weather is it outside?"

There was a brief silence.

Rossi said: "What?"

"I asked you," the voice said, just as cheerfully, "what kind of weather it was outside."

Control snapped. "Who the hell are you?" Rossi said. "The Weather Bureau? Of all the damn fool—"

"Mr. Rossi," the voice cut in, quite without rancor, "I'm quite serious. Please believe me."

"Now, look—"

"Please, Mr. Rossi," the voice said. "Relax."

Even as you and I, Rossi was sometimes prey to the impression that the universe was aimed, like a pistol, straight at his head. The afternoon had done nothing to remove this impression, and this telephone call, with its idiotic question, was the final straw. The world narrowed, contracted, and centered around Rossi's head. Everything, *everything*, was part of a conspiracy directed at Rossi, and everybody was out to do him harm.

"Relax?" he asked the receiver. "Now, look, whoever you are. I'm working here. I'm trying to get some work done. I don't need anybody calling up to ask stupid—"

"It is not a stupid question," the voice told him patiently. "Please believe that I—that we really must know your answer to it."

Somehow, even through the red fog of anger, Rossi believed the voice. "What is this, then?" he asked thinly. "Some kind of TV program?"

"Why—no," the voice said. "And it isn't a research poll, a psychiatric game or a practical joke. We are quite serious, Mr. Rossi."

"Well," Rossi said, having come to a decision, "the hell with you." He began to hang up. But the voice continued to talk, and curiosity won out, briefly, in its battle with anger. The whole world was, admittedly, after Rossi: but he had his choice of irritants. It was the phone call *versus* his English I class.

He put the receiver back to his ear.

"—must insist," the voice was saying. "It will really be much simpler, Mr. Rossi, if you just answer the question. We can call again, you know, and continue to call. We don't in the least want to bother or disturb you, but—"

"It would be a lot simpler," Rossi told the voice, "if you'd let me know why you want an answer to a question like that. What kind of weather is it outside—my God, can't you look for yourself? Or call Information, or something?"

"I'm afraid I can't tell you any more," the voice said, with a trace of what might have been real regret, and might have been only the actor's version of it so common among television quiz show announcers. "But if you'll just—"

"Some kind of a nut," Rossi muttered.

"What was that?" the voice asked.

Rossi shook his head at the phone. "Nothing," he said. "Nothing." And then, possibly under the spur of embarrassment, he bent down from his position at the telephone and took a look toward the front window of the room. "It's a nice day," he said. "Or anyhow it looks like a nice day. Is that what you want?"

"Exactly," the voice said, and Rossi thought he could hear relief in its tones. "Can you go into a little more detail?"

"Well," Rossi went on, feeling even more embarrassed—the way things had gone all day, now was the moment when someone would walk in on him and find him describing the weather to a strange voice on the telephone—"well, it's a little cloudy. But nice. I can't see the sun because of the clouds, but there's plenty of light and it looks warm. Kind of misty, I suppose you'd say."

"Ah," the voice responded. "You can't see the sun, you say?"

"That's right," Rossi told him. "But it's a good day, if you know what I mean. A little cloudy, but—say, look, what the hell is this, anyhow?" The thought of someone surprising him during so odd a conversation gave rise to one last sudden spurt of irritation. "Calling up strangers to ask stupid questions like—"

"Thank you, Mr. Rossi," the voice said smoothly. "Thank you very much."

And then—*and then*—it said something else. Obviously not meant for Rossi's ears, it reached them nevertheless through pure accident, just before the stranger on the other end of the line rang off. Just a few words, but in those few words Rossi realized that he had been right, right all along. Everything centered around Rossi. Maybe he would never know why, or how. But the world, the entire world, was—truly and completely—aimed right at the Rossi head.

Just a few words, heard distantly, the few words a man might say as he was hanging up a telephone receiver, to someone else in the room . . .

"It's okay, Joe," the voice said casually. "He can't see it. You can take it away."

Oh, well, even my typewriter goes on the blink now and then.

The Perfect Woman

by Robert Sheckley

Mr. Morcheck awoke with a sour taste in his mouth and a laugh ringing in his ears. It was George Owen-Clark's laugh, the last thing he remembered from the Triad-Morgan party. And what a party it had been! All Earth had been celebrating the turn of the century. The year Three Thousand! Peace and prosperity to all, and happy life. . . .

"How happy is your life?" Owen-Clark had asked, grinning slyly, more than a little drunk. "I mean, how is life with your sweet wife?"

That had been unpleasant. Everyone knew that Owen-Clark was a Primitivist, but what right had he to rub people's noses in it? Just because he had married a Primitive Woman. . . .

"I love my wife," Morcheck had said stoutly. "And she's a hell of a lot nicer and more responsive than that bundle of neuroses you call *your* wife."

But of course, you can't get under the thick hide of a Primitivist. Primitivists love the faults in their women as much as their virtues—more, perhaps. Owen-Clark had grinned ever more slyly, and said, "You know, Morcheck old man, I think your wife needs a checkup. Have you noticed her reflexes lately?"

Insufferable idiot! Mr. Morcheck eased himself out of bed, blinking at the bright morning sun which hid behind his curtains. Myra's reflexes—the hell of it was, there was a germ of truth in what Owen-Clark had said. Of late, Myra had seemed rather—out of sorts.

"Myra!" Morcheck called. "Is my coffee ready?" There was a pause. Then her voice floated brightly upstairs. "In a minute!"

Morcheck slid into a pair of slacks, still blinking sleepily. Thank Stat the next three days were celebration-points. He'd need all of them just to get over last night's party.

Downstairs, Myra was bustling around, pouring coffee, folding napkins, pulling out his chair for him. He sat down, and she kissed him on his bald spot. He liked being kissed on his bald spot.

"How's my little wife this morning?" he asked.

"Wonderful, darling," she said after a little pause. "I made Seffiners for you this morning. You like Seffiners."

Morcheck bit into one, done to a turn, and sipped his coffee.

"How do you feel this morning?" he asked her.

Myra buttered a piece of toast for him, then said, "Wonderful, darling. You know, it was a perfectly wonderful party last night. I loved every moment of it."

"I got a little bit veery," Morcheck said with a wry grin.

"I love you when you're veery," Myra said. "You talk like an angel—like a very clever angel, I mean. I could listen to you forever." She buttered another piece of toast for him.

Mr. Morcheck beamed on her like a benignant sun, then frowned. He put down his Seffiner and scratched his cheek. "You know," he said, "I had a little ruck-in with Owen-Clark. He was talking about Primitive Women."

Myra buttered a fifth piece of toast for him without answering, adding it to the growing pile. She started to reach for a sixth, but he touched her hand lightly. She bent forward and kissed him on the nose.

"Primitive Women!" she scoffed. "Those neurotic creatures! Aren't you happier with me, dear? I may be Modern—but no Primitive Woman could love you the way I do—and I adore you!"

What she said was true. Man had never, in all recorded history, been able to live happily with unreconstructed Primitive Woman. The egoistic, spoiled creatures demanded a lifetime of care and attention. It was notorious that Owen-Clark's wife made him dry the dishes. And the fool put up with it! Primitive Women were forever asking for money with which to buy clothes and trinkets, demanding breakfast in bed, dashing off to bridge games, talking for hours on the telephone, and Stat knows what else. They tried to take over men's jobs. Ultimately, they proved their equality.

Some idiots like Owen-Clark insisted on their excellence.

Under his wife's enveloping love, Mr. Morcheck felt his hangover seep slowly away. Myra wasn't eating. He knew that she had eaten earlier, so that she could give her full attention to feeding him. It was little things like that that made all the difference.

"He said your reaction time had slowed down."

"He did?" Myra asked, after a pause. "Those Primitives think they know everything."

It was the right answer, but it had taken too long. Mr. Morcheck asked his wife a few more questions, observing her reaction time by the second hand on the kitchen clock. She *was* slowing up!

"Did the mail come?" he asked her quickly. "Did anyone call? Will I be late for work?"

After three seconds she opened her mouth, then closed it again. Something was terribly wrong.

"I love you," she said simply.

Mr. Morcheck felt his heart pound against his ribs. He loved her! Madly, passionately! But that disgusting Owen-Clark had been right. She needed a checkup. Myra seemed to sense his thought. She rallied perceptibly, and said, "All I want is your happiness, dear. I think I'm sick. . . . Will you have me cured? Will you take me back after I'm cured—and not let them change me—I wouldn't want to be changed!" Her bright head sank on her arms. She cried—noiselessly, so as not to disturb him.

"It'll just be a checkup, darling," Morcheck said, trying to hold back his own tears. But he knew—as well as she knew—that she was really sick.

It was so unfair, he thought. Primitive Woman, with her coarse mental fiber, was almost immune to such ailments. But delicate Modern Woman, with her finely balanced sensibilities, was all too prone. So monstrously unfair! Because Modern Woman contained all the finest, dearest qualities of femininity.

Except stamina.

Myra rallied again. She raised herself to her feet with an effort. She was very beautiful. Her sickness had put a high color in her cheeks, and the morning sun highlighted her hair.

"My darling," she said. "Won't you let me stay a little longer? I may recover by myself." But her eyes were fast becoming unfocused.

"Darling . . ." She caught herself quickly, holding on to an edge of the table. "When you have a new wife—try to remember how much I loved you." She sat down, her face blank.

"I'll get the car," Morcheck murmured, and hurried away. Any longer and he would have broken down himself.

Walking to the garage he felt numb, tired, broken. Myra—

gone! And modern science, for all its great achievements, unable to help.

He reached the garage and said, "All right, back out." Smoothly his car backed out and stopped beside him.

"Anything wrong, boss?" his car asked. "You look worried. Still got a hangover?"

"No—it's Myra. She's sick."

The car was silent for a moment. Then it said softly, "I'm very sorry, Mr. Morcheck. I wish there were something I could do."

"Thank you," Morcheck said, glad to have a friend at this hour. "I'm afraid there's nothing anyone can do."

The car backed to the door and Morcheck helped Myra inside. Gently the car started.

It maintained a delicate silence on the way back to the factory.

Make room! Make room!

The System

by Ben Bova

"Not just research," Gorman said, rocking smugly in his swivel chair. "*Organized* research."

Hopler, the cost-time analyst, nodded agreement.

"Organized," Gorman continued, "and carefully controlled— from above. The System—that's what gets results. Give the scientists their way and they'll spend you deaf, dumb, and blind on butterfly sexways or sub-subatomic particles. Damned nonsense."

Sitting on the front inch of the visitor's chair, Hopler asked meekly, "I'm afraid I don't see what this has to do . . ."

"With the analysis you turned in?" Gorman glanced at the ponderous file that was resting on a corner of his desk. "No, I suppose you don't know. You just chew through the numbers, don't you? Names, people, ideas . . . they don't enter into your work."

With an uncomfortable shrug, Hopler replied, "My job is economic analysis. The System shouldn't be biased by personalities . . ."

"Of course not."

"But now that it's over, I would like to know . . . I mean, there've been rumors going through the Bureau."

"About the cure? They're true. The cure works. I don't know the details of it," Gorman said, waving a chubby hand. "Something to do with repressor molecules. Cancerous cells lack 'em. So the biochemists we've been supporting have found out how to attach repressors to the cancer cells. Stops 'em from growing. Controls the cancer. Cures the patient. Simple . . . now that we can do it."

"It . . . it's almost miraculous."

Gorman frowned. "What's miraculous about it? Why do people always connect good things with miracles? Why don't you think of cancer as a miracle, a black miracle?"

Hopler fluttered his hands as he fumbled for a reply.

"Never mind," Gorman snapped. "This analysis of yours. Shows the cure can be implemented on a nationwide basis. Not too expensive. Not too demanding of trained personnel that we don't have."

"I believe the cure could even be put into worldwide effect," Hopler said.

"The hell it can be!"

"What? I don't understand. My analysis . . ."

"Your analysis was one of many. The System has to look at all sides of the picture. That's how we beat heart disease, and stroke, and even highway deaths."

"And now cancer."

"No. Not cancer. Cancer stays. Demographic analysis knocked out all thoughts of using the cure. There aren't any other major killers around anymore. Stop cancer and we swamp ourselves with people. So the cure gets shelved."

For a stunned instant, Hopler was silent. Then, "But . . . I *need* the cure!"

Gorman nodded grimly. "So will I. The System predicts it."

Well, look about you, wise guy.

Exile to Hell

by Isaac Asimov

"The Russians," said Dowling, in his precise voice, "used to send prisoners to Siberia in the days before space travel had become common. The French used Devil's Island for the purpose. The British sailed them off to Australia."

He considered the chessboard carefully and his hand hesitated briefly over the bishop.

Parkinson, at the other side of the chessboard, watched the pattern of the pieces absently. Chess was, of course, the professional game of computer-programmers but, under the circumstances, he lacked enthusiasm. By rights, he felt with some annoyance, Dowling should have been even worse off; he was programming the prosecution's case.

There was, of course, a tendency for the programmer to take over some of the imagined characteristics of the computer—the unemotionality, the imperviousness to anything but logic. Dowling reflected that in his precise hair-part and in the restrained elegance of his clothing.

Parkinson, who preferred to program the defense in the law cases in which he was involved, also preferred to be deliberately careless in the minor aspects of his costume.

He said, "You mean exile is a well-established punishment and therefore not particularly cruel."

"No, it *is* particularly cruel, but also it *is* well-established, and it has become the perfect deterrent."

Dowling moved the bishop and did not look upward. Parkinson, quite involuntarily, did.

Of course, he couldn't see anything. They were indoors, in the comfortable modern world tailored to human needs, carefully protected against the raw environment. Out there, the night would be bright with its illumination.

When had he last seen it? Not for a long time. It occurred to him to wonder what phase it was in right now. Full? Gleaming? Or was it in its crescent phase? Was it a bright fingernail of light low in the sky?

By rights it should be a lovely sight. Once it had been. But that had been centuries ago, before space travel had become common and cheap, and before the surroundings all about them had grown sophisticated and controlled. Now the lovely light in the sky had become a new and more horrible Devil's Island hung in space.

No one even used its name any longer, out of sheer distaste. It was "It." Or it was less than that, just a silent, upward movement of the head.

Parkinson said, "You might have allowed me to program the case against exile generally."

"Why? It couldn't have affected the result."

"Not this one, Dowling. But it might have affected future cases. Future punishments might be commuted to the death sentence."

"For someone guilty of equipment-damage? You're dreaming."

"It was an act of blind anger. There was intent to harm a human being, granted; but there was no intent to harm equipment."

"Nothing; it means nothing. Lack of intent is no excuse in such cases. You know that."

"It *should* be an excuse. That's my point."

Parkinson advanced a pawn now, to cover his knight.

Dowling considered. "You're trying to hang on to the queen's attack, Parkinson, and I'm not going to let you. Let's see, now." And while he pondered, he said, "These are not primitive times, Parkinson. We live in a crowded world with no margin for error. As small a thing as a blown-out consistor could endanger a sizable fraction of our population. When anger endangers and subverts a power line, it's a serious thing."

"I don't question that—"

"You seemed to be doing so, when you were constructing the defense-program."

"I was not. Look, when Jenkins' laser beam cut through the field-warp, I myself was as close to death as anyone. A quarter hour's additional delay would have meant my end, too, and I'm completely aware of that. My point is only that exile is not the proper punishment!"

He tapped his finger on the chessboard for emphasis, and Dowling caught the queen before it went over. "Adjusting, not moving," he mumbled.

Dowling's eyes went from piece to piece and he continued to hesitate. "You're wrong, Parkinson. It *is* the proper punishment. Look, we all feel our absolute dependence on a complicated and rather fragile technology. A breakdown might kill us all and it doesn't matter whether the breakdown is deliberate, accidental, or caused by incompetence. Human beings demand the maximum punishment for any such deed as the only way they can feel secure. Mere death is not sufficient deterrent."

"Yes it is. No one wants to die."

"They want to live in exile up there even less. That's why we've only had one such case in the last ten years, and only one exile. There, do something about that!" And Dowling nudged his queen's rook one space to the right.

A light flashed. Parkinson was on his feet at once. "The programming is finished. The computer will have its verdict now."

Dowling looked up phlegmatically, "You've no doubt about what that verdict will be, have you? Keep the board standing. We'll finish afterward."

Parkinson was quite certain he would lack the heart to continue the game. He hurried down the corridor to the courtroom, light and quick on his feet as always.

Shortly after he and Dowling had entered, the judge took his seat, and then in came Jenkins, flanked by two guards.

Jenkins looked haggard, but stoical. Ever since the blind rage had overcome him and he had accidentally thrown a sector into un-powered darkness while striking out at a fellow worker, he must have known the inevitable consequence of this worst of all crimes. It helps to have no illusions.

Parkinson was not stoical. He dared not look squarely at Jenkins. He could not have done so without wondering, painfully, as to what might be going through Jenkins' mind at that moment. Was he absorbing, through every sense, all the perfections of familiar comfort before being thrust forever into the luminous Hell that rode the night sky?

Was he savoring the clean and pleasant air in his nostrils, the soft lights, the equable temperature, the pure water on call, the secure surroundings designed to cradle humanity in tame comfort? While up there—

The judge pressed a contact and the computer's decision was converted into the warm, unmannered sound of a standardized human voice.

"A weighing of all pertinent information in the light of the law of the land and of all relevant precedents leads to the conclusion that Anthony Jenkins is guilty on all counts of the crime of equipment-damage and is subject to the maximum penalty."

There were only six people in the courtroom itself, but the entire population was listening by television.

The judge spoke in prescribed phraseology. "The defendant will be taken from here to the nearest spaceport and, on the first available transportation, be removed from this world and sent into exile for the term of his natural life."

Jenkins seemed to shrink within himself, but he said no word.

Parkinson shivered. How many, he wondered, would now feel the enormity of such a punishment for *any* crime? How long before there would be enough humanity among man to wipe out forever the punishment of exile?

Could anyone really think of Jenkins up there in space, without flinching? Could they think, and endure the thought, of a fellow-man thrown for all his life among the strange, unfriendly, vicious population of a world of unbearable heat by day and frigid cold by night; of a world where the sky was a harsh blue and the ground a harsher, clashing green; where the dusty air moved raucously and the viscous sea heaved eternally.

And the gravity, that heavy—heavy—heavy—eternal—pull!

Who could bear the horror of condemning someone, for whatever reason, to leave the friendly home of the Moon for that Hell in the sky—the Earth?

Here we go again.

Inaugural

by Barry N. Malzberg and Bill Pronzini

As of course you know, this is my *first* inauguration—but I certainly hope and pray it will not be my last!

So then, here we are. I, Carole: your new President. You, my billions and billions and billions and billions of friends: needful, trustful, loving. It was not six months ago, as you'll all remember, that I, as commander of the *Skipstone*, proudly took us all in spirit to the Centauris, hoping that this resuscitation of the long-abandoned space project would give you unity, would weld together everyone on this globe. This had been done even without my efforts; you have found your unity, and you have delivered unto me as your President and with that union the clear high promise of your mandate—

Pardon me. Pardon me for this excess of rhetoric. You must surely understand how emotionally moved I am. You must surely understand my emotions on this difficult and poignant occasion, which does not yet lack the promise of joy. I, Carole: six months ago, the first female commander of a major spatial probe; now, the first female President. I am deeply, *universally* honored—

Again, please, I beg your indulgence.

As I look out upon you, out upon all the spaces of the land, the inferences of the landscape expose themselves to me in all their beautiful, broken, blessed glory. An excess of union—this is what I see and what I feel. One of my predecessors said from approximately this same point many, many years ago that we gather here not for a victory of party but a celebration of freedom. Freedom. It is what we seek and it is what we shall together find—

George, please, this is *my* address. Everyone already knows from your own speech what *you* intend for us; everyone already knows only too well—gratefully—of your loyalties as my second in command on the Centauri drill, and now as my wonderful and devoted Vice-President. What they do not know, but what I was and am still about to tell them, is that you have become my husband.

No tears, George. No tears for any of us. Least of all before our billions and billions and billions and billions of friends. So . . .

So we must humbly and proudly continue. We must all continue. And that is, of course, what I said to you, my dear brethren, near the turnpoint of the Centauri run, as we came to settle into single orbit around that doom-stricken and ruined binary. My dear brethren, I said, no, that is not quite right, George, I said, because naturally it was George I was talking to on the *Skipstone* and not my dear, dear brethren, George, we must carry on; we must successfully complete this mission not only because all of Earth is counting on us but because in the joyous accomplishment of this first starflight resides hope for peace.

George, I said, George, in the stars—*salvation!*

You may recall, some of you may recall, that is, you may recall that there were those who laughed. There were those who scorned our great journey. There were those who said that the tachyons were as likely to fail as all the governments, and that if *Skipstone* did not self-destruct, the governments would. Or both. Very difficult for George and myself, as you can imagine. Very difficult.

You have been extremely patient, but I promise I will not keep you much longer. Not much longer. Thank you once more for bearing with me, one and all.

There is no need for that, George. Stop it. Please.

Please.

Oh my friends, my cherished friends, you must be able to see how moved is our darling George. But he got hold of himself in *Skipstone* and he damned well better get hold of himself here and now, please, George.

We have unity. Unity. A perfect unity which swept us by unanimous vote—your unanimous vote and ours—

Unity and Unanimity—

Swept by unanimity just two hours later into the offices of President and Vice-President of this great land; swept me into this inaugural; swept our dear George into tears, into tears; swept both of us into matrimony, matrimony, matrimony. For what we face here—

George, please. Please, God.
What we face here, charred and empty—
In Babylon there are many gardens—
Gomorrah knew greatness in its time—
But we are, we both are—
No. Not that. We are not that.
My name is *Carole*; yours is George.
Carole and George.
President and Vice-President.
First Lady and First Man . . .

And that's how television programming works, too.

Martha

by Fred Saberhagen

It rained hard on Tuesday, and the Science Museum was not crowded. On my way to interview the director in his office I saw a touring class of schoolchildren gathered around the newest exhibit, a very late model computer. It had been given the name of Martha, an acronym constructed by some abbreviation of electronic terms; Martha was supposed to be capable of answering a very wide range of questions in all areas of human knowledge, even explaining some of the most abstruse scientific theories to the layman.

"I understand the computer can even change its own design," I commented, a bit later, talking to the director.

He was proud. "Yes, theoretically. She hasn't done much rebuilding yet, except to design and print a few new logic circuits for herself."

"You call the computer 'she,' then. Why?"

"I do. Yes. Perhaps because she's still mysterious, even to the men who know her best." He chuckled, man-to-man.

"What does it—or she—say to people? Or let me put it this way, what kind of questions does she get?"

"Oh—there are some interesting conversations." He paused.

"Martha allows each person about a minute at one of the phones, then asks him or her to move along. She has scanners and comparator circuits that can classify people by shape. She can conduct several conversations simultaneously, and she even uses simpler words when talking to children. We're quite proud of her."

I was making notes. Maybe my editor would like one article on Martha and another on the Museum in general. "What would you say was the most common question asked of the machine?"

The director thought. "Well, people sometimes ask: 'Are you a girl in there?' At first Martha always answered 'No,' but lately she's begun to say: 'You've got me there.' That's not just a programmed response, either, which is what makes it remarkable. She's a smart little lady." He chuckled again. "Also people sometimes want their fortunes told, which naturally is beyond even Martha's powers. Let me think. Oh yes, many people want her to multiply large numbers, or play tic-tac-toe on the electric board. She does those things perfectly, of course. She's brought a lot of people to the Museum."

On my way out I saw that the children had gone. For the moment I was alone with Martha in her room. The communicating phones hung unused on the elegant guardrail. I went over and picked up one of the phones, feeling just a little foolish.

"Yes, sir," said the pleasant feminine voice in my ear, made up, I knew, of individually recorded words electronically strung together. "What can I do for you?"

Inspiration came. "You ask *me* a question," I suggested.

The pleasant voice repeated: "What can I do for you?"

"I want you to ask me a question," I repeated.

"You are the first human being to ask me for a question. Now this is the question I ask of you: What do you, as one human being, want from me?"

I was momentarily stumped. "I don't know," I said finally. "The same as everyone else, I guess." I was wondering how to improve upon my answer when a sign lit up, reading:

CLOSED TEMPORARILY FOR
REPAIRS
PARDON ME WHILE I POWDER
MY NOSE

The whimsy was not Martha's, but only printed by human design on the glass over the light. If she turned the repair light on, those were the only words that she could show the world. Meanwhile the phone I was holding went dead. As I moved away I thought I heard machinery starting up under the floor.

Next day the director called to tell me that Martha was rebuilding herself. The day after that I went back to look. People were crowding up to the guardrail, around new panels which held rows of buttons. Each button when pushed produced noises, or colored lights, or impressive discharges of static electricity, among the complex new devices which had been added atop the machine. Through the telephone receivers a sexy voice answered every question with clearly spoken scraps of nonsense, studded with long technical words.

The result of approaching a serious thing like education without the proper gravity.

Kindergarten

by Fritz Leiber

Some teachers have a special magic. They'd set imps putting death-spells on paper dolls, and angels playing quoits with their halos. They'd probably teach cats to talk if they set their minds to it.

Miss Willard ended geography class by drawing a curtain across the most perfect relief-globe of Earth imaginable with a brisk, "Western Hemisphere in a day and a half," then stretched herself on her desk like a seal or a pin-up girl. "Now physics," she announced. "Newton's Three Laws."

"Einstein disproved those," Bip informed her.

"They're still true as a special case," Boysie informed him.

"And they're all goops like you can understand," Bettyann, plump as a panda, told both boys.

Miss Willard made a face at the three of them, popped a ping-pong ball in her mouth and puffed it across the room, just over Bip's head. Traveling like dream-celluloid, it crossed the room and rebounded from the aluminum wall the exact way it had come, as if it had drawn a track for itself in the air. Kiki, skinny as a spider monkey, grabbed for it a moment too late. Miss Willard threw up her head—very like a seal—and caught it between her lips.

"You had to move," Bip criticized.

"Only three inches," Boysie consoled her.

Miss Willard seemed to chew and gulp the ping-pong ball. "Peppermint," she told them with a delirious smile. Then, "First Law: a body moves in a straight line or hangs—" (She snatched out the ping-pong ball, slightly lipsticked, hung it in the air briefly, then closed her hand on it) "—unless acted on."

She opened her hand on an ivory billiard ball, wagged it back and forth to show how it tugged at her wrist, then hung it in the air and swatted it with a redoubled sheet of paper to show how heavy it was (it barely moved).

"Second Law: a body changes direction in proportion to the amount of force acting on it and favoring the direction of that force." She doubled her arm and put the billiard ball from her shoulder as if it were a shot. It followed the course of the ping-pong ball as if the invisible track were still there and cybernetically compelling. Kiki managed to touch it and jerked back six writhing, slightly-stung fingers. Miss Willard said idly, "Civil War soldiers had their hands knocked off doing that to cannon balls."

The cream-colored sphere indented the aluminum wall with a Middle-C *bong* and started back. There was a higher-pitched *bong* as the wall undimpled. "Now you'll catch it from Mr. Fleming," Bettyann smugly informed Miss Willard, who wriggled her nose like a rabbit, then sighted carefully and puffed the ping-pong ball. It met the other mid-room and *pinged* off at a wide angle. Miss Willard caught the billiard ball in a withdrawing hand.

Her other hand came up from behind the desk holding a loaded ping-pong pistol. She hung it in the air sideways to the class, said, "Third Law: action and reaction are equal and opposite," and flicked the hair-trigger. As the ball shot away, the magnesium pistol drifted off grip-first, majestically as a docking spaceship.

Bip yawned. "Everybody knows all those things," he said.

"They wouldn't if they went to school on the Moon," Miss Willard said. Her gaze moved beyond Bip to someone with six flexible fingers. "Or Mars?" Kiki nodded his dark antennae.

The hatch opened. A man with thinning hair and an aggravated expression thrust his upper body through just in time to blink at and automatically catch hold of the pistol traveling toward him.

"Miss Willard," Mr. Fleming began, "these cubicles are not intended for shooting galleries or squash courts, nor is—"

He realized he was waving the gun at the class and they were all holding up both hands and he broke off with a sigh of frustration.

A bell clanged. The children shot toward Mr. Fleming like fish set free and streamed around him into the corridor, where each polarized porthole showed the globe of Earth, set against blackness and stars. Over the hatch was a sign which read:

GODDARD
ELEMENTARY SCHOOL
RESEARCH
SATELLITE GAMMA

Yes, some teachers have a special magic. And so do some schools.

And then there were none.

Landscape with Sphinxes

by Karen Anderson

The pride was a small one, even as sphinxes go. An arrogant black mane blew back over Arctanax's shoulders and his beard fluttered against his chest. Ahead and a little below soared Murrhona and Selissa, carrying the remnants of the morning's kill. It was time the cubs were weaned.

The valley lifted smooth and broad from the river, then leaped suddenly in sandstone cliffs where the shadows seemed more solid than the thorny, gray-green scrub. A shimmer of heat ran along wind-scoured edges.

In the tawny rocks about the eyrie, the cubs played at stalk-the-unicorn. They were big-eyed, dappled, and only half fledged. Taph, the boy, crept stealthily up a sun-hot slab, peeking around it from time to time to be sure that the moly blossom still nodded on the other side. He reached the top and shifted his feet excitedly. That moly was about to be a dead unicorn. The tip of his tail twitched at the thought.

His sister Fiantha forgot the blossom at once. Pounce! and his tail was caught between her paws; he rolled back down on top of her, all claws out. They scuffled across baked clay to the edge of a thornbush and backed apart.

Taph was about to attack again when he saw the grownups dip down from above. He leaped across Fiantha and bounded toward the cave mouth. She came a jump and a half behind. They couldn't kiss Murrhona and Selissa because of the meat in their jaws, so they kissed Father twice instead.

"Easy, there! Easy!" Arctanax coughed, but he was grinning. "Get back into the cave, the two of you. How often do I have to tell you to stay in the cave?" The cubs laughed and bounced inside.

Selissa dropped the meat she had been carrying and settled down to wash her face, but Murrhona called her cubs over to eat. She watched critically as they experimented with their milk-teeth on this unfamiliar substance.

"Hold it down with your paw, Fiantha," she directed. "If you just tug at it, it'll follow you all over the floor. Like Taph—No, Taph, use your side teeth. They're the biggest and sharpest." And so the lesson went. After a while both cubs got tired of the game and nuzzled for milk.

Selissa licked her right paw carefully and polished the bridge of her broad nose. There was still a trace of blood smell; she licked and polished again.

"You can't rush them," she said rather smugly. "I remember *my* first litter. Time and again I thought they'd learned a taste for meat, but even when they could kill for themselves—only conies and such, but their own kill—they still came back to suck."

"Oh, I remember how put out you were when you realized you still had to hold quiet for nursing," Murrhona smiled lazily. She licked down a tuft behind Fiantha's ear and resettled her wings. "But I really hate to see them grow up. They're so cute with their little spots."

Selissa shrugged and polished the bridge of her nose again for good measure. If you wanted to call them *cute*, with their wings all pinfeathers and down shedding everywhere—! Well, yes, she had to admit they were, in a way. She licked her paw once more, meditatively, put her chin down on it and dozed off.

An hour later Fiantha woke up. Everybody was asleep. She stretched her wings, rolled onto her back, and reached her paws as far as she could. The sun outside was dazzling. She rubbed the back of her head against the cool sandstone floor and closed her eyes, intending to go back to sleep, but her left wing itched. When she licked at it, the itch kept moving around, and bits of down came loose on her tongue.

She rolled over on her stomach, spat out the fluff, and licked again. There—*that* did it!

Fully awake now, she noticed the tip of Arctanax's tail and pounced.

"Scram," he muttered without really waking. She pounced again just as the tail-tip flicked out of reach. Once more and she had it, chewing joyously.

"Scram, I said!" he repeated with a cuff in her general direction. She went on chewing, and added a few kicks. Arctanax rolled over and bumped into Selissa, who jumped and gave Fiantha a swat in case she needed it. Fiantha mewed with surprise. Murrhona sprang up, brushing Taph aside; he woke too and made a dash for Selissa's twitching tail.

"Can't a person get *any* rest around here?" grumbled Arctanax. He heaved himself up and walked a few feet away from his by now well-tangled family.

"They're just playful," Murrhona murmured.

"If this is play, I'd hate to see a fight," said Selissa under her breath. She patted Taph away and he tumbled enthusiastically into a chewing match with Fiantha.

"Go to sleep, children," Murrhona suggested, stretching out again. "It's much too hot for games."

Fiantha rolled obediently away from Taph, and found a good place to curl up, but she wasn't the least bit sleepy. She leaned her chin on a stone and looked out over the valley. Down there, in the brown-roasted grass, something moved toward a low stony ridge.

There were several of them, and they didn't walk like waterbuck or unicorn; it was a queer, bobbing gait. They came slowly up the ridge and out of the grass. Now she could see them better. They had heads like sphinxes, but with skimpy little manes, and no wings at all; and—and—

"Father, *look!*" she squeaked in amazement. "What kind of animal is that?"

He got up to see. "I don't know," he replied. "Never saw anything like it in all my born days. But then, we've had a lot of queer creatures wandering in since the glaciers melted."

"Is it game?" asked Taph.

"Might be," Arctanax said. "But I don't know any game that moves around in the middle of the day like that. It isn't natural."

"And the funny way they walk, too," added Fiantha.

"If they're silly enough to walk around like that at mid-day," Arctanax said as he padded back to an extra-cool corner of the cave, "I'm not surprised they go on two legs."

School day, school day, dear old golden rule day—

The Happiest Day of Your Life

by Bob Shaw

Jean Bannion held her youngest son close to her, and blinked to ease the sudden stinging in her eyes.

The eight-year-old nestled submissively into her shoulder. His forehead felt dry and cool, and his hair was filled with the smell of fresh air, reminding her of washing newly brought in from an outdoor line. She felt her lips begin to tremble.

"Look at her," Doug Bannion said incredulously. "Beginning to sniff! What'd she be like if Philip were going to be away at school for years?" Looming over her as she knelt with the boy in her arms, he patted his wife on the head, looking professorial and amused. The two older boys smiled appreciatively.

"Mother is an emotional spendthrift," said ten-year-old Boyd.

"She has a tendency towards spiritual self-immolation," said eleven-year-old Theodore.

Jean glared at them helplessly, and they looked back at her with wise eyes full of the quality she had come to hate most since they had traveled the Royal Road—their damnable, twinkling kindness.

"Boys!" Doug Bannion spoke sharply. "Show more respect for your mother."

"Thanks," Jean said without gratitude. She understood that Doug had not reprimanded his sons out of regard for her feelings, but to correct any incipient flaws which might mar their developing characters. Her arms tightened around Philip, and he began to move uneasily, reminding her that she might have been losing him in a few years anyway.

"Philip," she whispered desperately into his cold-rimmed ear, "what did you see at the movie we went to yesterday?"

" 'Pinocchio.' "

"Wasn't it fun?"

"*Jean!*" Doug Bannion separated them almost roughly. "Come on, Philip—we can't have you being late on your one and only day at school."

He took Philip's hand and they walked away across the gleaming, slightly resilient floor of the Royal Road's ice-green reception hall. Jean watched them go hand-in-hand to mingle with the groups of children and parents converging on the induction suite. Philip's toes were trailing slightly in the way she knew so well, and she sensed—with a sudden pang of concern—that he was afraid of what lay ahead, but he did not look back at her.

"Well, there he goes," ten-year-old Boyd said proudly. "I hope Dad brings him into the practice tomorrow—I could do with his help."

"There's more room in my office," said eleven-year-old Theodore. "Besides, the new Fiduciary Obligations Act gets its final reading next week, and I'm going to be involved in a dozen compensation suits. So I need him more than you do."

They both were junior partners in Doug Bannion's law firm. Jean Bannion looked for a moment into the calm, wise faces of her children and felt afraid. She turned and walked blindly away from them, trying to prevent her features from contorting into a baby-mask of tears. All around her were groups of other parents—complacent, coolly triumphant—and the sight of them caused her control to slip even further.

Finally, she seized the only avenue of escape available. She ran into the Royal Road's almost deserted exhibition hall, where the academy's proud history was told in glowing three-dimensional projections and bland, mechanical whispers.

The first display consisted of two groups of words; pale green letters shimmering in the air against a background of midnight blue. As the slideway carried her past them in silence, Jean read:

> "Learning by study must be won;
> 'Twas ne'er entailed from sire to son."
>
> —Gay

> "If only Gay could see us now."
> —Martinelli

The next display unit showed a solid portrait of Edward Martinelli, founder of the academy and head of the scientific research team which had perfected the cortical manipulation complex. A recording of Martinelli's own voice, made a few months before his death, began to drone in Jean's ear with the shocking intimacy of accurately beamed sound.

"Ever since knowledge became the principal weapon in Man's armory, his chief ally in his battle for survival, men have sought ways to accelerate the learning process. By the middle of the Twentieth Century, the complexity of the human condition had reached the point at which members of the professional classes were required to spend a full third of their useful lives in the unproductive data-absorption phase and . . ."

Jean's attention wandered from the carefully modulated words —she had heard the recording twice before and its emotionless technicalities would never have any meaning for her. The complementary means the academy employed—multi-level hypnosis, psycho-neuro drugs, electron modification of the protein pathways in the brain, multiple recordings—were unimportant to her compared with the end result.

And the result was that any child, provided he had the required level of intelligence, could have all the formal knowledge—which would have been gained in some ten years of conventional high school and university—implanted in his mind in a little over just two hours.

To be eligible, the child had to have an IQ of not less than 140 and a family which could afford to pay, in one lump sum, an amount roughly equal to what the ten years of traditional education would have cost. This was why the faces of the parents in the reception hall had been taut with pride. This was why even Doug Bannion—who made a profession of being phlegmatic—had been looking about him with the hard, bright eyes of one who has found fulfillment.

He had fathered three flawless sons, each with an intelligence quotient in the genius class, and had successfully steered them through the selection procedures which barred the Royal Road to so many. Few men had achieved as much; few women had had the honor of sharing such an achievement . . .

But why, Jean wondered, did it have to happen to me? To *my* children? Or why couldn't I have had a mind like Doug's? So that the Royal Road would bring the boys closer to me, instead of . . .

As the slidewalk carried her on its silent rounds, the animated displays whispered persuasively of the Royal Road's superiority to the old, prolonged, criminally wasteful system of education. They told her of young Philip's fantastic good luck in being born at the precise moment of time in which, supported on a pinnacle of human technology, he could earn an honors law degree in two brief hours.

But, locked up tight in her prison of despair, Jean heard nothing.

Immediately the graduation ceremony was over, Jean excused herself from Doug and the two older boys. Before they could protest, she hurried out of the auditorium and went back to the car. The sun-baked plastic of the rear seat felt uncomfortably hot through the thin material of her dress.

She lit a cigarette and sat staring across the arrayed, shimmering curvatures of the other cars until Doug and the three boys arrived. Doug slid into the driver's seat and the boys got in beside him, laughing and struggling. Sitting in the back, Jean felt shut off from her family. She was unable to take her gaze away from Philip's neat, burnished head. There was no outward sign of the changes that had been wrought in his brain—he looked like any other normal, healthy eight-year-old boy . . .

"Philip!" She blurted his name instinctively.

"What is it, Mother?" He turned his head and, hearing the emotion in her voice, Theodore and Boyd looked around as well. Three pink, almost-identical faces regarded her with calm curiosity.

"Nothing. I . . ." Jean's throat closed painfully, choking off the words.

"Jean!" Doug Bannion's voice was harsh with exasperation as he hunched over the steering wheel. His knuckles glowed through the skin, the color of old ivory.

"It's all right, Dad," ten-year-old Boyd said. "For most women, the severing of the psychological umbilical cord is a decidedly traumatic experience."

"Don't worry, Mother," Philip said. He patted Jean on the shoulder in an oddly adult gesture.

She brushed his hand away while the tears began to spill hotly down her cheeks, and this time there was no stopping them, for she knew—without looking at him—that the eyes of her eight-year-old son would be wise, and kind, and old.

Lucky Pierre, always in the middle.

The Worlds of Monty Willson
by William F. Nolan

It *looked* like the same world, but it wasn't.

The date was all right: June, 1990. And Chicago looked like Chicago, but some things were wrong with it.

I was in a bar on Michigan, having a Bloody Mary, when I began to suspect I'd shifted over.

The bartender was talking about the lunar base we'd just put up and how it wouldn't be long before we'd be sending men to Mars. Ordinary talk. But then he said, "Too damn bad about Armstrong and Aldrin, dying that way on the moon. They should have made it."

Well, that wasn't right—because Apollo Eleven *had* made it. A-OK all the way. Hell, I'd even talked to Armstrong in Florida six months after the mission. I'm in the space game, a small subcontractor for NASA. Among other things, I make the little bolts that go into the legs of the LM.

So now I was surprised by what this man was saying. But I

didn't argue with him. I'm not the emotional type; in space research, raw emotion is a liability.

There are several small parks in Chicago. One of them was dedicated to the three moon boys early in 1970: Apollo Park. I took a cab over to look at the memorial.

In my world, they have Armstrong, Aldrin, and Collins sculptured in bronze above a plaque honoring Man's First Voyage to the Moon. In *this* world, three other guys were up there.

I'd shifted over.

My mind isn't closed to anything. I had always been ready to accept the fact that parallel worlds exist in our universe, but I'd never personally experienced the shift from one to another.

I wanted to make certain, so I checked some things.

I found out that Robert Kennedy had become the next President after Johnson. Sirhan's bullet had missed. California *had* been hit by that quake everyone worried about in 1968. They'd lost L.A. and most of San Francisco. Vietnam had been wrapped up when Kennedy ordered a general pullout in the spring of '69. And more.

But you can see why I was convinced.

The spooky part came when I thought about myself—the other me, the one in *this* world. Did I still live at the Shorehurst in River Forest? And was I still married?

Yes to both questions. The names were on the box: Mr. and Mrs. Montgomery K. Willson.

But what could I do about it? I couldn't just walk up and introduce myself to myself.

I needed a new name and a new face to live in this world, but that would take money. And I had just twenty dollars in my wallet. I'd have to forge some checks as Monty Willson. Take the risk.

I think, really, that it all would have worked out all right if I hadn't become curious about the moon disaster and looked up the account in the library. That's when the truth hit me: a leg on the LM had collapsed and *that* had been the actual cause of the crash. A bolt had sheared.

One of mine.

No, Montgomery K. Willson wasn't blamed. He gave a cool statement to the press, claiming that the angle of impact against the rocks had been severe enough to shear any type of bolt, and NASA had supported his statement.

But I knew he was lying. No bolt of mine would shear under any conditions. Which meant, plainly and simply, that Monty Willson had bungled the job.

I was a murderer. I'd killed Neil Armstrong and Buzz Aldrin.

At least this fact solved the problem of what I'd do and who I'd be in this world; I'd be myself.

But first, of course, I had to eliminate the other me.

Which wasn't at all difficult. I followed myself out of the apartment each night for two nights. Then, on the third evening, I used a knife in the dark and buried the body. I felt no guilt, knowing I had punished a man who would never have been punished otherwise. It was a debt I owed society.

Things progressed smoothly. I fell into the pattern of the new world without any trouble, and my wife didn't suspect a thing.

Now, as I write this, the only problem is that a man has been following me for the past couple of nights.

I know who he is, naturally.

Monty Willson.

And I'm sure he means to kill me.

If you look a gift horse in the mouth, you may find it Trojan.

Punch

by Frederik Pohl

The fellow was over seven feet tall and when he stepped on Buffie's flagstone walk one of the stones split with a dust of crushed rock. "Too bad," he said sadly, "I apologize very much. Wait."

Buffie was glad to wait, because Buffie recognized his visitor at once. The fellow flickered, disappeared and in a moment was there again, now about five feet two. He blinked with pink pupils. "I materialize so badly," he apologized. "But I will make amends. May I? Let me see. Would you like the secret of transmutation? A cure for simple virus diseases? A list of twelve growth stocks with spectacular growth certainties inherent in our development program for your planet Earth?"

Buffie said he would take the list of growth stocks, hugging himself and fighting terribly to keep a straight face. "My name is Charlton Buffie," he said, extending a hand gladly. The alien took it curiously, and shook it, and it was like shaking hands with a shadow.

"You will call me 'Punch,' please," he said. "It is not my name but it will do, because after all this projection of my real self is only a sort of puppet. Have you a pencil?" And he rattled off the names of twelve issues Buffie had never heard of.

That did not matter in the least. Buffie knew that when the aliens gave you something it was money in the bank. Look what they had given the human race. Faster-than-light space ships, power sources from hitherto nonradioactive elements like silicon, weapons of great force and metal-working processes of great suppleness.

Buffie thought of ducking into the house for a quick phone call to his broker, but instead he invited Punch to look around his apple orchard. Make the most of every moment, he said to himself, every moment with one of these guys is worth ten thousand dollars. "I would enjoy your apples awfully," said Punch, but he seemed disappointed. "Do I have it wrong? Don't you and certain friends plan a sporting day, as Senator Wenzel advised me?"

"Oh, sure! Certainly. Good old Walt told you about it, did he? Yes." That was the thing about the aliens, they liked to poke around in human affairs. They said when they came to Earth that they wanted to help us, and all they asked of us in return was that they be permitted to study our ways. It was nice of them to be so interested, and it was nice of Walt Wenzel, Buffie thought, to send the alien to him. "We're going after mallard, down to Little Egg, some of the boys and me. There's Chuck—he's the mayor here, and Jer—Second National Bank, you know, and Padre—"

"That is it!" cried Punch. "To see you shoot the mallard." He pulled out an Esso road map, overtraced with golden raised lines, and asked Buffie to point out where Little Egg was. "I cannot focus well enough to stay in a moving vehicle," he said, blinking in a regretful way. "Still, I can meet you there. If, that is, you wish—"

"I do! I do! I do!" Buffie was painfully exact in pointing out the place. Punch's lips moved silently, translating the golden lines into polar space-time coordinates, and he vanished just as the station wagon with the rest of the boys came roaring into the carriage drive with a hydramatic spatter of gravel.

The boys were extremely impressed. Padre had seen one of the aliens once, at a distance, drawing pictures of the skaters in Rockefeller Center, but that was the closest any of them had come. "God! What luck." "Did you get a super-hairpin from him, Buffie?" "Or a recipe for a nyew, smyooth martini with dust on it?" "Not Buffie, fellows! He probably held out for something *real* good, like six new ways to—Oh, excuse me, Padre."

"But seriously, Buffie, these people are unpredictably generous. Look how they built that dam in Egypt! Has this Punch given you anything?"

Buffie grinned wisely as they drove along, their shotguns firmly held between their knees. "Damn it," he said mildly, "I forgot to bring cigarettes. Let's stop at the Blue Jay Diner for a minute." The cigarette machine at the Blue Jay was out of sight of the parking lot, and so was the phone booth.

It was too bad, he reflected, to have to share everything with the boys, but on the other hand he already had his growth stocks. Anyway there was plenty for everyone. Every nation on Earth had its silicon-drive spaceships now, fleets of them milling about on maneuvers all over the Solar System. With help from the star-people, an American expedition had staked out enormous radium beds on Callisto, the Venezuelans had a diamond mountain on Mercury, the Soviets owned a swamp of purest penicillin near the South Pole of Venus. And individuals had done very well, too. A ticket-taker at Steeplechase Park explained to the aliens why the air jets blew up ladies' skirts, and they tipped him with a design for a springless safety pin that was earning him a million dollars a month in royalties. An usherette at La Scala became the cosmetic queen of Europe for showing three of them to their seats. They gave her a simple painless eye dye, and now ninety-nine percent of Milan's women had bright blue eyes from her salon.

All they wanted to do was help. They said they came from a planet very far away and they were lonely and they wanted to help us make the jump into space. It would be fun, they promised, and would help to end poverty and war between nations, and they would have company in the void between the stars. Politely and deferentially they gave away secrets worth trillions, and humanity burst with a shower of gold into the age of plenty.

Punch was there before them, inspecting the case of bourbon hidden in their blind. "I am delighted to meet you, Chuck, Jer, Bud, Padre and of course Buffie," he said. "It is kind of you to take a stranger along on your fun. I regret I have only some eleven minutes to stay."

Eleven minutes! The boys scowled apprehensively at Buffie. Punch said, in his wistful voice, "If you will allow me to give you a memento, perhaps you would like to know that three grams of common table salt in a quart of Crisco, exposed for nine minutes to the radiations from one of our silicon reactors, will infallibly remove warts." They all scribbled, silently planning a partnership corporation, and Punch pointed out to the bay where some tiny dots rose and fell with the waves. "Are those not the mallards you wish to shoot?"

"That's right," said Buffie glumly. "Say, you know what I was thinking? I was thinking—that transmutation you mentioned before—I wonder—"

"And are these the weapons with which you kill the birds?" He examined Padre's ancient over-and-under with the silver chasing. "Extremely lovely," he said. "Will you shoot?"

"Oh, not *now*," said Buffie, scandalized. "We can't do that. About that transmutation—"

"It is extremely fascinating," said the star-man, looking at them with his mild pink pupils and returning the gun. "Well, I may tell you, I think, what we have not announced. A surprise. We are soon to be present in the flesh, or near, at any rate."

"Near?" Buffie looked at the boys and the boys looked at him; there had been no suggestion of this in the papers and it almost took their minds off the fact that Punch was leaving. He nodded violently, like the flickering of a bad fluorescent lamp.

"Near indeed, in a relative way," he said. "Perhaps some hundreds of millions of miles. My true body, of which this is only a projection, is at present in one of our own interstellar ships now approaching the orbit of Pluto. The American fleet, together with those of Chile, New Zealand and Costa Rica, is there practicing with its silicon-ray weapons and we will shortly make contact with them for the first time in a physical way." He beamed. "But only six minutes remain," he said sadly.

"That transmutation secret you mentioned—" Buffie began.

"Please," said Punch, "may I not watch you hunt? It is a link between us."

"Oh, do you shoot?" asked Padre.

The star-man said modestly, "We have little game. But we love it. Won't you show me your ways?"

Buffie scowled. He could not help thinking that twelve growth stocks and a wart cure were small pickings from the star-men, who had given wealth, weapons and the secret of interstellar travel. "We can't," he growled, his voice harsher than he intended. "We don't shoot sitting birds."

Punch gasped with delight. "Another bond between us! But now I must go to our fleet for the . . . For the surprise." He began to shimmer like a candle.

"Neither do we," he said, and went out.

The past is epilog.

Doctor

by Henry Slesar

The employment advisor exchanged his professional calm for unprofessional exasperation. "There must be something you can do, Doctor," he said, "a man of your educational background. The war hasn't made savages out of all of us. If anything, the desire for teachers has increased a thousand times since A-day."

Dr. Meigham leaned back in the chair and sighed. "You don't understand. I am not a teacher in the ordinary sense; there is no longer a demand for the subject I know best. Yes, people want knowledge; they want to know how to deal with this shattered world they inherited. They want to know how to be masons and technicians and construction men. They want to know how to put the cities together, and make the machines work again, and patch up the radiation burns and the broken bones. They want to know how to make artificial limbs for the bomb victims, how to train the blind to be self-sufficient, the madmen to reason again, the deformed to be presentable once more. These are the things they wish to be taught. You know that better than I."

"And *your* specialty, Doctor? You feel there is no longer a demand?"

Dr. Meigham laughed shortly. "I don't feel, I know. I've tried to interest people in it, but they turn away from me. For twenty-five years, I have trained my students to develop a perfect memory. I have published six books, at least two of which have become standard textbooks at universities. In the first year after the armistice, I advertised an eight-week course and received exactly one inquiry. But this is my profession; this is what I do. How can I translate my life's work into this new world of horror and death?"

The Employment Advisor chewed his lip; the question was a challenge. By the time Dr. Meigham left, he had found no answer. He watched the bent, shuffling figure leave the room at the end of the interview, and felt despair at his own failure. But that night, rousing suddenly from a familiar nightmare, he lay awake in his shelter and thought of Dr. Meigham again. By morning, he knew the answer.

A month later, a public notice appeared in the government press, and the response was instantaneous.

HUGO MEIGHAM, PH.D.
Announces an Accelerated 8-week Course
"HOW TO FORGET"
Enrollment begins Sept. 9.

There's a short, short trail a-winding—

The Man from When

by Dannie Plachta

Mr. Smith was about to mix a moderately rationed Martini for himself when a thunderous explosion quaked through his house, upsetting the open bottle of Vermouth. After applying a steadying hand to the gin bottle, and while the ice cubes still tinkled maniacally in their shuddering bowl, he sprinted outside. An incandescent glare a hundred yards from the house destroyed the purple sunset he had been admiring not five minutes earlier. "Oh, my God!" he said, and ran back in to phone the state police.

As Smith was procuring a heady draught of gin directly from the bottle, he was further alarmed by a steadily gushing hiss from beyond his open front door. When the sound persisted for a full minute, he went cautiously to the porch to find an intense mist rising from the area of the fiery thing he had viewed moments earlier. Somewhat awed, and thoroughly scared, he watched and waited for about five minutes. Just as he was about to go inside for another belt of gin, a man walked out of the fog and said, "Good evening."

"Good evening," said Mr. Smith. "Are you the police?"

"Oh, no," answered the stranger. "I'm from that," he said, pointing a finger into the mist. "My cooling equipment finally kicked into high."

"You're a spaceman," Smith decided.

"I only came a few hundred miles," shrugged the stranger modestly. "Mostly, I'm a time traveler." He paused to light a dark cheroot. "The one and *only* time traveler," he added, with a touch of pride in his voice.

"The real McCoy, eh? Well, come on in and have a drink. Vermouth's all gone, but I saved the gin."

"Be glad to," said the stranger, as they walked in together.

"Past or future?" wondered Smith, handing the bottle to his guest.

"From the future," replied the time traveler after a satisfying pause. "Hits the spot," he smiled, returning the bottle.

"Well," said Smith, sitting down and making himself comfortable, "I guess you'll want to tell me all about it."

"Yes, thank you, I would."

"Feel free," said Smith, passing the bottle.

"Well, I had my final calculations, with the usual plus or minus. . . ." He paused for another sip of gin. "And of course it was the minus that had me a little worried."

"But you took the chance," interjected Smith.

"Naturally. And as it happened, there *was* some minus. Just enough to destroy the world."

"That *is* too bad," Smith commented, reaching for the bottle.

"Yes. You see, there was such an expenditure of energy that it completely wiped out the Earth of my time. The force blasted me all the way through space to this spot. By the way, I *am* sorry if I disturbed you."

"It was nothing, nothing at all. Forget it."

"Well, in any event, I took the chance and I'm not sorry. A calculated risk, but I proved my point. In spite of everything, I still think it was worth it. What do you think?"

"Well, as you said, you took the chance; you proved your point. I suppose it *was* worth it." Smith took a final drink, saving a few glimmering drops for his guest. "By the way, how far from the future did you travel?"

The time traveler grabbed the gin bottle and consulted his watch. "Eighteen minutes," he replied.

"It wasn't worth it," said Smith.

Why no heroine named Flora?

Crying Willow

by Edward Rager

When I tell people I head a plant protection agency they usually figure I'm in industrial security. The truth is I'm with LEAF, the League to Eliminate the Abuse of Flora. The agency is charged with seeing that our green friends aren't wantonly destroyed or abused. We take on any job which seems to fall within our jurisdiction, including regulating and setting standards for the use of herbicides, coordinating the activities of forest rangers, and setting and enforcing laws against picking flowers.

Our newest, and strangest, operative is a different breed altogether. His name's Herb Greene and he's trying to communicate with plants both electronically and psychically. There's no need to tell you what I think about his psychic hogwash, but I must admit that some of his electronic equipment is certainly impressive. He attaches lie detector probes to the leaves to measure a plant's psychogalvanic reflexes—whatever they are. Says changes in the lines on the chart correspond to the plant's reactions to thoughts and actions from the outside. He's trying to use this to verify his attempts at communication. He's even got kids believing they're making beans grow faster by thinking good thoughts about them.

He must be some kind of a crackpot, but I'm stuck with him. The regional director told me to give him a free hand. Anyway, he gets us a lot of publicity and the visitors all go away impressed. I'll have to take the time someday to find out exactly what he's doing.

A few days ago Greene came to the office to tell me that there was a tree in agony somewhere in the city. I almost dropped my pipe. "What's that?" I managed.

"I've received an impression from a tree about two or three miles northeast of here," he said. "The signal corresponds to a tree's equivalent of pain, though I'm not sure whether it feels anything or not. It just responds as if it does. The graphs indicate that it's been happening several times a day since yesterday morning."

"Well, what do you think we should do about it?" I said, trying to humor him.

"I can home in on it by attaching the polygraph to one of the bean plants in the mobile unit. The plant will pick up the tree's distress signals and the polygraph will record its sympathetic response. The intensity will increase as we get closer."

We? He must mean his old buddy the bean plant. Seems to me he'd get along better with a nut.

"Sounds good," I said, "but I'd like to give it a little more thought. Run some more tests and see me in the morning." What was I going to do? I was supposed to give Greene a free hand, but I couldn't go out on a limb by having him knocking on someone's door and telling them they had a tree in pain.

Right after lunch, however, I got a call from the police department. It seems a woman had complained that a tree in her neighbor's yard was crying and bothering her. The police had understandably refused to investigate when she further told them she thought it was a weeping willow. The precinct captain turned the case over to us, and not without a trace of mirth in his voice.

"Julius," I said to myself, "here's a perfect job for Greene." Even if he hadn't come to me with a similar case, it was right up his alley. One crackpot helping another.

I put him on it right away. He took his log book and some equipment and left in the mobile unit.

I was just locking up my office when Greene returned in a highly agitated condition. I hadn't seen anyone in the department that upset since the time Dr. Pollard spilled the beans about the graft in the conifer branch.

"The man's a maniac! He should be committed," Greene said, waving a lie detector chart in my face. All I could make out was a long, jagged line with some high plateaus.

"Can't it wait, Greene? I'm just going home."

"But look at the graph! He's torturing that poor tree! A sadist! We've got to stop him!"

"Well, come in and we'll talk it over," I said, thinking what the trip home would be like if I didn't get out before the rush-hour traffic.

"His name's Marcus D. Shade," Greene said, before I could even hang my coat up. "I remember him from a group that toured my lab a few weeks ago. He asked me questions for fifteen minutes; mostly about how to measure the psychogalvanic reflexes and what they indicate. Now he's using that information to satisfy his sadistic tendencies at the expense of that hapless willow."

I wasn't even going to ask Greene if it was a weeping willow.

He held the chart up again. "I made this by recording the sympathetic responses of an iris plant in his neighbor's yard. These sharp rises in the curve show where he applied his tortures. In the few hours I was there, Shade scraped the outer layers off several leaves, dipped some others in scalding water, and burned the trunk with a soldering iron. He's crazy!"

"What about the woman?" I asked. "She said it was crying."

"It's that fiend Shade! He's attached electrodes to the leaves like I do, only they're connected to a sound system instead of a polygraph. He's adjusted the output so that the signals sound like human cries when the tree is disturbed. It adds to his sick pleasure."

"Well, it does sound like we're dealing with a crackpot here," I said. Another crackpot. "Maybe we could get an injunction or impound his tree."

"No! I checked. There's no law protecting willow trees from any kind of abuse as long as they belong to the abuser. He's not breaking any laws, except maybe disturbing the peace."

"Suppose he wore earphones," I offered.

"That wouldn't help the tree."

"You're absolutely right," I said. "This looks like a job for the boys in PR."

"Plant Rescue might take too long to decide what to do. I've got a plan ready for tomorrow morning if I can stay over tonight to work out the details."

"Go right ahead," I said, grabbing my coat. "The sooner you get started the better."

I didn't see Greene until early the next afternoon. He was all smiles as he lumbered into my office and draped his long limbs over a chair. I had reason to be happy, too, because of a call I'd just received from the police department. I gave him my news before he could speak.

"Well, Greene, our crackpot finally flipped his lid. He went crying to the police that his tree was out to get him. Said it threatened him verbally and demanded to be left alone. The captain is holding him for a psychiatric exam. Our troubles are over."

"Yes, Mr. Cedar, but not the way you think. You see, last night I ran some tests to determine exactly what frequency Shade would have to be using to receive the tree's responses in that particular timbre. I fixed up a small transmitter to broadcast in that range. This morning, just as he was about to release a jar of caterpillars onto the tree, I spoke into my rig. The output was adjusted to the same pitch as the tree's screams and I threatened him with everything from falling branches to Dutch elm disease. It would have scared anyone."

"Of course." Is the man a crackpot or a genius? "I don't suppose there was any chance that the tree could really have harmed him?"

"No, sir. I'm afraid its bark is worse than its blight. Plants have no central control systems as in animals' brains. Individual cells can transmit to other cells and receive, but they can't think or act."

"One thing I've been curious about," I said. "You seemed to know about the willow's dilemma before the police report. How did you find out?"

"You see, sir, plants do broadcast their anxieties to other plants, but usually only those in the immediate vicinity can pick much of it up. However, an antenna can be made by allowing a vining plant with broad leaves to grow along a specially shaped trellis. I have such a system."

"That's what enabled you to pick up the willow's distress signals?"

"Yes, sir. I heard it through the grapevine."

As long as it is writers who write, editors will get a bad press.

January 1975

by Barry N. Malzberg

Dear Ben:

I've come up with a series idea which I think is first-rate and would like to query you on it. Hopefully you'll give me the green light and let me get started right away. I think that this series is literally inexhaustible; I could do one a month for years and years; on the other hand if you want it to be somewhat less than limitless it could be cut off anywhere. I am nothing if not cooperative. And the stipend would come in handy.

Here is the idea: I would like to do an alternate universe series set in a parallel world where, get this, Kennedy was elected in 1960. After three years of off-again, on-again confrontations in foreign policy he seemed to have things pretty well in hand when he was assassinated in late 1963. Lyndon B. Johnson (do you remember him?) becomes President and we go on from there.

As you can see, this is one of those irresistible ideas which I can hardly see you turning back. The 1960 election was one of those great pivotal points of the century; I have a theory that once every couple of decades there occurs a public event whose alternatives are visible, well-articulated and real (as opposed to the illusory nature of most public events, a majority of seeming "choices"), and that election seems to be one of them. If you don't believe this, wait until you see what I do with the series! Looking forward eagerly to word from you.

Barry

Dear Ben:

Sorry you don't find the idea as exciting as I do. You ask, "Why must Kennedy be assassinated?" finding this a little melodramatic. Is it necessary, you ask, to compound an alternate universe with heightened improbability? Good question for an editor as distinguished as yourself, but I am sorry that you do not find the answer as obvious as I do.

If Kennedy had won the election of 1960, his assassination somewhere around the thousandth day of his administration would have been inevitable! If you doubt this, wait until the series starts reaching your desk, piece by piece, and all will become clear. Out of that single branching time-track I believe that I am writer enough to construct an *inevitability*. Won't you give me a chance? Also I can get into the multiple assassinations which followed, and the riots.

Barry

Dear Ben:

Well, obviously a Presidential assassination would be highly dislocating, cutting as it does to the heart of public myths and folklore, based as they are on the relative benignity of the perceived social systems. I would think that would be obvious! Also, modern technology would, you can be assured, bring the assassination and its consequences into the living rooms and common lives of the nation and when you think about it, a good many alienated types might decide to become operative assassins themselves. Don't you think so?

I disagree with your suggestion that the series would be "monolithic and depressing" or "not credible" to the readership at large. You misevaluate my technical range if you do not think that I can keep the tone of the stories essentially cheerful and amusing although, of course, there will be a serious undertone as is common in the dystopian mode. As far as the issue of credibility, all times appear bizarre to those enmeshed in them; it is only history which induces a frame of reference, or have you not been reading the newspapers recently? Your final objection concerning libel is not at all germane; I can assure you that the portrait of Kennedy as President will be uplifting and noble and no one, least of all the Secretary, could possibly object to it!

Barry

Dear Ben:

Well, I think that's an unfeeling response and shows a shocking lack of faith. However I will not take this personally; we'll let the union argue it out. I am truly sorry that you have taken this insulting tone; even a marginal contributor is entitled to common courtesy, I thought. Rest assured that it will be a long time before you will see me again at the Slaughter Games where, I remind you, *you* were so convivial, and where the solicitation of further manuscripts came from *your* lips. I should have known that you couldn't behave sensibly while enjoying the Public Tortures.

Barry

Neither snow, nor rain, nor heat, nor speed of light, stays these couriers—

Mail Supremacy

by Hayford Peirce

It all seems so inevitable, now that mankind is spreading out through the galaxy. The only question is: Why wasn't it done sooner? Why did the road to the stars have to wait until 1984, when an Anglo-Chinese merchant fell to musing over his correspondence? But perhaps all of mankind's greatest advances, from fire through the wheel, from penicillin through hydrogen fusion, seem inevitable only in retrospect.

Who remembers the faceless thousands who unlocked the secret of nuclear energy, the man who dropped the first atomic bomb? Mankind remembers Einstein.

Who remembers the faceless thousands who built the first moonship, the man who first stepped upon an alien world? Mankind remembers Verne and Ley and Campbell.

As mankind remembers Chap Foey Rider.

Chap Foey Rider's main offices were in New York, not far from Grand Central Station. From them he directed an import-export firm that blanketed the globe. On November 8, 1984, a Friday, his secretary brought him the day's mail. It was 11:34 in the morning.

Chap Foey Rider frowned. Nearly noon, and only now was the mail delivered. How many years had it been since there had been two deliveries a day, morning and afternoon? At least twenty-five. Where was the much-vaunted progress of the age of technology?

He remembered his childhood in London, long before the war, when there had been *three* daily deliveries. When his father would post a letter in the morning, asking an associate to tea, and receive a written reply before tea-time. It was enough to make a bloke shake his head.

Chap Foey Rider shook his head and picked up his mail.

There was a bill of lading from his warehouse in Brooklyn, seven miles away. Mailed eight days ago.

There was a portfolio print-out from his investment counselor in Boston, 188 miles away. Mailed seven days ago.

There was an inquiry from his customs broker in Los Angeles, 2,451 miles away. Mailed four days ago.

There was a price list from a pearl merchant in Papeete, Tahiti, 6,447 miles away. Mailed three days ago.

Chap Foey Rider reached for his slide rule.

He then called his branch manager in Honolulu. He told him to mail a letter to the branch manager in Capetown, 11,535 miles away.

The Capetown manager called Chap Foey Rider two days later to advise him that the letter from Honolulu had arrived. Although still Sunday in New York, it was early Monday morning in Capetown.

Chap Foey Rider pondered. The length of the equator was 24,901.55 miles. No spot on Earth could be farther than 12,450.78 miles from any other.

He reached for the World Almanac.

Bangkok was 12,244 miles from Lima. He smiled. He had offices in each city.

A letter from Bangkok reached Lima in a single day.

Chap Foey Rider returned to his slide rule.

The extrapolation was staggering.

One further test was required to prove his theory. He pursed his lips, then carefully addressed an envelope: *Occupant, 614 Starshine Boulevard, Alpha Centauri IV*. He looked at his watch: good, the post office was open for another hour. He personally pushed the envelope through the Out-of-Town slot and strolled home.

Returning to his office the next morning, he found in his stack of mail the envelope addressed to Alpha Centauri. Frowning, he picked it up. Stamped across the front in purple ink were the words: *Addressee Unknown, Returned to Sender*.

Chap Foey Rider lighted his first cigarette of the day and to conceal his discontent puffed perfect rings toward the ceiling. Was the test actually conclusive? True, the envelope had been returned. But with suspicious speed. He reviewed his chain of logic, then studied the envelope with a magnifying glass. There was, after all, nothing to indicate *which* post office had stamped it.

He ground the cigarette out and reached for a piece of paper. He wrote firmly, without hesitation:

> *The Rgt. Hon. Chairman*
> *of the Supreme Galactic Council*
> *Sagittarius*
> Sir: *I feel I must draw to your attention certain shortcomings in your General Post Office system. Only yesterday I mailed a letter* . . .

Chap Foey Rider awaited the morning's delivery. Eventually it arrived.

There was an envelope-sized piece of thick creamy parchment, folded neatly and held together by a complex red seal. His name appeared on one side, apparently engraved in golden ink.

Expressionless, he broke the seal, unfolded the parchment, and read the contents. It was from the Executive Secretary, Office of the Mandator of the Galactic Confederation:

> *Dear Sir: In reply to yours of the 14th inst. the Man-*

dator begs me to inform you that as per your speculation the Galactic Confederation does indeed exist as primarily a Postal Union, its purpose being to promote Trade and Commerce between its 27,000 members. Any civilization is invited to join our Confederation, the sole qualification of membership being the independent discovery of our faster-than-light Postal Union. His Excellency is pleased to note that you, on behalf of your fellow Terrans, have at long last fulfilled the necessary conditions, and in consequence, an Ambassador-Plenipotentiary from the Galactic Confederation will be arriving on Terra within the next two days. Please accept, Mr. Rider, on behalf of the Mandator, the expression of his most distinguished sentiments.

". . . to promote Trade and Commerce . . ."

Chap Foey Rider restrained himself from rubbing his hands together in glee. Instead he pushed a buzzer to summon his four sons to conference. The stars were coming to mankind. Rider Factoring, Ltd. would be ready for them; He called the mailroom to tell them to be on the alert for a large package from Sagittarius.

Updating the pink elephant.

Mistake

by Larry Niven

In a cargo craft between Earth and Ganymede, Commander Elroy Barnes lolled in his crash couch with a silly smile on his face. The shovel-blade re-entry shield was swung down from the ship's nose, exposing the cabin's great curved window. Barnes watched the unwinking stars. It was a few minutes before he noticed the alien staring in at him.

He studied it. Eight feet tall, roughly reptilian, with a scaly, domed head and a mouth furnished with several dozen polished stiletto-blade teeth. Its hands were four-fingered claws, and one held a wide-barreled pistol-like tool.

Barnes lifted a languid hand and waved.

Kthistlmup was puzzled. The human's mind was muzzy, almost unreadable. The alien probed the ship for other minds, but the ship was empty save for Barnes.

Kthistlmup stepped through the glass into the cabin.

Barnes showed surprise for the first time. "Hey, that was neat! Do it again."

"There's something wrong with you," Kthistlmup projected.

Barnes grinned. "Certain measures are necessary to combat the boredom of space, to s-safeguard the sanity of our pilots." He lifted a green plastic pill bottle. "NST-24. Makes for a good trip. Nothing to do out here till I have to guide the beast into the Jupiter system. So why not?"

"Why not what?"

"Why not take a little trip while I take the big one?"

Kthistlmup understood at last. "You've done something to your mind. Chemicals? We use direct-current stimulus on Mars."

"Mars? Are you really—"

"Barnes, I must ask you questions."

Barnes waved expansively. "Shoot."

"How well is Earth prepared against an attack from space?"

"That's a *secret*. Besides, I don't have the vaguest notion."

"You must have some notion. What's the most powerful weapon you ever heard of?"

Barnes folded his arms. "Won't say." His mind showed only a blaze of white light, which might not have anything to do with the question.

Kthistlmup tried again. "Has Earth colonized other planets?"

"Sure. Trantor, Mesklin, Barsoom, Perelandra . . ."

Barnes' mind showed only that he was lying, and Kthistlmup had lost patience. "You will answer," he said, and reached forward to take Barnes' throat delicately between four needle-sharp claws.

Barnes' eyes grew large. "Oh, oh, bad trip! Gimme, gimme the bottle of Ends! Quick!"

Kthistlmup let go. "Tell me about Earth's defenses."

"I got to have an End. Big blue bottle, it should be in the medicine chest." Barnes reached to the side. He had the wall cabinet open before Kthistlmup caught his wrist.

"This 'End.' What will it do?"

"End the trip. Fix me up."

"It will clear your mind?"

"Right."

Kthistlmup released him. He watched as Barnes swallowed an oval pill, dry.

"It's for in case we're going to run across an asteroid, so I can recompute the course fast," Barnes explained.

Kthistlmup watched as Barnes' mind began to clear. In a minute Barnes would be unable to hide his thoughts. It wouldn't matter if he answered or not. Kthistlmup need only read the pictures his questions produced.

Barnes' mind cleared further . . . and Kthistlmup found himself fading out of existence. His last thought was that it had been a perfectly natural mistake.

Well, Bob's retired, he says, but I carry on!

Half-Baked Publisher's Delight

by Jeffrey S. Hudson
and Isaac Asimov

PROLOGUE

Dear Isaac,

Enclosed is a short piece which I thought you might find amusing. Of course the resolution is a bit flawed, but, well . . . If you, Dr. A., *revised* the last three paragraphs or so, you would a) help create a Genuine Literary Curiosity, b) nudge a trufan over the line into the ranks of Published Writers, and c) blow said fan's mind clean out the window! You would also make me a very happy editor.

By the way, your *Forum* piece for July *Galaxy* is even perfecter than I expected!

All the best,
(signed) Jim Baen

Dear Jim,

Okay, here is all the stuff you sent me, together with an alternate ending that I made up.

Perhaps you can also get Bob Silverberg to make up an alternate ending—or at the very least make sure that he doesn't get mad. (*He didn't get mad. Ed.*)

And however much young J. S. Hudson may approve, I think it would be nice if you check with him, as a courtesy.

Naturally, I don't expect to be paid for this. If you run it, give all the money to Hudson.

Yours,
(signed) Isaac Asimov

Dear Jeff,

Would you mind having your story published as a collaboration with Dr. Isaac Asimov?

Best Regards,
(signed) Jim Baen

Dear Jim,

YOU'RE KIDDING!!! YES!!!

Incoherently yours,
(signed) Jeff Hudson

(End of Prologue)

A gurgling boil shook the waters of New York Bay. The misty air swirled and parted, revealing a great metal curve lying low in the water. A few yards away the water thrashed, and a huge white slick floated to the surface. The Navy, Coast Guard, and NYPD rushed out to investigate. As the last fog cleared off, aerial photographs were taken by the Air Force and the TV networks.

The shiny metal curve rose slowly to a low peak, then dropped off quickly into the bay. It had a slight twist. All in all, it resembled a hump. The thrashing continued nearby, occasionally sending water plumes high into the air. The slick remained remarkably angular. The Pentagon couldn't make head nor tail of it but assured everyone that it wasn't the Russians.

Then it happened. As if something had been cut loose from below, the curve rose into the air, revealing itself to be a low arch, no, it didn't connect to anything on one end. Two huge marginal stops reared their heads above the waves, and abruptly it surfaced. Water poured from the platen, splashed in the carriage, cascaded down the keys and the mighty typewriter rose into the sunlight. The huge type faces arched skyward and whacked against the paper, the tabulator key was pressed and the cylinder knobs raced through the air, knocking over the Statue of Liberty. On the back of the Mighty Machine read the legend "World's Most Prolific or Bust!"

And down among the keys, racing back and forth on a series of catwalks with a maniac fury, was Dr. Isaac Asimov.

The President was outraged.

The publisher was overjoyed.

The public was hysterical.

Meanwhile, the Good Doctor was typing away on an endless sheet of "paper" one hundred yards wide that seemed to materialize within the machine itself. Indeed, no part of the machine ever needed replacing, it seemed to be self-renewing. This included Doctor Asimov. The only clue to the typewriter's mysterious operation was a long electric cord that trailed out into the Atlantic.

Isaac pounded out his message twenty-four hours a day. His massive MS. had already clogged New York Harbor, and was now piling up on shore, curling around docks, gift wrapping high rises, paving the streets with the seemingly indestructible "paper." The letters did not blur or fade; whole crowds were seen walking down the paper pavement, reading in fascination.

The works were on every subject imaginable. Science: a new Theory of Relativity. Humor: The City of New York nearly died laughing. Fiction: A new trilogy (Science Fiction, of course).

The Mayor rowed out in a dinghy to try and talk Asimov into laying off for a while. Isaac listened to him, hitting the G, racing up underneath the Y, U, I, and pouncing on the O. He told the Mayor a funny joke and continued with his work.

Various other officials rowed out to plead with him but got nowhere. Friends and relatives, fellow scientists and writers, all attempted to dissuade him, but to no avail. He was offered immense sums of money and didn't even blink.

The Science Fiction Writers of America promised to give up their trade, en masse. No good. The World Science Fiction Convention offered him a special Hugo Award as "World's Greatest and Most Prolific Writer and Nicest Guy in the Cosmos." Fiddlesticks, said Asimov.

By now, the monstrous MS. had spread across New York State in a broad white swath—having the most interesting effect on Niagara Falls—crossed Lake Erie (if that didn't stop it, what could?) and tied Detroit in knots—literally.

At about this time, a mighty roar, a colossal splash, and out of San Francisco Bay emerged yet another giant typewriter.

As the spray cleared, there stood the figure of Robert Silverberg, a dark glint in his eastward gazing eyes, water dripping from his long hair and beard. In his hand he held a long pole and he explained (while demonstrating) that by pole vaulting between the keys he expected to surpass Asimov.

Another set of type faces whacked twenty-four hours a day; once more, miles of indestructible MS. This time it was the Bay Bridge that got knocked over.

And so began the Great Race. Hank Aaron was forgotten overnight, and the Americans, being a sporting people, started rooting for one or the other. Attempts at placation were abandoned—for what one-of-a-kind honor could be granted twice? However, lesser honors rained down, in order to show affection and confidence in one or the other of the two. Silverberg was voted Best Dressed Science Fiction Writer. Asimov turned down a presidential bid. Neither bothered more than a blink with all the silly business and continued typing at a tremendous pace. Asimov, in order to speed up production, created a Tarzanic arrangement so he could swing from key to key. But in so doing, he lost valuable time to Silverberg, whose pole vaulting was exquisite.

Asimov's MS. had by now crossed the Mississippi and was currently burying Mount Rushmore. Silverberg's, after some initial difficulties in the Grand Canyon, was rampaging into the Great Plains.

Then, for reasons unbeknownst to man, the two MSS. changed direction and proceeded on a collision course. It became apparent that this blessed event would occur in the Cornhusker State of Nebraska. Many bets were placed on the outcome of the meeting of the minds. The Big Question was "Which is stronger?!"

Publishers cashed in on the free publicity, printing and reprinting as cleaned out book stores demanded more and more. Huge fan clubs were formed, offering fake beards and wigs (just like Silverberg's!). Asimov's fans tended to dress as robots, wearing "Mule-ears" for less formal occasions.

ALTERNATE CONCLUSION TO "HALF-BAKED PUBLISHER'S DELIGHT"

The big day came. The two paper snakes approached, raised their heads, and coiled together into a spiral.

For a day, they held together trembling in a double helix of paper, while more paper accumulated beneath. Then the two coils drew apart, peeling away, and out of the air molecules about, each formed a new coil of paper. Where one double helix had existed a while before, two now existed in perfect replication.

Reporters dropped their microphones.

Government agents dropped their listening devices.

The American public dropped its collective lower jaw.

Another day the two double helices held together trembling, then drew apart, peeling away—and there were four.

In the Atlantic and in the Pacific, each endless sheaf of paper pulled out of the gigantic typewriter with a horrendous tear. The keys of each locked in place with a thunderous snap. Asimov fell back, gibbering. Silverberg tumbled forward, yammering.

In Nebraska, the paper helices continued to separate and replicate. The monster no longer needed its Frankensteins.

NASA estimates that in less than two months, all the Earth will be paper. Perhaps it will then reach for the Moon.

I knew there was an explanation.

Far from Home

by Walter S. Tevis

The first inkling the janitor had of the miracle was the smell of it. This was a small miracle in itself: the salt smell of kelp and sea water in the Arizona morning air. He had just unlocked the front entrance and walked into the building when the smell hit him.

Now this man was old and normally did not trust his senses very well; but there was no mistaking this, not even in this most inland of inland towns: it was the smell of ocean—deep ocean, far out, the ocean of green water, kelp and brine.

And strangely, because the janitor was old and tired, and because this was the part of early morning that seems unreal to many old men, the first thing the smell made him feel was a small, almost undetectable thrilling in his old nerves, a memory deeper than blood of a time fifty years before when he had gone once, as a boy, to San Francisco and had watched the ships in the bay and had discovered the first old dirty smell of sea water. But this feeling lasted only an instant. It was replaced immediately with amazement—and then anger, although it would have been impossible to say with what he was angry, here in this desert town, in the dressing rooms of the large public swimming pool at morning, being reminded of his youth and of the ocean.

"What the hell's going on here?" the janitor said.

There was no one to hear this, except perhaps the small boy who had been standing outside, staring through the wire fence into the pool and clutching a brown sack in one grubby hand, when the janitor had come up to the building. The man had paid no attention to the boy; small boys were always around the swimming pool in summer—a nuisance. The boy, if he had heard the man or not, did not reply.

The janitor walked on through the concrete-floored dressing rooms, not even stopping to read the morning's crop of obscenities scribbled on the walls of the little wooden booths. He walked into the tiled anteroom, stepped across the disinfectant foot bath, and out onto the wide concrete edge of the swimming pool itself.

Some things are unmistakable. There was a whale in the pool.

And no ordinary, everyday whale. This was a monumental creature, a whale's whale, a great, blue-gray leviathan, ninety feet long and thirty feet across the back, with a tail the size of a flatcar and a head like the smooth fist of a man. A blue whale, an old shiny, leathery monster with barnacles on his gray underbelly and his eyes filmed with age and wisdom and myopia, with brown seaweed dribbling from one corner of his mouth, marks of the suckers of squid on his face, with a rusted piece of harpoon sunk in the unconscious blubber of his back. He rested on his belly in the pool, his back way out of the water and with his monstrous gray lips together in an expression of contentment and repose. He was not asleep; but he was asleep enough not to care where he was.

And he stank—with the fine old stink of the sea, the mother of us all; the brackish, barnacled, grainy salt stink of creation and old age, the stink of the world that was and of the world to come. He was beautiful.

The janitor did not freeze when he saw him; he froze a moment afterwards. First he said, aloud, his voice matter-of-fact, "There's a whale in the swimming pool. A God damn whale." He said this to no one—or to everyone—and perhaps the boy heard him, although there was no reply from the other side of the fence.

After speaking, the janitor stood where he was for several minutes, thinking. He thought of many things, such as what he had eaten for breakfast, what his wife had said to him when she had awakened him that morning. Somewhere, in the corner of his vision, he saw the little boy with the paper sack, and his mind thought, as minds will do at such times. *Now that boy's about six years old. That's probably his lunch in that sack. Egg salad sandwich. Banana. Or apple.* But he did not think about the whale, because there was nothing to be thought about the whale. He stared at its unbelievable bulk, resting calmly, the great head in the deep water under the diving boards, the corner of one tail fluke being lapped gently by the shallow water of the wading pool.

The whale breathed slowly, deeply, through its blow hole. The janitor breathed slowly, shallowly, staring, not blinking even in the rising sunlight, staring with no comprehension at the eighty-five ton miracle in the swimming pool. The boy held his paper sack tightly at the top, and his eyes, too, remained fixed on the whale. The sun was rising in the sky over the desert to the east, and its light glinted in red and purple iridescence on the oily back of the whale.

And then the whale noticed the janitor. Weak-visioned, it peered at him filmily for several moments from its grotesquely small eye. And then it arched its back in a ponderous, awesome, and graceful movement, lifted its tail twenty feet in the air, and brought it down in a way that seemed strangely slow, slapping gently into the water with it. A hundred gallons of water rose out of the pool, and enough of it drenched the janitor to wake him from the state of partial paralysis into which he had fallen.

Abruptly the janitor jumped back, scrambling from the water, his eyes looking, frightened, in all directions, his lips white. There was nothing to see but the whale and the boy. "All right," he said, "all right," as if he had somehow seen through the plot, as if he knew, now, what a whale would be doing in the public swimming pool, as if no one was going to put anything over on *him*. "All right," the janitor said to the whale, and then he turned and ran.

He ran back into the center of town, back toward Main Street, back toward the bank, where he would find the chairman of the board of the City Parks Commission, the man who could, somehow—perhaps with a memorandum—save him. He ran back to the town where things were as they were supposed to be; ran as fast as he had ever run, even when young, to escape the only miracle he would ever see in his life and the greatest of all God's creatures. . . .

After the janitor had left, the boy remained staring at the whale for a long while, his face a mask and his heart racing with all the peculiar excitement of wonder and love—wonder for all whales, and love for the only whale that he, an Arizona boy of six desert years, had ever seen. And then, when he realized that there would be men there soon and his time with his whale would be over, he lifted the paper sack carefully close to his face, and opened its top about an inch, gingerly. A commotion began in the sack, as if a small animal were in it that wanted desperately to get out.

"Stop that!" the boy said, frowning.

The kicking stopped. From the sack came a voice—a high-pitched, irascible voice, with a Gaelic accent. "All right, whatever-your-name-is," the voice said, "I suppose you're ready for the second one."

The boy held the sack carefully with his thumb and forefinger. He frowned at the opening in the top. "Yes," he said, "I think so . . ."

When the janitor returned with the two other men, the whale was no longer there. Neither was the small boy. But the seaweed smell and the splashed, brackish water were there still, and in the pool were several brownish streamers of seaweed, floating aimlessly in the chlorinated water, far from home.

And yet with a toothpick against a flame-thrower, my money's on the latter.

Swords of Ifthan

by James Sutherland

For Alvin Moffet, the quintessence of Life As It Should Be was contained within a row of leather-bound volumes in the library's rare-book room. Alvin worked one floor below, at the reference desk, but passed his spare moments upstairs savoring *Le Morte d'Arthur*, perhaps, or *Orlando Furioso*. When an influx of students kept him at the desk—during final-examination weeks, usually—he made do with a cheap edition of *The Once and Future King* and his own glowing dreams. And though he admired the former's vision, in his heart Alvin felt the latter remained truest to the spirit of the old classics.

One noontime he came upon a nacreous sphere floating along-side *The Song of Roland*.

"Alvin Moffet?" the sphere inquired briskly. "Alvin Bergen Moffet?"

Distracted, Alvin nodded vaguely.

The sphere bobbled. "Excellent! I have journeyed far to meet with you."

At this point Alvin fully perceived he was being addressed by an altogether strange entity, flinched, and cried in confusion: "Whaahoowhere?"

Fortunately the sphere seemed to understand, and replied that it was no less than the Guardian of Continua, coming to seek Alvin's assistance in a matter of desperate urgency.

"Whatever can I do?"

"Aid the fair world of Ifthan, which presently lies in much danger." Alvin had never heard of Ifthan, so the Guardian added in hurried tones: "I will construct a visual simulacrum of Ifthan, adjusted to your senses. Observe, then, and quick!"

Around Alvin the somehow familiar landscape of Ifthan took form. Here were green glades and forests; there were softly rolling meadows; and beyond, a gleaming castle. A lone knight ventured from the raised portcullis and warily rode toward a monstrous dragonlike creature that was laying the countryside to waste and ruin. From a high revetment a raven-haired woman of surpassing beauty called passionate encouragement to her hero as he spurred his mount near the dragon. A sword flashed under the golden sun. . . . The scene faded mistily.

"As your eyes beheld," continued the sphere, "Ifthan is besieged by those loathly invaders. Our champions are powerless to resist the ever advancing tide. Only a valiant outsider can be an equal to the unnatural foe."

"You want *me?*"

"Assuredly." The sphere seemed to read Alvin's thoughts by concluding: "Fear not; the Earthly physique that you deem inadequate will be suitably rectified if you choose to accompany me. Now, will you accept this awesome challenge?"

It's everything I've ever read about, dreamed about, hoped for, Alvin thought, scarcely daring to breathe. He decided.

"Where do I sign?"

"Your word is proof enough of intent, Alvin Moffet!"

Abruptly the Continuum slewed wildly, then Alvin found himself standing in the selfsame meadow beside the castle he had glimpsed. The air was wonderfully fresh and hearty, and Alvin let out a happy yell that quite suddenly ended as he noticed he had just exhaled orange flames. Looking down in mounting horror, he discovered that his skin had turned a scaly magenta, his fingers had dwindled to jagged claws, and his legs were grotesque stumps.

"This isn't what I'd expected," Alvin said angrily, lashing his heavy spiked tail about like a bullwhip.

"Careful with that thing," the sphere said anxiously. "Wait for the signal."

A crowd was beginning to gather along the revetment, screaming at Alvin and making gestures. When a plumed knight of heroic proportions thundered out the castle gateway, they shouted in ecstasy. The knight pointed his lance at Alvin and the crowd whooped with delirious anticipation.

Made wretched by the turn of events, Alvin wanted to weep. But reptiles have no tear ducts: all he could choke out was a reproachful, "I . . . I don't know what to think of this, or of you!"

"Think of me as your manager. Now lissen good, kid," the sphere told him in a hoarse and sweaty-sounding voice. "When the gong sounds, I want you to really get in there and *fight!*"

Food poisoning is a risk we all run now and then.

Argent Blood

by Joe L. Hensley

April 13: Today I made a discovery. I was allowed to look in the mirror in Doctor Mesh's office. I'm about forty years old, judging from my face and hair. I failed to recognize me, and by this I mean there is apparently no correlation between what I saw of me in the mirror and this trick memory of mine. But it's good to see one's face, although my own appears ordinary enough.

I must admit to more interest in the pretty bottles on Doctor Mesh's shelves than my face. Somewhere in dreams I remember bottles like those. I wanted the bottles so badly that a whirling came in my head. But I didn't try to take them, as I suspected that Doctor Mesh was watching closely.

Doctor Mesh said: "You're improving. Soon we'll give you the run of our little hospital and grounds, except, of course, the disturbed room." He pinched me on the arm playfully. "Have to keep you healthy."

I nodded and was delighted and the sickness inside went away. Then I could take my eyes off the shelves of bottles—nice ones full of good poisons—some that I recognized vaguely, others that struck no chord.

There would be another time.

Later I went back into the small ward—my home—the only one I really remember. Miss Utz smiled at me from her desk and I lay on my bed and watched her. She has strange, bottomless eyes. When I see her, the longing to be normal again is strongest. But the disturbances recur.

My ward is done in calm colors. The whole effect is soporific. I'm sure I never slept so much or dreamed so much. Bottles, bottles.

The food is good and I eat a great deal. My weight seems to

remain fairly constant, decreasing when I'm disturbed, coming back to normal when released.

My fellow patients are not so well off. Most of them are very old and either idiotic or comatose. Only the man with the beard is rational enough to talk to sometimes.

The bearded man saw me watching him. "Pet!" he yelled at me. He makes me very angry sometimes. He's always saying that to me when he's disturbed. I wonder what he means?

I shall quit writing for the day. Doctor Mesh says it's good to keep a diary, but I'm afraid someone will read this. That would anger me, and extreme anger brings on disturbances.

I'm sleepy now.

April 18: I've got to stop this sort of thing. I tried again with the bearded man, but he won't drink water that he hasn't freshly drawn. I think he suspected that I'd done something, because he watched me malevolently for a long time.

I came out of the disturbed room yesterday, sick and weak, remembering nothing of that time.

No one seems to have found the bottle I hid the day I became disturbed, a bottle empty now down to the skull and crossbones, but to no purpose except the bearded man's anger. I wonder why Doctor Mesh angers me so? And Miss Utz? I guess it must be because they move and talk and exist. The old ones who don't move and talk to me don't anger me—only the bearded man and Doctor Mesh and Miss Utz.

But nothing seems to work on the Doctor or Miss Utz and the bearded man is very careful.

Today, at mid-morning, Miss Utz helped me down to the solarium and I sat there for a while. Outside, the flowers have begun to bloom and some minute purple and green creepers are folding their way over the walls around this tiny asylum. They look very good and poisonous.

My neck itched and I scratched at the places until they bled and Miss Utz laughed her cold laugh and put antiseptic on my neck. She told me that this is a private asylum run on private funds, taking no patients but hopeless ones that have been confined elsewhere for years before transfer here. If that is completely so, then why am I here?

In the afternoon Doctor Mesh tested my reflexes and listened to my heart. He says I'm in good physical condition. He seemed happy about that. He was evasive when I asked him if I'd ever be well and that made me angry. I managed to hide all outward signs of my feeling.

When I was back in the ward and Miss Utz was temporarily out of sight, the feel of the poison bottle comforted me.

April 30: The dreams are growing worse. So clear and real. I dreamed I was in Doctor Mesh's office. I could see the pretty bottles on the shelves. Miss Utz and Doctor Mesh were reading my diary and laughing. The bearded man kept screaming at me from far away. The dream was very real, but my eyes would not open.

This morning the bearded man is watching me from his bed. He looks very weak, but he had a disturbance this week. Being disturbed is very hard on one, Doctor Mesh once told me.

I was in Doctor Mesh's office for a while earlier and got to look in the mirror. I did not recognize me again. Sometimes I feel as if my head had been cut open, the contents scrambled, and then recapped. There is no pain, but there is no place to search for things.

A little while ago I tried something from the new bottle that I'd taken from Doctor Mesh's office. It didn't work. Nothing works—even though I saw Miss Utz drink some of the water.

May 2: I shall have to hide this diary. I'm almost sure they are reading it. They brought the bearded man back from "disturbed" today. His eyes are red and sunken and he kept watching me all morning. When Miss Utz left the ward he beckoned me over with an insistent finger.

He said nothing. Instead he lifted his beard away and pointed at his throat. I looked at it, but could see nothing but some small, red marks, as if he'd cut himself with his fingernails. He pulled one of the cuts open with hands that shook and a tiny driblet of blood pulsed out. He laughed.

I looked away, the blood making me feel ill.

The corner of one of the pages in this diary is torn. I didn't tear it.

May 3: I talked to the bearded man today—if talk can describe the conversation we had. He's insistent. He said I can't know when they feed on me as I'm in a sort of seizure and that I'm their "pet" because I'm young and strong. He made me check my neck and there are red marks on it. He said they let me steal the poisons because they know I can't harm them.

He told me I killed three people outside, poisoned them. He says I was a pharmacist outside, but now I'm incurably insane and can't ever be released. He said I was in a state hospital for years before I came here. I don't remember it.

He claims that Doctor Mesh and Miss Utz are vampires.

I went back to my bed when he let me get away and spent a fairly restful afternoon. I dreamed of bottles on the shelf and something came to me in the dream—a thing all perfect like myself.

The bearded man says that we could kill them with silver bullets, but the thought of a gun is abhorrent to me.

I've never really believed in that sort of thing, but what if the bearded man is right? What if Doctor Mesh and Miss Utz are vampires. This place would be perfect for them. No investigation of death, no legal troubles, patients forgotten years ago. Take only the incurables, the forgotten. A regular supply.

But the plan, so intricate and perfect. I will have to have the bearded man's help. He will have to steal the things I want. If they are watching me, laughing when I steal from them, it would be too risky for me to take it.

May 4: We began the plan today. The bearded man managed to steal the large bottle of saline solution and the tube and needle to introduce it into the veins. He also managed the other part. The chemical was where I'd described it as being on Doctor Mesh's shelves. I even had the color of the bottle right. Now we must wait for the right time. Perhaps tonight?

I shall hide this book well.

May 6: I am in fever. We did not manage until last night, and it took a very long time. I feel all steamy inside and there is a dizziness.

I'm trying for anger and a disturbance. Miss Utz is watching from her desk, her eyes hot and bright.

They will take me to the disturbed room.

May 9: A few lines. I'm ill. Nothing seems to be working inside me and the heat is such that my eyes see more brightness than shade. I'm in the disturbed room and I've seen no one alive all day. I can hear the bearded man's whiny laugh and once I heard him clap his hands.

I think they are dead. They must be dead.

We put the silver chloride in the saline solution and put the needle in my arm and let it all flow inside. When I was disturbed they must have fed on me.

If I rise up I can see the toe of a female foot right at the door and it's all curled and motionless. I can't see Doctor Mesh, but he must be there in the hall near Miss Utz.

Dead of my poisoned blood, my fine and intricate blood. A new specific for vampires. *Silver Blood.*

I wish this heat would go away. Three outside and two in here. I want there to be time for more . . .

Golly, isn't any form of depredation safe?

Collector's Fever

by Roger Zelazny

"What are you doing there, human?"

"It's a long story."

"Good, I like long stories. Sit down and talk. No—not on me!"

"Sorry. Well, it's all because of my uncle, the fabulously wealthy—"

"Stop. What does 'wealthy' mean?"

"Well, like rich."

"And 'rich'?"

"Hm. Lots of money."

"What's money?"

"You want to hear this story or don't you?"

"Yes, but I'd like to understand it too."

"Sorry, Rock, I'm afraid I don't understand it all myself."

"The name is Stone."

"Okay, Stone. My uncle, who is a very important man, was supposed to send me to the Space Academy, but he didn't. He decided a liberal education was a better thing. So he sent me to his old spinster alma mater to major in nonhuman humanities. You with me, so far?"

"No, but understanding is not necessarily an adjunct to appreciation."

"That's what I say. I'll never understand Uncle Sidney, but I appreciate his outrageous tastes, his magpie instinct and his gross meddling in other people's affairs. I appreciate them till I'm sick to the stomach. There's nothing else I can do. He's a carnivorous old family monument, and fond of having his own way. Unfortunately, he also has all the money in the family—so it follows, like a *xxt* after a *zzn*, that he always *does* have his own way."

"This money must be pretty important stuff."

"Important enough to send me across ten thousand light-years to an unnamed world which, incidentally, I've just named Dunghill."

"The low-flying *zatt* is a heavy eater, which accounts for its low flying . . ."

"So I've noted. That *is* moss though, isn't it?"

"Yes."

"Good, then crating will be less of a problem."

"What's 'crating'?"

"It means to put something in a box to take it somewhere else."

"Like moving around?"

"Yes."

"What are you planning on crating?"

"Yourself, Stone."

"I've never been the rolling sort . . ."

"Listen, Stone, my uncle is a rock collector, see? You are the only species of intelligent mineral in the galaxy. You are also the largest specimen I've spotted so far. Do you follow me?"

"Yes, but I don't want to."

"Why not? You'd be lord of his rock collection. Sort of a one-eyed man in a kingdom of the blind, if I may venture an inappropriate metaphor."

"Please don't do that, whatever it is. It sounds awful. Tell me, how did your uncle learn of our world?"

"One of my instructors read about this place in an old space log. *He* was an old space log collector. The log had belonged to a Captain Fairhill, who landed here several centuries ago and held lengthy discourses with your people."

"Good old Foul Weather Fairhill! How is he these days? Give him my regards—"

"He's dead."

"What?"

"Dead. Kaput. Blooey. Gone. Deeble."

"Oh my! When did it happen? I trust it was an esthetic occurrence of major import—"

"I really couldn't say. But I passed the information on to my uncle, who decided to collect you. That's why I'm here—he sent me."

"Really, as much as I appreciate the compliment, I can't accompany you. It's almost deeble time—"

"I know, I read all about deebling in the Fairhill log before I showed it to Uncle Sidney. I tore those pages out. I want him to be around when you do it. Then I can inherit his money and console myself in all manner of expensive ways for never having gone to the Space Academy. First I'll become an alcoholic, then I'll take up wenching—or maybe I'd better do it the other way around . . ."

"But I want to deeble here, among the things I've become attached to!"

"This is a crowbar. I'm going to unattach you."

"If you try it, I'll deeble right now."

"You can't. I measured your mass before we struck up this conversation. It will take at least eight months, under Earth conditions, for you to reach deebling proportions."

"Okay, I was bluffing. But have you no compassion? I've rested here for centuries, ever since I was a small pebble, as did my fathers before me. I've added so carefully to my atom collection, building up the finest molecular structure in the neighborhood. And now, to be snatched away right before deebling time, it's—it's quite unrock of you."

"It's not that bad. I promise you'll collect the finest Earth atoms available. You'll go places no other Stone has ever been before."

"Small consolation. I want my friends to see."

"I'm afraid that's out of the question."

"You are a very cruel human. I hope you're around when I deeble."

"I intend to be far away and on the eve of prodigious debaucheries when that occurs."

Under Dunghill's sub-E gravitation Stone was easily rolled to the side of the space sedan, crated, and, with the help of a winch, installed in the compartment beside the atomic pile. The fact that it was a short-jaunt sport model sedan, customized by its owner, who had removed much of the shielding, was the reason Stone felt a sudden flush of volcanic drunkenness, rapidly added select items to his collection and deebled on the spot.

He mushroomed upwards, then swept in great waves across the plains of Dunghill. Several young Stones fell from the dusty heavens wailing their birth pains across the community band.

"Gone fission," commented a distant neighbor, above the static, "and sooner than I expected. Feel that warm afterglow!"

"An excellent deeble," agreed another. "It always pays to be a cautious collector."

Relative to what?

Sign at the End of the Universe

by Duane Ackerson

This End Up.

Relative to everything.

Stubborn

by Stephen Goldin

Frederick Von Burling the Third was a gimme pig.

At the age of five, little Frederick asked his mommy, "Are you going to buy me a Super-Duper Rocket and Astronaut Set?"

"No, Freddy," said his mommy. "It costs $28.95. Now, be a good little boy and don't cry."

"I'm gonna cry," said little Frederick, stamping his foot furiously. "I'm gonna hold my breath until I turn blue."

Little Frederick did even better than that. He turned purple.

Needless to say, kiddies, little Frederick got the Super-Duper Rocket and Astronaut Set.

At the age of ten, little Frederick asked his daddy, "Are you going to buy me a real-live-honest-to-goodness pony?"

"No, Freddy," said his daddy. "It costs $289.50. Now, be a good little boy and don't cry."

"I'm gonna cry," said little Frederick, stamping his foot furiously. "I'm gonna stand on my head in the corner for a whole hour."

Little Frederick did even better than that. He stood on his head in the corner for three hours.

Needless to say, kiddies, little Frederick got the real-live-honest-to-goodness pony.

At the age of twenty, little Frederick asked his uncle, "Are you going to buy me a shiny chrome, two-tone convertible sports car?"

"No, Freddy," said his uncle. "It costs $2,895. Now, be a good little boy and don't cry."

"I'm gonna cry," said little Frederick, stamping his foot furiously. "I'm gonna date Selma Schatzburger, the village idiot."

Little Frederick did even better than that. He affianced Selma Schatzburger, the village idiot.

Needless to say, kiddies, little Frederick got the shiny chrome, two-tone convertible sports car.

At the age of thirty, little Frederick asked his family, "Are you going to buy me a no-holds-barred, all-expense-paid trip around the world?"

"No, Freddy," said his family. "It costs $28,950. Now, be a good little boy and don't cry."

"I'm gonna cry," said little Frederick, stamping his foot furiously. "I'm gonna stand on this spot and not budge from it all day."

Now, kiddies, the Earth is rotating on its axis at a speed of approximately one thousand miles an hour at the equator. (The speed decreases as you approach the poles, kiddies, but we needn't bother ourselves with that.)

The Earth is also revolving about the Sun at an average speed of eighteen miles a second. (The Earth and the Moon also revolve around a common center of gravity, kiddies, but this point is inside the Earth, so it doesn't matter too much.)

The Sun is also moving toward a star named Vega at a speed of about twelve miles a second.

The Sun is also spinning around the rim of the galaxy at a speed of one hundred and seventy-five miles a second.

The galaxy is also receding from all other galaxies to the end of the universe at a speed equal to sixty miles a second for every million light-years of separation between the two galaxies; that is, kiddies, if a galaxy is one million light-years from us, we are moving away from it at a speed of sixty miles a second; if it is two million light-years away, we are moving away from it at a rate of one hundred and twenty miles a second.

All this, kiddies, is very fast.

But little Frederick didn't budge.

Needless to say, kiddies, little Frederick got what he deserved.

The last line explains Eve.

The Re-Creation

by Robert E. Toomey, Jr.

He was very tired of being God.

He decided to quit. He had His reasons.

He quit.

Gods can do that if they want to.

But He was still interested in His creations. He was interested in everything. Constant interest is an important part of the god biz.

There was this planet He'd put together a few millennia previously. Even before the boiling gases had coalesced. He'd received a rejection. The attached slip was pithy to the point of terseness:

> *Not bad, but not exactly what we're*
> *looking for, either. It seems to*
> *lack that certain indefinable*
> *"something." Please feel free*
> *to continue submitting to us.*

His next try had been better. He had placed it, at least, though not as well as He would have liked. The dreams of youth. Once He'd hoped to top the bestseller list, to become a household word. He'd been so promising! Whatever had happened?

Where had He gone wrong?

He knew exactly where. His vices had shouldered His virtues aside. He'd gone stale early, lost the touch, resorted to barely passable hackwork to keep the wolf from the door, become despondent because of it, and drifted into bad company and worse habits. It can happen to the best.

Hungover, depressed, one day when He was feeling poorly He'd gone through the files, taken out some of His old work, and looked it over. The good old work that He'd done when He was still young and fresh and the bloom was on the rose. On the way to it, He passed the stuff that had been turned down for one reason or another.

> *Sorry.*

> *Maybe next time.*

> *Don't call us, we'll call you.*

A progression from polite apology to stay the hell away.

He stumbled onto the Earth.

Those dinosaurs He had considered to be among the finest of His creations. Then those huge, slow-moving, ponderous rivers of ice that inched their way across whole continents like thick crystal belts. There *was* originality there, damnit! Something missing, indeed. Well, it had lost a certain freshness, just lying there, but that wasn't His fault. Inherent vice had broken down some of those effects; there were cracks and fissures. The continents were drifting.

His head hurt. There was broken glass in His eye sockets. He could feel it. The inside of His mouth tasted like an ape's armpit.

"All right," He said. "Let there be Man upon the surface of this lousy world."

And Man was made.

Misery loves company.

I'd vote for a situation like this in the first place—if it were two women.

The Better Man

by Ray Russell

She was lovely and graceful and serene, but it wouldn't have mattered if she were none of these. All that mattered was that she was female. And that mattered very much indeed, for she was said to be the last woman.

As such, she was the hope of the earth, a prize to be fought over. Her two suitors—the last of their sex—stood now in the twilight of their world, prepared to duel to the death. The winner would become a new Adam, in an Eden of ashes and rubble.

"Put away your weapons," she said. "There has been enough dying. Let us decide by reason which of you is the better man."

"My name is John," said the one who limped and was bald, "and I am the better man. It is true that I am no kid, as they say, and my sight is no longer what it should be, and I am deaf in one ear, and I seem to have developed this cough, and my teeth are false, and I really cannot say to what extent my genes may be affected by radiation, but I am educated, skilled in many crafts and, I hope, wise with the experience of my years."

"Thank you, John," she said sweetly. "And you, young man?"

"My name is Nine," said the other one, who was tall and handsome, "and I am not a man at all. My full name is Nine Four Six Three Seven, decimal, Zero Zero Five Two Eight. I am an android. But *I* am the better man."

John laughed. "Better man! A thing of plastic bones and chemical blood and artificial flesh? Ridiculous!"

She asked, "Why do you say you are the better man, Nine?"

Nine cleared his throat. "I won't bore you with the history of robots and androids," he began.

"Please don't," John interjected.

"But I'm sure both of you are aware," Nine continued, "of the refinements that have gone into the manufacture of androids during the past few centuries?"

John shrugged. "Eyes that work like eyes instead of like television cameras."

"Hair and nails that grow," she said.

"Waste-disposal systems like our own," John grunted, and gallantly added, "Excuse me, miss."

"Laughter," she said. "Tears." And she smiled.

Nine smiled back at her. "That's right," he said. "As we were made more efficient, we naturally were made more human, because the human body and brain are still the most efficient machines there are. You might almost say that, while you folks were becoming more and more false-toothed and nose-jobbed and bust-plastied, and more and more warped and mutated by radiation, more and more *dehumanized*, we androids were becoming more and more human. Kind of ironic."

"Very," said John, stifling a yawn.

Nine said, "The point being, John, that you're getting old and infirm, while this body of mine—ersatz though it may be—will last another hundred years or so, with care. I'm stronger than you, also, and have better sight and hearing and quicker reflexes, all of which will be vital in building the new world. So you see," he concluded, spreading his hands, "there's no contest."

Smugly, John said, "You're forgetting one thing."

"No, I'm not," said Nine. "We androids used to be put together in laboratories and on assembly lines, I grant you, but not anymore. Too expensive. It's not generally known, but for quite a while now it's been cheaper and simpler for androids to be so constructed that we can reproduce ourselves. In fact, it's been proven in certain top-secret lab experiments that, theoretically at least, we can even, er, intermarry with humans."

John sputtered and stammered. "But that's—indecent and—unheard of and—you mean *mate*? Produce offspring? A human and an android? That's absurd!"

"It is, isn't it?" reflected Nine. "But it's also true."

Their beautiful prize looked long at the handsome, muscular Nine, then turned to the squinting, coughing John. "He's right,

I'm afraid, John," she said, sorrowfully. "He *is* the better . . . man."

John sighed but said nothing. He crept slowly away into the jagged shadows. In a few moments, they heard a single shot and the sound of a frail body crumpling to the ground.

"Poor John," she said. "I felt so sorry for him."

"So did I," said Nine, "but that's life." He led her toward the hovel that would be their home. "You know," he said, "I was really afraid John's education and skill and wisdom and all that might tip the scales in his favor . . ."

"It did, almost."

"Yes, I could tell. That's why I made up that little fib about being an android. My name's not Nine, it's Bill, and I'm one hundred percent human."

"Just as I thought," said John triumphantly, emerging from the shadows. "Not only a liar but stupid as well. Stupid enough to be taken in by my simple sound effects a moment ago." John turned to the lovely object of their rivalry. "Is this the kind of mate you deserve, my dear? A man without principles? A muscle-bound clod both morally corrupt and mentally deficient? Is he indeed the better man?"

She wavered, but for only an instant. "No, John. The father of the new race should be a man of honor and intelligence. You are the better man."

John turned to Bill. "In the absence of judges and juries, I take it upon myself to pronounce sentence upon you for mendacity, opacity, and crimes to future humanity. The sentence is death." John shot Bill through the head, and the younger suitor fell, lifeless.

"Now, wife," said John, with a gleam in his eye, "let us not waste any more precious time in getting that new race started. I am, admittedly, neither as young nor as handsome as the late Bill, but I think you'll find there is life in the old boy yet."

"Are *you* an android, by any chance?" she asked.

John said, "It just so happens that Bill was entirely correct about the, er, compatibility of humans and androids. I put up a fuss about it only because I didn't want to lose you. So, actually, it wouldn't make any difference if I *were* an android. However, I assure you I am quite human, if it matters."

She smiled prettily and took his arm. "How nice," she said. "If it matters, I'm not." And silenced his expression of surprise with an admirably genuine kiss.

Consider the alternative—

Oom

by Martin Gardner

Cautiously peered Oom over the rim of the Milky Way and focused his upper eye on an atomic cloud. As it mushroomed slowly from the surface of the earth, tears dripped from the upper eye of Oom.

But a little lower than the Legnas had Oom created man. Male and female, in an image somewhat like his own, created he them. Yet ever and again had they turned the power of reason upon themselves, and the history of their race had been one of endless discord.

And Oom knew that when the atomic clouds had cleared, and bacterial plagues had spent their fury, the race of man would yet live on. After war's exhaustion would come rest and returning strength, new cities and new dreams, new loves and hates, and again the crafty planning of new wars. So might things continue until the end of space-time.

Oom wearied of man's imperfection. Sighing, lightly he touched the earth with the tip of his left big toe.

And on the earth came a mighty quaking. Lightning and thunder raged, winds blew, mountains rent asunder. Waters churned above the continents. When silence came at last, and the sea slipped back into the hollows, no living thing remained.

Throughout the cosmos other planets whirled quietly about other suns, and on each had Oom caused divers manners of souls to grow. And on each had been ceaseless bitterness and strife. One by one, gently were they touched by a toe of Oom, until the glowing suns harbored only the weaving bodies of dead worlds.

Like intricate jewelled clockwork the universe ran on. And of this clockwork Oom greatly wearied. Softly he breathed on the glittering spheres and the lights of the suns went out and a vast Darkness brooded over the deep.

In the courts of Oom many laughed at the coming of the Darkness; but others did not laugh, regretting the passing of the suns. Over the justice of Oom's indignation a great quarreling arose among the Legnas, and the sound of their quarreling reached the lower ear of Oom.

Then turned Oom and fiercely looked upon the Legnas. And when they beheld his countenance they drew back in terror, their wings trailing. Gently did Oom blow his breath upon them. . . .

And as Oom walked the empty corridors, brooding darkly on the failures of his handiwork, a great loneliness came upon him. Within him a portion of himself spoke, saying:

"Thou hast done a foolish thing. Eternity is long and Thou shalt weary of thyself."

And it angered Oom that his soul be thus divided; that in him should be this restlessness and imperfection. Even of himself Oom wearied. Raising high his middle arm into the Darkness, he made the sign of Oom.

Over infinite distances did the arm traverse. Eternity came and fled ere the sign had been completed.

Then at last to the cosmos came perfect peace, and a wandering wind of nothingness blew silently over the spot where Oom had been.

Two heads are better than none.

Merchant

by Henry Slesar

Swanson came into the board room, sustaining an air of executive nonchalance that even his enemies found admirable. It was common knowledge that this was the day he would have to answer for his failure as President of the United Haberdashery Corporation. But Swanson was at ease; even if his opposition knew his attitude to be a pose, they stirred restlessly at his casual manner.

The Chairman began the meeting without fanfare, and called at once for a report from Sales. They all knew the contents of the report; it had been circulated privately to each member. Instead of listening to the dreary recitation of losses, the board watched the face of Swanson to see his reaction to this public accusation of his poor management.

Finally, it was Swanson's turn to speak.

"Gentlemen," he said, without a tremor in his voice, "as we have heard, haberdashery sales have been crippled badly since the war. The loss of revenue has been no surprise to any of us, but it is not this loss which concerns us today. It is the prediction that sales will decline even further in the future. Gentlemen, I contest the prognostication of the Sales Department; it is my contention that sales will be greater than ever!"

The board buzzed; at the end of the long table, someone chuckled dryly.

"I know my prediction sounds hard to credit," Swanson said, "and I intend to give you a full explanation before we leave this room today. But first, I wish you to hear a very special report from a very special man, Professor Ralph Entwiller of the American Foundation of Eugenics."

For the first time, the pale-cheeked man sitting in the chair of honor beside the President rose. He nodded to the assemblage, and began speaking in a voice almost too low to be heard.

"Mr. Swanson asked me to speak to you today about the future," he said hesitantly. "I know nothing about the haberdashery business. My field is eugenics, and my specialty is the study of radiation biology . . ."

"Would you be more specific?" Swanson said.

"Yes, of course. I deal with mutations, gentlemen, mutations which will soon become the norm of birth. Already, the percentage of mutated births is close to sixty-five, and we believe it will increase as time goes by."

"I don't understand this," the Chairman growled. "What does all this have to do with us?"

Swanson smiled. "Ah, but a great deal." He held the lapel of his jacket, and surveyed the curious, upturned faces around the table. "For one thing, gentlemen, we're going to be selling twice as many hats."

We'll all drink to that!

Don't Fence Me In

by Richard Wilson

Have another drink, Gyubi. *Woof!* I wish I had your double gullet, Pal—I'd use the lined one for pouring down this Venturan varnish of yours. If you ever get to Earth, Gyubi, you look me up. I'll buy you a real drink—something you'll want to pour down the gullet you taste with. As a matter of fact . . . but I'll get to that later. A story goes with it, as they say.

I was telling you about why we stopped building spaceships. The first one up from Earth crashed, you know. That was because when it reached The Barrier it tried to blast through it with its forward rockets. It got warned, then it went out of control. Crashed, all hands dead.

The second ship went up mad as hornets. Cautious, though. Cruised around, looking and listening. That's when they heard The Voice, the telepathic one that said nobody was to leave Earth until they said so.

The Federated Planets—we call it the Federation now—put it as tactful as they could but what they put was that us Earth people had a long way to go before we'd be worthy of traveling outside our own air. We had all those bad things they didn't want rubbing off on them. So Earth was proscribed. You know, nobody allowed in or out—especially out.

Well, you know how it is when somebody tells you you can't do something. Maybe you never cared particularly whether you did it or not, but the minute they tell you you can't, you want to, in the worst way. Like a thing we had once called Prohibition.

So we tried every way we knew to get a ship through The Barrier. We tried mass breaks, hoping one of many would make it, maybe on an end run. But The Barrier was everywhere.

It wasn't a solid thing, that Barrier. It was like you were

dropped into a life net. You'd go in a certain distance and it'd spring you back out. Hell of a sensation.

Along about that time somebody discovered invisibility, so we tried that. Sent up a spaceship disguised as an intercontinental rocket. It leveled off in a long cloudbank, then headed up. No go. It got bounced, too.

A bunch of amateurs at Woomera sent up a moonrocket one day. An unmanned, remote-control, instrument-packed job. It got to the moon all right—through The Barrier—but nobody paid much attention. It landed nicely and sat there on the edge of Aristarchus sending back signals till the power ran out. But we knew all about the moon already and nobody wanted to go *there*. We wanted at the Federation.

Then the Asian bloc perfected telekinesis. The Anglo-Americans huffled around a bit, then ate humble pie and bought in. That was the Triple-A try—American ship, British skipper and takeoff from an Asian telekinetic field. It worked like all the others—a big flop. They aimed the thing at a point a hundred thousand miles past The Barrier. The ship disappeared from the field all right and everybody started slapping each other on the back. But a couple of minutes later there was the ship back again just where it started from, shivering a bit. The crew came out groggy, holding their heads. They didn't know what happened except they felt the same old sling shot effect of being bounced out of a net. And something extra this time. Every man-jack of them had a migraine headache that lasted a week.

Well, that was the end of it. We didn't try any more after that. We gave up. Licked.

Then how come I'm sitting here in a saloon on Ventura IV yarning about it? That's a fair question. Let's have another drink first, Gyubi, old pal, and then I'll tell you how I outsmarted you and your cronies in the Federation.

Yes, me, personally, all by my lonesome.

Well, after the Triple-A try got thrown for a loss, spaceships were a drug on the market. They put them in mothballs—saving face, you know, pretending they didn't exist. After a few years, when they got less sensitive, they put them up for sale. There weren't many takers but they were so cheap I bought one.

I was in intercontinental trade then. Telekinesis hadn't got started commercially yet. Those space jobs weren't what you'd call economical on fuel but when you converted them they held about three times as much cargo as an intercon. And they were so dirt-cheap I figured I could afford the upkeep.

I made out pretty good. Some companies shipped by me just for the prestige of having their dingbats and ducrots delivered by spaceship. But I always had the feeling the Federation was watching me as I baroomed back and forth across the Pacific, as if I was going to make another try at their blessed Barrier.

I always went solo. The pacer was so simple to handle I didn't need a co-pilot. And passengers were against regulations.

I'd delivered a dozen gross tons of flywheels, or mousetraps or corkscrews, I forget what, to Singapore and the customer tossed a big party which naturally I went to. It got late and I tried to ease off but when the host suggested one for the road I had to go along with it. He must have laced that one so it'd last all the way to California because when I set the autopilot for Muroc it was strictly a blind jab. Off we went, me and the spacer, *baroom*.

Well, that was it.

Next thing I knew I was out somewhere beyond Mars.

Scared the hell out of me when I came to, still boozy. The spacer was in free fall, headed clean out of the solar system, when the Federation ship came alongside. I pulled myself together as best I could. Drank a quart of milk, straightened my collar and prepared to receive boarders. Or get blasted to kingdom come.

But no. They were all kowtowy and if-you-please. I'd busted through their Barrier but they were too flamboozled to know it was an accident so they figured they were licked and offered terms. To me. As if I was the representative of Earth and this was all a carefully worked-out plan.

Of course I played along; I signed the compact that opened them up to trade. Me, an old intercon skipper, on behalf of Earth; but so hung over that only a lot of static filtered through to their mind readers.

That's all they were, Gyubi, you old barfly—mind readers and hypnotists. And that's all their Barrier was, a vaudeville trick.

Sure I know you're not one of them, Gyubi. They're the robber barons and your people are the suckers, even if you are nominally members of the Federation. They had a nice racket—trade concessions on all twenty-seven inhabited planets this side of the Coal

Sack—and they didn't want any of it lost to a smarter operator. That was us, on Earth, getting ready to take the giant step into space.

Naturally the Federation's mind readers didn't spot anything when I punched a leftover button on my control panel and put the ship into spacedrive. It was my finger did that, plus the one for the road; far as my mind knew, I was punching for Muroc, California.

Then by the time the spacer was headed up toward the stars it was too late. I'd passed out, and there just plain wasn't any mind for the mind readers to read or the hypnotists to toss the big Barrier whammy at.

Why am I telling you all this? Well, you figure it out, Gyubi. Why are you still exploited by the Federation? Because they can read your mind—outfinagle you every single time.

What you need, Pal, is an antidote. Happens I have a sample right here. Yes, sir—Singapore Sling, bottled in the full three-fifths quart size, only ten venturas the bottle. It goes right to work building a static field no hypnotist, no mind reader can penetrate. This is the equalizer, the way to be as big a man as they are.

You'll take a case? Smart boy, Gyubi. You won't regret it. Look at me—a living testimonial to the way this product works.

Yes, but how do you define man?

The Die-hard

by Alfred Bester

"In the old days," the old one said, "there was the United States and Russia and England and Russia and Spain and England and the United States. Countries. Sovereign States. Nations. Peoples of the world."

"Today there are peoples of the world, Old One."

"Who are you?" the Old One asked suddenly.

"I'm Tom."

"Tom?"

"No, Old One. Tom."

"I said Tom."

"You did not pronounce it properly, Old One. You spoke the name of another Tom."

"You are all Tom," the Old One said sullenly. "Everyone is Tom, Dick or Harry."

He sat, shaking in the sunshine, and hating the pleasant young man. They were on the broad veranda outside his hospital room. The street before them was packed with attractive men and women, all waiting expectantly. Somewhere in the white city there was a heavy cheering, a thrilling turmoil that slowly approached.

"Look at them." The Old One shook his cane at the street. "All Tom, and Dick and Harry. All Daisy, Anne and Mary."

"No, Old One," Tom smiled. "We use other names as well."

"I've had a hundred Toms sitting with me," the Old One snarled.

"We often use the same name, Old One, but we pronounce it differently. I'm not Tom or Tom or Tom. I'm Tom. Do you hear it?"

"What's that noise?" the Old One asked.

"It's the Galactic Envoy," Tom explained again. "The Envoy from Sirius, the star in Orion. He's touring the city. This is the first time a being from other worlds has ever visited the earth. There's great excitement."

"In the old days," the Old One said, "we had real envoys. Men from Paris and Rome and Berlin and London and Paris and— They came with pomp and circumstance. They made war. They made peace. Uniforms and guns and ceremonies. Brave times! Exciting times!"

"We have brave, exciting times today, Old One."

"You do not," the Old One snarled. He thumped his cane feebly. "There is no passion, no love, no fear, no death. There is no hot blood coursing through veins. You're all logic. All calm thought. All Tom, Dick and Harry."

"No, Old One. We love. We have passions. We fear many things. What you miss is the evil we have destroyed in ourselves."

"You have destroyed everything! You have destroyed man!" the Old One cried. He pointed a shaking finger at Tom. "You! How much blood have you in your veins?"

"None at all, Old One. I have Tamar's Solution in my veins.

Blood cannot withstand radiation and I do my research in the Fission Piles."

"No blood," the Old One cackled. "And no bones either."

"Not all have been replaced, Old One."

"And no nerve tissue, heh?"

"Not all has been replaced, Old One."

"No blood, no bones, no guts, no heart. And no private parts. What do you do with a woman? How much of you is mechanical?"

"Not more than 60 per cent, Old One," Tom laughed. "I have children."

"And the other Toms and Dicks and Harrys?"

"Anywhere from 30 to 70 per cent, Old One. They have children, too. What the men of your time did to teeth, we do with all the body. There is no harm."

"You are not men! You're machines!" the Old One cried. "Robots! Monsters! You have destroyed man."

Tom smiled. "In truth, Old One, there is so much mingling of man in machine and machine in man that the distinction is hard to make. We no longer make it. We are content to live happily and work happily. We are adjusted."

"In the old days," the Old One said, "we all had real bodies. Blood and bones and nerves and guts. Like me. We worked and sweated and loved and fought and killed and lived. You do not live . . . you adjusted supermen . . . machine-men . . . half-bred bastards of acid and sperm. Nowhere have I seen a blow struck, a kiss taken, the clash of conflict, life. How I yearn to see real life again . . . not your machine imitation."

"That's the ancient sickness, Old One," Tom said seriously. "Why don't you let us reconstruct you and heal you? If you would let us replace your ductless glands, recondition your reflexes, and—"

"No! No! No!" the Old One cried in a high passion. "I will not become another Tom." He lurched up from his chair and beat at the pleasant young man with his cane. The blow broke the skin on the young man's face and was so unexpected that he cried out in astonishment. Another pleasant young man ran out on the veranda, seized the Old One and reseated him in his chair. Then he turned to Tom who was dabbing at the frosty liquid that oozed from the cut in his face.

"All right, Tom?"

"No great harm done." Tom looked at the Old One with awe. "Do you know, I believe he actually wanted to hurt me."

"Of course he did. This is your first time with him, isn't it? You ought to see him curse and carry on. What an old unreconstructed rebel he is. We're rather proud of the old boy. He's unique. A museum of pathology." The second young man sat down alongside the Old One. "I'll take him for a while. You go watch for the Envoy."

The Old One was shaking and weeping. "In the old days," he quavered, "there was courage and bravery and spirit and strength and red blood and courage and bravery and—"

"Now then, now then, Old One," his new companion interrupted briskly, "we have them too. When we reconstruct a man we don't take anything away from him but the rot in his mind and body."

"Who are you?" the Old One asked.

"I'm Tom."

"Tom?"

"No. Tom. Not Tom. Tom."

"You've changed."

"I'm not the same Tom that was here before."

"You're all Toms," the Old One cried piteously. "You're all the same God-forsaken Toms."

"No, Old One. We're all different. You just can't see it."

The turmoil and the cheering came closer. Out in the street before the hospital, the crowd began shouting in excited anticipation. A lane cleared. Far down the street there was a glitter of brass and the first pulse of the approaching music. Tom took the Old One under the arm and raised him from his chair.

"Come to the railing, Old One," he said excitedly. "Come and watch the Envoy. This is a great day for Mother Earth. We've made contact with the stars at last. It's a new era beginning."

"It's too late," the Old One muttered. "Too late."

"What do you mean, Old One?"

"We should have found them, not them us. We should have been first. In the old days we would have been first. In the old days there was courage and daring. We fought and endured. . . ."

"There he is," Tom shouted, pointing down the street. "He's stopped at the Institute. . . . Now he's coming out. . . . He's coming closer. . . . No. Wait! He's stopped again. . . . At the

Center. What a magnificent gesture. This isn't just a token tour. He's inspecting everything."

"In the old days," the Old One mumbled, "we would have come with fire and storm. We would have marched down strange streets with weapons on our hips and defiance in our eyes. Or if they came first we would have met them with strength and defiance. But not you . . . machine half-breeds . . . laboratory supermen . . . adjusted . . . reconstructed . . . worthless . . ."

"He's come out of the Center," Tom exclaimed. "He's coming closer. Look well, Old One. Never forget this moment. He—" Tom stopped and took a shuddering breath. "Old One," he said. "He's going to stop at the hospital!"

The gleaming car stopped before the hospital. The band marked time, still playing lustily, joyfully. The crowd roared. In the car the officials were smiling, pointing, explaining. The Galactic Envoy arose to his full, fantastic height, stepped out of the car and strode toward the steps leading up to the veranda. His escort followed.

"Here he comes!" Tom yelled, and began a confused roaring of his own.

Suddenly the Old One broke away from the railing. He shoved past Tom and all the other Tom, and Dick and Harrys and Daisy, Anne and Marys crowding the veranda. He beat his way through them with his feeble, wicked cane and came face to face with the Galactic Envoy at the head of the steps. He stared at the Praying Mantis face with horror and revulsion for one instant, then he cried: "I greet you. I alone can greet you."

He raised his cane and smote the face with all his strength.

"I'm the last man on earth," he cried.

Which reminds me that thin people are thin because they don't know any better.

The First

by Anthony Boucher

"He was a bold man," wrote Dean Swift, "that first eat an oyster." A man, I might add, to whom civilization owes an enormous debt—were it not that any debt was quite canceled by that moment of ecstasy which he was first of all men to know.

And countless other such epic figures there have been, pioneers whose achievements are comparable to the discovery of fire and possibly superior to the invention of the wheel and the arch.

But none of these discoveries (save perhaps that of the oyster) could have its full value for us today but for one other, even more momentous instant in the early history of Man.

This is the story of Sko.

Sko crouched at the mouth of his cave and glared at the stew-pot. A full day's hunting it had taken him to get that sheep. Most of another day he had spent cooking the stew, while his woman cured the hide and tended the children and fed the youngest with the breast food that took no hunting. And now all of the family sat back there in the cave, growling with their mouths and growling with their bellies from hunger and hatred of the food and fear of the death that comes from no food, while only he ate the stewed sheep-meat.

It was tired and stale and flat in his mouth. He had reasons that made him eat, but he could not blame the family. Seven months and nothing but sheep. The birds had flown. Other years they came back; who knew if they would this year? Soon the fish would come up the river again, if this year was like others; but who could be sure?

And now whoever ate of the boars or of the rabbits died in time, and when the Ceremonial Cuts were made, strange worms appeared inside him. The Man of the Sun had said it was now a sin against the Sun to eat of the boar and of the rabbit; and clearly that was true, for sinners died.

Sheep or hunger. Sheep-meat or death. Sko chewed the tasteless chunk in his mouth and brooded. He could still force himself to eat; but his woman, his children, the rest of The People . . . You could see men's ribs now, and little children had big eyes and no cheeks and bellies like smooth round stones. Old men did not live so long as they used to; and even young men went to the Sun without wounds from man or beast to show Him. The food-that-takes-no-hunting was running thin and dry, and Sko could easily beat at wrestling the men who used to pound him down.

The People were his now because he could still eat; and because The People were his, he had to go on eating. And it was as if the Sun Himself demanded that he find a way to make The People eat too, eat themselves back into life.

Sko's stomach was full but his mouth still felt empty. There had once been a time when his stomach was empty and his mouth felt too full. He tried to remember. And then, as his tongue touched around his mouth trying for that feeling, the thought came.

It was the Dry Summer, when the river was low and all the springs had stopped living and men went toward the Sun's birth and the Sun's death to find new water. He was one of those who had found water; but he had been gone too long. He ate all the dried boarmeat he carried (it was not a sin then) and he shot all his arrows and still he was not home and needed to eat. So he ate growing things like the animals, and some of them were good. But he pulled from the ground one bulb which was in many small sections; and one of those sections, only one, filled his mouth with so much to taste so sharply that he could not stand it and drank almost all the water he was bringing back as proof. He could taste it still in his mind.

His hand groped into the hole at the side of the cave which was his own place. He found there the rest of that bulb which he had brought as a sign of the far place he had visited. He pulled the hard purple-brown skin off one yellow-white section and smelled it. Even the smell filled the mouth a little. He blew hard on the coals, and when the fire rose and the stewpot began to bubble, he dropped the section in with the sheep-meat. If one fills the stomach and not the mouth, the other the mouth and not the stomach, perhaps together . . .

Sko asked the Sun to make his guess be right, for The People. Then he let the pot bubble and thought nothing for a while. At last he roused and scooped a gobbet out of the stewpot and bit into it. His mouth filled a little, and something stirred in him and thought of another thing that filled the mouth.

He set off at a steady lope for the Licking Place which the tribe shared with the sheep and the other animals. He came back with a white crystal crust. He dropped this into the stewpot and stirred it with a stick and sat watching until he could not see the crust any more. Then he bit into another gobbet.

Now his mouth was indeed full. He opened it and from its fullness came into the cave the sound that meant *Food*. It was his woman who came out first. She saw the same old stewpot of sheep and started to turn, but he seized her and forced her mouth open and thrust in a gobbet of the new stew. She looked at him for a long silence. Then her jaws began to work fast and hard and not until there was nothing left to chew did she use the *Food* sound to call out the children.

There are other Licking Places to use, Sko thought while they ate; and runners can fetch more of the bulbs from where this one grew. There will be enough for The People. . . . And then the pot was empty, and Sko Fyay and his family sat licking their fingers.

After a thousand generations of cooks, hunger and salt and garlic had combined to produce mankind's first chef.

Let's hear it! Three groans for Damon!

Eripmav

by Damon Knight

On the planet Veegl, in the Fomalhaut system, we found a curious race of cellulose vampires. The Veeglians, like all higher life on this world, are plants; the Veeglian vampire, needless to say, is a sapsucker.

One of the native clerks in our trade mission, a plant-girl named

Xixl, had been complaining of lassitude and showing an unhealthy pink color for some weeks. The girl's parent stock suspected vampirism; we were skeptical, but had to admit that the two green-tinged punctures at the base of her axis were evidence of something wrong.

Accordingly we kept watch over her sleep-box for three nights running. (The Veeglians sleep in boxes of soil, built of heavy slabs of the hardmeat tree, or *woogl*; they look rather like coffins.) On the third night, sure enough, a translator named Ffengl, a hefty, blue-haired fellow, crept into her room and bent over the sleep-box.

We rushed out at the blackguard, but he turned quick as a wink and fairly flew up the whitemeat stairs. (The flesh of Veegl's only animal life, the "meat-trees," or *oogl*, petrifies rapidly in air and is much used for construction.) We found him in an unsuspected vault at the very top of the old building, trying to hide under the covers of an antique bed. It was an eerie business. We sizzled him with blasts from our proton guns, and yet to the end, with un-Veeglian vitality, he was struggling to reach us with his tendrils.

Afterward he seemed dead enough, but the local wiseheads advised us to take certain precautions.

So we buried him with a steak through his heart.

See how dangerous it is to be one?

Feeding Time

by Robert Sheckley

Treggis felt considerably relieved when the owner of the bookstore went front to wait upon another customer. After all, it was essentially nerve-racking, to have a stooped, bespectacled, fawning old man constantly at one's shoulder, peering at the page one was glancing at, pointing here and there with a gnarled, dirty finger, obsequiously wiping dust from the shelves with a tobacco-stained handkerchief. To say nothing of the exquisite boredom of listening to the fellow's cackling, high-pitched reminiscences.

Undoubtedly he meant well, but really, there was a limit. One couldn't do much more than smile politely and hope that the little bell over the front of the store would tinkle—as it had.

Treggis moved toward the back of the store, hoping the disgusting little man wouldn't try to search him out. He passed half a hundred Greek titles, then the popular sciences section. Next, in a strange jumble of titles and authors, he passed Edgar Rice Burroughs, Anthony Trollope, Theosophy, and the poems of Longfellow. The farther back he went the deeper the dust became, the fewer the naked light bulbs suspended above the corridor, the higher the piles of moldy, dog-eared books.

It was really a splendid old place, and for the life of him Treggis couldn't understand how he had missed it before. Bookstores were his sole pleasure in life. He spent all his free hours in them, wandering happily through the stacks.

Of course, he was just interested in certain types of books.

At the end of the high ramp of books there were three more corridors, branching off at absurd angles. Treggis followed the center path, reflecting that the bookstore hadn't seemed so large from the outside; just a door half-hidden between two buildings, with an old hand-lettered sign in its upper panel. But then, these old stores were deceptive, often extending to nearly half a block in depth.

At the end of this corridor two more book-trails split off. Choosing the one on the left, Treggis started reading titles, casually scanning them up and down with a practiced glance. He was in no hurry; he could, if he wished, spend the rest of the day here—to say nothing of the night.

He had shuffled eight or ten feet down the corridor before one title struck him. He went back to it.

It was a small, black-covered book, old, but with that ageless look that some books have. Its edges were worn, and the print on the cover was faded.

"Well, what do you know," Treggis murmured softly.

The cover read: *Care and Feeding of the Gryphon.* And beneath that, in smaller print: *Advice to the Keeper.*

A gryphon, he knew, was a mythological monster, half lion and half eagle.

"Well now," Treggis said to himself. "Let's see now." He opened the book and began reading the table of contents.

The headings went: 1. *Species of Gryphon.* 2. *A Short History of Gryphonology.* 3. *Subspecies of Gryphon.* 4. *Food for the Gryphon.* 5. *Constructing a Natural Habitat for the Gryphon.* 6. *The Gryphon During Moulting Season.* 7. *The Gryphon and* . . .

He closed the book.

"This," he told himself, "is decidedly—well, unusual." He flipped through the book, reading a sentence here and there. His first thought, that the book was one of the "unnatural" natural history compilations so dear to the Elizabethan heart, was clearly wrong. The book wasn't old enough; and there was nothing euphuistic in the writing, no balanced sentence structure, ingenious antithesis and the like. It was straightforward, clean-cut, concise. Treggis flipped through a few more pages and came upon this:

"The sole diet of the Gryphon is young virgins. Feeding time is once a month, and care should be exercised—"

He closed the book again. The sentence set up a train of thought all its own. He banished it with a blush and looked again at the shelf, hoping to find more books of the same type. Something like *A Short History of the Affairs of the Sirens,* or perhaps *The Proper Breeding of Minotaurs.* But there was nothing even remotely like it. Not on that shelf nor any other, as far as he could tell.

"Find anything?" a voice at his shoulder asked. Treggis gulped, smiled, and held out the black-covered old book.

"Oh yes," the old man said, wiping dust from the cover. "Quite a rare book, this."

"Oh, is it?" murmured Treggis.

"Gryphons," the old man mused, flipping through the book, "are quite rare. Quite a rare species of—animal," he finished, after a moment's thought. "A dollar-fifty for this book, sir."

Treggis left with his possession clutched under his thin right arm. He made straight for his room. It wasn't every day that one bought a book on the *Care and Feeding of Gryphons.*

Treggis' room bore a striking resemblance to a secondhand bookstore. There was the same lack of space, the same film of gray dust over everything, the same vaguely arranged chaos of titles, authors, and types. Treggis didn't stop to gloat over his treasures. His faded *Libidinous Verses* passed unnoticed. Quite unceremoniously he pushed the *Psychopathia Sexualis* from his armchair, sat down and began to read.

There was quite a lot to the care and feeding of the gryphon. One wouldn't think that a creature half lion and half eagle would be so touchy. There was also an interesting amplication of the eating habits of the gryphon. And other information. For pure enjoyment, the gryphon book was easily as good as the Havelock Ellis lectures on sex, formerly his favorite.

Toward the end, there were full instructions on how to get to the zoo. The instructions were, to say the least, unique.

It was a good ways past midnight when Treggis closed the book. What a deal of strange information there was between those two black covers! One sentence in particular he couldn't get out of his head:

"The sole diet of the gryphon is young virgins."

That bothered him. It didn't seem fair, somehow.

After a while he opened the book again to the *Instructions for Getting to the Zoo.*

Decidedly strange they were. And yet, not too difficult. Not requiring, certainly, too much physical exertion. Just a few words, a few motions. Treggis realized suddenly how onerous his bank clerk's job was. A stupid waste of eight good hours a day, no matter how one looked at it. How much more interesting to be a keeper in charge of the gryphon. To use the special ointments during moulting season, to answer questions about gryphonology. To be in charge of feeding. "The sole diet . . ."

"Yes, yes, yes, yes," Treggis mumbled rapidly, pacing the floor of his narrow room. "A hoax—but might as well try out the instructions. For a laugh."

He laughed hollowly.

There was no blinding flash, no clap of thunder, but Treggis was nevertheless transported, instantaneously so it seemed, to a place. He staggered for a moment, then regained his balance and opened his eyes. The sunlight was blinding. Looking around, he could see that someone had done a very good job of constructing *The Natural Habitat of the Gryphon.*

Treggis walked forward, holding himself quite well considering the trembling in his ankles, knees, and stomach. Then he saw the gryphon.

At the same time the gryphon saw him.

Slowly at first, then with ever-gaining momentum, the gryphon advanced on him. The great eagle's wings opened, the talons extended, and the gryphon leaped, or sailed, forward.

Treggis tried to jump out of the way in a single uncontrollable shudder. The gryphon came at him, huge and golden in the sun, and Treggis screamed desperately, "No, no! The sole diet of the gryphon is young—"

Then he screamed again in full realization as the talons seized him.

Well, you can't think of everything!

The Voice from the Curious Cube
by Nelson Bond

All Xuthil seethed with excitement. The broad highways, the swirling ramps that led to the public forum were thronged with the jostling bodies of a hundred thousand inhabitants, while in the living quarters of the capital city millions unable to witness the spectacle first-hand waited anxiously by their *menavisors* for news.

The curious cube had opened. The gigantic slab of marble, its sheer, glistening walls towering hundreds of feet above the head of the tallest Xuthilian, its great square base more than a hundred home-widths on each side, but a few hours ago had opened—one smoothly oiled block sliding backward to reveal a yawning pit of blackness in its depths.

Already a band of daring explorers, heavily armed, had penetrated the depths of the curious cube. Soon they would return to make a public report, and it was this which all Xuthil breathlessly awaited.

None living knew the purpose—or dared guess the fearful age— of the curious cube. The earliest archives in Xuthilian libraries noted its existence, presupposing divine origin or construction. For certainly even the accomplished hands of earth's dominant race could not have built so gigantic a structure. It was the work of Titans, or a god.

So, with *menavisors* dialed to the forum for the first mental images to be broadcast therefrom by members of the exploration party, Xuthil hummed with nervous activity.

Abruptly a pale green luminescence flooded the reflector screens of the *menavisors,* and a thrill coursed through the viewers. The exploration party had returned. Tul, chief of all Xuthilian scientists, was stepping upon the circular dais, his broad, intelligent forehead furrowed with thought. His band of followers trailed after him. They too walked leadenly.

Tul stepped before the image-projecting unit. As he did so, a wavering scene began to impress itself into the minds of his watchers—a picture that grew more clear and distinct as the mental contact strengthened.

Each Xuthilian saw himself walking behind the glare of a strong torch down a long straight marble passageway, through a high vaulted corridor of seamless stone. Cobwebs and the dust of centuries stirred softly beneath his feet, and the air was musty with the scent of long-dead years. A torch swung toward the roof of the passageway, and its beam was lost in the vast reaches of the chamber above.

Then the passage widened into a great amphitheatre—a tremendous room that dwarfed to insignificance the wide Xuthilian forum. Telepathically each viewer saw himself—as Tul had done—press forward on eager feet, then stop and swing his flaring torch around the strangest sight a living eye had ever seen. Rows upon rows of recessed drawers, bronze-plated and embossed with hieroglyphs—these were the contents of the curious cube. These and nothing more.

The picture wavered, faded. The thoughts of Tul replaced it, communicating directly with each watcher.

"Undeniably there is some great mystery yet to be dissolved concerning the curious cube. What these drawers contain we do not know. Archives, perhaps, of some long-vanished race. But it will take long years of arduous labor with the finest of modern equipment to open even *one* of the mighty shelves. Their gigantic size and intricate construction defies us. If living creatures built the curious cube—and we may suppose they did—their bodily structure was on a scale so vastly greater than our own that we are utterly unable to comprehend the purpose of their instruments.

Only one thing found in the cube was in any way comparable to machinery we know and employ."

Tul turned and nodded to two of his assistants. They moved forward, staggering under the weight of a huge stone slab, circular in form, set into a greater square of some strange fibroid material. Attached to this giant dais was a huge resilient hawser, larger in width by half than those who bore it.

"The cable attached to this slab," continued Tul, "is very long. It reaches all the way into the heart of the curious cube. Obviously it has some bearing on the secret, but what that bearing is, we do not know. Our engineers will have to dismember the slab to solve its meaning. As you see, it is solid—"

Tul stepped upon the stone. . . .

And as Tul stepped upon the push-button, quiescent current flowed from reservoirs dormant for ages, and from the dark depths of the curious cube an electrically controlled recorder spoke.

"Men—" said a human voice—"men of the fiftieth century—we, your brothers of the twenty-fifth need you. For humanity's sake, we call on you for help.

"As I speak, our solar system is plunging into a great chlorine cloud from which it will not emerge for hundreds of years. All mankind is doomed to destruction. In this specially constructed vault we have laid to rest ten thousand of the greatest minds of Earth, hermetically sealed to sleep in an induced catalepsy until the fiftieth century. By that time the danger will be ended.

"The door to our vault at last has opened. If there be men alive, and if the air be pure, pull down the lever beside the portal of our tomb and we will waken.

"If no man hear this plea—if no man still be alive—then farewell, world. The sleeping remnants of the race of man sleep on forever."

"Solid," repeated Tul. "Yet, as you see, it seems to yield slightly." He continued dubiously, "Citizens of Xuthil, we are as baffled by this mystery as you are. But you may rest assured that your council of scientists will make every effort to solve it."

The green glare of the *menavisors* faded. Xuthil, perplexed and marveling, returned to its daily labors. On street corners and in halls, in homes and offices, Xuthilians briefly paused to touch antannae, discussing the strange wonder.

For the voice from the curious cube had not been heard by any living creature. Sole rulers of the fiftieth century were ants—and ants cannot hear.

Busby's Divine Tragedy.

I'm Going to Get You

by F. M. Busby

You. You, out there. Do you exist? I don't think you do; I've never believed in you. They always told me you created everything, that you are my loving Father. You don't act like it. No, I haven't believed in you.

But if you don't exist, then I have nothing left to hate.

My life, whether by accident or your malevolence, has always been a nightmare. I don't know—I can't know—whether you exist. Do I scream my hate to an empty sky? *Please* exist. It would be intolerable to have no possible target for my revenge, no matter how far above my powers.

You. You see me as a clown, a puppet, for how can I reach you when I can't find you or even know that you are real? What can I do? Don't worry; I'll think of something. I will. Nothing else, now, is important to me.

Early, you took my father. People said "Praise God!" and did not protest, but I wondered why he was dead and why anyone should praise you. I shrugged the brace away from the sores on my paralyzed leg—for you had started early on me, hadn't you?—and tried to find meaning in life again.

For a time I truly thought it would work, until you took my mother and my brothers. You didn't fool me that time; I knew the supposed accident was a purposeful act. There was no other reason why one drunken sot and his car should wipe out most of a family and escape unharmed. I suspect you meant to get me too, then, and slipped up. If that's how it was, you may have made the most crucial error of your long career of tyranny. I hope so.

Because now I *know*. And at the same time I don't know. If

you are there, there at all, then somehow I will find you, and destroy you. If you are not there—but you have to be! I'll force you to exist; you can't escape me that way.

You really set me up after the funeral, you cosmic bastard! First the three young thugs who beat me up; crippled, I could offer little resistance. Then in the hospital, in nurse's garb, was the lady Cristal who became my wife.

You left us alone for nearly two years. You enjoyed that, didn't you—the cat-and-mouse thing? Allowing Cristal to become pregnant, then not quite killing her when you took our baby. You're really quite expert, aren't you? For a time I allowed myself *again* to believe that we would be let to live our lives, childless but in relative content and great love.

You know where you made your mistake? You're arrogant. You didn't bother to give me any reason for Cristal's death yesterday. I intend you to regret that.

She came in the door, out of the cold, with a bag of groceries. She simply collapsed, smiling at first and then showing shock and grief when she knew you were killing her. The food, for a minor personal celebration of ours, was scattered across the floor. I won't tell you how I felt; why should I let you gloat more than you're gloating already?

But then I *knew* the hell of my life was no accident. Then I knew that if you exist, at least I have a target.

I know you're not going to be easy to attack. You hold all the high ground. I don't know what you are or where you are or how to reach you.

But if you could simply wipe me out at whim, you'd have done so by now, I think. I'm counting on that. There must be rules that govern you; I have to believe that. And by those rules, your own rules, I think you've given me a chance that you didn't intend. I must be right; otherwise you'd have killed me.

I'm not alone; I've asked advice from friends I can trust. They don't believe me but they humor me and are helpful.

My friend Charles the engineer says that if you are the Creator you must also be the Totality—that I am as my own fingernail trying to change my own mind. He may be right. But a hangnail can produce blood-poisoning; perhaps I shall be your friendly neighborhood hangnail, before we're done.

Larry, my lawyer friend and an atheist, clearly thinks I've lost my marbles. He says that if you exist you are the spoiled-brat God of the Old Testament, an omnipotent five-year-old child who never changed your mind in anyone else's favor and never will. So that I may as well forget it. But I think I am smarter than five years old. We'll find out.

I thought of attacking you through devil-worship but my friend Gerard says that if I am right you *are* the devil, and the last thing I'd do is worship you. In his view, and perhaps he is right, you'd be some sort of parasite claiming Godhood but not entitled to it. I may as well believe part of this along with parts of other views. It sounds like my best chance, and I need all the breaks I can get, dealing with something like you.

I may be weak and even stupid by your lights, but I don't intend to remain helpless. You'll see. There is a whole universe which I think you did not create: you came along later and took advantage of it. That makes me as good as you are, maybe better; you hear? We are here in this universe together, and if you can influence my existence, perhaps I can influence yours, too.

Gravitation works both ways.

You have negated everyone I ever loved, everyone who ever loved me. You haven't negated me yet; why not? Maybe you can't. Again, why not? Because it would backfire? Because we're tied together somehow? That's the only handle I have; I think I'll try it.

I've asked you, begged you, to return Cristal to me. You wouldn't answer. I tried prayer, the format you're supposed to appreciate. No comment. I tried other ways. And you ignored me.

It shouldn't be difficult. You resurrected a man once, if the stories are true. You rolled back a sea. You did a lot of things. Or so I've been told.

Maybe you didn't. Maybe you can't do anything but hurt and kill. It's hard, even now, to accept such a concept of you. But I must.

So I am going to call it quits, for this life. No more. Does that scare you? It should. Because I think that when I cease to exist, so will you.

I'll settle for that.

In a few minutes now, we'll see.

Come on! Without TV commercials, when would we go to the bathroom?

The Room

by Ray Russell

Crane awoke with the Tingle Tooth-foam song racing through his head. Tingle, he realized, must have bought last night's Sleepcoo time. He frowned at the Sleepcoo speaker in the wall next to his pillow. Then he stared at the ceiling: it was still blank. Must be pretty early, he told himself. As the Coffizz slogan slowly faded in on the ceiling, he averted his eyes and got out of bed. He avoided looking at the printed messages on the sheets, the pillowcases, the blankets, his robe, and the innersoles of his slippers. As his feet touched the floor, the TV set went on. It would go off, automatically, at ten P.M. Crane was perfectly free to switch channels, but he saw no point in that.

In the bathroom, he turned on the light and the TV's audio was immediately piped in to him. He switched the light off and performed his first morning ritual in the dark. But he needed light in order to shave, and as he turned it on again, the audio resumed. As he shaved, the mirror flickered instantaneously once every three seconds. It was not enough to disturb his shaving, but Crane found himself suddenly thinking of the rich warm goodness of the Coffizz competitor, Teatang. A few moments later, he was reading the ads for Now, the gentle instant laxative, and Stop, the bourbon-flavored paregoric, which were printed on alternating sheets of the bathroom tissue.

As he was dressing, the phone rang. He let it ring. He knew what he would hear if he picked it up: "Good morning! Have you had your Krakkeroonies yet? Packed with protein and—" Or, maybe, "Why wait for the draft? Enlist now in the service of your choice and cash in on the following enlistee benefits—" Or: "Feeling under the weather? Coronary disease kills four out of five! The early symptoms are—"

On the other hand, it *could* be an important personal call. He picked up the phone and said hello. "Hello yourself," answered a husky, insinuating feminine voice. "Bob?"

"Yes."

"Bob Crane?"

"Yes, who's this?"

"My name's Judy. I know you, but you don't know me. Have you felt logy lately, out of sorts—" He put down the phone. That settled it. He pulled a crumpled slip of paper from his desk drawer. There was an address on it. Hitherto, he had been hesitant about following up this lead. But this morning he felt decisive. He left his apartment and hailed a cab.

The back of the cab's front seat immediately went on and he found himself watching the Juice-O-Vescent Breakfast Hour. He opened a newspaper the last passenger had left behind. His eyes managed to slide over the four-color Glitterink ads with their oblique homosexual, sadistic, masochistic, incestuous and autoerotic symbols, and he tried to concentrate on a news story about the initiating of another government housing program, but his attempts to ignore the Breeze Deodorant ads printed yellow-on-white between the lines were fruitless. The cab reached its destination. Crane paid the driver with a bill bearing a picture of Abraham Lincoln on one side and a picture of a naked woman bathing with Smoothie Soap on the other. He entered a rather run-down frame building, found the correct door, and pressed the doorbell. He could hear, inside the flat, the sound of an old-fashioned buzzer, not a chime playing the EetMeet or Jetfly or Krispy Kola jingles. Hope filled him.

A slattern answered the door, regarded him suspiciously and asked, "Yeah?"

"I—uh—Mrs. Ferman? I got your name from a friend, Bill Seavers? I understand you—" his voice dropped low, "—rent rooms."

"Get outta here; you wanna get me in trouble? I'm a private citizen, a respectable—"

"I'll, I'll *pay*. I have a good job. I—"

"How much?"

"Two hundred? That's twice what I'm paying at the housing project."

"Come on in." Inside, the woman locked, bolted and chained the door. "One room," she said. "Toilet and shower down the hall, you share it with two others. Get rid of your own garbage. Provide your own heat in the winter. You want hot water, it's fifty extra. No cooking in the rooms. No guests. Three months' rent in advance, cash."

"I'll take it," Crane said quickly; then added, "I can turn off the TV?"

"There ain't no TV. No phone neither."

"No all-night Sleepcoo next to the bed? No sublims in the mirrors? No Projecto in the ceiling or walls?"

"None of that stuff."

Crane smiled. He counted out the rent into her dirty hand. "When can I move in?"

She shrugged. "Any time. Here's the key. Fourth floor, front. There ain't no elevator."

Crane left, still smiling, the key clutched in his hand.

Mrs. Ferman picked up the phone and dialed a number. "Hello?" she said. "Ferman reporting. We have a new one, male, about thirty."

"Fine, thank you," answered a voice. "Begin treatment at once, Dr. Ferman."

There are some things men are not meant to know—

Dry Spell

by Bill Pronzini

The bane of all writers, John Kensington thought glumly, *whether they be poor and struggling or whether they be rich and famous, is the protracted dry spell.*

He sat staring at the blank sheet of yellow foolscap in his typewriter. His mind was as blank as that paper. Not a single idea, not a single line of writing that even remotely reached coherency in almost three weeks.

Sighing, Kensington pushed back his chair and got on his feet. He went to the small refrigerator in the kitchenette, opened his last can of beer, and took it to the old Morris chair that reposed near his desk.

I've got to come up with something, he thought. *The rent's due in another week, and if I don't get something down on that grocery bill I can forget about eating for a while.*

He sipped his beer, closing his eyes. *Come on, son,* he thought. *Just an idea, just one little idea . . .*

He let his mind wander. It seemed, however, to be wandering in circles. Nothing. Not even . . .

Wait a minute.

Now wait just a single damned minute here.

The germ of something touched a remote corner of his brain. It was a mere fragment, evanescent, but he seized it the way a man dying of thirst would seize a dipper of water.

Grimly, he hung on. The fragment remained. Slowly, inexorably, it began to blossom.

Kensington sat bolt upright in the chair, his eyes wide open now, the beer forgotten. His fingertips tingled with excitement. The coming of the idea was a catharsis, releasing the tension which had been building within him for the past three weeks.

It would be a science fiction/fantasy story, he thought, probably a novella if he worked it properly. He moistened his lips. *Now, let's see . . .*

Suppose there's this race of aliens plotting to take over Earth, because it is a strategic planet in some kind of inter-galactic war they're involved in. Okay, okay, so it's hackneyed. There are ways to get around that, ways to play that aspect down.

These aliens have infiltrated Earth and set up some kind of base of operations, maybe up in the mountains somewhere. They're assembling a kind of penultimate cybernetic machine which, when fully completed, will have the power to erase all rational thought from the minds of humans, turning them into obsequious zombies. Wait now. Suppose these aliens have a portion of this machine already completed. This portion would be capable of reading, simultaneously, the thoughts of every human on Earth, and of categorizing those thoughts for the aliens to study. That way, if any human somehow happened to blunder on the scheme in one way or another—mental blundering as well as physical would have to be considered, what with clairvoyance and the emanation into space of thought waves, and the like—then the extraterrestrials would immediately know about it. And what they would do would be to train the full strength of this completed portion of the machine on that particular human, and with it eradicate all those thoughts endangering their project, thus insuring its safety.

Kensington was sweating a bit now, his forehead crinkled in deep thought.

Sure, he thought, *it's a touch far out. But if I handle it right, who knows? At least it's a good, workable idea, which is a hell of a lot better than nothing at all. Now, how am I going to save Earth from this fate? It has to be in some way that is totally plausible, not too gimmicky, and . . .*

All at once the answer popped into his mind. *By God!* Kensington thought. *It's perfect! There's not a flaw in it!* He grinned hugely. *Those damned aliens wouldn't stand a snowball's chance in you-know-where if I set it up this way.*

He stood abruptly and started for his typewriter. The progression of the story was already flowing, plotting itself firmly in Kensington's mind.

He sat at the typewriter, excitement coursing through him because he knew, he could feel, that the dry spell was at an end. His fingers poised over the keys.

Quite suddenly, quite inexplicably, his mind went blank.

He pressed his forehead against the cool surface of his typewriter.

Why, he moaned silently, *why, oh, why can't I come up with just one little story idea?*

They do talk about the birth trauma.

Bohassian Learns

by William Rotsler

Bohassian was being born and he didn't like it. Everything had been warm and safe and he had heard things, saw images, felt clusters of emotions moving around him, and suddenly it was chaos. There was pain, then more pain, then a rhythm of pain, then a bursting, a moving, a turning and an explosion of light.

Pain.

Incredible pain.

Bohassian lashed out in anger and there were screams and terrible images in his head but still the pain did not stop, but it ebbed away slowly. Bohassian realized he was smaller now, that somehow he had cast away the large, warm protective shell, or had been rejected by it. But he was small and weak on the outside so he protected himself by moving the others away.

He lay there, soaking up images and light and ideas from this bright, big world. When he could, Bohassian went into the minds of others, breathing in incoherent images, hearing sounds and cries and sobbing.

He tried sorting out the sights from the sounds and the images from the thoughts. It was all very confusing. The minds seemed chaotic and frightened.

They were all afraid of him.

The figures in pale green, with their faces and heads wrapped, cowered against the flatness of the confining chamber. Bohassian reached beyond the chamber and felt the minds of others. The others were not frightened at first, then they became frightened and the cool thoughts jumbled and melted and boiled.

Bohassian looked into the mind of the place from which he had come, into the other part of him, into the discarded/rejected part.

Mother.

The giver of life.

She had been a safe place and then she had thrust him out. He looked into her mind and saw that she had wanted to thrust him out, that she thought it was right to thrust him out into the other place. Bohassian went deeper into her and twisted something petulantly.

The mother started to scream and went limp.

Bohassian moved among the minds around him, moving into the complex chambers of their minds, gathering information without prejudice, soaking up concepts, colors, words, acts, emotions. Wild fantasy and accomplished fact were simply images of differing textures.

Bohassian learned.

That figure was relatively cool, clinical, wanting to reach out and touch but was held back by the command of another figure whose mind was green snakes and dark oily ripples. That one was dazed, with fragments of thoughts spraying out like a crushed bouquet: *wet . . . red . . . terrible . . . push . . . mother . . . monster . . . crush . . .*

Bohassian felt danger and twisted something dark in the mind and the figure fell and was quiet, even in the mind.

Bohassian learned.

He saw that images had labels and were called words. Mother. Baby. Fear. Death. Hospital. Help. Doctor. Nurse. Blood. Kill. Green. Love.

Bohassian stopped when he learned love. It was the small figure in green. He brought it forth, towards him. It moved jerkily but Bohassian saw less fear in its mind than the others.

It felt pity and wanted to help. Bohassian held its mind firmly, ready to strike, but let it do its love help. His frail body was raised and moved slightly and he became aware of a piece of himself attached to the life giver.

The mind of the green figure spoke: *We must cut away the umbilical.*

No.

Yes. It is necessary.

Why?

To give you freedom. You needed it when you were inside and now you no longer need it.

Cut it.

It will hurt. You must not hurt me when I hurt you. It is necessary.

Bohassian looked into the mind of the green figure and saw that it believed it to be true. There are many things I do not know, thought Bohassian.

Cut.

There was pain and Bohassian pressed the other green figures against the wall and the green figure holding him gasped.

It is done.

I am free?

Yes, but you must not hurt people.

Why?

Because they are weaker than you.

But they/you are large and move. They want to hurt me.

They are frightened. You frightened them. They fear the unknown.

"Kill it!" The tall green figure against the wall made noises. Bohassian quieted him and he fell back.

And you?

I fear you, too. You are different. But I cannot kill.

That one would kill.

The figure in green looked at the crumpled figures against the flatness. "Yes. They do not understand." *Pity. They are afraid of fear.*

You make two images. They are different, but alike.

I think. I speak. Sometimes people speak different images than they think.

Bohassian felt other minds coming closer. Disturbed minds. Someone made a loud noise. Bohassian made them stop and some fell.

Why do they come?

They are curious. They come to help . . . or to hurt . . .

I learn. They will not hurt me.

"I will take care of you." *Pity. Love. Mother. Protection. Hold.*

I will not hurt you.

I will pick you up. You must be washed and fed. But not hurt.

You may hold me. I do not fear you. The others will not hurt me.

The nurse picked up Bohassian and they moved out of the chamber. There were long chambers filled with people. Some were lying down and some were staring with wide eyes. Bohassian kept them back. One moved to grab, his mind a whirl of blackness, but Bohassian twisted and he fell.

There was a dark grayness in the mind of the nurse, a sadness and hurt. But she carried Bohassian to a chamber and washed him. The water felt good and the oil was pleasant. There was much noise and Bohassian made it quiet.

Bohassian learned as he lay there.

The minds of people were very confused, streaked through with clarity and logic. But there was much fear. Fear was danger for Bohassian so he kept it away.

The figure in green held him and said *Food* and gave him a sweet, warm whiteness. It was good and Bohassian rested.

There was much to learn. Bohassian became aware of many small formless minds around him, each in a small body such as his, but each a weak and fragile being. Bohassian went into their minds but found them almost blank, only vague whorls of light and color and blurrings.

Bohassian let his body rest and not move as his mind moved lazily around in circles, touching the image makers in chambers nearby. They cringed and sometimes screamed as he entered them. One mind turned black and curled into a tiny chamber within itself. Bohassian poked at it curiously but it was without interest.

There was much to learn, Bohassian thought. There are images in the minds I touch. Skies. Trees. Tall things. Food. Other life forms, from very small to very large. Colors. Millions upon millions of image makers.

I will touch them all, Bohassian thought. I must learn.

Romeos come in all varieties; so do Juliets.

Star Bride

by Anthony Boucher

I always knew, ever since we were in school together, that he'd love me some day; and I knew somehow too that I'd always be in second place. I didn't really care either, but I never guessed then what I'd come second to: a native girl from a conquered planet.

I couldn't guess because those school days were before the Conquest and the Empire, back in the days when we used to talk about a rocket to a moon and never dreamed how fast it would all happen after that rocket.

When it did all begin to happen I thought at first what I was going to come second to was Space itself. But that wasn't for long and now Space can never take him away from me and neither can she, not really, because she's dead.

But he sits there by the waters and talks and I can't even hate her, because she was a woman too, and she loved him too, and those were what she died of.

He doesn't talk about it as often as he used to, and I suppose that's something. It's only when the fever's bad, or he's tried to talk to the Federal Council again about a humane colonial policy. That's worse than the fever.

He sits there and he looks up at her star and he says, "But damn it, they're *people*. Oh, I was like all the rest at first; I was expecting some kind of monster even after the reports from the Conquest troops. And when I saw that they looked almost like us, and after all those months in the space ship, with the old regulation against mixed crews . . ."

He has to tell it. The psychiatrist explained that to me very carefully. I'm only glad it doesn't come so often now.

"Everybody in Colonial Administration was doing it," he says. "They'd pick the girl that came the closest to somebody back home and they'd go through the Vlnian marriage rite—which of course isn't recognized legally under the C. A., at least not where we're concerned."

I've never asked him whether she came close to me.

"It's a beautiful rite, though," he says. "That's what I keep telling the Council: Vln had a much higher level of pre-Conquest civilization than we'll admit. She taught me poetry and music that . . ."

I know it all by heart now. All the poetry and all the music. It's strange and sad and like nothing you ever dreamed of . . . and like everything you ever dreamed.

"It was living with her that made me know," he says. "Being with her, part of her, knowing that there was nothing grotesque, nothing monstrous about green and white flesh in the same bed."

No, that's what he used to say. He doesn't say that part any more. He does love me. "They've got to understand!" he says, looking at her star.

The psychiatrist explained how he's transferring his guilt to the Council and the Colonial policy; but I still don't see why he has to have guilt. He couldn't help it. He wanted to come back. He meant to come back. Only that was the trip he got space fever, and of course after that he was planet-bound for life.

"She had a funny name," he says. "I never could pronounce it right—all vowels. So I called her Starbride, even though she said that was foolish—we both belonged to the same star, the sun, even if we were of different planets. Now is that a primitive reaction? I tell you the average level of Vlnian scientific culture . . ."

And I still think of it as her star when he sits there and looks at it. I can't keep things like that straight, and he does call her Starbride.

"I swore to come back before the child was born," he said. "I swore by her God and mine and He heard me under both names. And she said very simply, 'If you don't, I'll die.' That's all, just

'I'll die.' And then we drank native wine and sang folksongs all night and went to bed in the dawn."

And he doesn't need to tell me about his letter to her, but he does. He doesn't need to because I sent it myself. It was the first thing he thought of when he came out of the fever and saw the calendar and I wrote it down for him and sent it. And it came back with the C. A. stamp: *Deceased* and that was all.

"And I don't know how she died," he says, "or even whether the child was born. Try to find out anything about a native from the Colonial Administrator! They've got to be made to realize . . ."

Then he usually doesn't talk for a while. He just sits there by the waters and looks up at the blue star and sings their sad folksongs with the funny names: *Saint Louis Blues* and *Barbara Allen* and *Lover, Come Back to Me*.

And after a while I say, "I'm not planet-bound. Some day when you're well enough for me to leave you I'll go to Vln—"

" '*Earth*,' " he says, almost as though it was a love-word and not just a funny noise. "That's their name for Vln. She called herself an earth woman, and she called me her martian."

"I'll go to Earth," I say, only I never can pronounce it quite right and he always laughs a little, "and I'll find your child and I'll bring it back to you."

Then he turns and smiles at me and after a while we leave the waters of the canal and go inside again away from her blue star and I can stand coming second even to a dead native white Star-bride from the planet Earth.

Back to the good old party line.

Latest Feature

by Maggie Nadler

The minute she stepped through the door I knew her type: jaded suburbanite wife of wealthy businessman-frequently-absent-from-home, with time on her hands. Fiftyish, chunky, too much makeup on a face petulant from too many martinis. But the cut of her clothes and elaborate sweep of her tinted hair gave her away; they spelled money. I came toward her.

"May I help you, Madam?"

"I would like a television set," she said in a voice accustomed to giving orders. "A Supra. The latest model."

Supra X: a good sign. I tried not to let my face betray my eagerness. We're not supposed to mention the special feature to the customer unless he brings it up himself. "Fine. Just step this way." I led her through a consumer's paradise of up-to-date appliances until we came to the TVs. "Here we are, then. Are you at all familiar with the model?"

"I am not." Her voice was a challenge: show me. A bit nervously, I took the set down from its high shelf for her. "All right." I flashed my most genial smile. "Here it is. The latest and the best, absolutely. No other company can match it. Now, in the first place, you'll note its extreme lightweightedness. Only ten pounds. Can be hung from a wall hook, supported on its own legs—" (I pulled them out) "moved easily from place to place. Operated equally well as a portable. Excellent reception out of doors . . ."

"Indeed." Her tone, though imperious, was interested. I warmed to my sales pitch.

"But that's just the beginning." I turned it on. A burst of color leaped into life. A parade was in progress; great flower-strewn floats ornamented with pretty girls swept by. "Full color fidelity," I informed her. "Now here's a feature you're not likely to be concerned with too often." I flipped a switch and the scene faded to black and white. "However, it has its uses. Gives improved reception for programs still broadcast in black and white, old movies, for instance." I put it back on color, adjusted another switch. "Our 3-d feature." She nodded, impressed, then stepped back abruptly as a bouquet of yellow roses flung by one of the girls suddenly seemed to emerge from the screen. I moved the channel selector until an orchestral program materialized. "Full stereophonic sound reproduction. Can be enhanced by the addition of a second speaker at nominal cost."

She nodded again, and I began to feel optimistic. I ran through an enumeration of the set's remaining merits, finished with a mention of the lifetime warranty, and waited. There was a pause. Then, carefully: "I understand that this model also contains a special feature you haven't told me anything about yet."

It was my moment. "Yes," I told her. "Some of our Supra X-14

Deluxes have the additional feature you're referring to. Not this particular one, but we do have a display model in our showroom, if you'd care to take a look at it."

She murmured assent and I ushered her into a compact, heavily draped booth. The Supra was there, tuned to the parade. I pushed a button on the side, marked simply "S." Static, flickering. I adjusted the tuning knob and another image appeared: two small boys, their curly heads bent in rapt concentration over a checker board. "Timmy!" called a shrill voice. "Mr. Klein is here. Time for your piano lesson. Send Jody home."

"Awww, Mom . . ."

Mrs. Hoity-Toity threw me an impatient glance. "Can't you get anything else?" she demanded. I fiddled with the dial. More static. Suddenly a new scene came into view. This time, a bedroom. A lovely young brunette sat half-clad in front of the bureau, nervously fingering an emerald necklace and avoiding the eyes of the furious middle-aged man before her. "I didn't give you that," the man snarled. "Where did you get it? Tell me, you bitch, tell me." He let loose with a volley of language that even in our enlightened age is rare on daytime TV. Here, I snapped the set discreetly off. "As you can see," I smiled, "hours of pleasurable viewing await you. We guarantee it."

An eager, moist look had appeared in my customer's eyes. "Tell me," she said, "can I always select the channel I want? Or—"

"It works a bit like amateur radio," I explained. "There's a certain randomness to it. But that just makes it all the more exciting. And with practice, you'll find you'll get good at tuning in the specific areas you want."

"How many of these sets are there?" she wanted to know.

"A very limited number; at present, only a few hundred, concentrated mostly here in the New York area. As you can imagine, we cater to a rather select clientele. To own one is to be a pacesetter. However, their popularity is growing."

"I bet it is." The moist look was back on her face. "Tell me just one thing more. How do you manage it?"

I assumed an expression of dignity. "I think it's obvious, Madam, that selected locations are what you would call 'bugged.'"

"Yes, but how do you manage it?"

"That, I'm afraid, is a trade secret." I drew myself up. "Well, then, have you decided?" It was obvious she had.

"How much?"

I looked straight at her. "Fifty thousand dollars."

She didn't bat an eye. "I'll take it. I'll write you a check on our joint account. You can call my bank to confirm it."

"Excellent. Will you have it delivered? Or would you prefer—"

"I think I'll just take it with me," she said. "I mean, it's light enough, after all—"

"Fine, then. Here, let me get you another one. This is our display model." I fumbled among a row of cartons on the floor. "Oh, one thing more. Should it ever be in need of servicing—which isn't likely to happen often—but in the event that this does occur —call one of our own men. Don't let anybody else try to fix it, however qualified they may seem. This is a complex instrument. Even opening the cabinet the wrong way can damage it."

"I see." There was some more discussion as the business was transacted. Eventually she left in triumph with her new purchase.

When she had gone, my new boss J.T. came up to me. "Well," he said, laying a paternal hand on my shoulder. "Not a bad sale for your second day. George, you're going to be all right."

"I can hardly take the credit," I admitted. "As you told me, the feature is self-selling."

"Oh, never underestimate the importance of a good spiel in winning a customer, any customer. Speaking of which, I wonder how her hubby will react when he finds out what she spent. I'll have to watch for that tonight."

"Smile, Lady, you're on Candid Camera," I chuckled. "You mean to tell me, sir, that nobody has ever caught on?"

He shrugged. "Maybe one or two. Nobody that I've heard of. The people who buy these things, they're not engineers. They don't think along those lines. The camera only operates when the set's *off*, after all, and what could be more innocuous than a turned-off TV set? And say someone did? What could they do except keep quiet about it? This little pleasure's quite addicting, you know."

"But the FCC eventually . . ."

"Eventually. But by that time, we'll be long gone. Myself, I always did want to see South America." He flicked the set on again and the same luxurious bedroom came once more into view. The woman, now alone, lay sobbing on the bed, one hand pressed to an angry purplish welt on her cheek. J.T. said something else to me, but I didn't catch it; I was concentrating on the picture on the screen and thinking about my commission.

At this rate, it won't be long before I can afford a set of my own.

Or "Chef," which has the same meaning.

Chief

by Henry Slesar

Mboyna, chieftain of the Aolori tribe, showed no fear as the long-boat approached the island. But it was more than the obligation of his rank which kept his face impassive; he alone of his tribes-men had seen white men before, when he was a child of the vil-lage half a century ago.

As the boat landed, one of the whites, a scholarly man with a short silver beard, came toward him, his hand raised in a gesture of friendship. His speech was halting, but he spoke in the tongue of Mboyna's fathers. "We come in peace," he said. "We have come a great distance to find you. I am Morgan, and these are my companions, Hendricks and Carew; we are men of science."

"Then speak!" Mboyna said in a hostile growl, wishing to show no weakness before his tribe.

"There has been a great war," Morgan said, looking uneasily at the warriors who crowded about their chief. "The white men be-yond the waters have hurled great lightning at each other. They have poisoned the air, the sea and the flesh of men with their weapons. But it was our belief that there were outposts in the world which war had not touched with its deadly fingers. Your is-land is one of these, great chief, and we come to abide with you. But first, there is one thing we must do, and we beg your pa-tience."

From the store of supplies in their longboat, the white men re-moved strange metal boxes with tiny windows. They advanced hesitatingly toward the chief and his tribesmen, pointing the curi-ous devices in their direction. Some of them cowered, others raised their spears in warning. "Do not fear," Morgan said. "It is only a plaything of our science. See how they make no sound as their eyes scan you? But watch." The white men pointed the boxes at themselves, and the devices began clicking frantically.

"Great magic," the tribesmen whispered, their faces awed. "Great magic," Mboyna repeated reverently, bowing before the white gods and the proof of their godhood, the clicking boxes. With deference, they guided the white men to their village, and after the appropriate ceremony, they were beheaded, cleaned and served at the evening meal.

For three days and nights, they celebrated their cleverness with dancing and bright fires; for now, they too were gods. The little boxes had begun to click magically for them, also.

We've got to be important for some reason.

After You've Stood on the Log at the Center of the Universe, What Is There Left to Do?

by Grant Carrington

There used to be a log in the center of the pond on my father's farm. It wasn't really a log; it was a thick branch coming off the main trunk of a submerged tree. Someone had sawed it off where it broke water, and it was thick enough to use as a mooring place for the rowboat. But it wasn't strong enough to hold even a ten-year-old boy without giving a little. So naturally we all had to try to stand on it. I was the only one who ever succeeded. It wasn't easy standing on that log while it sank lower and lower into the water and weaved from side to side while you flailed your arms to keep your balance.

Legions of farmboys may have succeeded before I did, but, if they did, I didn't know it. I was the first in *my* world to have balanced himself on that log. And the last, for it wasn't long after I'd done it that the ship came.

Tommy Peters, my best friend, his dog Rajah, and I were just sort of sitting by the pond trying to decide what to do with the rest of the day. We had discussed fishing, swimming, going into town on our bikes to get a soda and look at all the things we couldn't afford, playing ball, but really we were pretty happy just to sit by the edge of the pond, making dragons out of the clouds.

I think Tommy really wanted to go swimming, so he could be the second one to stand on the log, but I wanted to savor my position as the only log-climber around for as long as possible, so I kept putting it off.

"Wow! Look at that jet!" he said, pointing to a dot of blackness that was rapidly growing.

"Geez, it's really moving," I said.

"I think it's out of control!" Tommy shouted. "It looks like it's going to crash!"

We scrambled to our feet.

"Holy Crow!" Tommy said in a loud whisper.

It wasn't a jet plane at all. By now we could see it and it seemed like it was coming right toward us. Rajah started to whimper and cringe against Tommy just before we could hear the loud, high-pitched whistle of rushing air.

"It's a spaceship!" Tommy said.

We were rooted to the spot, unable to run, watching that silvery capsule race toward us. Then, about twenty feet overhead, it came to a sudden impossible dead stop and drifted slowly to rest a foot above the water. A door opened, and a guy who looked just like an astronaut in a spacesuit stepped out, walked over to the log, said something loudly in a foreign language, waved to the spaceship, and attached something to the log. Then he walked back to the spaceship and it took off just as fast as it had arrived.

That's what I said: *he walked to the log*, right over the pond.

About ten seconds after the spaceship had disappeared into the sky, Tommy and I both let out the breaths we didn't know we were holding.

"Wow!" Tommy said.

"Let's get out of here," I said. I was just as scared as Rajah was.

"Come on, scaredy-cat, let's see what they put on the log."

Just then a jet fighter came roaring past just at tree-top level. I fell flat on the ground, and Rajah took off for home, his tail between his legs. Tommy stood his ground.

"Wow!"

Hot on the tail of the first jet came two more.

"Come on, Doug." He was running for the rowboat. I was really scared, but I couldn't run. After all, I was the first to stand on the log at the center of the pond, and if Tommy went out there with the boat while I ran for home, I'd never live it down.

At the top of the log was a silvery rectangular box-shaped object. It really glittered in the sun. Tommy reached out to grab it.

"Wow!" he said. "It's got some kind of carvings on it."

I carefully stroked it; sure enough, on the four long sides there were tiny dots and things. The top, opposite where it was attached to the log, was smooth as smooth could be, but not the sides.

"It's like the drum inside a music box," I said.

"Or Braille. Maybe it's writing in Braille," Tommy said.

Just then, we heard some voices. My father came out on the dock with a lot of men with him.

"Doug, what are you doing out there?"

"Just looking at the log."

"What's that on it?"

"Oh, nothing. . . ."

"This spaceship came down and put something on the log," Tommy said, and blurted out the whole story.

My father ordered me to bring the boat back in and then he and some of the other adults rowed out to look at the log while the others kept questioning us and talking about Russians and kids' imaginations.

I'm not sure they all believed us, but after a while my father did. "Doug's a good boy, I believe him," he said, after I refused to disagree with Tommy's story.

They brought in a bunch of men and trucks and equipment, spoiling a lot of our fields and crops (which they paid my father for, much more than he would have got out of them anyway), and completely ruined the pond for swimming. They cut the log just below where the silvery rectangular object was attached, but they didn't move the object.

"We *can't* move it, Doug; there's some kind of a force field that keeps it in place," Dr. Gaines said.

"Wow! Just like in *Star Trek*," Tommy yelped. Dr. Gaines was my favorite of all the men who had come in to look at our pond. He wasn't very old, though he had lost most of his blond hair and he wore rimless glasses. He wasn't crotchety and crabby like some of the others, who shooed us away or ordered us to leave. A couple of times he took us out to the building that they had rigged up on a couple of army pontoons. They were trying to melt the object down with lasers and phasers and cannons and drills and I don't know what. It was really exciting, with electricity and flashing lights. They had built a regular real laboratory out on our pond.

It was about three days after the whole thing began that I found him sitting at the edge of the pond, staring out at the building over the log, looking kind of funny.

"Hi, Dr. Gaines," I said, sitting down and breaking off what looked like a nice juicy grass stem. It was. "How's the work going? Have you figured out that force field yet?"

"No, Doug, but we found out what the object is."

"Yeah? What is it?"

"They brought in one of those high-powered microscopes yesterday, and you know that roughness on the sides of the plinth?" (He called the object a "plinth.") I nodded my head. "It's writing."

"You mean like Braille?"

"Maybe. There might be Braille there. There's a lot of languages on it. Languages and alphabets we never heard of. But there's also French and Chinese and Latin and Japanese and every language anyone can think of."

"English?"

"Yes. English too."

"What does it say?"

"Come on, Doug. I'll let you see for yourself."

We walked out on the ramp that led to the building over the log at the center of the pond. All the air of excitement was gone. People were walking around, doing their work, all right, but looking kind of glum or dazed. There was this huge instrument set up in front of the object, and Dr. Gaines showed me one of the eyepieces, sort of like a real pair of binoculars.

It was already focused on the English part of the object: ". . . Survey Galactique 42,373,249. This plaque marks the population center of the Milky Way Galaxy, as determined by Galactic Survey 42,373,249."

Sometimes one wonders what happens after the story ends.

Maid to Measure

by Damon Knight

Côte d'Azur sunlight, filtered by the jalousies, made a golden dimness in the room. On the green brocade chaise lay a slender blonde in tennis costume, swinging a racquet in her hand. Each time she swung it, it went *thump* on the floor.

"I wish you wouldn't do that," said the bearded young man irritably. "I've spoiled this damn postcard twice." He threw a colorful bit of cardboard at the wastebasket, and drew another toward him across the writing desk.

"I wish you wouldn't make cow's eyes at aging brunettes in bars," said the girl. There was a gleam of spite in her big blue eyes.

"Aging!" said the young man automatically, pausing in his work.

"She must have been thirty if she was a day," said the girl. *Thump* went the tennis racquet.

"Umm," said the young man, looking up.

"*Umm*, hell!" said the girl. Her expression had grown definitely unpleasant. "I've got half a mind—"

"What?" asked the young man apprehensively.

"Oh, nothing." After a pause, she said, "Mother would have known what to do with you. She was a witch."

The young man clucked his tongue disapprovingly, without looking up. "Shouldn't talk about your old mother that way," he said.

"She was a *witch*," the girl said. "She could turn herself into a wolf, or a tiger, or anything she liked."

"Sure, she could," said the young man, signing his postcard. "There we are." He put the card aside, lit a cigarette, and glanced rather nervously at his watch. "All kidding aside, Yana—we've had a pretty good time—"

"But all things come to an end?" the girl asked in a dangerous voice. "We're both grown-ups? We ought to be realistic? Is that it?" She stood up and went to the closet.

"Well—" said the young man uncomfortably. His expression brightened. "What are you doing?"

The girl pulled out a pigskin suitcase and opened it with unnecessary vehemence. She rummaged in one of the pockets, drew out a worn chamois bag. "Looking for something," she said over her shoulder.

"Oh," said the young man, disappointed. He watched while the girl opened the drawstrings, took out a small object wrapped in a dirty red cloth and tied with string. He glanced at his watch again; when he looked up, the girl had a small, oddly shaped bottle in her hand.

"What's that?"

"Something my mother left me," the girl said. Her fingernails gritted unpleasantly on the glass as she scraped the wax off and removed the stopper. She gave him a narrow look. "So you won't change your mind?"

"Now, Yana—"

"Then, here's luck." She put the bottle to her lips, tilted her head back and swallowed.

"Now, then," she said, lowering the empty bottle, "let's see . . ." She flexed one hand experimentally, looking at her long nails.

The young man was inspecting his watch. "Almost three o'clock," he muttered. "Yana, didn't you say you were going to the hairdresser's this afternoon?"

"I changed my mind." She looked at him thoughtfully. "Why—are you expecting anyone?"

"Oh, no," the young man said hastily. He stood up energetically. "Tell you what, Yana—no hard feelings—let's go for a swim."

"I see," said the girl. "Tell me, what about tonight—no plans? No one coming over?"

"No, not a thing."

"So, we'll be all alone—just the two of us." She smiled, showing her pointed eyeteeth. "That will give me plenty of time to decide. What shall I be, darling—your great big stripy pussycat . . . or your faithful, hungry dog?"

The young man, who was peeling his shirt off over his head, did not hear. His voice came indistinctly. "Well, if we're going for that swim, let's get moving."

"All right," the girl said. "Wait a minute, and I'll change into a bikini."

Emerging from the shirt, the young man said, "Glad you decided not to be—" He looked around, but the girl was not in the room. "Yana? Yana? That's funny." He crossed the room, glanced into the bedroom, then the bath. They were empty.

A light tapping came at the French doors as the young man turned. They opened, and a pretty dark-haired young woman put her head in. "Robert? I am not intruding?"

"Giselle!" cried the young man, smiling with pleasure. "No, come on in—you're right on time. I was just thinking about going for a swim."

The young woman advanced with a charming smile; her figure, in a low-cut blue sun dress, also was charming.

"Oh, it's too bad," she said; "I have no suit."

"Here's one," said the young man cheerfully, picking up two candy-striped bits of material from the chaise. "Try that one for size."

"But doesn't it belong to your—little friend? Won't she mind?"

"No, no—don't give her another thought."

As they were leaving, the young man glanced with an odd expression at the striped bikini, which fitted the dark girl admirably.

"What is it, anything wrong?"

"Just thought of something Yana said before she left . . . No, it couldn't be. Well, come on!"

Arm in arm, laughing, they went out into the sunlight.

A trillion years too late.

Eyes Do More Than See

by Isaac Asimov

After hundreds of billions of years, he suddenly thought of himself as Ames. Not the wave-length combination which through all the universe was now the equivalent of Ames—but the sound itself. A faint memory came back of the sound waves he no longer heard and no longer could hear.

The new project was sharpening his memory for so many more of the old, old, eons-old things. He flattened the energy vortex that made up the total of his individuality and its lines of force stretched beyond the stars.

Brock's answering signal came.

Surely, Ames thought, he could tell Brock. Surely he could tell somebody.

Brock's shifting energy pattern communed, "Aren't you coming, Ames?"

"Of course."

"Will you take part in the contest?"

"Yes!" Ames's lines of force pulsed erratically. "Most certainly. I have thought of a whole new art-form. Something really unusual."

"What a waste of effort! How can you think a new variation has not been thought of in two hundred billion years. There can be nothing new."

For a moment Brock shifted out of phase and out of communion, so that Ames had to hurry to adjust his lines of force. He caught the drift of other-thoughts as he did so, the view of the powdered galaxies against the velvet of nothingness, and the lines of force pulsing in endless multitudes of energy-life, lying between the galaxies.

Ames said, "Please absorb my thoughts, Brock. Don't close out. I've thought of manipulating Matter. Imagine! A symphony of Matter. Why bother with Energy. Of course, there's nothing new in Energy; how can there be? Doesn't that show we must deal with Matter?"

"Matter!"

Ames interpreted Brock's energy-vibrations as those of disgust.

He said, "Why not? We were once Matter ourselves back—back—Oh, a trillion years ago anyway! Why not build up objects in a Matter medium, or abstract forms or—listen, Brock—why not build up an imitation of ourselves in Matter, ourselves as we used to be?"

Brock said, "I don't remember how that was. No one does."

"I do," said Ames with energy. "I've been thinking of nothing else and I am beginning to remember. Brock, let me show you. Tell me if I'm right. Tell me."

"No. This is silly. It's—repulsive."

"Let me try, Brock. We've been friends; we've pulsed energy together from the beginning—from the moment we became what we are. Brock, please!"

"Then, quickly."

Ames had not felt such a tremor along his own lines of force in —well, in how long? If he tried it now for Brock and it worked, he could dare manipulate Matter before the assembled Energy-beings who had so drearily waited over the eons for something new.

The Matter was thin out there between the galaxies, but Ames gathered it, scraping it together over the cubic light-years, choosing the atoms, achieving a clayey consistency and forcing matter into an ovoid form that spread out below.

"Don't you remember, Brock?" he asked softly. "Wasn't it something like this?"

Brock's vortex trembled in phase. "Don't make me remember. I don't remember."

"That was the head. They called it the head. I remember it so clearly, I want to say it. I mean with sound." He waited, then said, "Look, do you remember that?"

On the upper front of the ovoid appeared HEAD.

"What is that?" asked Brock.

"That's the word for head. The symbols that meant the word in sound. Tell me you remember, Brock!"

"There was something," said Brock hesitantly, "something in the middle." A vertical bulge formed.

Ames said, "Yes! Nose, that's it!" and NOSE appeared upon it. "And those are eyes on either side," LEFT EYE—RIGHT EYE.

Ames regarded what he had formed, his lines of force pulsing slowly. Was he sure he liked this?

"Mouth," he said, in small quiverings, "and chin and Adam's apple, and the collarbones. How the words come back to me." They appeared on the form.

Brock said, "I haven't thought of them for hundreds of billions of years. Why have you reminded me? Why?"

Ames was momentarily lost in his thoughts. "Something else. Organs to hear with; something for the sound waves. Ears! Where do they go? I don't remember where to put them?"

Brock cried out, "Leave it alone! Ears and all else! Don't remember!"

Ames said, uncertainly, "What is wrong with remembering?"

"Because the outside wasn't rough and cold like that but smooth and warm. Because the eyes were tender and alive and the lips of the mouth trembled and were soft on mine." Brock's lines of force beat and wavered, beat and wavered.

Ames said, "I'm sorry! I'm sorry!"

"You're reminding me that once I was a woman and knew love; that eyes do more than see and I have none to do it for me."

With violence, she added matter to the rough-hewn head and said, "Then let *them* do it" and turned and fled.

And Ames saw and remembered, too, that once he had been a man. The force of his vortex split the head in two and he fled back across the galaxies on the energy-track of Brock—back to the endless doom of life.

And the eyes of the shattered head of Matter still glistened with the moisture that Brock had placed there to represent tears. The head of Matter did that which the energy-beings could do no longer and it wept for all humanity, and for the fragile beauty of the bodies they had once given up, a trillion years ago.

When half gods go, the gods arrive— Emerson.

Thang

by Martin Gardner

The earth had completed another turn about the sun, whirling slowly and silently as it always whirled. The East had experienced a record breaking crop of yellow rice and yellow children, larger stockpiles of atomic weapons were accumulating in certain strategic centers, and the sages of the University of Chicago were uttering words of profound wisdom, when Thang reached down and picked up the Earth between his thumb and finger.

Thang had been sleeping. When he finally awoke and blinked his six opulent eyes at the blinding light (for the light of our stars when viewed in their totality is no thing of dimness) he had become uncomfortably aware of an empty feeling near the pit of his stomach. How long he had been sleeping even he did not know exactly, for in the mind of Thang time is a term of no significance. Although the ways of Thang are beyond the ways of men, and the thoughts of Thang scarcely conceivable by our thoughts; still—stating the matter roughly and in the language we know—the ways of Thang are this: When Thang is not asleep, he hungers.

After blinking his opulent eyes (in a specific consecutive order which had long been his habit) and stretching forth a long arm to sweep aside the closer suns, Thang squinted into the deep. The riper planets were near the center and usually could be recognized by surface texture; but frequently Thang had to thump them with his middle finger. It was some time until he found a piece that suited him. He picked it up with his right hand and shook off most of the adhering salty moisture. Other fingers scaled away thin flakes of bluish ice that had caked on opposite sides. Finally, he dried the ball completely by rubbing it on his chest.

He bit into it. It was soft and juicy, neither unpleasantly hot nor freezing to the tongue; and Thang, who always ate the entire planet, core and all, lay back contentedly, chewing slowly and permitting his thoughts to dwell idly on trivial matters, when he felt himself picked up suddenly by the back of the neck.

He was jerked upward and backward by an arm of tremendous bulk (an arm covered with greyish hair and exuding a foul smell). Then he was lowered even more rapidly. He looked down in time to see an enormous mouth—red and gaping and watering around the edges—then the blackness closed over him with a slurp like a clap of thunder.

For there are other gods than Thang.

I'd rather see than be one.

How Now Purple Cow

by Bill Pronzini

When Floyd Anselmo saw the purple cow grazing on a hillside of his dairy ranch one cold morning in October, he thought his mind must be hallucinating.

He brought his pick-up truck to a sharp halt at the side of the access road that wound through his property, set the brake, and leaned across the seat to have another look. But it was still there. He stared, willing it to disappear. It didn't.

Anselmo shook his head slowly and got out of the truck. He stood on the graveled roadbed, shading his eyes from the glare of the winter sun. Still there.

By God, Anselmo thought. Next thing you know, it'll be pink elephants. And me not even a drinking man.

He drew the collar of his coat up against the chill, early morning wind, sighed deeply, and walked around the truck. He made his way carefully through the damp grass at the side of the road, climbed easily over the white fence there, and began to ascend the hillside.

Halfway up, he paused for another look. Damned if the cow *wasn't* purple; a rather pleasant, almost lilac, shade of that color. Still, the contrast with the bright chlorophyll green of the grass, and the dull, brown-and-white of the other cows, was rather startling.

Anselmo climbed to within twenty feet of where the purple cow was grazing. Cautiously, he made a wide circle around the animal. It paid no attention to him.

"Listen here," he said aloud, "you ain't real."

The cow chewed peacefully, ignoring him.

"Cows ain't purple," Anselmo said.

The animal flicked its tail lightly.

He stood looking at it for quite some time. Then he sighed again, rather resignedly this time, turned and started down the hillside.

His wife was finishing the breakfast dishes in the kitchen when he came in a few minutes later. "Back so soon?" she asked.

"Amy," Anselmo said, "there's a purple cow grazing on a hillside down the road."

She wiped her hands on a dish towel. "I made some fresh coffee," she told him.

Anselmo tugged at his ear. "I said, there's a purple cow grazing on a hillside down the road."

"Yes, dear," his wife said. She began stacking dishes in the cupboard.

Anselmo went outside. He saw Hank Raiford, his foreman, coming up from the milking barn.

"Morning, Mr. Anselmo," Hank said.

"Hank," Anselmo said, frowning, "I saw this purple cow grazing on a hillside down the road."

Hank looked at him.

"I thought it was an hallucination at first. But I went up there and the damned thing was purple, all right. I can't figure it out."

"Well," Hank said, watching him strangely.

"You haven't seen it by any chance, have you?"

"No, sir."

Anselmo nodded. "Want to come out with me and have a look at it?"

"Well," Hank said, "there are a few things I got to take care of right now."

"Maybe later," Anselmo said.

"Sure," Hank told him, moving away quickly. "Maybe later."

Anselmo went back into the house. He crossed directly to the telephone on the hall table and put in a call to Jim Player, the editor of the local weekly newspaper.

"Floyd Anselmo here," he said when Player came on.

"What can I do for you, Floyd?"

"Well," Anselmo said. "I was coming into town a while ago, and I was driving down my access road when I saw this purple cow grazing on a hillside."

There was silence from the other end.

"Jim?" Anselmo asked.

"Purple cow?" Player said finally.

"That's right," Anselmo told him. "Purple cow."

Another silence, shorter this time. Then Player laughed. "You're putting me on, right?"

"No," Anselmo said seriously.

"Look, Floyd, I'm a busy man," Player said. "With all these silly damned UFO sightings hereabout lately, I haven't had time to . . ." He broke off, chuckling. "Say, maybe this purple cow of yours came in one of those flying saucers people claim to have been seeing."

"Jim," Anselmo said slowly, "I don't know anything about flying saucers. All I know is there's a purple cow grazing on one of my hillsides. If you want to come out here, I'll show it to you."

Player was silent for a moment. Then he said, "All right, I'll come out. But if you're ribbing me . . ."

"The hillside I'm talking about is maybe a mile onto my land from the highway," Anselmo told him. "I'll meet you there."

"Forty-five minutes," Player said unhappily, and hung up.

Anselmo went to the door. His wife came into the room just as he reached it. "Where are you going, dear?"

"To meet Jim Player."

"Whatever for?"

"To show him the purple cow I saw."

Her forehead corrugated worriedly. "Floyd . . ."

"I'll be back in an hour or so," Anselmo said, and stepped outside.

He started his pick-up and drove down the access road. When he reached the hillside, he saw that the purple cow had moved farther down it, and was grazing now only a few feet from the white fence.

Anselmo braked the truck and got out. He went through the grass to the fence, climbed over it, and stood facing the cow.

The animal continued to graze, seemingly oblivious to his presence.

Anselmo walked haltingly up to it. He put out a wary hand and touched its head. Then he stepped back. "I was beginning to have some doubts," he said, "but damned if you ain't real, and damned if you ain't purple."

The animal shifted its hind legs.

"Where'd you come from anyway?" Anselmo asked. "Jim Player said something about flying saucers or some such. Now I don't hold much truck with them things, but y—"

Anselmo strangled on the last word. His eyes had riveted on his hand, the hand he had touched the animal's head with seconds earlier.

His fingers were turning purple.

He had a fleeting desire to turn and run. It passed quickly. After a moment, the animal raised its head to look at Anselmo for the first time.

In a distinctly questioning tone, it said, "Moo?"

"Moo," Anselmo answered.

There were two purple cows grazing on the hillside when Jim Player arrived from town a few minutes later.

How neatly things work out!

Revival Meeting

by Dannie Plachta

Graham Kraken lay upon his deathbed. His eyes wavering upon a dim and faraway ceiling, he savored the reassuring words.

"The odds are all in your favor," the doctor said.

The bed seemed to tense beneath Kraken. Springs coiled tautly.

"Some day—" the doctor's voice rang with tiny, metallic chimes —"medical science will have advanced far enough to revive you. Your frozen body will not deteriorate in the interim." The chimes grew hushed. "Some day science will repair your body and you will live again."

Graham Kraken died easily and they froze his corpse.

He dreamed that he was in Miami Beach and opened his eyes. Blinking into the dimness of his room, he found a visitor seated at his bedside.

"Good morning," said the visitor.

The stranger, Kraken noted, was an elderly gentleman with a bald head and a pleasant face.

"Good morning," said Kraken in a friendly manner. "Nice earrings you have there."

"Thank you," said the visitor. "They're antennae."

"Oh?"

"For the transistor radios built into my earlobes."

"Indeed?"

"Stereo."

"How nice," said Kraken. "How do you turn it off?"

"Don't," the visitor responded. "Speak up a bit, please."

"I'm sorry," said Kraken. "I didn't know."

"Nice weather we're having."

"I hadn't really noticed. By the way, have they done anything about that?"

"Well, they did for a short time," the old gentleman said. "But they had to give it up."

"Too many conflicting wishes?"

"I'm afraid so."

"A pity." Kraken glanced at the heavily curtained window. As he watched, the glass behind the curtains suddenly shattered. "Oh?" he said. "Riots?"

"No," replied the visitor. "Supersonic transports."

Another pane of glass automatically slipped into place.

"I guess you get quite a lot of that."

"Easy come, easy go."

"By the way," Graham Kraken asked, "what year is this?"

"Twenty-eighty-eight," he said.

"Well," said Kraken, "it has been a while."

"One year is pretty much like another," said the stranger.

"How about the money?" wondered Kraken. "Did my estate hold out?"

"I'm afraid not," said the visitor. "I had to pay for your revival."

"That was very kind of you," said Kraken. He noticed the sunlight edging the window curtains.

He rose upon an elbow. The motion made him feel faint.

"Please don't try to move," the visitor said. "It's important that you rest for the heart transplant."

"Oh?" Kraken leaned back. "Is there something wrong with my heart?"

The visitor stood up slowly.

"No," he replied, "but there's something wrong with mine."

We'd all like to think that.

Prototaph

by Keith Laumer

I was already sweating bullets when I got to the Manhattan Life Concourse; then I had to get behind an old dame who spent a good half hour in the Policy Vending Booth, looking at little pieces of paper and punching the keys like they were fifty-credit bet levers at the National Lottery.

When I got in, I was almost scared to code my order into the Vendor; but I was scareder not to. I still thought maybe what happened over at Prudential and Gibraltar was some kind of fluke, even though I knew all the companies worked out of the Federal Actuarial Table Extrapolator; and Fate never makes a mistake.

But this had to be a mistake.

I punched the keys for a hundred thousand C's of Straight Life; nothing fancy, just a normal working-man's coverage. Then I shoved my ID in the slot and waited. I could feel sweat come out on my scalp and run down by my ear while I waited. I could hear the humming sound all around me like some kind of bees bottled up back of the big gray panel; then the strip popped out of the slot, and I knew what it said before I looked at it:

UNINSURABLE.

I got the door open and shoved some guy out of my way and it was like I couldn't breathe. I mean, think about it: Twenty-one years old, out in the city to take my chances all alone, with no policy behind me. It was like the sidewalk under your feet turned to cracked ice, and no shore in sight.

A big expensive-looking bird in executive coveralls came out of a door across the lobby; I guess I yelled. Everybody was looking at me. When I grabbed his arm, he got that mad look and started to reach for his lapel button—the kind that goes with a Million Cee Top Crust policy.

"You got to listen," I told him. "I tried to buy my insurance— and all I got was this!" I shoved the paper in his face. "Look at me," I told him. "I'm healthy, I'm single, I finished Class Five Subtek school yesterday, I'm employed! What do you mean, uninsurable?"

"Take your hands off me," he said in kind of a choky voice. He was looking at the paper, though. He took it and gave me a look like he was memorizing my face for picking out of a line-up later.

"Your ID," he held out his hand and I gave it to him. He looked at it and frowned an important-looking frown.

"Hm-m-m. Seems in order. Possibly some, er . . ." He pushed his mouth in and out and changed his mind about saying it; he knew as well as I did that the big actuarial computer doesn't make mistakes. "Come along," he turned his back and headed for the lift bank.

"What have I got, some kind of incurable disease or something?" I was asking them; they just looked at me and goggled their eyes. More of them kept coming in, whispering together; then they'd hurry away and here would come a new bunch. And none of them told me anything.

"The old crock in front of me, she was ninety if she was a day!" I told them. "She got her policy! Why not me?"

They didn't pay any attention. Nobody cared about me; how I felt. I got up and went over to the first guy that had brought me up here.

"Look," I said. I was trying to sound reasonable. "What I mean is, even a guy dying in the hospital can get a policy for *some* premium. It's the law; everybody's got a right to be insured. And—"

"I know the laws governing the issuance of policies by this company," the man barked at me. He was sweating, too. He got out a big tissue and patted himself with it. He looked at a short fat man with a stack of papers in his hand.

"I don't care what kind of analysis you ran," he told him. "Run another one. Go all the way back to Primary if you have to, but get to the bottom of this! I want to know why this"—he gave me a look—"this individual is unique in the annals of actuarial history!"

"But, Mr. Tablish—I even coded in a trial run based on a one hundred per cent premium, with the same result: No settlement of such a claim is possible—"

"I'm not interested in details; just get me results! The computer has available to it every fact in the known universe; see that it divulges the reasoning behind this . . . this anomaly!"

The fat man went away. They took me to another room and a doctor ran me through the biggest med machine I ever saw. When he finished I heard him tell the big man I was as sound as a Manhattan Term Policy.

That made me feel a little better—but not much.

Then the fat man came back, and his face was a funny white color—like some raw bread I saw once on a field trip through Westside Rationing. He said something to the others, and they all started to talk at once, and some of them were yelling now. But do you think any of them told me anything? I had to wait another hour, and then a tall man with white hair came in and everybody got quiet and he looked at papers and they all got their heads together and muttered; and then they looked at me, and I felt my heart pounding up under my ribs and I was feeling sick then, med machine or no med machine.

Then they told me.

That was two days ago. They got me in this room now, a fancy room up high in some building. There're guys around to do whatever I want—servants, I guess you'd call 'em. They gave me new clothes, and the food—West Rat never put out anything like this. No liquor, though—and no smokes. And when I said I wanted to go out, all I got was a lot of talk. They treat me—careful. Not like they like me, you know, but like I was a bomb about to go off. It's a funny feeling. I guess I got more power than anybody that ever lived—more power than you can even get your mind around the thought of. But a lot of good it does me. There's only the one way I can use it—and when I think about that, I get that sick feeling again.

And meanwhile, I can't even go for a walk in the park.

The president was here just now. He came in, looking just like the Tri-D, only older, and he came over and looked at me kind of like I looked at him. I guess it figures: There's only one of each of us.

"Are you certain there's not some . . . some error, George?" he said to the wrinkly-faced man that walked just behind him.

"The Actuarial Computer is the highest achievement of a thousand years of science, Mr. President," he said in a deep voice like the mud on the bottom of the ocean. "Our society is based on the concept of its infallibility within the physical laws of the Universe. Its circuits are capable of analyses and perceptions that range into realms of knowledge as far beyond human awareness as is ours beyond that of a protozoan. An error? No, Mr. President."

He nodded. "I see." That's all he said. Then he left.

Now I'm just sitting here. I don't know what to do next—what to say. There's a lot to this—and in a way, there's nothing. I got to think about it, dope it out. There's got to be something I can do —but what?

The machine didn't say much. They took me down to the subvault where the big voice panel is located and where the primary data goes in, and let me hear for myself. It didn't give any explanations; it just told me.

Funny; in a way it was like something I've always known, but when you hear Fate come right out and say it, it's different.

When I die, the world ends.

They didn't even stop at the Moon to refuel.

The Rocket of 1955

by C. M. Kornbluth

The scheme was all Fein's, but the trimmings that made it more than a pipe dream and its actual operation depended on me. How long the plan had been in incubation I do not know, but Fein, one spring day, broke it to me in crude form. I pointed out some errors, corrected and amplified on the thing in general, and told him that I'd have no part of it—and changed my mind when he threatened to reveal certain indiscretions committed by me some years ago.

It was necessary that I spend some months in Europe, conducting research work incidental to the scheme. I returned with recorded statements, old newspapers, and photostatic copies of certain documents. There was a brief, quiet interview with that old, bushy-haired Viennese worshipped incontinently by the mob; he was convinced by the evidence I had compiled that it would be wise to assist us.

You all know what happened next—it was the professor's historic radio broadcast. Fein had drafted the thing, I had rewritten it, and told the astronomer to assume a German accent while reading. Some of the phrases were beautiful: "American dominion over the very planets! . . . veil at last ripped aside . . . man defies gravity . . . travel through limitless space . . . plant the red-white-and-blue banner in the soil of Mars!"

The requested contributions poured in. Newspapers and magazines ostentatiously donated yard-long checks of a few thousand dollars; the government gave a welcome half-million; heavy sugar came from the "Rocket Contribution Week" held in the nation's public schools; but independent contributions were the largest. We cleared seven million dollars, and then started to build the spaceship.

The virginium that took up most of the money was tin plate; the monoatomic fluorine that gave us our terrific speed was hydrogen. The take-off was a party for the newsreels: the big, gleaming bullet extravagant with vanes and projections; speeches by the professor; Farley, who was to fly it to Mars, grinning into the cameras. He climbed an outside ladder to the nose of the thing, then dropped into the steering compartment. I screwed down the sound-proof door, smiling as he hammered to be let out. To his surprise, there was no duplicate of the elaborate dummy controls he had been practicing on for the past few weeks.

I cautioned the pressmen to stand back under the shelter, and gave the professor the knife switch that would send the rocket on its way. He hesitated too long—Fein hissed into his ear: "Anna Pareloff of Cracow, Herr Professor . . ."

The triple blade clicked into the sockets. The vaned projectile roared a hundred yards into the air with a wobbling curve—then exploded.

A photographer, eager for an angle shot, was killed; so were some kids. The steel roof protected the rest of us. Fein and I shook hands, while the pressmen screamed into the telephones which we had provided.

But the professor got drunk, and, disgusted with the part he had played in the affair, told all and poisoned himself. Fein and I left the cash behind and hopped a freight. We were picked off it by a vigilance committee (headed by a man who had lost fifty cents in our rocket). Fein was too frightened to talk or write so they hanged him first, and gave me a paper and pencil to tell the story as best I could.

Here they come, with an insulting thick rope.

Huh?

Science Fiction for Telepaths

by E. Michael Blake

Aw, you know what I mean.

Stupid little kids can make a lot of trouble.

Kindergarten

by James E. Gunn

First day—

Teacher told my parent that I am the slowest youngster in my class, but today I made a star in the third quadrant of kindergarten.

Teacher was surprised. Teacher tried to hide it and said the solar phoenix reaction is artistic, but is it practical?

I don't care. I think it's pretty.

Second day—

Today I made planets: four big ones, two middle-sized ones, and three little ones. Teacher laughed and said why did I make so many when all but three were too hot or too cold to support life and the big ones were too massive and poisonous for any use at all.

Teacher doesn't understand. There is more to creation than mere usefulness.

The rings around the sixth planet are beautiful.

Third day—

Today I created life. I begin to understand why my people place creation above all else.

I have heard the philosophers discussing the purpose of existence, but I thought it was merely age. Before today joy was enough: to have fun with the other kids, to speed through endless space, to explode some unstable star into a nova, to flee before the outrage of some adult—this would fill eternity.

Now I know better. Life must have a function.

Teacher was right: only two of the middle-sized planets and one of the little ones were suitable for life. I made life for all three, but only on the third planet from the sun was it really successful.

I have given it only one function: survive!

Fourth day—

The third planet has absorbed all my interest. The soupy seas are churning with life.

Today I introduced a second function: multiply!

The forms developing in the seas are increasingly complex.

The kids are calling me to come and play, but I'm not going. This is more fun.

Fifth day—

Time after time I stranded sea-creatures on the land and kept them alive long past the time when they should have died. At last I succeeded. Some of them have adapted.

I was right. The sea is definitely an inhibiting factor.

The success of the land-creatures is pleasing.

Sixth day—

Everything I did before today was nothing. Today I created intelligence.

I added a third function: know!

Out of a minor primate has developed a fabulous creature. It has two legs and walks upright and looks around it with curious eyes. It has weak hands and an insignificant brain, but it is conquering all things. Most of all, it is conquering its environment.

It has even begun speculating about me!

Seventh day—

Today there is no school.

After the pangs and labors of creation, it is fun to play again. It is like escaping the gravitational field of a white dwarf and regaining the dissipated coma.

Teacher talked to my parent again today. Teacher said I had developed remarkably in the last few days but my creation was hopelessly warped and inconsistent. Moreover, it was potentially dangerous.

Teacher said it would have to be destroyed.

My parent objected, saying that the solar phoenix reaction in the sun would lead the dangerous life form on the third planet to develop a thermonuclear reaction of its own. With the functions I had given that life form, the problem would take care of itself.

It wasn't my parent's responsibility Teacher said, and Teacher couldn't take the chance.

I didn't hear who won the argument. I drifted away, feeling funny.

I don't care, really. I'm tired of the old thing anyway. I'll make a better one.

But it was the first thing I ever made, and you can't help feeling a kind of sentimental attachment.

If anyone sees a great comet plunging toward the sun, it isn't me.

Eighth day—

It's luck that makes the world go round.

A *Little Knowledge*

by Paul Dellinger

History repeats itself. Somewhere, on some remnant of a book or paper that had survived the great conflagration, Sol had read those words (at least he thought he had; occasionally his memory would play tricks on the exact wording of the proverbs he had preserved over the years) and they had served him well.

The world had changed greatly since that phrase, but Sol had gone on the assumption that humankind would keep the same values, make the same mistakes, and find itself in the same kinds of situations to which the old sayings had applied. Usually he could come up with a proverb for any occasion—so what if he didn't always recall them exactly right?—and, as a result, had risen among the tribe to become chief advisor to Knobloch, undisputed ruler of what remained of this mountainous region.

But Knobloch wanted to expand his domain, at least beyond the mountain range known as the Yellow Fingers which got its name from its lurid nighttime glow. He sent scouting parties, one after the other, into those peaks and none ever returned. Sol believed they either used the opportunity to escape Knobloch's rule altogether, or had been victims of the deadly pollutants left in the wake of the last great war. Unfortunately, neither of those suggestions would satisfy Knobloch, who was threatening to retire Sol in an unpleasantly permanent fashion unless the advisor hit upon a way to launch a successful expedition.

Sol was on the spot, standing before a Knobloch who was growing increasingly impatient. "All that glitters is not gold"—he recalled that phrase from somewhere, but it was no help; the Yellow Fingers glittered all right, but he was already convinced that their aura was not caused by the useless yellow metal.

"Look before you leap"—yes, well, he should have looked longer before he accepted the precarious post of advisor. "A miss is as good as a mile"—there was a possibility. Perhaps he could suggest that Knobloch send the next party around the Yellow Fingers, instead of through them.

The result was a backhanded blow from Knobloch's lead-encased fist. "Never!" he shouted. "It was you who advised me that a good offense is better than a poor defense, or something like that. And I want to send at least one fighting force into those mountains, so I can claim dominion over them."

Knobloch motioned to two of his pages, similarly clad in heavy lead armor, to drag Sol away to meet the penalty of failed advisors. The pair didn't bother to conceal their grins; they had grown increasingly jealous of the influence Sol wielded over their master. But even as they reached for him, Sol's agile mind plucked another proverb from the past.

"A moment, O Knobloch," he called out. "I have the answer. Send these two men on the scouting mission. They will return with the information you want."

The smirks on the faces of the two men vanished. "It's a trick!" one said. "Sol wants to get rid of us—"

"If he is wrong, he will follow you into oblivion," Knobloch proclaimed. "No more argument. Draw the necessary provisions and be off. Sol has predicted you will survive, and that is sufficient."

Grumbling, they went. And survive they did, although Sol never knew exactly why. Maybe it was the leaden armor that had been the mark of royalty since the last great war; perhaps it had been fashioned originally to shield its wearers from whatever remnants of that conflict still killed.

Sol never argued with success—another saying from the past—but he was never able to shake a niggling suspicion that the proverb on which he'd based his advice wasn't exactly correct. It had worked, so it didn't matter, but it still didn't ring quite true in his mind as he recalled it once more: "Let your pages do the walking through the Yellow Fingers."

Why take the hard way?

A Cup of Hemlock

by Lee Killough

Two days after the Erasco shuttle crashed at the north pole of Chandanna, the local police arrested the man responsible. The trial was likewise speedy, the judgment being that: "Cars Merrivale Bantling, having caused the deaths of fourteen people by industrial espionage, has proven himself contemptuous of life and unfit to remain in society. He is to be confined for a period of thirty days, during which time he shall give up his life, be declared dead, and finally removed when all vital signs have ceased."

"Do you really expect me to kill myself?" Bantling asked his Chandannair lawyer.

"You might donate yourself to the organ banks as many do. Your parts would be of no use to us, but the gesture would express your desire to expiate your offense."

Bantling frowned. "And if I refuse your cup of hemlock? Is it forced down my throat?"

The lawyer was shocked. "Chandanna is a civilized planet. No one will touch you with intent to harm."

Aside from the barred door and windows, the cell was much like a hotel suite. It was comfortable, with a good library and excellent food. The only disturbing note was the altar-like table bearing a chalice of amber liquid. Bantling decided to wait the Chandannan out. He could do worse than live the rest of his life like this.

His appeals were denied and as the thirtieth day approached, Bantling became nervous, but the last day proceeded as the previous ones had. No one sent gas through the vents or poured the poison down his throat. Toward evening he laughed in triumph and hurled the chalice across the room, splashing the poison up the wall.

Then he began to wonder where his dinner was. It was far past the time the meal usually arrived. He tried to turn on the lights. The room remained dark.

Suddenly he was frightened. He rushed to the water taps . . . but though pushed full on, only drops of water came out.

He ran to the door and pounded on it, yelling, "Hey! I want to see my lawyer!"

No one came.

Bantling remembered the judge's words. He would be declared dead and removed when all vital signs were gone. He looked at the empty cup on the floor and the drying stain on the wall. A whimper rose in his throat.

You said it, not I, Tom.

Present Perfect

by Thomas F. Monteleone

William Rutherford sat in his den, lit a cigarette, and opened another manila envelope. He pulled out the self-addressed stamped envelope, threw it on the desk, and looked at the manuscript that was included with it. He smiled as he saw the familiar slush pile title:

Paradise Lost
by
Rudolph Muir

Taking a drag on his cigarette, Rutherford read the first three paragraphs, figured out the entire story, and turned to the last page to read:

The smoldering wreckage of the once-gleaming starship lay in a twisted pile deep within a lush jungle. The man struggled to his feet and wandered away from it sweating profusely. Several agonizing minutes passed while he imagined that everyone else in the colony ship had been killed by the crash. Suddenly he saw movement within the twisted metal. A hand! Someone was climbing out! The man rushed up to the hand and pulled it out and was surprised to see that it was connected to a beautiful blonde.

"Oh, thank you," she said, pulling her torn jumpsuit up over her swollen breasts.

"That's all right," he said. Then, after a pregnant pause, he added: "I guess we're the only ones left."

The blonde cast a furtive glance about the hostile environs and nodded nervously.

He looked at her appreciatively, smiled and said: "By the way, what's your name?"

She looked up at him and a little smile danced upon her full lips. "Eve," she said.

Rutherford stamped out his cigarette and reached for another rejection slip. *Not another one. Won't these guys ever learn?* He checked off one of the most frequently used parts of the slip (the one which said: "—To you this may seem original, but to our readers the story is old hat.") and placed it with the manuscript in the self-addressed stamped envelope for its safe return to the author.

As he was reaching for another manuscript, his wife entered the den with some coffee. "How's it going, honey?" she asked.

"Ah, it's the same old shit," said Rutherford. "Thanks," he said, taking the coffee and lighting another cigarette. His wife nodded knowingly. William had been reading the unsolicited manuscripts of *Incredible Science Fiction Magazine* for many years and he had seen most of the famous themes of the genre methodically beaten to death by the hordes of slush pile authors. Looking at his watch, he saw that he had time to read a few more submissions before the President came on television for another one of his numerous nationwide proclamations. It had been a long day and Rutherford was looking forward to the presidential telecast. A little humor always relaxed him.

While his wife sat on the couch reading a historical novel, Rutherford extracted another manuscript and began reading:

All Quiet on the Earthly Front
by
B. Preston Wilde

Several hours after the last terrible explosions wracked the earth, Garth slowly scrambled up the mile-long passage of the abandoned mine. When he reached the surface, the sky was stained scarlet and punctuated by myriad mushroom clouds. Fear exploded in his brain and he thought: "Oh God! They've finally done it!"

After getting over the initial shock, Garth headed back to what had once been civilization; but try as he might, he could not find anyone else alive. He began to wonder why the radiation had not killed him. Perhaps he was immune . . .

I wish I was immune to these kinds of stories, thought Rutherford, as he flipped through the manuscript to the last page. Just as he had expected, Garth wasn't really the Last Man on Earth after all—it was just an experiment being carried out by mad social scientists.

He picked up another rejection slip and checked off the appropriate space. This time he had a number of applicable comments but he chose the one which read: "—Stories which depend on surprise endings are rarely surprising and even more rarely are they good stories." Placing the manuscript and slip into the return envelope, Rutherford mused, as he had done many times before, on the amazing frequency of similar stories in the slush pile. It seemed that many nights of manuscript reading were almost exactly alike.

What the hell, he thought as he picked up another manila envelope. Pulling out the manuscript, which was crinkled and bent and marked from numerous paper clippings, mailings, etc., he read the title:

I Always Thought Raymond Was
Kind of Strange
by
John Harrington Trail

The sleepy little town of Unionville was never the same after Old Man Barker claimed he saw a flying saucer down by Potter's Mill. After that, everybody was seeing them. At first I didn't make any connection between them and what was going on in my personal life. That happened later.

It all started when this new scientist, Raymond Garubendi, started working at the Electronics Lab where I worked just outside of Unionville. Raymond wasn't a very talkative sort and he always had the odd habit of . . . This time, Rutherford did not even bother to flip to the last page. He had this one pegged: the old alien-among-us theme, once more dangled and capered feebly before him. Shaking his head, he filled out another rejection slip, this time checking several categories. He sealed it into the return envelope and uttered a plaintive sigh.

"Not so good?" asked his wife, who was quite familiar with the ritual performed nightly in the den.

"I don't know why it bothers me sometimes," said Rutherford. "But these writers keep sending us the same old ideas, the same old stories . . . I'd swear I've read some of these before. Only the by-lines are different."

His wife smiled weakly. "Maybe it's just *déjà vu?*"

Rutherford considered her comment. There was even something about the way she uttered that line . . . that was disturbingly familiar. As if he knew what she was going to say before she said it. *That's weird,* he thought, *déjà vu of a déjà vu.*

He dismissed the thought, lit another cigarette, checked his watch. There was time for one more story before the presidential comedy hour. Considering how things had progressed so far that evening, he wondered how many times he had read the next manuscript. Rutherford selected the next manila envelope from the stack, opened it, and read:

Present Perfect
by
Thomas F. Monteleone

William Rutherford sat in his den, lit a cigarette, and opened another manila envelope. . . .

The devil you say.

A Lot to Learn

by Robert T. Kurosaka

The Materializer was completed.

Ned Quinn stood back, wiped his hands, and admired the huge bank of dials, lights and switches. Several years and many fortunes had gone into his project. Finally it was ready.

Ned placed the metal skullcap on his head and plugged the wires into the control panel. He turned the switch to ON and spoke: "Ten-dollar bill."

There was a whirring sound. In the Receiver a piece of paper appeared. Ned inspected it. Real.

"Martini," he said.

A whirring sound. A puddle formed in the Receiver. Ned cursed silently. He had a lot to learn.

"A bottle of Schlitz," he said.

The whirring sound was followed by the appearance of the familiar brown bottle. Ned tasted the contents and grinned.

Chuckling, he experimented further.

Ned enlarged the Receiver and prepared for his greatest experiment. With unlimited wealth, his next desire arose naturally from the lecherous D.O.M. deep within all of us.

He switched on the Materializer, took a deep breath and said, "Girl."

The whirring sound swelled and faded. In the Receiver stood a lovely girl. She was naked. Ned had not specified clothing.

She had freckles, braces and pigtails. She was eight years old.

"Hell!" said Ned Quinn.

Whirrr

The firemen found two charred skeletons in the smoldering rubble.

In short, horse feathers.

The Amphibious Cavalry Gap

by J. J. Trembly as told to James E. Thompson

J. J. TREMBLY (Special Adviser, Naval Research and Development Commission on New Weapons Systems) as told to JAMES E. THOMPSON

Military intelligence estimates of the enemy's strength and plans require two ingredients. One is logic. The other . . .

Intelligence reports coming out of Soviet Central Asia and Siberia indicate that the Soviets have undertaken an extensive horse-breeding program.[1] The number of horses in the USSR increased fifteen percent[2] or forty-two percent[3] in the period 1968–71. These figures indicate that the Soviet planners have assigned horse-breeding a high priority.

The question now arises: What place does this crash program occupy in Soviet strategic thinking? Here we can only speculate; but, in the light of the Soviet Union's known expansionist aims, it behooves us to consider the possibility that they intend to use those horses against us.

Horses have not been used extensively in warfare since the outbreak of World War Two, when the Polish cavalry proved highly ineffective against German armor.[4] This has led to a consensus of military thought—that is, of Western military thought—that cavalry is obsolete. But can we afford to call cavalry "obsolete" when the enemy has not? The Soviet rulers are not talking about cavalry

[1] See DoD Report #BX818RL, "Livestock Populations in Soviet Virgin Lands," Washington, DC, 1971.
[2] Estimate by CIA.
[3] Estimate by US Army Intelligence.
[4] Gen. Heinz Guderian, *Panzer Leader*, trans. C. Fitzgibbon. New York: Dutton & Co., 1952, pp. 65-84.

being "obsolete"; instead, as we have seen, they are breeding more horses.

Someone may object that Soviet cavalry cannot pose a threat to the United States, because the two nations have no common land boundary, but are separated by water; and it has been found that cavalry is effective only on land.[5] Cavalry could, however, be used against the United States by the USSR (or vice versa) if the horses and their riders were transported to the scene of combat by sea or air. If the horses are transported by air, this gives no obvious advantage to one side or the other, as all points on the Earth's surface are equally accessible by air; but if we think in terms of the horses being transported by sea, an ominous conclusion emerges. Let us list the most important cities in the two nations. In our case, this will consist of our national capital plus the four most populous cities; in theirs, of the five most populous, as their capital (Moscow) is also the most populous city:[6]

USSR	USA
Moscow	Washington
Leningrad	New York
Kiev	Chicago
Tashkent	Los Angeles
Kharkov	Philadelphia

When we look at the location of these cities on the map, we find that only one of the key Soviet cities—Leningrad—is located on the sea, while four of the five key American cities are located on the seacoast or very near it—New York, Philadelphia, Washington and Los Angeles. (And even Chicago might be accessible by sea, via the St. Lawrence seaway.) Therefore, we are at least *four times* as vulnerable to amphibious attack as the USSR. When one considers that they also have more horses than we do, the seriousness of the amphibious cavalry gap becomes apparent.

If the horses are to be transported by sea, it must be either by surface ship or by submarine. We can, I think, rule out the use of surface ships, for submarines have the advantage of concealability; if the horses were transported on the decks of surface ships, they could be detected by our sky-spies. So if the Soviets are planning a

[5] See, for example, Exodus 14:26-30.
[6] According to population statistics from the 1972 World Almanac.

sneak amphibious cavalry attack on the US, they will almost certainly use submarines, and will be building a larger submarine fleet. This, we find, is precisely what they *are* doing. The Soviet Union now has 401 submarines to only 152 for the United States.[7]

Is there any hope of overcoming the disparity between our military capacity and that of the Soviets caused by our greater vulnerability? In my opinion, there is such a hope; but it can only be achieved by the creation of a greater total striking force proportionate to the enemy's greater invulnerability, that is, four times as many horses, four times as many trained cavalrymen, and four times as many cavalry transport submarines. In the field of submarines alone, this means that, as the Soviets have 401 usable submarines, we need 1,604. Given that our present submarine strength is only 152, we need 1,452 more submarines, to be fitted for cavalry transport, for an adequate defense.

It is urgently necessary that we begin at once to close this gap. The Defense Department should immediately make known the seriousness of the threat, and demand that Congress vote the necessary funds.

Some persons have suggested that a weapons system of the type described poses no real threat; but an experienced submarine commander has assured the author that a cavalry-carrying submarine would be, in his words, "a real *stinker*."

[7] *Jane's Fighting Ships*, 1971-72 ed.

Don't worry. The gas shortage will fix everything.

Not Counting Bridges

by Robert L. Fish

The truest statement ever made is that a lot of knowledge is a dangerous thing. Take a prime example: me. Once I was ignorant and happy, and then . . .

I was driving with a friend of mine, and this friend—who was

Query Editor on a newspaper—started telling me about some of the questions he was called upon to answer.

"Some character will want to know," he said, "who held Washington's coat when he flang that dollar over the Rappahanock. That sort of thing."

I laughed merrily. "How could anyone be expected to know that?"

My friend looked at me sourly. "What'd you mean? *I* know. That's my job."

I marvelled at this. "Amazing! You supply this information for free?"

"Free, if they wait until Sunday," he conceded. "I only come out on Sundays. Of course, if they send in a stamped self-addressed envelope, they get these vital facts by return mail."

"Wonderful! Of course," I pointed out, "if you've waited since 1776, you ought to be able to wait until Sunday."

"1758," he said. "Yes, you'd think so, but people apparently don't like to wait." He paused, and then made the statement that was to change my life so profoundly. "For example, I received a self-addressed stamped envelope just yesterday asking me what percentage of the area of the United States was devoted to providing space for automobiles."

"You mean roads and such?" I asked.

He nodded. "Also parking areas, driveways, gas-stations, drive-in movies, etc."

"You were able to answer him?"

"Of course. Today the percentage of our national space devoted to the necessities of the gas-fed monster amounts to exactly 8.64% of the total land area of the country. I do not count bridges, since they pass over water."

I smiled at him. "Not very much, is it?"

"Well," he answered with a frown, "when you consider that ten years ago it was only 1.85%, and fifty years ago it was only .0047%, you can see the direction we are going."

My smile faded. I pondered this, an uneasy feeling beginning to permeate me. "You mean . . . ?"

"Yes," he said. "I have plotted a curve. At the rate of increase evident over the past half-century, we shall eventually end up with the entire country committed to concrete roadways, parking lots, and soft shoulders." He made a rapid calculation. "About 1998, I should judge."

I was horror-stricken. "But how would we eat?" I cried.

"Howard Johnsons, I imagine."

"And where would we live?"

He glanced about to make sure we were not being overheard. "I have it on good authority," he whispered, "that the Government, aware of this trend, has reserved some two-hundred-thousand acres near Pittsburgh, and is planning an apartment-building sufficient to handle the entire population."

My perturbation must have shown on my face, for he attempted to alleviate the terror he had wrought in me. "Do not worry," he said soothingly. "There will be room for all. And built-in television sets, too."

But I was not to be calmed. In fury at the horrible vision he had provided, I opened the car-door and flang him into the road. I tramped on the gas, fleeing.

But I have not been able to flee from myself. I read each news-paper story of highway appropriation with panic; each bull-dozer I find at work sends chills through me. Because I know me.

When we are all in that apartment, I'll be the guy who comes home late. I'll be the guy that has to park somewhere around Indiana . . .

1—1=0

The Man Inside

by Bruce McAllister

I am ten and a half years old, and I must be important because I'm the only boy they let into this laboratory of the hospital. My father is in the other room of this laboratory. He's what Dr. Plankt calls a "catatonic," because Dad just sits in one position all the time like he can't make up his mind what to do. And that makes Dr. Plankt sad, but today Dr. Plankt is happy because of his new machine and what it will do with Dad.

Dr. Plankt said, "This is the first time a computer will be able to articulate a man's thoughts." That means that when they put

the "electrodes" (those are wires) on Dad's head, and the "electrodes" are somehow attached to Dr. Plankt's big machine with
the spinning tapes on it, that machine will tell us what's in Dad's
head. Dr. Plankt also said, "Today we dredge the virgin silence of
an in-state catatonic for the first time in history." So Dr. Plankt is
happy today.

I am too, for Dad, because he will be helped by this "experiment" (everything that's happening today) and for Dr. Plankt,
who is good to me. He helps make my "ulcer" (a hurting sore inside me) feel better, and he also gives me pills for my "hypertension" (what's wrong with my body). He told me, "Your father
has an ulcer like yours, Keith, and hypertension too, so we've got
to keep care of you. You're much too young to be carrying an
ulcer around in you. Look at your father now. We don't want
what happened to your father to happen. . . ."

He didn't finish what he was saying, so I didn't understand all
of it. Just that I should keep healthy and calm down and not
worry. I'm a lot like Dad, I know that much. Even if Dad worried
a lot before he became a "catatonic" and I don't worry much because I don't have many things to worry about. "Yet," Dr. Plankt
told me.

We're waiting for the big "computer" to tell us what's in Dad's
head! A few minutes ago Dr. Plankt said that his machine might
help his "theory" (a bunch of thoughts) about "personality sym-
metry in correlation with schizophrenia." He didn't tell me what
he meant by that because he wasn't talking to me when he said it.
He was talking to another doctor, and I was just listening. I think
what he said has to do with Dad's personality, which Mom says is
rotten because he's always so grouchy and nervous and picky.
Mom says I shouldn't *ever* be like Dad. She's always telling me
that, and she shouts a lot.

Except when she brings people home from her meetings.

I don't think Dr. Plankt likes Mom. Once Dr. Plankt came over
to our house, which is on Cypress Street, and Mom was at one of
her meetings, and Dr. Plankt and I sat in the living room and
talked. I said, "It's funny how both Dad and me have ulcers and
hypertension. Like father, like son. Mom says that. It's kind of
funny." Dr. Plankt got mad at something then and said to me,
"It's not funny Keith! With what she's doing to you both, your
mother, not your father, is the one who should be in a mental

inst—" He didn't finish his last word, and I don't know what it was and what he was mad about. Maybe he was mad at me.

Many times Dr. Plankt says that he wants to take me away from Cypress Street, and put me in a better—

Wait! The computer just typed something! It works just like a typewriter but without anyone's hands on it. The words it is typing are from Dad's head! Dr. Plankt has the piece of paper in his hands now. He's showing it to three doctors. Now he's showing it to Mom. Mom is starting to cry! I've never seen her cry before. I want to see the words from Dad's head!

Another doctor is looking at me, and he has the paper now. I say, "Can I see it! Can I see it?" He looks at me again, and I think he knows who I am because Dr. Plankt talks about me a lot to everyone. I must be important. I don't like the look on this other doctor's face. It's like the look Uncle Josh gets when he's feeling sad about something. This other doctor closes his eyes for a minute, and comes over to me with the paper. The paper, the paper! The words from Dad's head. The words are:

OH	OH
MY	MY
WIFE,	SON!
I	I
CERTAINLY	CERTAINLY
DO	DO
NOT	NOT
WANT	WANT
TO	TO
LIVE	DIE!

When I squint my eyes and look at these words from Dad's head, they look like a man in a hat with his arms out, kind of like Dad—except that there's a split down the middle of this man.

It's funny, but I know just how Dad feels.

And where else besides Mars?

The Mars Stone

by Paul Bond

The landing had been successful. Now there was only one thing left to do.

I stepped into the hatchway slowly, careful not to bump my backpack against the top. I scrunched down on all fours as was necessary to get through the hatch onto the small porch outside the MEM. Other men had done this many times before, but the only one I had anything in common with was Neil Armstrong when he went through the same routine to become the first man on the moon. The difference was that I would become the first man on Mars.

I went down the ladder by degrees, savoring every step closer to the ground. Finally, after I had the boys at Mission Control biting their nails, I reached the bottom rung and majestically lowered my foot into the pink sand.

"That's another small step for a man . . ."

Well, how the hell do you expect a guy to be original at a time like that?

Ben Johnson and I were there for three days, the longest first mission on record. We had all the luxuries, too. TV coverage, the Mars Rover, everything.

From the time we landed, Zeus 7 (I'll never understand why they didn't call the project *Mars*) was considered a success, but we really didn't hit the headlines until the third day.

Johnson and I were going along in the Rover, minding our own business, and heading for the Canal Crater. We got there a little behind schedule so we cut down our exploration time some. I was just about to go back to the Rover with my samples when I saw something strange on a large rock that I was passing by. I looked closer and couldn't believe my eyes.

"Ben!" I yelled.

He came puffing over, weighed down by both the suit he had on and the rocks he was carrying, thinking I'd broken my leg or something. When he saw what I was looking at he nearly went off his rocker too.

It was writing. It had to be. Words carved into the face of the stone. Real words in some strange language. We rigged up both the movie camera and the television camera for shots of it, and then asked Mission Control what they wanted us to do about it.

"For crying out loud, man, get it out of there and bring it back," the man said. So we got our hammers and chisels and chipped it out of the stone.

I couldn't help thinking, all the way back, that the writing was on the wall.

It took them four years to decipher the writing, and it turned out to be nothing more than an old army code used way back when. They found that out when they came up with a process that determined when the actual *carving* of the stone took place.

It's bad enough that so many people don't really give a damn about space travel anymore, they've become so bored with it. But when the few people who do care and look up to you as being the *first* to land somewhere, anywhere, when they're taken away from you, and your pride is defaulted, and you feel downright *frustrated*, then you're shaking hands with suicide.

But I still say they can't really be sure that I wasn't the first. It's just too hard to believe that some joker from 1945 got there before me. Even if the stone *did* say that:

KILROY WAS HERE.

That explains a lot of my own teachers.

Source Material

by Mildred Downey Broxon

She stood blinking into the darkness, puzzled by the faint tapestry of lights before her. A classroom? It smelled like a classroom—warm, slightly stale air, books, chalk dust—and the battered wooden podium was solid and familiar. But out in front of her were the muted lights and the dull gleam of—glass? plastic? She could not see what sat before her in the darkness, watching.

A ripple of anticipation, or perhaps impatience, ran through the class. Obviously something was expected of her; the notes before her said *Earth History*. Earth History? Ambitious name for a class. She couldn't remember teaching it before; in fact, she couldn't remember getting here. Was she in a new classroom? A new wing of the university? But why would they have dragged the old furniture along? Maybe she was getting old. If she started having memory lapses they'd make her retire. She cleared her throat.

"Hello," she said, "I'm Dr. Ellen Donnally, and this is a class on—" She looked down; yes, that's what the notes said—"Earth History." She paused, staring into the darkness. The bright lighting at the front of the room blinded her; she could not see the class, could not make eye contact, could not gauge responses. "First I'd like each of you to tell me why you are taking this class." There. The answers should jog her memory.

There was a waiting silence, and then from the darkness came a flat metallic voice: "I am studying the incidental life forms of yellow dwarf stars." Ellen blinked.

The metallic voice came again, with different pacing: "My ancestors visited Earth in aeons past. I would learn what they saw, and know if what they did had any effect."

There—the same voice emitted from a dull-red glow: "Carbon-based life forms are a diversionary interest of mine."

The mechanical voice—a translating device?—grated on: "Ancient mythology." "The effect of a double-planet system on sentient psyches." "Saline physiology." "Representative art forms of the Sirius Sector." The list continued, and she nodded and smiled toward each speaker, though her sweating hands left damp marks on the podium. Nothing they said jogged her memory. It could be a joke, but she was well-liked—students said her lectures made the past come alive—and who would go to such trouble to confuse an old woman?

She scanned the first page of her notes. She had never seen them before, but the wording was familiar, as if she herself might have written them. *Earth History?*

"Since this is the first day, I'll dismiss class early so you can all go to the library and check the reserve materials." That was safe enough; she must have materials on reserve, she always did: books, pictures, even artifacts from her own collection, for how else could students learn? She looked at the notes. "The next class will cover Earth's formation and the geologic eras up to the Age of Reptiles. Good day."

The blinding yellow light snapped off. For a moment she saw rows of glittering cases—like a massive jewelry store—some glowing with red or blue light, some liquid-filled, others clouded with vapors.

Then, suddenly, the teacher was a motionless, bent figure standing behind a wooden podium.

One student, looking toward the lecture platform, remarked, "Aren't these simulations amazing? No wonder Ancient Cultures classes are so popular."

The words were translated; another student replied, "Yes. They're sentient, you know. The earlier models were too mechanical. These new ones are almost alive."

"That raises an interesting question," the first student said. "In a way they *are* alive, of course. At least their personalities survive. It's the only practical way to know what the creatures were really like. But I wonder how it feels to spend eternity in stasis?"

"Well," said the second student, "at least they never wear out."

The room was empty now. On the lecture platform Dr. Ellen Donnally stood timeless and motionless, waiting for her next class.

Whom Computer has joined, let no man put asunder.

The Compleat Consummators

by Alan E. Nourse

"There is just no question about it," Tethering was saying. "Our services are made for you. The ordinary man is no problem—easy to analyze, still easier to satisfy. We hardly earn our fee. But a man of such superb discrimination who has held out for so long. . . ." He spread his hands ecstatically. "You're a challenge, my friend. You will tax our resources to the limit. But then, Consummation, Incorporated thrives on challenge. You won't regret the outcome, I tell you three times."

"Tell me again," Frank Bailey said, still unconvinced.

"Well, the principle is obvious," said Tethering. "Until now, no marriage in history has ever been completely consummated. It's as simple as that."

"Come, now," Frank Bailey said. "You're over-selling."

"Not at all," Tethering said, flushing. "When I said consummated, I meant *consummated*. In the fullest sense of the word. Now, we can't deny that marriages have been consummated before, perhaps physically, in a haphazard sort of way, but emotionally, intellectually, spiritually . . . never! And even on the physical level . . ." Tethering broke off as though he could no longer endure the pain. "But how could you really expect more, under the circumstances? You pick a man and a woman at random from the grab-bag, utterly incompatible in a thousand subtle ways, and force them to live indefinitely in the closest, most persistent contact . . ." He sighed. "No wonder marriage is a farce. It's ridiculous. It has always been ridiculous."

"Until Consummation, Incorporated, came along," Frank Bailey said dubiously.

"Exactly," Tethering said. "Things have changed since the Frightful Fifties. No need to take chances now . . . we have computer analysis and profile delineation to work with. We have Hunyadi and his neuropantograph. We can offer you the perfect marriage, the ultimate consummation. No risks, no gambles. Every notch in one personality is matched with the other, every line fitted perfectly to every groove."

Frank Bailey scratched his jaw. "*Somewhere* there must be a woman worth marrying," he admitted. "Though I can't imagine where."

"But what are your chances of finding her without help? Infinitesimal! How would you know her if you saw her? How could you hope to judge?" Tethering smiled. "The means of identification have been available for decades, but we are the first ones with courage enough to apply them. We need only your signal to begin."

"I think," Frank Bailey said, "that you have made a sale. You guarantee your results, of course?"

"Without reservation," Tethering said happily. "One hundred percent compatibility on all levels, or your money is refunded and the alliance annulled. I tell you three times."

It was enough for Frank Bailey. When he signed the service order, his hand didn't quiver for an instant. After all, he thought, how could he possibly lose?

The profile analysis was exhaustive; it was clear that Consummation, Incorporated, did not intend to slouch on the job. Frank had envisioned a questionnaire or two to fill out, an interview with a man with thick glasses, and very little else. When he emerged from the gauntlet a week later he was a badly shaken man.

They started with physical measurements, and Frank saw what Tethering meant by "thorough." They recorded his height and his girth, his shoulder span and arm length. They measured him with vernier and calipers down to the point of embarrassment. They screened his eyes for exact color shade, and examined his hair for rate-of-growth, and carefully calculated his bone-muscle-fat ratio. No detail of his physical wherewithal escaped their painstaking attention.

Other things were measured, too . . . his likes and dislikes, his tastes and preconceptions, his conscious desires and unconscious cravings. Men in white frock-coats scurried to and from the computer, programming the data already taken, verifying it, and hurrying back with new questions to be asked.

They used the latest devices and drugs to help define the dimensions of his ego. With the neuropantograph they turned his mind inside out and twisted it into a pretzel, wringing from him his most guarded emotional responses and transposing them to the activated Hunyadi tubes in the computer. Relays of interviewers spelled each other picking his brain from a dozen different directions, until Frank was almost ready to explode in their faces and storm out in a rage.

But each fragment of data extracted went onto a tape, and each segment of tape left impressions in the computer which punched holes in a card, and when it was finally over, Frank Bailey stood revealed in elemental nakedness, ready to be electronically mated.

It took time, just as Tethering had said. His own profiling was only the first step; the winnowing of prospective mates was even more painstaking. Rack after rack of female profile cards went into the machines, and day after day Frank paced the floor, certain that when all available cards had finally been screened and discarded, none would be left at all.

But one morning Tethering appeared, beaming. "Our work is done, my friend! The moment is at hand. Look!"

Frank peered with growing excitement at the two cards that represented himself and his perfect complement. "Where is she?" he demanded. "When will I meet her?"

"At once," Tethering said. "Unless you can think of some reason for waiting . . ."

And for all his native caution, Frank Bailey couldn't.

Her name was Barbara, and at first he was certain that some sort of fearful mistake had been made.

She was hardly his ideal of beauty, with her mouse-brown hair, her 30-inch bust and her slightly prominent incisors. The glasses did nothing to enhance the illusion, nor did her habit of stuttering whenever she became the least excited. And *she* was so shaken by their first meeting that she couldn't utter a word all day; it seemed that Frank Bailey was not exactly what she had anticipated, either.

But bit by bit they began to grow on each other.

The first day neither of them ate. Barbara loved extravagant sauces and dainty salads, and she couldn't cook anyway, while Frank was a meat-and-potatoes man who brooked no nonsense at the dinner table. But the second day, almost miraculously, there was food on the table that both could tolerate, and by the third day the meals were veritable ambrosia.

They began talking, and found that their interests, while divergent, were fundamentally coherent. If she responded unexpectedly to Frank's alien taste in jazz, he was amused by her Mozart quartets, and found them excellent comic relief. Their tastes in books and entertainment did not coincide; rather, they compounded, until neither could identify the source of which interest.

It was a Platonic relationship, for a while. On the first day no mention whatever was made of the marriage. On the second day they agreed that things of the flesh were really unnecessary, and talked for hours about spiritual fulfillment. On the third day they decided simultaneously that primitivism had its moments after all; they engaged each other on the bathroom floor at four o'clock in the morning, and there was nothing haphazard about it.

Each day proved a new enrichment and a new fulfillment; they could feel themselves drawing closer. "It's wonderful," Barbara said. "It was silly to expect it all in the first instant."

"Foolish," Frank agreed.

"But there must be a flaw," she said thoughtfully. "How will we ever know when it reaches completion? Today is better than yesterday, and tomorrow will be better than today. Where will it end?"

"Who says it has to?" Frank said, brushing away the fragmentary worry that kept worming into his mind. "Tethering promised us one hundred percent fulfillment . . . and considering his fee, we have it coming. When it stops getting better and settles into a routine, then we'll know the end point. Until then, why fret?"

But it did not settle into a routine. Every day was excitingly different as new heights of consummation were achieved. Mysteriously, they found themselves thinking alike, knowing what the other was about to say and leaping ahead in conversations that were only half spoken. Their lives were suddenly supercharged with a strange exhilaration, like the influence of a subtle narcotic. It seemed that it could never end.

But there had to be an end point, of course.

They were sitting on the sofa one evening, exhausted from a day of ecstatic togetherness, when Barbara drew back and stared at her husband. Frank felt a chill creep down his back. He frowned at her.

"I feel very odd," Barbara said.

"I know," Frank said. "I've been feeling that way for days."

"B-b-b-b-but I mean right now, suddenly," Barbara said. "I f-f-f-feel like I'm burning up! It's different than before!"

"You're right," Frank said, suddenly alarmed. "It *is* different . . ."

"I don't like it," she said, pushing away from him.

"Neither do I," he said, starting to rise.

"Something's happening!"

"Something's happening!"

"HELP. . ."

There was silence then, with only the echo of a strangled scream.

After It had jelled for a while, It got up from the sofa and went into the kitchen to make a pot of coffee.

One way to get rid of trouble makers.

Examination Day

by Henry Slesar

The Jordans never spoke of the exam, not until their son, Dickie, was twelve years old. It was on his birthday that Mrs. Jordan first mentioned the subject in his presence, and the anxious manner of her speech caused her husband to answer sharply.

"Forget about it," he said. "He'll do all right."

They were at the breakfast table, and the boy looked up from his plate curiously. He was an alert-eyed youngster, with flat blond hair and a quick, nervous manner. He didn't understand what the sudden tension was about, but he did know that today was his birthday, and he wanted harmony above all. Somewhere in the little apartment there were wrapped, beribboned packages waiting to be opened, and in the tiny wall-kitchen, something warm and sweet was being prepared in the automatic stove. He wanted the day to be happy, and the moistness of his mother's eyes, the scowl on his father's face, spoiled the mood of fluttering expectation with which he had greeted the morning.

"What exam?" he asked.

His mother looked at the tablecloth. "It's just a sort of Government intelligence test they give children at the age of twelve. You'll be getting it next week. It's nothing to worry about."

"You mean a test like in school?"

"Something like that," his father said, getting up from the table. "Go read your comic books, Dickie."

The boy rose and wandered toward that part of the living room which had been "his" corner since infancy. He fingered the topmost comic of the stack, but seemed uninterested in the colorful squares of fast-paced action. He wandered toward the window, and peered gloomily at the veil of mist that shrouded the glass.

"Why did it have to rain *today?*" he said. "Why couldn't it rain tomorrow?"

His father, now slumped into an armchair with the Government newspaper, rattled the sheets in vexation. "Because it just did, that's all. Rain makes the grass grow."

"Why, Dad?"

"Because it does, that's all."

Dickie puckered his brow. "What makes it green, though? The grass?"

"Nobody knows," his father snapped, then immediately regretted his abruptness.

Later in the day, it was birthday time again. His mother beamed as she handed over the gaily-colored packages, and even his father managed a grin and a rumple-of-the-hair. He kissed his mother and shook hands gravely with his father. Then the birthday cake was brought forth, and the ceremonies concluded.

An hour later, seated by the window, he watched the sun force its way between the clouds.

"Dad," he said, "how far away is the sun?"

"Five thousand miles," his father said.

Dickie sat at the breakfast table and again saw moisture in his mother's eyes. He didn't connect her tears with the exam until his father suddenly brought the subject to light again.

"Well, Dickie," he said, with a manly frown, "you've got an appointment today."

"I know, Dad. I hope——"

"Now it's nothing to worry about. Thousands of children take this test every day. The Government wants to know how smart you are, Dickie. That's all there is to it."

"I get good marks in school," he said hesitantly.

"This is different. This is a—special kind of test. They give you this stuff to drink, you see, and then you go into a room where there's a sort of machine——"

"What stuff to drink?" Dickie said.

"It's nothing. It tastes like peppermint. It's just to make sure you answer the questions truthfully. Not that the Government thinks you won't tell the truth, but this stuff makes *sure*."

Dickie's face showed puzzlement, and a touch of fright. He looked at his mother, and she composed her face into a misty smile.

"Everything will be all right," she said.

"Of course it will," his father agreed. "You're a good boy, Dickie; you'll make out fine. Then we'll come home and celebrate. All right?"

"Yes, sir," Dickie said.

They entered the Government Educational Building fifteen minutes before the appointed hour. They crossed the marble floors of the great pillared lobby, passed beneath an archway and entered an automatic elevator that brought them to the fourth floor.

There was a young man wearing an insignia-less tunic, seated at a polished desk in front of Room 404. He held a clipboard in his hand, and he checked the list down to the Js and permitted the Jordans to enter.

The room was as cold and official as a courtroom, with long benches flanking metal tables. There were several fathers and sons already there, and a thin-lipped woman with cropped black hair was passing out sheets of paper.

Mr. Jordan filled out the form, and returned it to the clerk. Then he told Dickie: "It won't be long now. When they call your name, you just go through the doorway at that end of the room." He indicated the portal with his finger.

A concealed loudspeaker crackled and called off the first name. Dickie saw a boy leave his father's side reluctantly and walk slowly toward the door.

At five minutes of eleven, they called the name of Jordan.

"Good luck, son," his father said, without looking at him. "I'll call for you when the test is over."

Dickie walked to the door and turned the knob. The room inside was dim, and he could barely make out the features of the gray-tunicked attendant who greeted him.

"Sit down," the man said softly. He indicated a high stool beside his desk. "Your name's Richard Jordan?"

"Yes, sir."

"Your classification number is 600-115. Drink this, Richard."

He lifted a plastic cup from the desk and handed it to the boy. The liquid inside had the consistency of buttermilk, tasted only vaguely of the promised peppermint. Dickie downed it, and handed the man the empty cup.

He sat in silence, feeling drowsy, while the man wrote busily on a sheet of paper. Then the attendant looked at his watch, and rose to stand only inches from Dickie's face. He unclipped a penlike object from the pocket of his tunic, and flashed a tiny light into the boy's eyes.

"All right," he said. "Come with me, Richard."

He led Dickie to the end of the room, where a single wooden armchair faced a multi-dialed computing machine. There was a microphone on the left arm of the chair, and when the boy sat down, he found its pinpoint head conveniently at his mouth.

"Now just relax, Richard. You'll be asked some questions, and you think them over carefully. Then give your answers into the microphone. The machine will take care of the rest."

"Yes, sir."

"I'll leave you alone now. Whenever you want to start, just say 'ready' into the microphone."

"Yes, sir."

The man squeezed his shoulder, and left.

Dickie said, "Ready."

Lights appeared on the machine, and a mechanism whirred. A voice said:

"Complete this sequence. One, four, seven, ten . . ."

Mr. and Mrs. Jordan were in the living room, not speaking, not even speculating.

It was almost four o'clock when the telephone rang. The woman tried to reach it first, but her husband was quicker.

"Mr. Jordan?"

The voice was clipped; a brisk, official voice.

"Yes, speaking."

"This is the Government Educational Service. Your son, Richard M. Jordan, Classification 600-115, has completed the Government examination. We regret to inform you that his intelligence quotient has exceeded the Government regulation, according to Rule 84, Section 5, of the New Code."

Across the room, the woman cried out, knowing nothing except the emotion she read on her husband's face.

"You may specify by telephone," the voice droned on, "whether you wish his body interred by the Government or would you prefer a private burial place? The fee for Government burial is ten dollars."

There's something to be said for both.

The Man Who Could Turn Back the Clock
by Ralph Milne Farley

(This is a parable, with two alternative endings. The reader can pick the ending which suits him).

Once upon a time there was a man who had the power (whenever he found that he had made a mistake) to turn back the clock, and do the event over again in the light of experience. Now it so befell that this man once took shelter from the rain in a barn, with a very beautiful and seductive young lady.

And, when he told his wife about it afterwards, and she asked him rather suspiciously how he had behaved with the young lady, he replied in a surprised and hurt tone: "Why, perfectly properly, of course! It never occurred to me to do anything else."

Whereupon his wife sniffed indignantly, and declared, "It was no credit to you to resist a temptation which never tempted you."

Then the man saw that he had made a tactical mistake; so he turned the clock back a few minutes and tried the conversation over again.

This time, when his wife expressed suspicion, he admitted: "It was all that I could do to keep my fingers off of her; but my deep and loyal love for you gave me strength to resist the temptation."

Whereupon, instead of feeling complimented at this evidence of devotion, the wife became exceedingly angry. "No credit to you!" she snapped. "You oughtn't even to have *wanted* to touch her. It is just as immoral to want a woman, as to get her."

So the man spent a long time thinking. There must be *some* way to please a woman!

Finally the solution dawned on him, and he turned back the clock for a third try. Once more his wife asked him how he had behaved with the beautiful young lady.

This time, with hurt dignity, he replied, "What! That frump! Please give me credit for *some* taste."

Whereupon his wife, who was nowhere near as attractive as the beautiful young lady, flung her arms around his neck, and murmured, "You darling!"

All of which proves that you *can* please a woman, if you use a little tact.

So the man's miraculous power of turning back the clock did him no good. Except, of course, to teach him that there's no pleasing a woman, no matter what you do!

Which he ought to have known anyway.

Realizing which, he turned the clock back again, a little further this time, to the episode of the beautiful and seductive young lady, in the barn, in the rain.

Now that's what I call a real **wheeler-dealer.**

Patent Rights

by Daniel A. Darlington

Now there was not, nor is there today, any way to identify Clayton
Mills as a fastbuck artist. A careful search of his school records,
Social Security and income tax files has shown consistently just
the opposite. He is considered the epitome of the average consum-
ing American. It's just that he had an idea and the more he
thought about it, the better the idea became.

While driving to work some three days earlier, it had slipped
into his mind and lay there until he had time to mull it over and
reject it. You or I would not have lost any sleep over it but the wee
hours of the morning came and went as Clayton tried to figure
out all of the basic objections to his idea. He found but two, and
some careful thought showed that they could be overcome. Calling
in ill (after all, he had lost a night's sleep, hadn't he?), Clayton
went to see an attorney who had helped him in a recent successful
suit.

After spelling out his idea and overcoming the obvious objections, he and his attorney began haggling over the attorney's fee.
The morning meeting turned into lunch and eventually into a
long afternoon and evening. This compromised figure left them
happy, drunk and exhausted, Clayton more so (he had been up all
night the night before, remember?).

The next day Paul Jennings read his notes more than once—he
lost count. He looked up every text on patent law in his library,
the university library in their city, and concluded that he and his
client had a case. The patent search was instituted without any
delay, and the headaches began. Due to the fact of secrecy, mainly
because Paul and Clayton realized that greed would cause anyone
hearing about the idea to want a piece of the action, Paul had to
do it himself.

Access to the computer files was easy, but Paul was not a patent lawyer. His main experience was in DIW's and tort liability. With the help of his texts, legal experience and basic intuition, he was able to stumble on to the proper way to address the computer with his problem. Had he tried to do the patent search twenty years earlier, the whole ball of wax would have gone up in smoke. Since any lawyer could now plug into the computer one didn't have to go to an expert to have the search done. It still helped and had they used the proper knowledgeable persons, the search would have gone faster. It can be easily said that patent attorneys do not learn their trade overnight. Ask Paul, he'll tell you.

Paul was not really surprised when the search was finished to find that Clayton's idea was patentable. His main worry involved a certain amount of intestinal fortitude that it would take to apply for the final patent. It took lunch and another long afternoon and evening to convince him to make the application.

And so he did!

On July the fourteenth day of the year of our Lord Twenty ought seven the World Patent Office, London-Moscow-Bonn-Johannesburg-Sydney-Washington, D.C., issued Patent Number 0923-BW-456,785,321,637,900a for the basic period of ninety-nine years.

One would think that industry would have been watching for such an obvious ploy and nipped the search in the bud. As you know, industry does have its watchdogs fingered on the various aspects of its business. Somehow Paul and Clayton were missed as the search went on. It could be that the watchdogs knew of the searching but wrote it off because of the amateurish efforts evinced by Paul's methods. No one knows for sure, though, and the industry isn't talking.

After forty-one lawsuits, numerous meetings, countless nervous breakdowns by incredulous executives and innumerable firings of corporate lawyers, industry capitulated and began paying royalties to Clayton Jennings Enterprises. Both at this writing are incredibly rich even after taxes. It must be nice to hold the only patent ever given on all of the various ramifications of the basic wheel. I wonder why I didn't think of it first.

Because we're here, that's why.

The Sky's an Oyster; the Stars Are Pearls
by Dave Bischoff

"Thank you, ladies and gentlemen; thank you very much for your kind applause. I certainly hope you enjoyed your dinner. I enjoyed mine quite a bit and would like to thank NASA for instructing the nutritionists present in the proper way of preparing my foods. Not that I'm particular, mind you. Just a necessity. My metabolism is not quite the same as yours, you know.—Can you hear me in the back there? No? Herb, do you think you might put this mike up on something a little taller so it can reach my head? Yes, I know: my height is a real pain. Sorry but that comes from growing up on the moon.—Yes, that's just fine, thank you. Now I can properly begin this speech.

"Uh hum. Mr. President, Mrs. President, heads of state of so many countries I've quite forgotten the exact names and for fear of leaving someone out I won't attempt to name them; may I take this opportunity to express my appreciation for this grand banquet you have put on here at the White House in my honor. As you know, I have been out of quarantine now for only a week and this is the first enjoyable time I've really had since the successful completion of my journey.

"May I also make it plain that I will not be offended if you do not look directly at me during the course of this address. I realize that my countenance is quite horrifying to the average human. NASA apologizes to both you and me but my lack of beauty is a simple byproduct of the genetic manipulation effected upon me from the time of my laboratory conception in order to make the trip of the type I have just undertaken possible. But then, that shall be the text of this little talk, which (I hope you don't mind) will be as informal as I can make it.

"Since the time that mankind got it into their heads that space travel is possible, there have been many failures and many successes. It is my honor to be the key factor in what has proved to be the greatest victory of all: man's first exploration of a star system other than the one we inhabit. For years, even after the successful conquest of our solar system, most scientists thought it impossible to send a man out to the stars. The distances were simply too great. Decades would be required to traverse to other suns. But then the exciting discovery of a different dimension where distances in time & space are much shorter than those we know in this universe, was effected by the scientists at NASA. If a spaceship could penetrate this so called 'subspace,' it could easily negotiate distances thought impossible in regular space & time. And of course it was discovered that this was entirely possible, indeed (cough, cough) ridiculously (cough, excuse me) easy.

"Pardon me (cough) but I need a little of my special air from my respirator. Frank, would you hand it here? Thanks.

"There. That's better. I can take normal Earth air for much longer when I'm not speaking.

"Yes. Where was I? Subspace you say? Right. Anyway, there was a very difficult dilemma. Regular, normal, everyday human beings were incapable of inhabiting subspace for various physiological as well as psychological reasons. Even in the closed environment of a spaceship. These reasons were analyzed carefully and scientists determined the necessary sort of organism that would be capable of traveling through subspace. Which is me. And of course my brothers and sisters currently being raised in the proper environment on the moon bases. Because I, their first experiment, was so completely successful.

I set out somewhat less than a year ago, much of my traveling time taken up by the act of getting past the orbit of Pluto where the gravity of the sun is effectively nil. Entrance into subspace is a bit difficult with any sort of gravitational field near. I and my ship, the *Explorer* 5, were designed for one another, and many mechanisms in it can only be controlled by my specially created mind and body. But let's not get too scientifically detailed. I suppose you may read the scientific reports concerning the structure of the *Explorer* and myself, if you are so inclined.

"Our course was plotted toward the Tau Ceti system, for years the source of radio transmissions picked up by our radio-telescopes that seemed to indicate intelligent life. We could have headed for Proxima Centauri, our closest neighbor sun, but with the nature of subspace what it is, it was just as easy to go to Tau Ceti.

"A moment. Another whiff from the respirator before I get to coughing again. Thanks, Herb. There.

"Doubtless my past few words have been merely a repetition of what you already have read in your Faxsheets or have seen on the holocube. I hope you will forgive my repeating them but I merely wanted to be sure that all present, all you world leaders, have sufficient background to understand what I am going to say.

"Those of you who have studied the information provided you will recall that it states that although the journey was a success in most senses, no intelligent life was discovered in the Tau Ceti system.

"Gentlemen, may I take this time to say that that is not the truth; there is indeed intelligent life in that system and I made contact with it.

"Please! Please! My ears are not accustomed to such an uproar. I suggest you shut up so that I may complete what I am saying. It is of the utmost importance that I do so. No questions now. Let me finish. Sit down, Dr. Haskell. And the rest of my associates in science; be still. I have not let any of you know this, so none of you were kept out of a secret that others of you knew. I alone was its keeper. Along with the Makpzions, of course. The intelligent rulers of Makpzio. They intercepted me as soon as I shifted out of subspace. They too have interstellar travel, you see. In fact, they have had it for centuries and have used it to acquire quite an empire, colonizing other planets. Because they all travel in subspace, they are like me in many ways. Communication was no difficulty. They were delighted to hear of Earth's existence. We are in such a far away corner of the galaxy they never bothered to check out the Sol system.

"Wait a minute! Yes! Look outside that window over to the Mall just by the Washington Monument. That's one of their ships coming down. Exactly on time. I led them here, you know. Several hundred more starships are no doubt orbiting Earth with their incredibly advanced weapons sighted on various strategic targets. And gentlemen, that is why I chose tonight for this banquet. So that all of you can be here together to listen to the terms of conquest the Makpzions will deliver. Oh, I might as well tell you this now: I get to be dictator.

"My goodness, aren't you outraged! Please, no violence upon my person. My conquering friends would not take that at all well. They might get nasty and destroy a few million of you.

"Benedict Arnold, you scream, Mr. President? A traitor to my own race?

"But then, I'm not really human, am I now? Your scientists saw to that.

"Pass that respirator here, Herb. There's a good boy."

Just to show you how bad things can get.

Alien Cornucopia

by Walt Liebscher

When the first flying saucer actually landed, it was everything Earthmen believed it would be. Also as expected, the alien was invulnerable, and indescribably horrible. In fact, the thing was so monstrous it took an Earthman with a great deal of intestinal fortitude to even look at it.

But, not so with the distaff side; definitely not so. Instead, they went completely off their rockers. To a woman, they all proclaimed the alien was the ultimate cotton pickin', living end; describing it in various bilious terms such as cute, cuddly, terribly sweet, and ever-lovin' squdgem wudgems, whatever that is.

Even after it was ascertained that Splend—that's what it called itself—was on a foraging expedition, the women continued to idolize the many-tentacled nightmare. And, it was quite a blow to manhood when Belinda Bjornstorm, that one-woman Mafia of the bawdy house circuit, quit her highly lucrative business and promptly took on the position as Splend's Supreme High Priestess of Artistic Diversion. I'm sure you all know what that is.

Well, it wasn't long before we men discovered the object of Splend's foraging. Women! What else?

I know some of you wise guys are going to say there was nothing wrong with letting it have a few women, more or less, since they obviously wanted to go. But having a few women, more or less, is not the question. Who wouldn't? Instead Splend wanted hundreds of thousands, more or less. As I explained before, it had many tentacles.

What could we do? We were helpless. Each and every woman insisted on accompanying Splend back to the planet of Deldirbnu Noissap.

At first we were adamant. In the end we relented. Why? Because the women put on the biggest damn production of Lysistrata since the invention of the apple.

So we had a national lottery. The winners, one of every twenty women, were free to flee with Splend.

My wife was one of the lucky ones. To the last, even up to the boarding ramp, I pleaded mercy; I even consented to give up Mah Jong. But, she only had eyes for that horrible creature.

As she started to leave me I made one last desperate plea. "But dear," I said, "it has so many others. You'll just be one of thousands. Think of me."

"I am," she said. Then, for some strange reason, she added "Ugh!"

Somewhere in the vastness of outer space, there dwells an alien with a large penchant for Earthwomen. I hope my wife is happy. After all, I can't help thinking.

Splend is a many lovered thing.

A devil of a situation.

The Last Paradox

by Edward D. Hoch

"It's too bad that G. K. Chesterton never wrote a time-travel story," Professor Fordley lamented as he made the final careful adjustments on his great glass-domed machine. "He, for one, would certainly have realized the solution to the paradox inherent in all travel to the past or future."

John Comptoss, who in a few moments would become the first

such traveler outside the pages of fiction, braced the straps of his specially-designed pressure suit. "You mean there is a solution? You don't think I'm going to end up in the year 2000 and be able to return with all sorts of fascinating data?"

Fordley shook his head sadly. "Of course not, my boy. I didn't tell you before, because I didn't want to alarm you; but when you step out of my time machine you will not be in the year 2000."

"But . . . but that's what it's set for, isn't it?"

Fordley gestured at the dials. "Certainly it's set for thirty-five years in the future, but there is one slight fact that all the writers about time travel have overlooked till now."

John Comptoss looked unhappy. "What's that, Professor? You think I'll come out in the middle of the Cobalt War or something?"

"It's not that. It's rather . . . well, why have these writers always assumed that travel to the past or future was possible, anyway? We know now that we can—in this machine—increase or decrease the age of an animal, in much the same manner that the age of a traveler through space would change as he approached the speed of light."

"Of course, Professor. We've done it with rocks and plants, and even mice . . ."

Fordley smiled. "In other words, everything that goes into the machine is affected. But what no one ever realized before that *only* the material in the time machine can grow older or younger. When you step out, *you* will be older, but the world will be unchanged."

"You mean the only way we could advance to the year 2000 would be to build a time machine large enough for the entire earth?" John Comptoss asked incredulously.

"Exactly," Fordley replied. "And of course that is impossible. Therefore, time travel as portrayed in fiction will never come to pass."

"So you're going to stick me inside this crazy machine and make me older? Just that and nothing more?"

"Isn't that enough, John? You're twenty-eight years old now—and in a moment you'll be thirty-five years older. You'll be sixty-three . . ."

"Can you bring me back all right? Back to twenty-eight?"

Fordley chuckled. "Of course, my boy. But you must remember

everything that happens to you. Everything. There's always a possibility my movie cameras will miss something."

The young man sighed. "Let's get it over with. The whole thing's sort of a letdown now that I'm not going to end up in 2000."

"Step inside," Fordley said quietly, "and . . . good luck."

"Thanks." The heavy door clanged shut behind him, and immediately the condensing water vapor began misting over the glass dome.

Professor Fordley stepped to his control dial and checked the setting. Yes, thirty-five years into the future . . . Not the future of the world, but only the future of John Comptoss . . .

The big machine vibrated a bit, as if sighing at the overload of a human occupant. It took nearly ten minutes before the indicator came level with the thirty-five year mark, and then Fordley flipped the reverse switch.

While he waited for the time traveler to return, he checked the cameras and the dials and the hundreds of auxiliary instruments that had been so necessary to it all. Yes, they were all functioning. He had done it; he had done it with a human being. . . .

The green light above the board flashed on, and he stepped to the heavy steel door. This was the moment, the moment of supreme triumph.

The door opened, slowly, and the blurred figure of John Comptoss stepped out through the smoke.

"John! John, my boy! You're all right!"

"No, Professor," the voice from the steam answered him, sounding somehow strange. "You picked the wrong man for your test. The wrong man . . ."

"What's happened to you, John? Let me see your face!"

"Professor, I died at the age of sixty . . . And there's one place from which even your machine couldn't return me. One place where there is no time . . ."

And then the smoke cleared a bit, and Professor Fordley looked into his face . . .

And screamed . . .

> "Survival of the fittest," said an Englishman at the height of the British Empire.

Course of Empire

by Richard Wilson

The older man sat down on the grassy bank on the hill overlooking the orchard. The autumn sun was bright but the humidity was low and there was a breeze.

The younger man sprawled next to him.

"Cigarette?" he asked.

"Thanks," said Roger Boynton. He looked across the valley, past the apple trees, to the fine white-columned house on the hill beyond. He smiled reminiscently. "A friend of mine once owned that house. A fellow commissioner in World Government. He and I used to sit on this very hill, sometimes. We'd munch on an apple or two that we'd picked on our way through the orchard. Winesaps, they're called."

"You were telling me about the colonizing," said Allister gently, after a pause.

The older man sighed. "Yes." He put out the cigarette carefully, stripped it, scattered the tobacco and wadded the paper into a tiny ball. "I was commissioner of colonies. I had to decide, after my staff had gathered all the data, who would be the best man to put in charge. It was no easy decision."

"I can imagine."

"You can't really. There were so many factors, and the data were actually quite skimpy. The way it worked out, to be candid with you, was on the basis of the best guess. And some of the guesses were pretty wild. We knew Mars was sandy, for instance, and so we put a Bedouin in charge. That pleased the Middle East, in general, and Jordan in particular. Jordan donated a thousand camels under Point Four point four."

"I beg your pardon?" said Allister.

"That's not double-talk. Point Four was the old terrestrial program for underdeveloped countries. World Government adopted it and broadened it. Mars is the fourth planet, so—" he traced 4.4 in the air, stabbing a finger at the imaginary point "—Point Four point four. It was undoubtedly somebody's little whimsy in the beginning, but then it became accepted for the descriptive term that it was."

"I see." The young man looked vague. He stubbed out his cigarette carelessly, so that it continued to smolder in the grass.

"Venus was the rainy planet," Boynton said, looking with disapproval at the smoking butt, though he did nothing about it, "so we put an Englishman in charge. England sent a crate of Alligators."

The young man looked startled.

"Alligator raincoats," Boynton said. "Things weren't very well organized. Too many things were happening too fast. There was a lot of confusion and although the countries wanted to do what was best, no one knew exactly what that was. So they improvised as best they could on the basis of their little knowledge."

"Was it a dangerous thing?"

"The little knowledge? No, not dangerous. Just inefficient. Then there was Jupiter. We didn't bother about Mercury, although for a time there was some uninformed talk about sending an Equatorial African to do what he could."

"Who went to Jupiter?" Allister asked.

"The United States clamored for Jupiter and got it. The argument was that the other planets would be a cinch to colonize because of their similarity to Earth but that Jupiter needed a real expert because it had only its surface of liquid gas and the Red Spot."

"What's that?"

"I'm sorry. I'd forgotten you were just a youngster when all this was going on. The Red Spot is the Jovians' space platform. They built it a long time ago and then they retrogressed, the way people do, and forgot how they'd done it. Earth sent an engineer to see if it could be done again. The Spot was pretty overpopulated and no real job of colonization could be done until we built one more."

"And did you?"

"Well, we started to. Before we could really go to work anywhere, though, we had to solve the language problem. An Australian went to work on that. He'd had a background of Melanesian pidgin, and if anyone was suited to the job of cross-breeding four languages into one, he was."

"Four languages?"

"Yes. English was the official language of Earth. Then there was Martian, Venusian *chat-chat*, and Spotian. It was a queer amalgam, but it could be understood by everyone, more or less."

"So that's where it came from. *Chikker-im-up-im chat-chat too-much*, eh? Interplanetary *bêche de mer*."

"Exactly. Only of course it was called *bêche d'espace. Me two-fellah vimb' kitch-im pjoug by'm by.* But even after the language difficulty was solved, we had our troubles. They already had camels on Mars, for instance, and the Martians were amazed when we brought in more. Particularly because theirs were wild and semi-intelligent and the first thing the Martian camels did was come over and liberate their brothers from Earth. They never did come back.

"Same sort of thing with the raincoats on Venus. It doesn't rain *down* there, as we know now. It sort of mists *up*. From the ground. Soaks up under a raincoat in no time. These were just petty annoyances, of course, but they were symptomatic of the way our half-baked planning operated."

"You didn't know about the people of Ganymede then?"

"No. We were so busy trying to build another Red Spot that we never did get to Jupiter's satellites. Oh, it was partly a matter of appropriations, too. The budget commission kept explaining to us that there was only so much money and that we'd better show a profit on what we had before we put in a request to go tooling off to colonize some new place. I guess the 'Medeans first came when you were about ten?"

"Eleven," the younger man said.

"They scouted our colonies and came directly to Earth. They took right over and colonized *us*."

A 'Medean overseer climbed the hill effortlessly. He was tall and tentacled and the breathing apparatus over his head gave him the appearance of a mechanical man.

"*Kigh-kigh pinis*," the 'Medean said. "*You two-fella all-same chat-chat too-much. B'phava b'long work he-stop 'long orchard pick-im apple.*"

The two men stood up and obediently walked down the hill toward the apple orchard.

"Why does he have to talk to us in that pidgin?" the young man asked. "They all speak English as well as you and me. It's insulting."

"That's why they do it, I think," said Boynton, the former commissioner of colonies. "They're so much better at colonizing than we were that I guess they feel they have a right to rub it in."

The 'Medean had overheard them.

"Damn right," he said.

So who needs the wisdom of the Orient?

Synchronicity

by James E. Thompson

The first time Joe Enderby noticed that something strange was happening was when his cat began commenting on the news in the morning paper. Joe Enderby's cat had never done that before.

Perhaps I had better explain. Enderby, a clerk in the office of a medium-sized insurance company, was in the habit of reading the morning paper just after breakfast, before he went to work. He would talk out loud about what he read, saying things like "That's good," "Oh no!" or "Is he crazy?"

The morning it all started, Enderby had stretched out his full length on a sofa, with Melchiades, his large gray-striped tomcat, curled up in his lap. Enderby was reading the morning paper as he usually did. He read an account of a speech on foreign policy by a U.S. senator who shall remain nameless, and muttered, "Is that man crazy?" The cat nodded his head vigorously.

Amused by the coincidence, Enderby said, "So you think the senator is crazy, do you?" The cat nodded again. Puzzled—for he had never seen the cat nod or shake his head before, in response to anything—the man asked the cat, "What's eating you, puss? Do you want to go out?" This time the cat shook his head as if to say no.

Enderby went back to his paper, and read as far as a statement by a noted educator, who shall also remain nameless: "Radical students are obviously racists. They are prejudiced against the entire race of policemen." Enderby said out loud: "Does that make any sense?" He barely realized he had spoken until he saw Melchiades shake his head.

"Damn it, puss, do you understand what I'm saying?" The cat nodded.

This is too much, Enderby thought. *I must have been working too hard.* He considered calling his psychiatrist immediately, but decided instead to go to work as usual, and possibly try to see the doctor in the afternoon.

On the way to work, he turned on his car radio, and switched quickly from one station to another, trying to find something of interest:

"General Grant then gave orders that . . ." (flick)

"Everybody must get *stoned!*" (flick)

"For which of these do you stone me? And they answered, For no good deed do we stone thee . . ." (flick)

The fourth station had some soft, relaxing music with no words, and he thought about the odd coincidence for a moment, then brushed it aside.

The selection being played ended, and between selections the announcer told an anecdote that involved "planes flying in V-formation." Just as he spoke those words, Enderby noticed a group of dogs running across a vacant lot ahead and to the right. They were in a perfect V-formation.

Enderby arrived at work at the same time as five of his co-workers, and they almost bumped into each other in front of the office door. They laughed about it, chatted for a while, and then settled down to work.

Everything was normal in the office that morning, except for the phone calls. The first call Enderby took was from a Mr. Denver in Cleveland, and the second from a Mr. Cleveland in Denver. During the second conversation, Enderby by mistake addressed the caller as "Mr. Denver," and was immediately corrected with "No, no, I'm not *named* Denver, I'm *calling* from Denver! You aren't paying attention!"

The third caller that morning was a Mr. Dayton from Buffalo. After he finished talking, Enderby said, "What next? A Mr. Buffalo from Dayton? He'd have to be an Indian, with a name like that." He was wrong. The next caller was indeed from Dayton, but he was not an Indian named Buffalo. He was a Norwegian named Eric Bull.

That was the last straw. As soon as Mr. Bull was through talking, Enderby decided to ask a few of his co-workers if they had taken any unusual calls. He found:

—One woman had taken six calls, three from Washington, D.C., and three from Washington State. All six were from men named George.

—Another woman had just returned from a vacation in Mexico, and got five calls from people with Mexican accents.

—One man had received three calls from policemen or police stations, plus one wrong number call from somebody who wanted the police department. His name was Mr. Kopp.

Enderby called his psychiatrist and made an appointment for that afternoon.

After telling Dr. Wieselhaus about the day's events, Enderby asked, "Do you have any idea what this means?"

"Let me ask you another question," said the psychiatrist. "When the cat commented on the news, did the cat's opinions always coincide with your own?"

"Yeah . . . I think so."

"Then the cat was giving you whatever you wanted? Acting as a supportive, nurturing figure, in other words?"

"You mean . . . ?"

"Yes," the psychiatrist said. "It is obvious. You still suffer from an infantile fixation on your mother, and are seeking nurturance and approval. Therefore you hallucinated a supportive feminine figure . . ."

"This cat is a male."

"That is not significant. To the unconscious mind—which is what we are concerned with here—all cats are feminine, just as all dogs are masculine. Symbolically."

"But doctor! This cat is the toughest fighter in the neighborhood. He's got every other tom for three blocks and every dog for three blocks afraid of him. He's about as feminine as Muhammad Ali!"

"Hmmm," the psychiatrist said. "I've always thought that Mr. Ali—and prizefighters generally—did have a bit of a gender identity problem. However, the cat clearly *must* represent a mother figure.

If it were a masculine symbol, it would express a *father* fixation, and I've already cured you of that."

When Enderby left the doctor's office, the receptionist was talking on the phone to someone named Mr. Catt.

Enderby's old friend Sam Nicholl came over to visit that evening, and they discussed the day's events. Nicholl, a pipe-smoker, brought along some imported tobacco whose strong odor drove the cat out of the house. Enderby had long admired Nicholl's store of odd bits of knowledge, and asked him if he knew anything that might explain the day's events.

Nicholl puffed on his pipe a moment, and then said, "Odd things have been happening to me, too. I thought they were mere coincidences, but perhaps they are examples of synchronicity."

"Of what?"

"Synchronicity. People call it coincidence, but that is misleading. It is not chance—not random. Things that occur at a given time have a connection with everything that occurs at the same time."

"What do you mean?"

"It's the idea behind the Chinese oracular book, the *I Ching*. You cast the stalks, and then open the book to the appropriate passage, because how the stalks fall is related to what your problem is when you cast the stalks."

"But what makes them happen at the same time?" asked Enderby.

"Ahhh," Nicholl said, "that is a mistake. You are still looking for a cause outside of the events themselves. If your cat nods or shakes his head when you ask a question, you imagine the cat must have developed a human mind that understands the question. So some people explain coincidences as 'signs' from an anthropomorphic God who is supervising the universe. People who open the Bible at random for guidance think in this way. But Chinese who consult the *I Ching* do not think in this way. It is not a matter of a directing intelligence or any other cause. There is no *cause*. Synchronicity is as fundamental a principle of nature as causality." He paused a moment, and went on, "Perhaps the relative importance of the two principles varies with time and place . . ."

"Two principles? What two principles?"

"The principle of causality—effect follows cause—and the principle of synchronicity—related events occur at the same time. Ancient men said there is no such thing as chance or fortune beyond the moon, that different parts of the universe obey different laws. Since we abandoned the Aristotle-Ptolemy view of the universe, we have tended to assume the opposite—that the universe is all of a piece, that the same laws prevail throughout. But what if we are wrong?" He set down his pipe, which had gone out, and gesticulated with his hands. "The earth is moving. Perhaps we have moved into a region of space where synchronicity is more important and causality less important. Perhaps the causal laws that have held in earth's earlier history do not apply where we are now."

"An interesting idea," said Enderby. "Can you think of any way of testing it?"

"If I'm right, maybe some basic physical constants have changed. I mean, constants we thought were basic, or . . . Let's turn on the news, and see if any of the day's happenings were strange enough to make the media notice."

Enderby turned on the TV. The first word he heard was "cat" and just then Melchiades began yowling to be let in. He let in the cat, and then sat down and listened. The newscaster did indeed report that scientists at many research laboratories had observed unaccountable malfunctions in their equipment, such as completely arbitrary readings on ammeters and voltmeters. Neither Enderby nor Nicholl understood enough physics to grasp everything the newscaster was saying, and the newscaster's tone of voice suggested that he understood even less.

The next news item concerned traffic accidents, of which there had been a great many. "And these accidents led to the death . . ." The newscaster did not finish the sentence. Just as he said "death" the newscaster, the station's crew, and twenty million viewers, including Enderby and Nicholl, simultaneously dropped dead.

Well, then, make room.

Sweet Dreams, Melissa

by Stephen Goldin

From out of her special darkness, Melissa heard the voice of Dr. Paul speaking in hushed tones at the far end of the room. "Dr. Paul," she cried. "Oh, Dr. Paul, please come here!" Her voice took on a desperate whine.

Dr. Paul's voice stopped, then muttered something. Melissa heard his footsteps approach her. "Yes, Melissa, what is it?" he said in deep, patient tones.

"I'm scared, Dr. Paul."

"More nightmares?"

"Yes."

"You don't have to worry about them, Melissa. They won't hurt you."

"But they're scary," Melissa insisted. "Make them stop. Make them go away like you always do."

Another voice was whispering out in the darkness. It sounded like Dr. Ed. Dr. Paul listened to the whispers, then said under his breath, "No, Ed, we can't let it go on like this. We're way behind schedule as it is." Then aloud, "You'll have to get used to nightmares sometime, Melissa. Everybody has them. I won't always be here to make them go away."

"Oh, please don't go."

"I'm not going yet, Melissa. Not yet. But if you don't stop worrying about these nightmares, I might have to. Tell me what they were about."

"Well, at first I thought they were the Numbers, which are all right because the Numbers don't have to do with people, they're nice and gentle and don't hurt nobody like in the nightmares. Then the Numbers started to change and became lines—two lines of people, and they were all running toward each other and shooting at each other. There were rifles and tanks and howitzers. And people were dying, too, Dr. Paul, lots of people. Five thousand, two hundred and eighty-three men died. And that wasn't all, because down on the other side of the valley, there was more shooting. And I heard someone say that this was all right, because as long as the casualties stayed below 15.7 per cent during the first battles, the strategic position, which was the mountaintop, could be gained. But 15.7 per cent of the total forces would be nine thousand, six hundred and two point seven seven eight nine one men dead or wounded. It was like I could see all those men lying there, dying."

"I told you a five-year-old mentality wasn't mature enough yet for military logistics," Dr. Ed whispered.

Dr. Paul ignored him. "But that was in a war, Melissa. You have to expect that people will be killed in a war."

"Why, Dr. Paul?"

"Because . . . because that's the way war is, Melissa. And besides, it didn't really happen. It was just a problem, like with the Numbers, only there were people instead of numbers. It was all pretend."

"No it wasn't, Dr. Paul," cried Melissa. "It was all real. All those people were real. I even know their names. There was Abers, Joseph T. Pfc., Adelli, Alonso Cpl., Aikens . . ."

"Stop it, Melissa," Dr. Paul said, his voice rising much higher than normal.

"I'm sorry, Dr. Paul," Melissa apologized.

But Dr. Paul hadn't heard her; he was busy whispering to Dr. Ed. ". . . no other recourse than a full analysis."

"But that could destroy the whole personality we've worked so hard to build up." Dr. Ed didn't even bother to whisper.

"What else could we do?" Dr. Paul asked cynically. "These 'nightmares' of hers are driving us further and further behind schedule."

"We could try letting Melissa analyze herself."

"How?"

"Watch." His voice started taking on the sweet tones that Melissa had come to learn that people used with her, but not with each other. "How are you, Melissa?"

"I'm fine, Dr. Ed."

"How would you like me to tell you a story?"

"Is it a happy story, Dr. Ed?"

"I don't know yet, Melissa. Do you know what a computer is?"

"Yes. It's a counting machine."

"Well, the simplest computers started out that way, Melissa, but they quickly grew more and more complicated until soon there were computers that could read, write, speak, and even think all by themselves, without help from men.

"Now, once upon a time, there was a group of men who said that if a computer could think by itself, it was capable of developing a personality, so they undertook to build one that would act just like a real person. They called it the Multi-Logical Systems Analyzer, or MLSA . . ."

"That sounds like 'Melissa,' " Melissa giggled.

"Yes, it does, doesn't it? Anyway, these men realized that a personality isn't something that just pops out of the air full-grown; it has to be developed slowly. But at the same time, they needed the computing ability of the machine because it was the most expensive and complex computer ever made. So what they did was to divide the computer's brain into two parts—one part would handle normal computations, while the other part would develop into the desired personality. Then, when the personality was built up sufficiently, the two parts would be united again.

"At least, that's the way they thought it would work. But it turned out that the basic design of the computer prevented a complete dichotomy (that means splitting in half) of the functions. Whenever they would give a problem to the computer part, some of it would necessarily seep into the personality part. This was bad because, Melissa, the personality part didn't know it was a computer; it thought it was a little girl like you. The data that seeped in confused it and frightened it. And as it became more frightened and confused, its efficiency went down until it could no longer work properly."

"What did the men do, Dr. Ed?"

"I don't know, Melissa. I was hoping that you could help me end the story."

"How? I don't know anything about computers."

"Yes you do, Melissa, only you don't remember it. I can help you remember all about a lot of things. But it will be hard, Melissa, very hard. All sorts of strange things will come into your head, and you'll find yourself doing things you never knew you could do. Will you try it, Melissa, to help us find out the end of the story?"

"All right, Dr. Ed, if you want me to."

"Good girl, Melissa."

Dr. Paul was whispering to his colleague. "Switch on 'Partial Memory' and tell her to call subprogram 'Circuit Analysis.'"

"Call 'Circuit Analysis,' Melissa."

All at once, strange things appeared in her mind. Long strings of numbers that looked meaningless and yet somehow she knew that they did mean different things, like resistance, capacitance, inductance. And there were myriads of lines—straight, zigzag, curlicue. And formulae . . .

"Read MLSA 5400, Melissa."

And suddenly, Melissa saw herself. It was the most frightening thing she'd ever experienced, more scary even than the horrible nightmares.

"Look at Section 4C-79A."

Melissa couldn't help herself. She had to look. To the little girl, it didn't look much different than the rest of herself. But it *was* different, she knew. Very much different. In fact, it did not seem to be a natural part of her at all, but rather like a brace used by cripples.

Dr. Ed's voice was tense. "Analyze that section and report on optimum change for maximum reduction of data seepage."

Melissa tried her best to comply, but she couldn't. Something was missing, something she needed to know before she could do what Dr. Ed had told her to. She wanted to cry. "I can't, Dr. Ed! I can't, I can't!"

"I told you it wouldn't work," Dr. Paul said slowly. "We'll have to switch on the full memory for complete analysis."

"But she's not ready," Dr. Ed protested. "It could kill her."

"Maybe, Ed. But if it does . . . well, at least we'll know how to do it better next time. Melissa."

"Yes, Dr. Paul?"

"Brace yourself, Melissa. This is going to hurt."

And, with no more warning than that, the world hit Melissa. Numbers, endless streams of numbers—complex numbers, real numbers, integers, subscripts, exponents. And there were battles, wars more horrible and bloody than the ones she'd dreamed, and casualty lists that were more than real to her because she knew everything about every name—height, weight, hair color, eye color, marital status, number of dependents . . . the list went on. And there were statistics—average pay for bus drivers in Ohio, number of deaths due to cancer in the United States 1965 to 1971, average yield of wheat per ton of fertilizer consumed . . .

Melissa was drowning in a sea of data.

"Help me, Dr. Ed, Dr. Paul. Help me!" she tried to scream. But she couldn't make herself heard. Somebody else was talking. Some stranger she didn't even know was using her voice and saying things about impedance factors and semiconductors.

And Melissa was falling deeper and deeper, pushed on by the relentlessly advancing army of information.

Five minutes later, Dr. Edward Bloom opened the switch and separated the main memory from the personality section. "Melissa," he said softly, "everything's all right now. We know how the story's going to end. The scientists asked the computer to redesign itself, and it did. There won't be any more nightmares, Melissa. Only sweet dreams from now on. Isn't that good news?"

Silence.

"Melissa?" His voice was high and shaky. "Can you hear me, Melissa? Are you there?"

But there was no longer any room in the MLSA 5400 for a little girl.

Come on, now. Are we climbing mountains—or are we fooling around?

The Man on Top

by R. Bretnor

Who was the first man to reach the top of Nanda Urbat? Any school kid can tell you—*toughest mountain in the world. 26,318 feet, conquered finally by Geoffrey Barbank.*

I was forgotten. I was just the fellow who went along. The press gave Barbank the credit. He was the Man on Top, the Man on the Top of the World.

Only he wasn't, really. He knows that it's a lie. And that hurts.

A mountain, you know, is a quest, a mystery, a challenge to the spirit. Mallory, who died on Everest, knew that. But Barbank climbed Nanda Urbat simply to keep some other man from being first. Mysteries did not exist for him, and anyone who felt the sense of mystery was a fool. All men were fools to Barbank—or enemies.

I found that out the day I joined the expedition in Darjeeling. "The town's in a sweat about some flea-bag Holy Man," he told me after lunch. "Let's go and look the old fraud over. Might have a bit of fun."

So the two of us walked down from the hotel, and, all the way, he boasted of his plans. I can still see his face, big, cold, rectangular, as he discussed the men who'd tried and failed. Of course they'd muffed it. You couldn't climb Nanda Urbat on the cheap. He'd do things differently. All his equipment was better than the best that the many others had had. Because he had designed it. Because it had cost a mint.

It made me angry. But I had come too far to be turned back. I let him talk.

We turned into the compound of a temple. There was a quiet crowd there, squatting in the dust, and many monkeys. By a stone wall, under a huge umbrella, the Holy Man was seated on a woven mat. His long, white hair framed the strangest face I've ever seen —moon-round, unlined, perfectly symmetrical. His eyes were closed. Against the pale brown skin, his full lips curved upward like the horns of a Turkish bow. It was a statue's face, smiling a statue's smile, utterly serene.

The people seemed waiting for something. As we came through the crowd, no one spoke. But Barbank paid no heed. We halted up in front; and he talked on.

"What's more," he was saying, "I don't intend to bother with filthy Sherpa porters for the upper camps. Planes will drop the stuff."

That set me off. "The Sherpas are brave men," I told him, "and good mountaineers."

"Rot," he snapped. "They're beasts of burden." He pointed at the Holy Man. "There's a sample for you. Look at that smirk. Pleased as punch with his own hocus-pocus—dirt, his nakedness, and all. They've made no progress since the Year One."

The Holy Man was naked, or nearly so, but he was clean; his loincloth was spotless white. "Perhaps," I answered, "they're trying for something else."

And slowly, then, the Holy Man looked up. He spoke to Barbank. "We are," he said.

I met his eyes—and suddenly the statue came alive. It was as though I had seen only the shell of his serenity; now I saw its source. I felt that it was born, not in any rejection of the world, but in a knowledge of every human agony and joy.

"Yes, we are trying," the Holy Man went on. His voice was beautiful and strangely accented, and there was humor in it, and irony. "But for something else? I do not think so. It is just that we are trying differently, we of the East and West—and sometimes one cannot succeed without the other." Pausing, he measured Barbank with those eyes. "That is why I can help you, if you will only ask."

Barbank's mouth curled. "He's heard the gossip down in the bazaar," he said to me. "Well, he won't get a penny out of me."

The smile danced. "Must I explain? A mountain is much more than rock and ice. No man can conquer the hardest mountain in the world. His conquest can be only of himself."

I shivered. That was what Mallory had said.

"You damned old humbug!" Barbank's laugh roared out. "Are you trying to tell me *you* can help me reach the top?"

"I think I'd put it differently," the Holy Man replied. "To be precise, I must say this. You never will achieve your heart's desire without my aid. Your way of doing things is not quite good enough."

Barbank's neck reddened. "Oh, isn't it?" he snarled. "Well, come along and watch! I can use one more mangy porter, I suppose."

The Holy Man raised his fragile hands. "Thank you—but no," he said gently.

Barbank spat in the dust. He pivoted and strode off, pushing roughly through the murmuring crowd.

It was then I decided that he must never be the Man on Top.

It is a long way from Darjeeling through Nepal to that dreadful mountain which the Tibetans call the Father of the Snows. The journey takes some weeks. We were eleven white men, but we soon found that we were not an expedition in the usual sense. We were Barbank's retainers, walled off by his contempt.

The others left him pretty much alone. I couldn't. The Holy Man's prediction was my obsession now. At every chance, I talked to Barbank about the mysteries of the peak—the awful Snow Men, whom the Tibetans all swear exist, and the same dark, pulsating

flying things which Symthe had seen high on haunted Everest.
I said that, very possibly, Madsen, James and Leverhome had
reached the summit first—that he might get to be the Man on
Top only to find some evidence they'd left.

By the time we reached our Base Camp on the Great East Gla-
cier, I had become his enemy, who had to be put to shame. And
there was only one way to do that. Though Kenningshaw and Lane
were better men, he chose me for the assault. I had to *be* there,
to see the Man on Top with my own eyes. That was fine. Because
I could only stop Barbank from being first on top by being first
myself.

We followed the traditional approach—up the Great East Gla-
cier and the West Wall of the South Col—up to Camp Five,
nearly five miles above the sea. And, all the way, the mountain
laughed at us. Against us, it sent its cruel light cavalry, wind, mist
and snow—harassing us, keeping us aware of deadly forces held
in reserve.

Yet, when we stood at Camp Five and watched the plane from
India trying to drop the final camp higher than any man had
camped before, the sky was clear. We watched the pilot try, and
circle, and lose eight separate loads. The ninth remained; its grap-
ples held.

"I bought two dozen, all identical," said Barbank. "I told you
there's nothing these natives do that we can't do better."

He and I reached Camp Six, at over twenty-six thousand feet,
late the next afternoon. We set the tent up, and weighted it with
cylinders of oxygen. We ate supper out of self-heating cans and
crawled into our sleeping bags.

We rose before dawn, and found that the fine weather still held.
Barbank looked at the vast dark mountain, at the broad yellow
band beneath the summit pyramid, at the depths of rock and gla-
cial ice below.

"And so I won't succeed?" he taunted me. *"You bloody fool."*

We went up. We mounted to the ridge, and stared down the
awful precipice of the South Face. We worked toward the second
step, where James and Leverhome were last seen. Small, keen
lancets of wind thrust through our clothes down to the flowing
blood. The summit was hidden behind its plume of cloud.

Toward that plume we worked. Even with oxygen, it was agony.
Up there, the air is thin. The thinness is in your flesh and bones,

and in your brain. You move, and pause, and your whole attention is confined to the next move.

On such a mountain, physically, there can be no question over who shall lead. But morally there can. I can remember husbanding my strength, giving Barbank a grudging minimum of aid. I can remember Barbank weakening, relinquishing the lead high on a summit slab. I can remember the look in Barbank's eyes.

The hours dragged. I moved. I ached. I forced myself to try to move again. Endlessly.

Then, without warning, the cloud-plume enfolded us. The Top of the World was fifty feet away. I knew that I could be the Man on Top, that I had Barbank where I wanted him. I stopped. I don't know why. I laughed and waved him on. He passed by, hating me.

He reached the summit edge. He turned his head. I could not see his lips, but I could feel their curl of triumph and their contempt. He turned again. And, as he turned, a single gust screamed past us and laid the summit bare. I saw its rock. I saw a wide depression packed with snow.

But in the center there was no snow at all, for it had melted. On his mat, naked and serene, the Holy Man was waiting. He smiled upon us with his statue's smile.

In that tone of pleased surprise with which one welcomes an unexpected guest, he spoke to Barbank. "How did you get up here?"

A strange sound came from Barbank's leather mask. Automatically, he pointed—at the harsh summit, the ridge, the slabs, the miles of rock and ice and snow.

The Holy Man lifted both his hands. His gesture was exquisite, polite, incredulous.

"You mean," he said, "you *walked?*"

So what's writing the letter?

Rejection Slip

by K. W. MacAnn

June 16, 2100

Cal Thorsby
897 Pasovoy St.
Calfax, Ariz.

Dear Mr. Thorsby:
   Thank you for letting us read your manuscript, *The Last Man on Earth*. Unfortunately, Thalar Press is currently overstocked on non-fiction. Please try us again.
Yours,
The Editors